凱信企管

用對的方法充實自己，
讓人生變得更美好！

凱信企管

用對的方法充實自己，
讓人生變得更美好！

超好學

English
Conversation

每天5分鐘的

英文會話課

詹瑩玥、張帆、呂游◎合著

效率最高！

每天只要短短5分鐘，記得快、用得準！

利用零碎時間打造你的英語力

使用說明 User's Guide

每天5分鐘的學習奇蹟，900常用句這樣就記住！

本書每一頁都是一個獨立的學習單元，每次只要短短5分鐘即可學到一個完整概念，你可以翻到任何一頁開始學起。不刻意安排學習進度，避免讀者倍感壓力，只要有耐心學習，長期累積自然能看出成效。

真好記！每句英文最多4個單字，初學者也能琅琅上口

【Part1日常實用超短句】精選老外「使用率高」的口語句，每句話最多四個單字，最短的甚至只有一個字，即使初學者也能輕鬆上手，好說又道地。

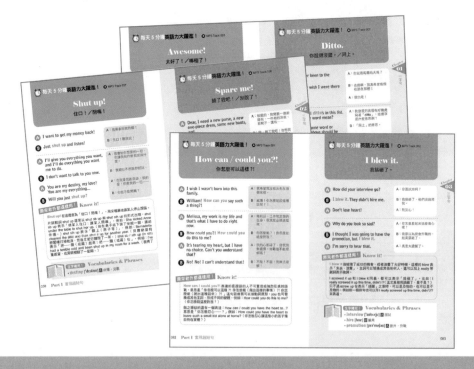

最道地！詳盡解析看透透，老外道地用法一目瞭然

每個單元都有1個英文主句，並搭配2組對話幫助讀者進一步學習句子用法；此外，更貼心加附詳細解析，不但讓讀者學會主句怎麼用，還可以延伸學習更多相關用法。

> **原來老外都這樣用！ Know it!**
>
> How can / could you?! 表達的是說話的人不可置信或強烈反感的語氣，意思是「你怎麼可以這樣？! 你怎麼能（做出這樣的事情）?! 你怎麼能（說出這種話來）?! 」這句話後面可以接動詞原形，you 也可替換成其他主詞，形成不同的變體，例如：How could you do this to me?（你怎麼能這麼對我？）
>
> 與之類似的還有一個表達：How can / could you have the heart to...? 意思是「你怎麼忍心……？」例如：How could you have the heart to leave such a small kid alone at home?（你怎麼忍心讓這麼小的孩子獨自待在家裡？）

超精準！短句依照情境功能分類，便於查找、使用

【Part2傳情達意好用句】依功能分類，例如表達「喜悅、興奮」時的句子，表達「尷尬、彆扭」時的口語……，共有20種情境，希望能幫助你用豐富的語句以及最貼近老外的口語方式，精準地表達自己的心情與感受。

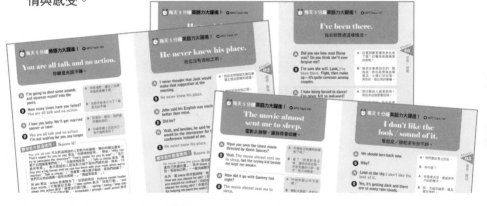

好流利！外師親錄英語會話MP3，邊聽邊說效果顯著

精益求精，學英文也一樣！請善用隨書附贈的MP3進行練習，第一遍練聽力，第二遍練習跟著說，第三遍試著揣摩老外口音語調，時時聽、常常練，英語自然聽得輕鬆、說得標準流暢。

● MP3 Track 001

親愛的讀者，感謝你翻開這本書。如果你對簡潔道地的常用英語口語感興趣，如果你想在每一天有限的時間裡學到老外在日常生活中「使用率」高的口語表達，如果你想在和外國人的交流中隨時就能脫口而出一句漂亮又讓人驚豔的英語，那麼歡迎你，這本書可以說是為你量身定做的。

全書一共分為兩個部分：第一部分是「實用超短句」，每一句都是老外生活裡常會說的口語，最多四個單字，最短的甚至只有一個字，就能讓你達到「記得快，用得準」的超高效率；第二部分是「傳情達意好用句」，精選一些好用的口語句，將它們按照表達情緒的功能分類，例如表達「喜悅、興奮」時的句子，表達「尷尬、彆扭」時的口語，或表達「鄙視、鄙夷」時最合宜的用句等，希望能幫助你用豐富的句子以及最貼近老外的口語方式，精準地表達自己的心情與感受。

本書最大的特點：就是沒有刻意地安排學習進度，才不致讓你在一開始的學習就倍感壓力，進而排斥，然後放棄。你可以翻到任何一頁開始學起，因為每一頁的內容和架構都

是獨立的。不論想學哪一句常用語，從主句的認識，到兩組對話的設計，讓你完全了解並掌握如何應用在生活情境裡；接下來，輕鬆活潑的解析，以及適時拉出介紹的單字，也能讓你更深度了解你所學的每一句話的用法，舉一反三，延伸學更多，不僅能避免表錯情會錯意，也讓英語說得更道地。

很多讀者都有因為生活忙碌而沒有時間學好英語的困難。其實在語言學習領域早有研究顯示，「細水長流」比「暴風驟雨」效果好，意思就是：每天5分鐘的短暫學習比隔幾天狂讀2小時效果好，因為提高語言能力，貴在堅持，而不在所謂的「速成」。

再忙的人總有零碎的「片刻時間」，把這些時間拿來學習，相信經過積少成多的累積收穫會更可觀的。這本書就是非常符合現代人生活步調的「化零為整學習材料」，希望即使每天只是5分鐘，每位讀者都能利用本書，感受到學習的樂趣和英文進步的快樂。

目錄 **Contents**

Part **1**
實用超短句

Chapter01 一字句

Chapter02 二字句

Chapter03 三字句

Chapter04 四字句

Part 2
傳情達意好用句

Chapter09 冷漠、無所謂

Chapter10 迷茫、困惑

Chapter11 難受、不舒服

Chapter12 譴責、不贊同

Chapter13 傷心、難過

Chapter14 深情、熱愛

Chapter15 生氣、憤慨

Chapter19 厭煩、憎惡

Chapter20 遺憾、悔恨

Part 1

實用超短句

每天 5 分鐘英語力大躍進！ O MP3 Track 001

Awesome!

太好了！／棒極了！

Ⓐ How was your date with that blonde girl?

Ⓑ **Awesome!** We had a great time.

A：你跟那位金髮女孩的約會如何呀？

B：太讚了！我們在一起很開心。

Ⓐ Oh my God, I'm gonna be on TV!

Ⓑ That's **awesome!** Can't wait to see you on the screen!

Ⓐ Oh, in fact you can't "see" me there. I'm playing a corpse covered by a white sheet.

Ⓑ ...

A：天哪，我要上電視了！

B：太棒了！我迫不及待想看你出現在螢幕上呢！

A：哦，其實你「看」不到我的。我演一具死屍，蓋著白床單呢。

B：……

原來老外都這樣用！ **Know it!**

awesome 是很常用的一個字，表示「很好，棒極了」。它的用法很靈活，既可單獨成句，也可放在句子中，具體說明你讚揚的對象，如：This is an awesome place!（這地方真棒！）不過，這個字近幾年有點被濫用了。

順帶一提，英語中還有一個類似的字很好用—— gorgeous。它通常用來稱讚女生漂亮，例如，看到一位女性朋友穿了件漂亮的晚禮服，就可以誇她：You look gorgeous today.（你今天美極了。）表示讚美的形容詞還有：wonderful、amazing、stunning、superb、marvelous、impressive 等。

 生字補充！ **Vocabularies & Phrases**

• corpse [kɔrps] 名 屍體

Ditto.

你說得沒錯。／同上。

A Have you ever been to the Maldives?

B Yeah, I really wish I were there now!

A Ditto!

A：你去過馬爾地夫嗎？

B：去過啊，我真希望我現在就在那裡！

A：我也是！

A I found several **ditto**'s in this list. What does the word mean?

B It means the same word or phrase as the above should be used here.

A：我發現列表裡有好幾處寫著「ditto」，這個字是什麼意思啊？

B：「同上」的意思。

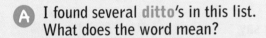 原來老外都這樣用！ **Know it!**

ditto 可以用來表示你與某人有著相同的觀點或感受（如第一個對話），在口語中可以簡潔有力地表達情緒，例如，你和某人吵架了，對方生氣地說：I hate you!（我討厭你！），此時你就可以回應：Ditto!（我也討厭你！）ditto 還可以表示「同上」（如第二個對話），這個意思主要用於表格中，指此處應該用與上一格相同的詞語或表達，填表時也可以用符號「"」來表示 ditto 這個字。

另外，不要混淆 ditto 和 ibid 的用法。後者通常用於正式寫作中，出現在引用的內容之後，表示「出處同前」。

 生字補充！ **Vocabularies & Phrases**

• **Maldives** [ˈmældaɪvz] 名 馬爾地夫

Exactly.

正是。／沒錯。

A So you think we should buy the castle?

B Exactly.

A：這麼說你認為我們應該把城堡買下來？

B：正是。

A I think we need to find a warm place for our vacation. I miss the sunshine so much.

B Exactly! What do you say, Olivia? And we can wear our new dresses!

A OK, I'm for it.

A：我覺得我們應該選一個溫暖的地方度假。我太想念陽光了。

B：沒錯！奧莉維亞，你覺得如何？我們還可以穿新裙子！

A：可以啊，我同意。

原來老外都這樣用！ **Know it!**

exactly 在這裡是對話中的一種回應，用於肯定對方說的話，表示你認為對方說的話完全正確。大家在附和別人時不妨試著多用用這個表達，比一直用 yes 要好得多。

exactly 是常用副詞，表示「精確地，確切地」，如：It's exactly half past five.（一分不差，正好 5 點半。）exactly 也可以表示「恰好，正好」，如：That's exactly what I've been trying to tell you.（那正是我一直想告訴你的。）口語中還經常使用 not exactly 這個表達，表示「不完全如此」或「並不是」。例如："You hate your boss, don't you?" "Not exactly. I just think he is a bit too mean."（「你恨你的老闆，是不是？」「不完全是這樣。我只是覺得他有點太刻薄了。」）

 生字補充！ **Vocabularies & Phrases**

· castle [ˋkæsḷ] 名 城堡

Interesting.

有意思。／有趣。／呵呵。

A These are all pictures I took with big stars!

B Interesting.

A：這些都是我跟大明星們的合照！

B：真有趣。

A The HR Department has invited an expert to give us a talk this weekend.

B What's it about?

A It's about "how to stay in a good mood when you're working overtime."

B Interesting.

A：人事部這個週末請了專家為我們開講座。

B：是關於什麼的？

A：關於「如何在加班時保持良好情緒」。

B：呵呵。

原來老外都這樣用！ Know it!

interesting 的本義為「有趣的，吸引人的」。在英文交談中，人們常用 Interesting. 或 That's interesting. 來表示對談話的內容或話題感興趣。但基於禮貌，人們在並不感興趣的時候，可能也「虛偽地」用 interesting 回應，而且現在逐漸有負面含義超過正面含義的趨勢，所以在跟老外說話時，就要特別小心分辨其個中之意。

另外介紹一組可用來表示「有趣的，吸引人的」這一含義的字：fascinating（迷人的，引人入勝的）；stimulating（饒有趣味的，激發思考的）；intriguing（〔由於不尋常、神祕或出人意料而〕非常有趣的）；absorbing / engrossing（很吸引人的，引人入勝的）；gripping / riveting / compelling（〔故事、電影等〕扣人心弦的，引人入勝的）；enthralling（〔尤指表演〕精彩的，有趣的）；spellbinding（極有趣的，使人入迷的）。

Look.

看。／瞧。／聽著。

Ⓐ Where are you going?

Ⓑ **Look**, I've had enough of this. I'm going home.

A：你去哪兒啊？

B：聽著，我已經受夠了。我要回家。

Ⓐ Rick, are you interested in translating the book?

Ⓑ When should it be finished?

Ⓐ By the end of April.

Ⓑ You know, I'll be super busy in February and March.

Ⓐ **Look.** Why don't you think about it and give me your answer tomorrow?

A：瑞克，你有沒有興趣翻譯那本書？

B：什麼時候要完成？

A：四月底。

B：你知道的，我二月和三月會超級忙。

A：這樣吧，你考慮一下，明天給我答覆好嗎？

原來老外都這樣用！ **Know it!**

look 在這裡用於讓人注意你接下來要說的話，表示「瞧，聽好」，相當於一個「引子」。類似這種功能的表達還有："you know"，意為「你知道的」（對某事進行解釋和描述時想要提供更多的資訊）；listen 或 listen to this，意為「聽著，聽好」（用於提示對方留意你要說的話）；guess what，意為「猜猜看」（用於提示對方留意你要說的話，往往是你認為會讓人驚訝的話）。

 生字補充！ **Vocabularies & Phrases**

• **have had enough of...** 片 對……受夠了

Oops.

哎喲。／哎呀。

A Could you please fill out this table?

A：你可以把這個表格填好嗎？

B Sure. **Oops**, I think I spelled that wrong.

B：沒問題。哎呀，我想我拼寫錯了。

A **Oops**! My new shoes are slippery on this wet floor!

A：哎呀！我穿新鞋走在有水的地上好滑啊！

B Be careful! Hold my hand.

B：小心點！抓著我的手。

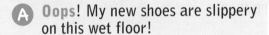 **Know it!**

原來老外都這樣用！

oops 是感嘆詞，當你摔倒或出了點小差錯時可以用，相當於中文裡的「哎喲」或「哎呀」。在同樣情形下，中文和英文使用的感嘆詞不同。有人說：衡量一個人英文水準的標準之一，就是看他能否自然地使用英文感嘆詞，例如突然被人踩一腳時，下意識喊的是「哎喲」還是 "ouch"。ouch 也是一個感嘆詞，表示突然感到疼痛時的叫聲，相當於中文裡的「哎喲」。

類似的例子還有：hooray 是表示高興的呼喊聲，相當於中文的「好哇」。psst 是一種暗中引起某人注意的聲音，相當於中文的「噓」。eek 表示突然的驚嚇，相當於中文的「喲」或「呀」，例如：Eek! A mouse!（呀！老鼠！）gee 用於表達驚訝或生氣，相當於中文的「哎呀」或「哇」，例如：Gee, Mom, do we have to go?（哎呀，媽媽，我們非去不可嗎？）eww 表示厭惡，例如：She kissed him? Eww!（她親他了？真噁心！）yuck 表示強烈的厭惡，常用於表示討厭某種食物，相當於中文的「哎喲」或「矮油」，例如：Oh yuck! I hate mayonnaise.（哎喲！我討厭美乃滋。）

 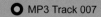

Period.

到此為止。

A You won't go dancing with me tonight, right?

B I'm going to the bar with John.

A I hate to say it, but you would rather go out with John than dance with me?

B I don't want to talk about it, **period!**

A Mom, may I go to the party tonight?

B Have you finished your homework?

A I can do it at the weekend, or...

B You're not going out tonight, **period.** Homework first!

A：今晚你不陪我去跳舞了，是吧？

B：我要和約翰去酒吧。

A：我真是不想說，你寧願和約翰出去也不願和我跳舞？

B：我不想談這個，到此為止吧！

A：媽，我今晚能去參加聚會嗎？

B：你做完作業了嗎？

A：我可以在週末做，或者……

B：今晚你哪兒也不能去，沒什麼好說的了。做完作業再說！

原來老外都這樣用！ **Know it!**

period 有「句號」的意思，句末出現句號就表示一句話結束了，所以 Period 在口語中有「到此為止」之意，表示不耐煩不想再談下去了。

End of story 同樣也表示拒絕再談下去，態度生硬，所以也要看場合使用。例如：I bought it because I wanted to. End of story.（我買是因為我想要。就是這樣，沒什麼好說的。）

Shoot!

說吧！／糟糕！

A Can I ask you a question?

A：能問你個問題嗎？

B OK, **shoot!**

B：可以，問吧！

A Thanks for the meal! It's really delicious.

A：謝謝你請我吃飯，真的很美味！

B You're welcome. Oh, **shoot!** I forgot my wallet!

B：別客氣。啊，完蛋了！我忘了帶錢包！

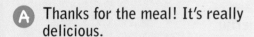 **Know it!**

Shoot! 在口語中主要用於兩種場合：一是告訴對方有什麼想說的就說吧（如第一個對話）；二是表達驚嚇、失望、生氣等情緒（如第二個對話），例如，當你關上門之後才發現鑰匙忘在屋裡時，就可以用 Ah, shoot!（哎呀，糟了！）來表達鬱悶之情，或者當你買的彩券差一號就中獎了，你也可以說：Shoot! I lost the lotto by one number!（真悶，差一號就中獎了！）

Shoot! 表明說話人心裡有火但是又不想罵人，所以不算髒話，大人小孩都可以說。

不過，當你低聲地放慢速度說 shoot 的時候，它的意思就發生了變化，表示的是不在乎或者討厭。例如，你跟朋友說你考試才考了 60 分，結果你朋友回答道：Shoot! At least you passed the exam! I only got 59!（夠囉，至少你考試及格了！我才 59 分！）

 生字補充！ **Vocabularies & Phrases**

• **wallet** [ˈwɑlɪt] **名** 錢包

So (what)?

那又怎樣？

A I'm marrying Bill next month.

A：我下個月要跟比爾結婚了。

B What? He's twenty years older than you!

B：什麼？他比你大二十歲呢！

A **So?** He cares about me and he's gonna make a wonderful husband.

A：那又怎樣？他在乎我，他會是個好丈夫的。

A You mean she knows our secret?

A：你是說她知道我們的祕密？

B Yes, she does. **So what?**

B：對，她是知道。那又怎麼樣？

A She might tell someone!

A：她可能會跟別人說呀！

B Oh, come on. Nobody will believe her.

B：哦，拜託，她說了也沒人信啊。

原來老外都這樣用！ **Know it!**

So? 或者 So what? 意為「那又怎樣？／那有什麼關係？」，表示對方說的事情並不重要，或者表示說話者不以為然的態度。這種說法不是特別客氣，有時甚至有點挑釁的意味，所以在上司、長輩，或不太熟悉的人面前要慎用。當然，非常要好的朋友則另當別論，你大可在丟出 So what? 的同時朝他／她翻個白眼。

除單獨成句外，so what 也可放在句首使用，常以 so what if... 的形式出現，表示「……又怎樣」，如：So what if we are a little late?（我們遲到一會兒又怎樣？）

Sure.

不客氣。

Chapter 01

一字句

A Thank you, dude.

A：謝啦，兄弟。

B Sure.

B：別客氣。

A I wouldn't have made it without you. Thank you so much.

A：沒有你我不會成功。太感謝了。

B Sure.

B：不用客氣。

原來老外都這樣用！ Know it!

sure 的基本含義是「肯定的，確信的」，但在這裡顯然不是這種含義。這裡 sure 是對對方感謝的回應，相當於中文的「不客氣」。我們最熟悉的回應感謝的方式可能是 That's OK. 和 You're welcome.，但其實在日常口語中，回應方式遠不止於此。

如果要求不是特別嚴謹的話，為了便於理解總結，我們可以把回應感謝的方式進行大致分類。

• 「樂意幫助」派：You're welcome. It's my pleasure. Anytime. Glad that I could help. Be my guest. My job.

• 「小事一樁、不足掛齒」派：Not at all. It was nothing. Don't mention it. Never mind. No problem. No sweat.

• 「不用謝」派：That's OK. That's all right. Sure. You bet.

不過相對來說，還是 You're welcome 最為常用，尤其是在比較正式的場合，或跟不是很熟的人交流時。

每天 **5** 分鐘**英語力大躍進！** ○ MP3 Track 011

There.

瞧。／好啦。

A **There!** I've done it!
I've resigned.

B Good for you!

A：瞧！我做到了！我已
經辭職了。

B：好樣的！

A Justin and I broke up.

B Again. It's the second time this
year.

A We're done. Really. I won't see
him again.

B **There!** What did I tell you?
I knew it wouldn't work.

A Why didn't you stop me? I hate
your I-told-you-so remarks.

A：我和賈斯汀分手了。

B：又來。這是今年第二
次了。

A：這次真的完了。我不
會再見他了。

B：你看，我怎麼跟你說
的？我就知道不行。

A：你幹嘛不攔著我？我
最煩你放馬後炮了。

原來老外都這樣用！ **Know it!**

there 在這裡是感嘆詞，意為「瞧，好啦」，表示一種滿意的語氣，可以是因為終於做了自己想做的事而滿意（如第一個對話），也可以是因為自己以前說的話被證明是正確的（如第二個對話）。see 有時也可以表示這種含義，例如：See? I told you it's still hot and you'll get burned!（看吧，我告訴過你它還熱著呢，你會燙到的！）

there 還可以表示安慰，這時常以 there, there 或 there, now 的形式出現。例如：There, there, don't get so upset.（好啦，好啦，別那麼難過。）

 生字補充！ **Vocabularies & Phrases**
• **resign** [rɪˋzaɪn] 動 辭職

Whatever.

隨便。／都行。／無所謂。

A If you leave me, I'll kill myself!

A：你要是敢離開我，我就死給你看！

B Whatever.

B：隨你便。

A Do you know who Plato is?

A：你知道柏拉圖是誰嗎？

B Mickey Mouse's pet dog.

B：米老鼠的寵物狗。

A No, he is an ancient Greek philosopher.

A：不是，他是一位古希臘的哲學家。

B Whatever.

B：管他是誰呢。

原來老外都這樣用！ Know it!

whatever 在這裡是副詞，表示「隨便，都行，無所謂」，表達說話的人一種無所謂的態度，例如不在乎從若干選項中具體選擇哪一個，不在乎某事物的具體細節，或不在乎對方的說法、做法，不想與對方爭辯。

類似可以表達「不在乎，無所謂」的說法還有：So what?（那又怎樣？）Who cares?（誰在乎？／我才不在乎呢。）I don't give a damn / shit / fuck.（我才不在乎呢。）What does that have to do with me?（那跟我有什麼關係？）要注意，以上說法都不是很客氣哦。

生字補充！ Vocabularies & Phrases

• **ancient** ['enʃənt] 形 古代的
• **Greek** [grik] 形 希臘的

Bottoms up!

乾杯！

A I've been planning this trip for a month. By this time tomorrow, I'll be on the plane.

B Then we shouldn't waste the drink. **Bottoms up!**

A：這次出遊我計畫了一個月，明天這個時候我就在飛機上了。

B：那我們別讓酒浪費了，乾杯！

A You've been my best friend my whole life and I hope everything will go well for you in the new school. Everyone, to Johnny.

B Thank you, Kevin. I would like to thank you for all the support you've given me. **Bottoms up**, everyone!

A：你是我這輩子最好的朋友，我希望你在新學校一切順利。各位，我們一起敬強尼一杯。

B：謝謝，凱文，謝謝你一直以來對我的支持。朋友們，乾杯！

原來老外都這樣用！ **Know it!**

Bottoms up! 在喝酒時使用，相當於中文裡的「乾杯」，用以表達良好的祝願或感激、高興等心情（如上述兩個對話），正所謂「感情深，一口悶」嘛！不過，Bottoms up! 這個說法在如今略顯老套，Cheers! 更加常用一些。例如，大家歡迎你的到來，一起吃了頓飯，那麼席間你就可以舉著酒杯說：Thank you for the warm welcome. Everyone, cheers!（感謝你們的熱情歡迎，乾杯！）但是，根據語境的不同，cheers 還有其他含義，可不要混淆了。cheers 還可以表示「謝謝」，比如："Here is the magazine you wanted to borrow." "Oh, cheers."（「這是你想借的那本雜誌。」「哦，謝謝。」）cheers 也可以表示「再見」，比如：Cheers then. See you next week.（那麼，再見，下週見啦。）

Butt out!

別插嘴！／不要管！

A Don't be mad at Candice. She meant well.

B This has nothing to do with you, so just **butt out!**

A：別生坎迪絲的氣，她是好意。

B：這件事與你無關，不要管！

A We are really sorry for the inconvenience caused to you.

B I don't need your apology. I want a refund.

A But it's not our fault...

B **Butt out!** I'm talking to your boss!

A：為您造成不便，我們非常抱歉。

B：我不用你道歉，我要退款。

A：可是，這又不怪我們……

B：別插嘴！我跟你經理在說話！

原來老外都這樣用！　Know it!

Butt out! 是一種粗魯的說法，用於告訴對方不要參與某件事情或對話，可譯為「不要管！／別插嘴！」表達相似的意思還可以用：It's none of your business.（這不關你的事。）It has nothing to do with you.（這跟你沒關係。）Mind your own business.（管好你自己的事情吧。）Don't interrupt me.（不要打斷我。）Don't cut in. / Don't chip in.（別插嘴。）

也可以用 Don't butt in.（別插嘴。）butt in 的意思和 butt out 完全相反。butt in 有兩重含義，一是「插嘴」，例如：Stop butting in!（別插嘴！）；二是「插手，管閒事」，例如：They don't want outsiders butting in on their decision-making.（他們不希望有外人插手他們的決策。）

Cheer up!

振作起來！／高興點！

A Can you just leave me alone?

B No. You've been here in this gloomy room for a whole day. What you need now is a shower and a good meal. **Cheer up!** Let's get out of here.

A：你讓我一個人靜一靜嗎？

B：不行。你都在這個陰暗的房間裡待了一整天了。你現在需要洗個澡，吃頓美食。高興點！咱們出去吧。

A I failed again. Do I really have what it takes to be a good cook?

B Of course you do. I'm a big fan of yours. **Cheer up!** You are the most gifted cook I've ever met.

A：我又失敗了。我真的是當廚師的料嗎？

B：你當然是。我是你的鐵粉。振作起來！你是我見過最有天賦的廚師了。

原來老外都這樣用！ **Know it!**

cheer up 表示「（使）高興起來，（使）振作起來」。當你看到別人灰心喪氣、情緒低落時，你就可以對他或她說 Cheer up! 鼓勵對方振作起來，打起精神。這是將 cheer up 作為祈使句來使用。cheer up 作為片語，也可以用在句子當中，例如：They cheered up when they saw us coming along.（他們看到我們來了，就高興了起來。）

cheer up 還可以表示「裝飾，裝點」，常以 cheer sth up 的形式出現，例如：I bought some pictures to cheer the place up a bit.（我買了些畫，把這地方裝飾佈置得漂亮一點。）

與 cheer 相關的常用表達還有 cheer on，表示「（在比賽中）為……加油，為……打氣」，例如：They gathered around the swimming pool and cheered her on.（他們聚集在游泳池邊為她加油。）

Come on!

快點！／加油！／夠囉！

A We lost the football match again. That was absolutely humiliating.

B Oh, **come on!** Some battles you win, some battles you lose.

A：我們又輸了足球賽，簡直丟臉丟到家了。

B：哦，這有什麼！勝敗乃兵家常事嘛。

A Where's my muffin gone?

B Er... A cat came running in, went straight for your muffin and took it away.

A Oh, **come on!** Can you come up with a worse lie?

A：我的鬆餅去哪裡了？

B：呃……一隻貓跑進來，朝著你的鬆餅就過去把它叼走了。

A：哦，夠囉！你還能再誇張點兒嗎？

原來老外都這樣用！ **Know it!**

Come on! 可以說是日常生活口語中最常見的表達之一。據統計，在美國經典劇集《六人行》中，六位主角使用 come on 達八百多次。

Come on! 可以表達多種意思和情緒。例如，當電影快要開場，而你的朋友仍在拖拖拉拉時，你可以用 Come on! 來催他／她快一點：Come on! We're running late!（快點，我們要遲到了！）當有人灰心喪氣時，你可以用 Come on! 給他／她加油鼓勵！當有人說了一句不可靠的話，或是企圖耍什麼花招時，你同樣可以回敬他／她一句 Come on!（拜託！／別逗了！／別跟我來這套！），表示你絕不買帳。

生字補充！ **Vocabularies & Phrases**

• **humiliating** [hjuˋmɪlɪˌetɪŋ] 形 丟臉的，不光彩的

Drop it.

別說了。／別鬧了。／住手吧。

A Why did you give it up then?

A：你當時為什麼放棄了？

B Just **drop it**, will you? I don't want to talk about it any more.

B：到此為止，可以嗎？我不想再談這個問題了。

A Take this ball. Can you hit the tree over there with it?

A：拿著這個球。你能用這個球擊中那邊的那棵樹嗎？

B Come on. I'm not interested in your silly game.

B：拜託，我對你的弱智遊戲沒興趣。

A Take it, please. Take it, take it...

A：拿著吧，求求你。拿著吧，拿著吧……

B **Drop it**. I'm totally worn out.

B：別鬧了。我都快累死了。

原來老外都這樣用！ Know it!

Drop it 在口語中常用來表達兩種意思，一種是「停止談論某事，別談了」（如第一個對話），另一種是「別鬧了，住手吧」（如第二個對話）。

如果想表達「別談這個話題了」，還可以使用 drop the subject，例如：To her relief, Julius dropped the subject.（讓她欣慰的是，朱力斯停止了那個話題。）也可以用 let it drop，例如："What about the tuition fee?" "We've agreed to let it drop."（「學費怎麼辦？」「我們已經說好不再提了。」）

 生字補充！ Vocabularies & Phrases
• **worn out** 片（因工作賣力而）精疲力竭的

Fat chance!
不可能！

A Would your car be easy to steal?

A：你的汽車容易被盜嗎？

B Fat chance! I've got a device that shuts down the gas and ignition.

B：不可能！我有個裝置，可關閉油門和點火開關。

A I have only 200 yuan left with me.

A：我只剩200塊錢了。

B But we won't get paid until next month.

B：可是我們要下個月才能拿到薪水呢。

A I'm going to borrow some money from my sister.

A：我打算找我姐借一點錢。

B You think she'll lend you any money? Fat chance!

B：你覺得她會借給你嗎？別做夢了！

原來老外都這樣用！ Know it!

Fat chance! 通常用來強調你認為某事不可能發生。不要被fat迷惑了，以為它是表示機會很大呢！除了 fat chance，還有一個關於 fat 的用法要特別注意，那就是 a fat lot of good / help / use。千萬別誤以為這是「很有幫助，很有用」的意思，它其實是「無濟於事，毫無用處」之意。

No chance at all! 也是「不可能！」之意，可以和 Fat chance! 替換。

 生字補充！ **Vocabularies & Phrases**

• **device** [dɪˋvaɪs] 名 設備，裝置
• **ignition** [ɪgˋnɪʃən] 名（汽車引擎的）點火裝置

Forget it.

別想了。／不行。

A How much do I owe you for dinner yesterday?

B Oh, forget it—it's nothing.

A：昨天的晚餐我該給你多少錢？

B：哦，別在意——那沒什麼。

A Any chance of you working the night shift for me?

B Forget it—I've been on two night shifts!

A：你能不能替我值夜班？

B：別想了——我已經值了兩個夜班了！

原來老外都這樣用！ Know it!

Forget it 這個小短句可表示多種意思，也可用於不同場合：當你想告訴對方不用在意某事時，可以用 Forget it. 表示「區區小事，何足掛齒」之意（如第一個對話）；當你要拒絕對方的請求時，可以用 Forget it. 表示「不行」之意（如第二個對話）；當你不想重複剛才說的話時，也可以用 Forget it. 表示「沒什麼」之意，例如，對方沒聽清楚你說的話，問你剛才說什麼了，你就可以回答：Forget it, it doesn't matter.（沒什麼，不是什麼重要的事。）；當某人跟你反覆嘮叨某事而讓你厭煩時，可以用 Forget it 表示「別再說了」之意，例如，好友一直責備你遲到，你可以回應：Just forget it, OK?（別再說了，行嗎？）

 生字補充！ Vocabularies & Phrases

• **owe** [o] 動 欠（錢）
• **night shift** 片 夜班

Get lost!

走開！／滾開！

A Are you OK?

A：你還好嗎？

B **Get lost** and leave me alone!

B：走開，讓我一個人靜一靜！

A Don't get mad at me, honey. I didn't mean to hurt you.

A：別生我的氣，寶貝。我不是故意要傷害你的。

B But you did hurt me!

B：但你就是傷害了我！

A I'm sorry. But she needs me.

A：對不起，但是她需要我。

B Go to hell! **Get lost!**

B：你去死吧！你給我滾！

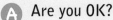 **Know it!**

Get lost! 是一種很粗魯的說法，用於讓某人走開，不要煩你，相當於中文的「走開！滾開！」類似的表達還有以下幾種：Go away! 表示「走開！」；Get out of here! 表示「滾（出去）！」；Go fly a kite! 意為「走開！閉嘴！別煩我！」，是不太客氣的說法；Go to hell! 意為「下地獄吧！去死吧！」，表示對某人很生氣，也是一種很粗魯的讓別人滾開的表達；Fuck off! 意為「滾開！」，是非常粗魯的表達，請大家慎用。

再介紹幾個與 lost 相關的常用表達。feel / be lost 表示「迷惘，困惑，不知所措」，如：It's not unusual to feel lost when you first start college.（剛上大學時感到迷惘不足為奇。）get lost (in sth) 表示「（在複雜的過程或忙碌中）被遺忘或忽略」，如：It's easy for your main points to get lost in a long speech.（做長篇演說容易偏離要點。）

 生字補充！ **Vocabularies & Phrases**

• **mean** [min] 動 意欲，打算

每天 5 分鐘**英語力大躍進！**

 每天 5 分鐘**英語力大躍進！**　○ MP3 Track 021

Get real!
別傻了！／現實點！

A Let's just say it was an accident.

> A：就說這是個意外。

B **Get real!** She'll never buy that.

> B：別傻了！她才不會相信呢。

A Maybe you can sneak out of the house when your parents are asleep.

> A：說不定你可以趁你爸媽睡著的時候溜出來。

B Oh, **get real!** If my mom finds out, I'll never hear the end of it.

> B：哦，別傻了！要是被我媽發現了，她會嘮叨個沒完的。

原來老外都這樣用！ Know it!

Get real! 意為「別傻了！／現實點！」當你認為對方的看法或提議很傻很天真時，便可用這句話給他／她潑潑冷水。

能表示類似含義的表達還有：Don't be silly! 意為「別傻了！」Grow up! 意為「你是三歲小孩嗎？」還有更生動的，pigs might fly（或 when pigs fly）的字面意思是「豬可能會飛（當豬飛的時候）」，但豬會飛嗎？顯然不會啊，所以它表示的是某事不可能發生，相當於中文裡的「太陽從西邊來」，如："This time he might behave himself." "Yes, and pigs might fly."（「這一次他也許可以規規矩矩的呢。」「是啊，太陽還能從西邊出來呢。」）

 生字補充！ Vocabularies & Phrases

- **buy** [baɪ] **動** 接受，相信（尤指不大可能屬實的事情）
- **sneak out of 片** 偷偷溜出……

Go ahead!

繼續吧！／開始吧！

A Hey, man, you should tell her you're into her. Now imagine that I was the girl, and tell me!

A：嘿，兄弟，你應該告訴她你喜歡她。現在把我想像成那個女孩，對我表白吧！

B OK, but I just don't want you staring at me when I'm doing this.

B：倒是可以，但我就是不想在表白的時候被你盯著看。

A All right, I'll turn around. **Go ahead!**

A：好吧，我轉過身。你説吧！

- -

A You know I'm a good joke teller. I have a good one about my prom.

A：你知道我很會講笑話。我有一個關於我高中舞會的笑話，很好笑。

B **Go ahead**, please!

B：那你講吧！

原來老外都這樣用！ Know it!

在口語中常用 Go ahead! 來表達「說吧！／去吧！」之意，用於鼓勵（如第一個對話）或允許（如第二個對話）別人做某事。再舉兩個例子：If you wanna watch TV, go ahead!（如果你想看電視的話，去看吧！）"Do you mind if I smoke here?" "No, go ahead."（「我能在這兒抽菸嗎？」「沒關係，抽吧。」）此外，Go ahead! 還可以表示請對方先走或先行做某事，例如你和另外一個人在門口「狹路相逢」，你就可以很有風度地說：Go ahead, please.（您先請吧。）

 生字補充！ **Vocabularies & Phrases**

- **stare** [stɛr] 動 盯著看
- **prom** [prɑm] 名（常在學年末舉行的）高中生正式舞會

Got it!
知道了！／明白！

A If you take the baby out for a walk, you might wanna bring his hat, and there's extra milk in the fridge, and there are extra diapers in the bag.

A：你要是帶寶寶出去散步，記得帶著他的帽子，冰箱裡還有牛奶，袋子裡還有些尿布。

B Hat, milk, diapers. Got it!

B：帽子、牛奶、尿布。知道了！

A Three short whistles, and you start to run, okay?

A：聽到三聲短促的哨音，你就開始跑，明白了嗎？

B Got it!

B：明白！

原來老外都這樣用！ Know it!

Got it! 用於回應別人的吩咐，語氣通常十分爽快，表示你已明白並準備照做。問句 Got it? 意為「明白了嗎？」，如：He's got a weak ankle. One hard kick and he'll back off. Got it? （腳踝是他的薄弱之處。用力踢上一腳，他就沒辦法囂張了。明白了嗎？）

與 Got it! 類似的表達還有 Roger (that)! 這本是一句無線電的通訊用語，意為「收到！／明白！」，後來漸漸成為生活俚語，表示「好！／了解！／明白！」。

 生字補充！ Vocabularies & Phrases
- **extra** [ˈɛkstrə] 形 額外的，另外的
- **diaper** [ˈdaɪəpɚ] 名 尿布，尿片

Grow up!

成熟點！／要像個大人樣！

A I want those shoes! Candice bought those shoes, and I want just the same!

B **Grow up**, please! You can't have everything Candice has. Even if you got everything she has, you couldn't be her.

A：我想要那雙鞋！坎迪絲買了那雙鞋，我也想要同款的！

B：成熟點吧！你不能看坎迪絲有什麼就要什麼。就算你擁有了她有的一切，你也成為不了她。

A Just you wait! I'll kick your ass next time!

B Come on. **Grow up!** Can you do anything better than cry like a baby?

A：等著瞧！我下次會狠狠教訓你的！

B：拜託，有點大人的樣子吧！你除了會哭得像小孩一樣，還會什麼？

原來老外都這樣用！ **Know it!**

Grow up! 意為「要有個大人樣！」，用於告誡別人要成熟一些，像個成年人一樣有理性和責任感。類似的意思還可以用 Don't be so childish! 或 Behave like an adult! 來表示。childish 的意思是「幼稚的，孩子氣的」，含有貶義。adult 的意思是「成年人」。所以 Don't be so childish! 的意思就是「別這麼幼稚！」，Behave like an adult! 的意思是「要像個大人的樣子！」

grow up 還可以表示「形成，興起，發展」，例如：Trading settlements grew up by the river.（河的兩岸形成了一些貿易定居點。）再介紹幾個與 grow 相關的表達 grow apart 指「（彼此的關係）越來越疏遠」，如：The couple had been growing apart for years.（這對夫婦多年來日漸疏遠。）grow on 表示「逐漸為（某人）所喜歡」，如：I hated his music at first, but it grows on you.（我一開始討厭他的音樂，可慢慢卻越來越喜歡。）grow out 指「（使）頭髮長長而讓原來的髮型消失」，如：I'm growing my fringe out.（我準備把瀏海留長不要了。）

Hold on.

等會兒。／等等。／別掛電話。

A It's snowing outside. Let's go out and take some photos.

A：外面下雪呢。我們出去拍照吧。

B **Hold on** a minute. I'll just grab my coat.

B：等一下。我去拿外套。

A Clara and James are going to the United States next week.

A：克拉拉和詹姆斯下週要去美國了。

B **Hold on.** Isn't Clara supposed to be with Mike?

B：等等，克拉拉不是應該和麥克在一起嗎？

A Oh, they broke up ages ago.

A：哦，他們八百年前就分手了。

原來老外都這樣用！ Know it!

hold on 也是英語口語中很常見的表達，既可單獨成句（如第二個對話中），也可與 a minute, a second, a sec 等連用（如第一個對話中）。

hold on 在不同場合可以表達不同的意思。它可以表示「等會兒，稍等」，相當於 wait (a minute, a second, a sec)（如第一個對話中）；也可表示注意到、聽到或記起令人感興趣或不好的事（如第二個對話中）；還可用在接電話時，表示「等一等，不要掛」，如：Hold on. Let me check and see if she's here.（請稍等，讓我看看她在不在。）Can you hold on a second? I have another call.（先別掛好嗎？我得接個別的電話。）

 生字補充！ **Vocabularies & Phrases**

• **grab** [græb] 動 抓住，抓取
• **break up** 片 分手
• **ages ago** 片 很久以前

I quit.

我退出。／我不幹了。

A This task is so hard. **I quit.**

B Oh, come on! Let's have another try. It's worth it.

A：這項任務太難了。我要退出。

B：哎，別這樣！我們再試一試。這件事兒值得我們努力的。

A Hey, what's wrong with you? This salad tastes terrible!

B You're yelling at me again! Can't believe I ever thought of cooking for you! **I quit!**

A：喂，怎麼回事？這沙拉怎麼這麼難吃！

B：你又對著我大呼小叫！我竟然還幫你做飯！我不幹了！

原來老外都這樣用！ **Know it!**

I quit 既可以表示因困難而退出某項正在從事的活動（如第一個對話中），又可以表示因生氣、厭煩而停止不幹了（如第二個對話中）。這裡的 quit 是非正式用法，有「離開」之意，如辭職就是 to quit one's job，輟學就是 to quit school，某明星退出娛樂圈則可以說 to quit show business。

quit 還常常用來表示停止、戒除壞事或令人厭煩的事，例如：to quit smoking（戒菸），to quit drinking（戒酒），Quit bothering me!（別煩我！）在口語中，有時用 quit 會比用 stop 顯得更道地一些呢。

生字補充！ **Vocabularies & Phrases**

• **yell** [jɛl] 動 喊，叫

I'm flattered.

過獎了。

A Lily, I have had feelings for you for a long time. I think you are the girl whom I'm looking for.

B I'm flattered, but I think we are better as friends.

A：莉莉，我喜歡妳很久了，我覺得妳就是我一直在尋找的女孩。

B：我受寵若驚，但我想我們做朋友比較好。

A Did you hear that John would run for the chairman's seat?

B Yeah, he's awesome!

A Actually, I think you are the better candidate. Why don't you enter the election?

B Well, I'm flattered, but I don't think I am the person for the job.

A：你聽說約翰要競選主席了嗎？

B：聽說了，他真了不起！

A：其實我覺得你是更合適的人選，你為什麼不參加競選？

B：您過獎了，我覺得自己不是那塊料。

原來老外都這樣用！ Know it!

I'm flattered 通常用來表示覺得自己對他人的誇獎受之有愧（如第二個對話中）。這個「受之有愧」可能是你發自肺腑的感慨，也可能只是你的自謙之詞，其實心裡說不定多開心呢！還有一種情況就是拒絕對方的邀請、告白時（如第一個對話中），說一句 I'm flattered 會讓你的拒絕顯得委婉禮貌些，不會那麼不客氣。

動詞 flatter 有「討好，奉承」之意，告誡對方「不要自以為是！」時可以用 Don't flatter yourself! 這句表達。

 生字補充！ Vocabularies & Phrases
• candidate [ˈkændəˌdet] **名** 候選人

It sucks.

太糟糕了。／真差勁。／太遜了。

Chapter
02
二字句

A I made up the joke myself.
It's funny, isn't it?

B No, **it sucks.**

A:這是我自己編的笑話。
好笑吧?

B:才不是呢,特別爛。

A Susan invited you to her home for dinner?

B Yeah, she made several so-called specialties.

A Delicious?

B Her cooking was terrible.
It sucked!

A:蘇珊邀請你去她家吃晚
飯了?

B:是的,她做了幾道所謂
的拿手菜。

A:好吃嗎?

B:她的廚藝糟透了。那頓
飯真難吃!

原來老外都這樣用! **Know it!**

除了上述兩個對話外,**It sucks** 還可用在多種場合表達「糟透了」的意
思。舉幾個例子:閨蜜和男友分手了,你安慰她說沒事的,一切都會好
的,但是傷心的閨蜜會說:No, it's not OK! It sucks! (不,一點兒都不
好!糟透了!)朋友不再幻想天上掉下錢來,決定腳踏實地生活,你可
以幽默地鼓勵:Welcome to the real world! It sucks, but you're going to
love it! (歡迎來到現實世界。它很差勁,但是你會愛上它的!)

生字補充! **Vocabularies & Phrases**

• **make up** 片 創作,編寫
• **specialty** [ˈspɛʃəltɪ] 名(某人、飯館或地方的)特色食品

Just because.

不為什麼。╱沒有為什麼。

A Why do you like reptiles? I heard you keep two lizards as pets.

B Just because.

A：你為什麼喜歡爬行動物？我聽說你養了兩隻蜥蜴當寵物。

B：喜歡就是喜歡囉。

A Why are you hanging out with Steve? He is such a loser!

B Just because.

A：你為什麼跟史蒂夫約會？那傢伙那麼沒出息！

B：不為什麼。

A Is it because he's good-looking? Beauty is only skin deep!

B Yeah, I'm just a superficial woman!

A：是因為他長得好看嗎？可外貌是膚淺的啊！

B：是啊，我就是一個膚淺的女人啊！

原來老外都這樣用！ Know it!

just because 除了像對話中那樣單獨使用，還可以在句子中作某成分使用，表示「僅僅因為……」，例如：Don't say yes just because they ask.（不要因為別人有求於你，你就什麼都答應。）

它還有一個很常見的用法是與 doesn't mean 連用，即 just because... doesn't mean...，意為「僅僅因為……並不意味著……」，表示一個條件的成立並不意味著另一個條件的成立，兩者沒有必然因果關係。例如：Just because you are my brother doesn't mean I have to like you.（你是我兄弟，那也不代表我必須得喜歡你呀。）

 生字補充！ Vocabularies & Phrases

• lizard [ˈlɪzəd] 名 蜥蜴

Nice try.

說的好。／好是好。

A My dog ate my homework.

A：我的作業被我的狗吃了。

B **Nice try.** I know you don't have a dog.

B：很不錯的說法。不過我知道你沒養狗。

A Maybe we could call on her!

A：我們可以去看看她呀！

B **Nice try**, Steve, but we don't know where she lives.

B：史蒂夫，這主意好是好，可是我們不知道她住哪兒呀。

原來老外都這樣用！ **Know it!**

Nice try 用於表達你認為對方的說法或提議不錯，只可惜行不通（如第二個對話中），或某種說法太牽強，不能說服你（如第一個對話中），後面往往跟著一個大大的、堅決的 but，陳述你的異議。

還有一個類似的表達是 Good question（或說成 That's a good question），其意思是對方的問題很好，只可惜你不知道怎麼回答。如："How can we raise the fund then?" "Good question!"（「那麼我們怎麼籌集資金呢？」「問得好！」）

 生字補充！ **Vocabularies & Phrases**
• **call on** 片 拜訪

No biggie.
沒關係。／不要緊。

A Sorry, I forgot to bring you the exercise book.

B Oh, **no biggie.**

A：抱歉，我忘了把練習本帶來給你。

B：哦，沒關係。

A I spilled the beer on the carpet. I'm so sorry!

B **No biggie!** I'll take care of it.

A：我把啤酒灑到地毯上了。太對不起了！

B：不要緊！我會處理的。

原來老外都這樣用！ Know it!

No biggie 用於表示認為某事不重要（如第一個對話中）或並沒有為某事感到生氣或煩惱（如第二個對話中）。它常可用來回應對方的 I'm sorry 或 sorry。

另外，It's no biggie 也是英語口語中常用的形式，表示「沒什麼大不了的」，常常用於安慰他人。比如，好朋友演講比賽失利了，你就可以安慰他／她說：It's no biggie. I'm sure you will do a better job next time.（這沒什麼大不了的，我相信你下次一定會表現得更棒。）it's no biggie 也可以後接 if 從句，表示「如果……也沒關係」。比如：I was going to use the computer but it's no biggie if you want to use it first.（我本打算用電腦的，不過要是你想先用也沒關係。）

生字補充！ Vocabularies & Phrases
- spill [spɪl] **動** 使濺出，使潑灑
- carpet [ˈkɑrpɪt] **名** 地毯

每天 5 分鐘英語力大躍進！　○ MP3 Track 032

No offence.

沒有冒犯的意思。／別見怪。

A How do you like my mom's cooking?

B No offence, but this cheese really doesn't taste very good.

A Tomorrow you'll quit your job at the café?

B Yes! And no offence to everybody who still works here, you have no idea how good it feels when you never have to make coffee again!

A：你覺得我媽媽的廚藝如何？

B：我說了你可別生氣。這乳酪真的不太好吃。

A：明天起你就不在咖啡館工作了？

B：是呀！我沒有冒犯同事們的意思，但你們不知道再也不用煮咖啡的感覺有多爽！

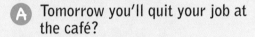 **原來老外都這樣用！** **Know it!**

當你在交談中即將說出可能讓對方感覺不快的話時，便可用 no offence 禮貌地表達一下歉意，接著再用 but 引出你要說的話（如第一個對話中）。no offence 後面也常用 to 引出你要表達歉意的事（如第二個對話中），即「沒有冒犯……的意思」。

可以較為禮貌地表達不同意見的說法還有：I'm sorry / I hate to say this, but...（我真不願意這麼說，但是……）；With (the greatest / due / all due) respect, but...（不是我不尊重你，但是……）；No hard feelings, but...（請別見怪，不過……）。適當地使用這些說法，可以緩和語氣，使交流更加順暢。

 生字補充！ **Vocabularies & Phrases**
• quit [kwɪt] 動 辭去（工作）

No problem.
沒問題。／沒什麼。

A Can I bring a friend?

A：我能帶個朋友來嗎？

B Sure, **no problem.**

B：當然，沒問題。

A Thanks for all your help.

A：感謝你所有的幫助。

B **No problem!**

B：沒什麼！

原來老外都這樣用！ **Know it!**

No problem 有兩個含義，一個用於表示同意，可譯為「沒問題」，如在第一個對話中；另一個用於回應對方的感謝或道歉，可譯為「沒什麼」，如在第二個對話中。have no problem (in) doing sth 表示「做某事沒問題」，例如：I've had no problem recruiting staff.（我招聘員工沒問題。）

problem 的基本含義是「問題；難題；困難」，有不少近義字可表達類似的含義。

- setback 意為「挫折，阻礙」，例如：The space program suffered a major setback when the space shuttle exploded.（該太空梭爆炸使航太計畫遭到嚴重挫折。）

- snag 意為「（尤指意外的）問題」，例如：There is a snag—I don't have his number.（有個小麻煩——我沒有他的號碼。）

- hitch 意為「小問題，小故障」，例如：There have been a few last-minute hitches.（最後一刻出現了一些小問題。）

- trouble 意為「麻煩；故障」，例如：The plane developed engine trouble.（飛機發生了引擎故障。）

- hassle 意為「麻煩；困難」，例如：Just trying to store all this stuff is a hassle.（單是把這些所有的東西儲藏起來就是個麻煩。）

No way!

不行！／不可能！

Ⓐ Can I borrow your car?

Ⓑ No way!

A：我能借用你的汽車嗎？

B：不行！

Ⓐ I've heard about the news.
Phil has told me.

Ⓑ No way!

A：我聽說那個消息了。菲爾告訴我了。

B：不可能！

原來老外都這樣用！ Know it!

No way! 是句很常見的口語，通常用於兩種場合：一是表示斷然拒絕做某事，意為「不！不行！」（如在第一個對話中）；二是表示不相信或驚訝，意為「不會吧！不可能！」（如在第二個對話中），再看一個例句：She's 45? No way!（她45歲？不會吧！）在第一種用法中，有時也可說成 No way Jose! 以示強調，即「絕對不做！」

no way 除了單獨成句外，也可用在句中，後接從句，如：There's no way I'll ever get married again.（我決不再婚。）There's no way the building work will be finished by today.（建築工作在今天完工是絕不可能的。）但要注意這種用法與 there's no way of doing sth 的區別，後者指「沒有做某事的辦法」，如：There's no way of knowing if the treatment will work.（沒有辦法知道這種治療方法是否有效。）

 生字補充！ **Vocabularies & Phrases**

• **borrow** [ˋbaro] 動 借東西，借錢
• **news** [njuz] 名 新聞

每天 5 分鐘英語力大躍進！ 🔘 MP3 Track 035

Not bad.

還不錯。／還可以吧。

A Hey, your studio looks great!

B Yeah, **not bad**, right? I spent weeks looking for a place like this!

A：嘿，你這工作室看起來不錯呀！

B：是呀，不錯吧？找這地方可是花了我好幾個星期呢！

A How's everything going lately?

B Oh, **not bad.**

A：近來如何啊？

B：哦，還可以。

原來老外都這樣用！ **Know it!**

not bad 可以用來回答別人關於你近況的詢問，或用於對某人或某事物的評價。從字面上看，這個片語的意思是「還不錯」，但在不同語境中，配上說話人不同的語氣和表情，其實可以表達不同的意思。比如別人問你某幅畫怎麼樣，如果你覺得這畫真的不錯，讓你眼前一亮，就可以豎起大拇指以讚歎的語氣說一句 Not bad!（不錯嘛！）如果你覺得這畫一般般，又不好直接表現出亮無興趣的樣子，也可以泛泛地評價一句 Not bad.（還可以吧。），讓對方通過你的語氣和表情來判斷你的意思吧。

 生字補充！ **Vocabularies & Phrases**

• studio [ˈstjudɪo] 名（畫家或攝影師的）工作室

Say cheese!

笑一個吧！

A Would you please take a photo for us?

B OK. Is everybody ready? Say cheese!

A：請問您能幫我們拍張照片嗎？

B：好的。大家都準備好了嗎？笑一個吧！

A A question for you!

B I'm ready!

A What is the expression used by photographers to get people to smile?

B So easy! It's "Say cheese!"

A：考你一道題！

B：放馬過來吧！

A：照相時，攝影師會告訴大家笑一個，這個「笑一個」怎麼說？

B：太簡單了！是 Say cheese!

原來老外都這樣用！ Know it!

Say cheese! 專門用於照相的場合，是拿相機的人鼓勵被拍照者笑一笑時說的話（如第一個對話中）。我們平時拍照時都會要大家「笑一個吧」，英文中與之相對應的表達應該就是 say cheese，因為說 cheese 這個字時，嘴型跟微笑的樣子是相似的，所以當攝影師說完 Say cheese! 之後，大家就可以齊聲高喊 Cheese! 這樣照出來的照片肯定笑得很開心！

有一款手機應用叫 Say Cheese Camera，顧名思義，當你喊完 cheese 之後，手機就會自動拍照，所以，它的中文名字就叫「聲控相機」。

生字補充！ Vocabularies & Phrases

- **photographer** [fə`tɑgrəfə] 名 攝影師

Shut up!

住口！／閉嘴！

A I want to get my money back!

B Just **shut up** and listen!

A：我要拿回我的錢！

B：住口！聽我說！

A I'll give you everything you want, and I'll do everything you want me to do.

B I don't want to talk to you now.

A You are my destiny, my love! You are my everything...

B Will you just **shut up**?

A：我會給你想要的一切，你讓我做什麼我就做什麼。

B：我現在不想跟你說話。

A：你就是我的宿命，我的愛！你是我的一切……

B：你能不能閉嘴？

原來老外都這樣用！　Know it!

Shut up! 在這裡意為「住口！閉嘴！」，用來粗暴地讓某人停止說話。

片語動詞 shut up 還常以 shut sb up 和 shut sth up 的形式出現。shut sb up 表示「使某人住口；讓某人閉嘴」，例如：She kicked Anne under the table to shut her up.（她在桌子底下踢了安妮一腳，讓她住嘴。）shut sth up 表示「關上（房子等）」，例如：Bernadette cleaned the attic and then shut it up for another year.（貝爾納黛特把閣樓打掃乾淨，然後又把它關閉了一年。）shut sb / sth up (in sth) 表示「把……關（或藏）起來；把……關（或藏）在」，例如：I've had a terrible cold and been shut up in my room for a week.（我得了重感冒，在房間裡關了一星期。）

生字補充！　Vocabularies & Phrases

• **destiny** [ˈdɛstənɪ] 名 命運，定數

Spare me!

饒了我吧！／別說了！

A Dear, I need a new purse, a new one-piece dress, some new boots, and...

B Oh, **spare me!** You can get anything you want! Just leave me alone!

A：親愛的，我需要一個新錢包、一件新的洋裝、新靴子，還有……

B：哦，饒了我吧！你想買什麼都行，別煩我了！

A They have three houses: one in the country, one at the seaside, and...

B **Spare me!**

A：他們有三間房產，一間在鄉下，一間在海邊，還有……

B：別說了！

原來老外都這樣用！ Know it!

Spare me! 用於打斷別人的話，以免聽到讓自己不快或厭煩的細節。當有人像唐僧一樣在你耳邊不停嘮叨時，你就可以用 Spare me! 叫他／她閉嘴。

打斷別人嘮叨的表達方式還有很多，如：Knock it off! Cut it out! Stop nagging me! Give me a break! 以及最常見的 Shut up! 不過，這些表達大多帶點火藥味，使用時要注意對象和場合哦！

生字補充！ Vocabularies & Phrases

- **one-piece** [ˋwʌn͵pis] 形 上下連身的

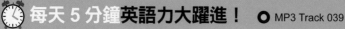

That figures.

意料之中。／這很合理。

A I heard that Jim invited Jane to his birthday party.

B But Jane didn't show up.

A That figures.

A：我聽說吉姆邀請簡參加他的生日聚會了。

B：但是珍沒有去。

A：早就料到了。

A I can't believe that I have to fill in five forms to submit my application.

B Well, in my opinion, that figures.

A：真不敢相信，我得填五份表格才能提交申請。

B：嗯，其實我覺得這挺合理的。

原來老外都這樣用！ **Know it!**

That figures 既可以表示「早就知道會這樣」（如第一個對話中），也可以表示「這是合情合理的」（如第二個對話中）。也可以說成 It figures 或 Figures，三者意思相同，可以互換使用。例如："We're out of milk and bread." "Figures."（「我們沒有牛奶和麵包了。」「意料之中。」）

注意不要把 Go figure 和 That figures 搞混。Go figure 表示認為某事很奇怪，解釋不通。例如："He didn't even make a call." "Go figure."（「他甚至沒打一通電話。」「這就怪了。」）

 生字補充！ **Vocabularies & Phrases**

• application [ˌæpləˈkeʃən] **名** 申請（書）

That's gross!

真噁心！

A Ouch! I've got a jellyfish sting! It hurts! Ow!

B Well, there's really only one thing you can do. You're gonna have to pee on it.

A What?! **That's gross!**

B I saw it on Discovery Channel.

A：哎喲！我被水母螫了！好疼！啊！

B：唉，看來你只有一個辦法了。在傷口上撒點尿吧。

A：什麼？！太噁心了！

B：我是在探索頻道看到的。

A I think the guy opposite is watching us with a telescope!

B Eww! **That's gross!**

A：我覺得對面那男人在拿望遠鏡看我們呢！

B：呀！真噁心！

原來老外都這樣用！ **Know it!**

That's gross! 在口語中用於表示某人或某事物讓你感到噁心、討厭，這種厭惡感既可以是感官上的，也可以是心理上的。這句話常常可以簡化為 Gross! 如：Ooh, gross! I hate onions!（喔，噁心！我討厭吃洋蔥！）

你可能已經注意到，人們在說 That's gross! 時前面往往配上豐富的語氣詞，常見的有：Eww! Ooh! Yuk! Ugh! 這些字均表示厭惡和不悅。英語中常見的語氣詞還有很多，如：Ouch! Ow! 表示疼痛，Oops! 表示犯錯、狼狽，Uh-oh 表示做錯了事或壞事即將發生等。

生字補充！ **Vocabularies & Phrases**
• jellyfish [ˈdʒɛlɪ.fɪʃ] 名 水母

That's right!

沒錯！／夠了喔！

A Some people find it very difficult to work quickly.

B **That's right**, and they often find exams very stressful.

A：有些人覺得想要快速地工作是困難的。

B：沒錯，他們往往也覺得考試壓力很大。

A Things just got out of control.

B I told you so! You were not fully prepared!

A **That's right!** Just blame me for everything, as usual!

A：事情失控了。

B：我早跟你說過了！你還沒有做好準備！

A：夠了喔！總是這樣，什麼事都怪我！

原來老外都這樣用！ **Know it!**

That's right! 一般有兩種含義。第一種表示同意別人說的話，類似於 yes，可譯為「對，沒錯」，第一個對話中就是這種用法。第二種含義是用於對某人所說的話或所做的事表示憤怒，可譯為「好啦，夠啦」，也可以把它理解為一種反話、氣話，依然譯為「對，沒錯」，第二個對話中就是這種用法。

這裡的 right 意為「對的，正確的，如實的」。如果想表達類似的含義，還可以用：correct，意為「正確的」，比 right 正式；accurate，意為「（資訊、描述、尺寸等）準確的」；exact，意為「（數字、數量或時間）精確的，確切的」；spot-on，意為「（尤指猜測或人們說的話）完全正確的」。

 生字補充！ **Vocabularies & Phrases**

• **stressful** [ˈstrɛsfəl] 形 充滿壓力的
• **blame** [blem] 動 責怪，指責

Time's up.

時間到。

A Hey, **time's up!** It's my turn!

B That was half an hour?

A Well, time flies when you're having fun.

A：喂，時間到了！該我啦！

B：半小時這麼快就過去了？

A：玩得高興時，時間就過得快。

A Fourteen... Fifteen... Oh, my God! Sixteen...

B **Time's up.** Less than twenty situps in one whole minute? You're so weak!

A：十四……十五……天啊！十六……

B：時間到。一分鐘才做了不到二十個仰臥起坐？你弱爆了！

原來老外都這樣用！ **Know it!**

Time's up 是終止計時的常用語，相當於中文裡的「時間到」。這裡的 up 是「耗盡、用光」的意思，例如我們可以說：We've used up all our savings.（我們把積蓄都花光了。）

如果要表示時間快到了、時間不多了，則可以說 Time's running out 或 We're running out of time. 如：Time's running out. We must hurry.（時間不多了。我們得快點。）表示其他事物用光、耗盡，也可用 sth run out 或 run out of sth，如：My patience was running out.（我漸漸失去耐心了。）Her luck has run out.（她的好運用完了。）They ran out of money and went home penniless.（他們把錢花光了，兩手空空地回了家。）

生字補充！ **Vocabularies & Phrases**

• **situp** [ˈsɪtˌʌp] 名 仰臥起坐

Watch out!

小心！／注意！

Ⓐ Turn left! Turn left! **Watch out!**

A：左轉！左轉！小心啊！

Ⓑ If you stop making such a fuss, I'm sure we both can arrive home alive.

B：要是你能別這麼大驚小怪的，我肯定我們都能平安到家。

Ⓐ **Watch out**—you're going to hit the door!

A：小心——你差點撞上門了！

Ⓑ I was zoning out.

B：我剛剛在放空。

原來老外都這樣用！ Know it!

Watch out! 表示提醒他人小心，留意可能會發生的危險，與其功能相似的還有 Look out! 和 Be careful! 通常來說，要留意的危險都是近在眼前的，比如：There's some ice there—be careful!（地上有冰——小心！）Look out! There's a car coming.（小心！有車開過來了。）值得一提的是，watch out 和 look out 這對很相似的「兄弟」在用法上略有差別：watch out 除了獨立成句外，也可以在 if 從句中用來談論假設的危險，如：You could have a nasty accident if you don't watch out.（不特別小心的話，可能會發生嚴重的事故。）；而 look out 則主要用於祈使句中，用來提醒注意眼前的危險。有時候和別人吵架，為了避免衝突變大，你想要抽身，如何不表現出落荒而逃的尷尬呢？放出一句：If we ever do meet again, you'd better watch out!（再讓我遇到你的話，你最好小心點！）挺霸氣吧？

生字補充！ Vocabularies & Phrases

- **make a fuss** 片 大驚小怪；大吵大鬧
- **zone out** 片 恍神放空；注意力不集中

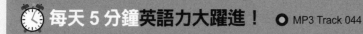

What gives?

怎麼回事？／出什麼問題了？

A I heard you quarrel with the waiter just now. **What gives?**

B Nothing, just a little misunderstanding.

A：我剛才聽到你和服務生吵架了。怎麼回事？

B：沒什麼，只是一點小誤會。

A Are you here to bring me the extra concert ticket?

B Sorry, I 've given it to Bob.

A You've promised me the ticket! **What gives?**

A：你是來送多的演唱會的票給我的嗎？

B：對不起，我已經給鮑勃了。

A：你答應給我的！怎麼回事啊？

原來老外都這樣用！ Know it!

What gives? 可用於多種場合，表示不明白某人為什麼做某事、怎麼會出現眼前的這種狀況（如上述兩個對話中）等。這句話既可以用來詢問別人，也可以表示對自己的處境感到不解。例如，逛公園時你發現手機不見了，此時就可以說：Where is my cell phone? What gives?（我的手機在哪裡？怎麼不見了呢？）如果想加強語氣，也可以與 My God! My goodness! 等一起使用。例如，你一進屋發現地毯全濕了，Oh my God! What gives?（天哪！發生什麼事了？）這句話就可以充分表達你當時的心情。

與 What gives? 可以進行替換使用的有 What happened? What went wrong? What's the problem? 等。

 生字補充！ **Vocabularies & Phrases**

- **misunderstanding** [ˌmɪsʌndəˈstændɪŋ] 名 誤會
- **extra** [ˈɛkstrə] 形 額外的

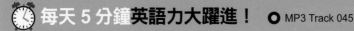

What's up?
出什麼事了?／怎麼了?

A Honey, **what's up?** You sounded weird on the phone.

A:親愛的,出什麼事了? 你在電話裡聽起來怪怪的。

B Nothing, I just wanted to see you.

B:沒事,就是想見你。

A Oh, come on. There must be something wrong.

A:唉,算了吧。肯定有什麼事。

- -

A Hey, man. **What's up?**

A:嘿,兄弟,怎麼了?

B Maybe you can tell me. My girlfriend would like to know why I didn't show up at the restaurant today. How could you not give me her message?!

B:你說怎麼了?我女朋友問我今天為什麼沒去飯店。你怎麼能不把她的訊息告訴我呢?!

原來老外都這樣用! **Know it!**

What's up? 意為「怎麼了?」,用來關心他人出了什麼事情,有哪裡不對勁。如果你是向對方詢問另一個人的情況,就可以用 What's up with...?(……怎麼了?)如:What's up with your mom?(你媽媽怎麼了?)此外,What's up? 也可作為打招呼的用語,相當於 How's it going? How're you doing?

用來詢問「怎麼了?」的表達方式還有很多,如:What's (all) this? What's with...? What's going on? What's the matter (with...)? What's wrong (with...)? Is everything okay? 等等。

 生字補充! **Vocabularies & Phrases**
· **weird** [wɪrd] 形 奇怪的

Wise up!

別傻了！／清醒點！

A I heard your ex-boyfriend had come back to you?

B Yeah, he said he still loved me. I was wondering if I should...

A Hey, wise up! Don't get yourself hurt again!

A：我聽説你前男友回來找你了？

B：是的，他説他仍然愛我。我在想我是不是應該……

A：喂，別傻啊！別再讓自己受傷了！

A Which horse are you going to bet on?

B The Flash.

A Come on, wise up! The Flash has never been a winner!

A：你要把錢押在哪一匹馬身上？

B：閃電俠。

A：拜託，別傻了！閃電俠可從來沒贏過！

原來老外都這樣用！ Know it!

當發現別人因不瞭解糟糕的真相，可能會作出愚蠢的決定時，你可以用 Don't be stupid!（別做傻事！）或者 Don't be silly!（別傻了！）來提醒他。但這兩種說法非常不禮貌，雖然你是好意，聽起來有嘲諷之意，比較傷感情。Wise up! 則是較為客氣的說法，可以比較放心地使用。

當 wise up 不獨立成句時，它表示知道某種不好狀況的真相，並因此開始改變行動。例如：Clients need to wise up to the effect advertising has on the consumers.（客戶需要搞清楚廣告對消費者的影響。）

生字補充！ Vocabularies & Phrases

• **wonder** [ˈwʌndɚ] 動 想知道
• **bet** [bɛt] 動 下賭注

You bet!

當然！／你說的沒錯！

A Are you ready? We're leaving in a few minutes.

B You bet!

A：你準備好了嗎？我們幾分鐘後就出發。

B：當然好了！

A You must be tired after such a long walk.

B You bet! I'm exhausted.

A：你走了這麼遠，肯定累了。

B：沒錯！我都累癱了。

原來老外都這樣用！ Know it!

You bet! 用於強調很贊同對方所說的話，或很樂意按照對方的建議去做。在非常親密、隨意的交談中，You bet! 也常常變身為 You betcha! 如："Going to the party tonight?" "You betcha!"（「你會去今晚的聚會嗎？」「當然去啊！」）

此外，you bet 也可以放在句子開頭，後接從句，表示「當然……」的意思。如："Are you thirsty?" "You bet I am!"（「你渴了嗎？」「當然渴了！」）"You must like her very much. I can see that from the way you look at her." "You bet I do."（「你肯定特別喜歡她。從你看她的眼神就能看出來。」「沒錯，我是很喜歡她。」）

 生字補充！ Vocabularies & Phrases
· **exhausted** [ɪgˈzɔstɪd] 形 筋疲力盡的

Are you insane?

你瘋了嗎？

A I've eaten too much. Let's go home on foot.

B Are you insane? That's 10 miles!

A：我吃得太撐了。我們走路回家吧。

B：你瘋了嗎？有 10 英哩遠呢！

A I think we should stop driving Jack to school. Let him go there by bike.

B What? Are you insane? He might get hit by a car!

A Honey, relax. He's not a baby anymore.

A：我覺得我們不該再開車送傑克上學了。讓他自己騎單車去吧。

B：什麼？你瘋了吧！他會被汽車撞到的！

A：親愛的，別這麼緊張。他不是小娃娃了。

原來老外都這樣用！　Know it!

insane 在口語中可以表達「愚蠢的，瘋狂的」之意。當你覺得對方的想法或做法太傻、太離譜時，就可以皺著眉頭問一句：Are you insane?

類似的表達還有 Are you crazy? 和 Are you out of your mind? 如：Go out for a walk?! Are you out of your mind? It's pouring outside!（出去散步?! 你瘋了嗎？外面下著傾盆大雨呢！）當然，如此誇張的說法要注意場合和對象哦。

生字補充！　Vocabularies & Phrases

• **mile** [maɪl] 名 英哩

Are you kidding?

不會吧？／開玩笑吧？

A I just checked the lecture hall. There're probably 20 to 25 people in there.

B **Are you kidding?** Is that all?

A In particle physics, 25 is Woodstock.

A：我剛才觀察了一下講堂，裡面大概有 20 到 25 人吧。

B：不會吧？才這麼一點點人？

A：在粒子物理學領域，25 人就相當於伍德斯托克音樂節了。

A I can't find the tickets.

B **Are you kidding?** The movie starts in five minutes.

A：我找不到票了。

B：你開玩笑吧？電影還有五分鐘就要開始了。

原來老外都這樣用！ Know it!

Are you kidding?（或 No kidding?）中的 kid 是動詞，表示「開玩笑」的意思，kid 還可以有其他用法，如：No kidding around.（少在這兒胡鬧。）If you don't behave yourself, you'll be grounded for a week—no kidding.（你要是不乖，就罰你一星期不許出門—絕不是開玩笑。）作為女生，當有男生恭維你今天穿得真漂亮，簡直像仙女下凡時，你也可以故作矜持地回他一句：Oh, you're kidding me.（哎喲，別取笑我了。）

生字補充！ Vocabularies & Phrases

- **particle physics** 片 粒子物理學（又稱高能物理學），物理學的一個分支
- **Woodstock** [ˈwudˌstɑk] 名 伍德斯托克音樂節（全球重要的搖滾音樂節，首屆即有四五十萬人參加）

Are you there?

你有沒有在聽啊？

A You know what, when I said "yes," he was happy as a clam. And then... hey, hey, **are you there?**

B Oh, of course. You were talking about some seafood.

A ...

A：當我說「是」的時候，你不知道他有多開心。然後……哎，哎，你有沒有在聽啊？

B：哦，當然在聽啊，你剛剛說到海鮮了嘛。

A：……

A **Are you there?** Have you heard what I said?

B Sorry, I was distracted.

A Can you try to concentrate on what I'm saying? It's important and I don't want to keep repeating it.

B Sure. I'm very sorry.

A：你在聽嗎？你聽到我說的話了嗎？

B：對不起，我剛剛分心了。

A：你能集中注意力嗎？我說的話很重要，我不想一遍一遍地重複。

B：當然。實在抱歉。

原來老外都這樣用！ **Know it!**

Are you there? 意為「你有沒有在聽啊？」，用於詢問對方有沒有跟上你的思路，有沒有理解你的話。這裡的 there 不是指某個具體的地方，而是指思路所在。表達類似的意思，還可以用 Are you listening (to me)? 或 Are you with me? 這裡的 with 指「跟……一起」，Are you with me? 就是指「你跟上我的思路了嗎？你聽明白我的意思了嗎？」

回答時如果表示「沒在聽、分心了」，可以用：I was distracted.（我分心了。／我注意力不集中。）Sorry, my mind was somewhere else.（對不起，我剛才想別的了。）Sorry, I just spaced out / zoned out.（不好意思，我剛剛放空了。）

Be my guest.

請便。

A Do you mind if I use your bathroom?

A：我能用一下你的洗手間嗎？

B Be my guest.

B：請隨意。

A Are you driving out today, Jim?

A：吉姆，你今天要開車出去嗎？

B No, I'll stay home preparing for my exams.

B：不，我要待在家裡復習考試。

A Can I borrow your car?

A：那我能借你的車嗎？

B Sure. Be my guest.

B：當然，儘管開。

原來老外都這樣用！ Know it!

Be my guest 可以表示「請便、請吧」，用於同意別人的請求。在表示同意別人的請求時，還可以用 Of course you can 或 Go ahead，如："Can I have the sports section?" "Yeah, go ahead. I've read it." （「我可以看看體育版嗎？」「可以，拿去吧，我已經看過了。」）

Be my guest 中的 guest 雖然含有「客人」之意，但這句話並不表示「請客」的意思。能表示「我請客」之意的表達有：1. My treat 或 It's my treat 表示「我付錢、我請客」。例如：Let's go out to lunch—my treat.（我們出去吃午飯吧—我請客。）2. Put it on my tab 表示「記在我帳上」，這裡 tab 意為「帳目」。例如：You can order what you like and put it on my tab.（你可以點你喜歡的東西，記在我帳上。）3. The dinner is on me 意為「晚餐我付錢、晚飯我請客」，其中 be on sb 表示「由某人支付」。例如：Each table will get a bottle of champagne on the house.（每桌都將得到一瓶本店奉送的香檳。）

Bear with me.

請等我一會兒。／請你稍等。

A Good morning. I have an appointment with Mr. Lincoln.

A：早安。我跟林肯先生有約。

B Good morning. Bear with me a minute, and I'll check if Mr. Lincoln is in.

B：早安。請稍等，我看看林肯先生在不在。

A Hello, Sunshine Hotel.

A：你好，陽光賓館。

B Hello. I've booked a room for Saturday under the name of Mr. Harold White. I'd like to change it to Sunday.

B：你好。我用哈樂德‧懷特先生的名字預訂了一間週六的房間。我想改到週日。

A Bear with me, madam, I'll check the information.

A：請稍候，女士，我查詢一下。

A Sorry, madam. I didn't find the name Mr. Harold White. But there are still vacant rooms for Sunday.

A：對不起，女士。我沒找到哈樂德懷特先生的名字。但我們現在還有空房間可供週日預訂。

原來老外都這樣用！ **Know it!**

Bear with me 用於禮貌地請求別人等你找出資訊、完成手上的事情等，相當於「請等我一會兒、請你稍等」。要表達類似的含義，還可以使用：Just a minute. Just a moment. Please wait a minute / a moment. Give me a second. I'll be back in a minute.

bear with 除了能表示「稍等」的意思外，它還可以表示「容忍、忍耐」，例如：It's boring, but please bear with it.（這很無聊，但請你忍耐一下。）動詞 bear 本身就有「忍耐、忍受、經受住」的含義，例如：Humiliation was more than he could bear.（羞辱是他萬萬不能忍受的。）

Bring it on!
放馬過來吧！

A I know the intensive training will last for a week. Good luck!

B It's nothing. **Bring it on!**

A：我知道強化訓練會持續一週，祝你好運！

B：這沒什麼，放馬過來吧！

A How is the negotiation going?

B We'll have the third round next week.

A The negotiation could be a tough one.

B **Bring it on!** We're sure to have the last laugh!

A：談判進行得怎麼樣？

B：下週我們將進行第三輪談判。

A：估計這次談判不會那麼容易。

B：放馬過來吧！我們肯定會笑到最後的！

原來老外都這樣用！ **Know it!**

Bring it on! 這句話用於表示已經準備好面對不好的事情，意為「放馬過來吧、就讓它來吧」，有一種勇敢無畏的氣勢。bring on 通常表示如下含義：可表示「導致」之意，例如：Stress can bring on a stomachache.（壓力會導致胃痛。）What's brought this on? Who has upset you?（怎麼啦？誰惹你生氣了？）也可表示「使壞事發生在某人身上」，此時可以和 bring upon 互換使用，例如：The manager accused him of bringing shame on the whole company.（經理指責他給全公司帶來恥辱。）

 生字補充！ **Vocabularies & Phrases**
- **negotiation** [nɪ͵goʃɪˋeʃən] 名 談判，協商
- **tough** [tʌf] 形 棘手的，難辦的

Catch you later!
一會兒見！

A Let's have a picnic this weekend!

A：我們週末去野餐吧！

B Good idea! But I don't know if I'm available.

B：好主意！不過我不知道是否有空。

A Call me when your schedule is fixed!

A：等你行程安排確定了之後再打電話給我吧！

B OK, catch you later!

B：好的，一會兒見！

A The meeting will finish at around 5 pm and let's have dinner together at 7 pm.

A：會議大概下午 5 點結束，我們 7 點的時候一起吃晚飯吧。

B OK, catch you later!

B：好的，一會兒見！

原來老外都這樣用！ Know it!

Catch you later! 是日常口語中表示「再見」的常用說法，與 goodbye 相比，更強調預期能很快見到對方（如第一個對話中），甚至指預期能在說話的當天就見到（如第二個對話中）。See you later! 可以和 Catch you later! 互換使用，兩者表示的意思相同。類似的說法還有：See you (in a bit / in a while / soon)! I'll be / Be seeing you! 這些都表示「很快會再相見」的意思。

生字補充！ Vocabularies & Phrases

- **available** [əˋveləb!] 形（人）有空的
- **schedule** [ˋskɛdʒul] 名 計畫表，行程表

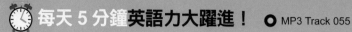 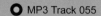
Cut it out!

停！／夠了！／別鬧了！

Ⓐ You never listen to me!

Ⓑ **Cut it out!** I don't want to argue with you now.

A：你從來不聽我的話！

B：夠了！我現在不想跟你爭論。

Ⓐ Give it to me! It's mine, you thief!

Ⓑ It's mine!

Ⓒ Hey, you guys, **cut it out**—Mom's trying to get some sleep.

A：給我！那是我的，你這個小偷！

B：這是我的！

C：嘿，你們別鬧了——媽媽要睡一會兒。

原來老外都這樣用！ Know it!

Cut it out! 在口語中通常表示說話的人因受到某人干擾為讓其停下來，可以譯為「停！夠了！別鬧了！」例如，在別人喋喋不休地對你說你不愛聽的話時，在你很累了但別人卻跟你玩笑打鬧時，或者在你不想繼續爭吵時，都可以用這句話。

Knock it off! 也可以表達類似的含義，例如：Knock it off! I'm just trying to finish my homework today.（別吵了！我正努力在今天之內完成作業呢。）

片語動詞 cut out 除了以 cut it out 的形式出現之外，還可以表達多種含義，例如：In the end, I decided I wasn't cut out for the army.（我最後得出結論，自己不是當兵的料。）The new rules will cut out 25% of people who were previously eligible to vote.（這些新規定會把 25% 原來有合法投票權的人排除在外。）The idea behind these forms is to cut out fraud.（這些做法背後的意圖是要杜絕欺詐行為。）

Go for it!

好好爭取吧！／你用吧！

A Do you know, I really want that job.

B Go for it!

A：你知道嗎，我真的想要那份工作。

B：那就好好爭取吧！

A My car just ran out of gasoline. May I borrow yours?

B Of course, go for it!

A：我的車沒油了，能借你的車開嗎？

B：當然，你用吧！

原來老外都這樣用！ **Know it!**

Go for it! 常用來鼓勵某人努力達成目標（如第一個對話中）。當朋友想要競選學生會主席時，你可以說：Go for it! You can win the election!（好好爭取！你能贏得選舉的！）當同事告訴你一個不錯的工作創意時，你可以說：It sounds a great idea. Go for it!（這想法聽起來棒極了，好好幹吧！）此外，Go for it! 還可以表示說話的人同意對方的請求，通常譯為「用吧！去吧！」（如第二個對話中）。這時的 Go for it! 可以替換為 Go ahead! 比如：“May I use your bathroom?” “Sure, go ahead!”（「我能用你的洗手間嗎？」「當然，請吧！」）

 生字補充！ **Vocabularies & Phrases**

- **run out of** 片 用完，耗盡
- **gasoline** [ˋɡæsəˌlin] 名 汽油

Good for you!

做的好！／好樣的！

A I've decided to accept the position.

B Good for you.

A：我決定接受那個職位了。

B：好樣的。

A Excuse me. You are Lauren, aren't you?

B Oh, hi! Haven't seen you for years! You two are still together?

A Yes. We got married after college, and now we have a boy and a girl.

B Great! Good for you guys!

A：不好意思，你是勞倫，對吧？

B：哦，嗨！好多年沒見了！你們倆還在一起？

C：對。我們大學畢業後結了婚，現在有一兒一女。

B：太棒了！你們倆真好啊！

原來老外都這樣用！ **Know it!**

Good for you! 意為「做得好！／好樣的！」，表示對對方所做得事情的贊同。再看幾個與 good 相關的常見表達：

it's a good thing 意為「幸好、幸虧」，例如：It's a good thing you are at home. I've lost my keys.（幸虧你在家。我的鑰匙丟了。）be good and ready 意為「完全準備好了」，例如：We'll go when I'm good and ready and not before.（等我準備就緒我們就走，沒弄好不能走。）that's a good one 意為「我不信，開玩笑吧」，例如：You won 5 million dollars? That's a good one!（你中了五百萬？開玩笑吧！）be good for a laugh 意為「可博得一笑，很好玩」，例如：It's Hazel's party tomorrow. Should be good for a laugh.（明天黑茲爾開派對，應該很好玩。）if you know what's good for you 意為「你要是知道好歹（用於威脅某人做某事）」，例如：Do as he says, if you know what's good for you!（如果你知道好歹的話，就照他說的做吧！）

Good to know.

知道這個很有用。／謝謝你告訴我。

A What are you doing, John?

A：約翰，你在幹嘛？

B I'm getting that paper ready for Friday.

B：我在準備週五用的論文。

A The syllabus says it's for Thursday.

A：大綱上寫的是週四。

B Oh, good to know.

B：哦，幸虧你告訴我。

A Andrew, did you know that after the queen bee mates with a drone bee, the drone bee dies.

A：安德魯，你知道嗎，女王蜂和公蜂交配後，公蜂就會死。

B ... Good to know.

B：……很有用的知識。

原來老外都這樣用！　Know it!

Good to know 的常用含義有兩種，一種是表示帶有很願意知道或幸虧知道了的感覺；另一種是用來敷衍對方的表達。

如果別人跟你說了什麼尷尬的話題，你不知道怎麼接，又不好意思什麼都不說時，就可以說 all right，例如："I got divorced." "All right."（「我離婚了。」「好吧。」）如果有人問了你問題，而你不知道該怎麼回答才好時，就可以說 That's a good question. 例如："How can we afford this?" "That's a good question."（「我們如何能負擔得起這個呢？」「問得好！」）

生字補充！　Vocabularies & Phrases

- **syllabus** [ˋsɪləbəs] 名 教學大綱
- **drone** [dron] 名 雄蜂，公蜂

每天 **5 分鐘 英語力大躍進！** ○ MP3 Track 059

Hang in there!

堅持下去！／挺住！

A You look so exhausted. Is everything OK?

B I have two essays to submit by the end of this Friday, and I AM exhausted!

A Hang in there! You can do it!

A：你看起來特別累。一切都還好吧？

B：這週五前我得交兩篇文章，我的確是累死了！

A：堅持住啊！你沒問題的！

A Everything is in such a mess. I think I'd better quit.

B Hang in there! Things will work out.

A：所有的事情都是一團糟，我想我還是放棄吧。

B：挺住！一切都會好的。

原來老外都這樣用！ **Know it!**

Hang in there! 在英語口語中多用來鼓勵他人不要放棄，即使面臨困難也要堅持下去（例如上面兩個對話中）。同樣的意思還可以用 Hang on in there! 表示。例如，你的朋友在付出了精力和努力後還是未能達到預期目標，沮喪得想要放棄，此時你就可以對他／她說：Hang on in there, and you never know what you might achieve!（堅持住，你永遠無法預知你會取得什麼樣的成就！）

大家千萬不要混淆Don't hang up! 和 Hang in there!這兩個「假朋友」。Don't hang up! 可不是在幫朋友加油打氣，這是一句打電話時的常用口語，意為「別掛電話！」比如：Don't hang up! I can explain it!（別掛電話！我可以解釋的！）

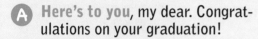
Here's to you!

敬你一杯！／為你乾杯！

Chapter **03**

三字句

A **Here's to you**, my dear. Congratulations on your graduation!

A：為你乾杯，親愛的。祝賀你畢業！

B Thanks, Ma.

B：謝謝媽。

A Honey, **here's to you!** I'm so glad we got engaged!

A：親愛的，敬你一杯！真開心我倆訂婚了！

B Me too. To our engagement!

B：我也是。為訂婚乾杯！

原來老外都這樣用！ **Know it!**

Here's to you! 是常見的敬酒用語，意為「敬你一杯！／為你乾杯！」如果敬酒物件是其他人或事物，則可用 Here's to sb / sth 或直接用 To sb / sth。如：Here's to the happy new couple!（敬幸福的新人！）To friendship!（為友誼乾杯！）

如果在酒宴上，你想提議大家一起為某人或某事乾杯，則可以說 I'd like to propose a toast to...（我提議為……乾杯）如：I'd like to propose a toast to the beautiful bride.（我提議為美麗的新娘幹一杯。）這時，在座的各位賓客就可舉起酒杯，齊聲說 To the bride!（敬新娘！）或 Cheers!（乾杯！）

生字補充！ **Vocabularies & Phrases**

• **graduation** [ˌɡrædʒʊˋeʃən] 名 畢業
• **engaged** [ɪnˋɡedʒd] 形 已訂婚的
• **engagement** [ɪnˋɡedʒmənt] 名 訂婚，婚約

How can / could you?!

你怎麼可以這樣 ?!

A I wish I wasn't born into this family.

B William! **How can you** say such a thing?!

A：我希望我沒有出生在這個家裡。

B：威廉！你怎麼能説這種話呢？！

A Melissa, my work is my life and that's what I have to do right now.

B How could you?! **How could you** do this to me?

A It's tearing my heart, but I have no choice. Can't you understand that?

B No! No! I can't understand that!

A：梅莉莎，工作就是我的生命，我現在必須這麼做。

B：你怎麼能？！你怎麼能這麼對我？

A：我的心都碎了，但我別無選擇。妳難道不能理解嗎？

B：不能！不能！我無法理解！

原來老外都這樣用！ Know it!

How can / could you?! 表達的是說話的人不可置信或強烈反感的語氣，意思是「你怎麼可以這樣 ?! 你怎麼能（做出這樣的事情）?! 你怎麼能（說出這種話來）?!」這句話後面可以接動詞原形，you 也可替換成其他主詞，形成不同的變體，例如：How could you do this to me?（你怎麼能這麼對我？）

與之類似的還有一個表達：How can / could you have the heart to...? 意思是「你怎麼忍心……？」例如：How could you have the heart to leave such a small kid alone at home?（你怎麼忍心讓這麼小的孩子獨自待在家裡？）

I blew it.

我搞砸了。

A How did your interview go?

A：你面試如何？

B **I blew it.** They didn't hire me.

B：我搞砸了。他們沒錄用我。

A Don't lose heart!

A：別灰心！

A Why do you look so sad?

A：你怎麼看起來這麼傷心呢？

B I thought I was going to have the promotion, but **I blew it.**

B：我原以為我會升職的，結果搞砸了。

A I'm sorry to hear that.

A：真是太遺憾了。

原來老外都這樣用！ **Know it!**

I blew it 指破壞了成功的機會，或者浪費了大好時機。這裡的 blow 表示「失去、浪費」，主詞可以替換成其他任何人，還可以加上 really 等副詞表示強調。

I screwed it up 和 I blew it 同義，都可以表示「搞砸了」。比如：I really screwed it up this time, didn't I?（這次真被我搞砸了，是不是？）只不過 screw up 在表示「搞砸」之意時，可以是及物的，也可以是不及物的。例如前一個例句也可以用 I really screwed up this time, didn't I? 來表達。

 生字補充！ **Vocabularies & Phrases**

- **interview** [ˈɪntəˌvju] **名** 面試
- **hire** [haɪr] **動** 雇用
- **promotion** [prəˈmoʃən] **名** 晉升，升職

I got goosebumps.
我都起雞皮疙瘩了。

A I'm frozen. Nothing can compare with a hot drink right now. You feel cold?

A：我要凍僵了。現在能來一杯熱飲就好了。你冷嗎？

B Of course. Can't you see? **I got goosebumps.**

B：當然。你沒看見嗎？我都起雞皮疙瘩了。

A He sang so emotionally. **I got goosebumps.** He is a natural singer.

A：他唱得特別有感情，我都起雞皮疙瘩了。他是個天生的歌者。

B Yes. He did a good job. He could win this thing.

B：對，他表現得很好。他可能會贏得這次比賽。

原來老外都這樣用！ Know it!

英文中表示「雞皮疙瘩」的詞彙與「雞」沒有關係，倒是與「鵝」（goose）有關，用的是 goosebumps 這個字。一般 I got goosebumps 是表示寒冷或恐懼，不過有時候人們聽到一首歌或看到一段表演後，被深深地感動了，也會用這個字來表達。如果想要表達得更誇張一點，類似中文的「雞皮疙瘩掉一地」，可以說：I got goosebumps on goosebumps.

中文裡與「鵝」有關的固定表達很少，而英文裡卻有不少與 goose 相關的表達，例如：wouldn't say boo to a goose 表示「非常羞怯，膽小如鼠」；kill the goose that lays the golden egg 意為「殺雞取卵，竭澤而漁」；what's sauce for the goose is sauce for the gander 意為「應該一視同仁，適於此者亦應適於彼」。

 生字補充！ **Vocabularies & Phrases**
- **natural** [ˈnætʃərəl] 形 天賦的，天生具有某種素質的

I knew it!

我就知道!

A You know, Jill said that she liked me.

A：你知道嗎,吉爾說她喜歡過我。

B Oh! I knew it! I could see that from the way she treated you.

B：哦!我就知道!從她對待你的方式我就能看出來。

A Turns out that it's the guy next door who steals our *TV Guide* every week!

A：原來是隔壁那傢伙每個禮拜都偷我們的《電視指南》!

B Oh, I knew it!

B：哦,我就知道是他!

原來老外都這樣用! **Know it!**

I knew it! 在口語中意為「我就知道!我早猜到了!」,用於表示你早已料到對方所說的情況,常常帶有得意(如第一個對話中)或憤怒(如第二個對話中)的意味。

I knew it! 往往是指你早已料到某種情況但沒有說出來,而如果想要表達你早已料到某種情況、而且早就提醒過對方,則可以用 I told you so 或 Told you / ya!

生字補充! **Vocabularies & Phrases**

- **(it) turns out...** 片 原來是……,結果是……
- **TV Guide** 片 《電視指南》(美國銷量最大的電視刊物)

I mean it.

我是認真的。／我說到做到。

A Are you kidding?

B No. I mean it.

A：你是在開玩笑嗎？

B：不，我是認真的。

A It's time to go to bed. You shouldn't stay up late.

B But Dad, I want to watch this movie.

A OK. But you must go to bed before 11:00.

C Go to bed right now. Unlike your dad, if I say "no," I mean it.

A：到睡覺時間了，你不可以熬夜。

B：但是爸爸，我想看這部電影。

A：好吧，但你一定要在 11:00 前睡覺。

C：馬上去睡覺。我可不像你爸爸，如果我說「不行」，我就說到做到。

原來老外都這樣用！ **Know it!**

動詞 mean 在這裡表示「當真，說到做到」，所以 I mean it 意為「我是認真的，我說到做到」，表示態度嚴肅，不是在開玩笑。表達相同的意思還常說 I mean what I said.。

再看幾個 mean 作動詞時的常用表達。See what I mean? 意為「我說得沒錯吧？（表示發生的事恰好證明了你先前說過的話）」，例如：See what I mean? Every time she calls me up she wants me to do something for her.（我說得沒錯吧？她每次打電話給我都是要我幫她辦事。）That's what I mean 意為「我就是這個意思（用於表示某人說的話正是你剛才想說的）」，例如："We might not have enough money." "That's what I mean, so we'd better find out the price first."（「我們也許錢不夠。」「我也是這個意思，所以我們最好先弄清楚價錢。」）

每天5分鐘英語力大躍進！ ● MP3 Track 066

I'll fix it.
我來搞定。

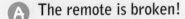

A The remote is broken!

A：遙控器壞了！

B Don't worry, **I'll fix it.**

B：別著急，我會搞定的。

A My flashlight doesn't work.

A：我的手電筒不亮了。

B Maybe it is out of power.

B：可能是沒電了。

A Oh, no, I have no spare battery.

A：哦，不會吧，我可沒有備用電池。

B No big deal. **I'll fix it.**

B：沒什麼大不了的，我有辦法。

原來老外都這樣用！ **Know it!**

I'll fix it 獨立成句時表達的是「我會想辦法解決」的意思，it 可以用於指具體的東西（如上面兩個對話中），也許你本身就會修理，也許你不會修理，但你會去找人把東西修好；也可以用於指抽象的問題。比如，同事需要馬上購買一張機票，可是正巧無法上網支付，這時能夠提供幫助的你可以說：I'll fix it.（我幫你付款吧。）

I'll take care of it. 可以表達和 I'll fix it. 同樣的意思。例如："I have to go now, but my sister will come in ten minutes for the camera." "Don't worry, I'll take care of it."（「我現在就得走了，可是我妹妹 10 分鐘後會來拿相機。」「別擔心，我幫你給她。」）

生字補充！ **Vocabularies & Phrases**

• **flashlight** [ˈflæʃˌlaɪt] **名** 手電筒
• **out of power** **片** 沒電了
• **spare** [spɛr] **形** 備用的

I'm all ears.

我聽著呢。／我洗耳恭聽。

A Hey, buddy, I want to talk to you about this paper.

B I'm all ears.

A：嘿，兄弟，我想和你談談這篇論文的事。

B：我洗耳恭聽。

A You broke my iPad?

B I'm so sorry, and I know I owe you a big apology.

A I'm all ears!

A：你弄壞了我的 iPad？

B：太對不起了，我知道我該好好跟你道歉的。

A：我聽著呢！

原來老外都這樣用！ **Know it!**

I'm all ears 表示說話的人已準備好認真聽對方要說的話了，生活中會在很多場合用到或聽到這句話。例如，你準備向經理彙報事情，經理可能會說：Go ahead—I'm all ears.（說吧，我聽著呢。）當有人要告訴你某件事的真相時，你可以說：Well, I'm all ears.（好，我洗耳恭聽。）既然 all ears 是「認真聽」的意思，那麼 with half an ear 是什麼意思呢？它表示「心不在焉地聽」。例如：She was listening with half an ear in the class.（她聽課時心不在焉。）

I'm listening 可以與 I'm all ears 互換使用。以第一個對話為例，B 也可以回答說：I'm listening.（我正聽著呢。）

 生字補充！ **Vocabularies & Phrases**

• **buddy** [`bʌdɪ] **名** 老兄
• **apology** [ə`pɑlədʒɪ] **名** 道歉

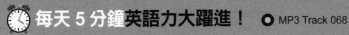

I'm on it.

我正在處理。

A I need to know how much the project will cost exactly.

B I know, and **I'm on it.**

A：我需要知道這個專案具體會花多少錢。

B：我知道，我正在計算。

A What's wrong with my computer?

B It was just attacked by a virus.

A：我的電腦怎麼了？

B：中毒了。

A Would you please fix it for me? I've got homework to do.

B Don't worry, **I'm on it.**

A：你能幫我修一下嗎？我還有作業要寫。

B：別著急，我正在修呢。

原來老外都這樣用！　Know it!

I'm on it. 和 I'm working on it. 可以互換使用，兩者均表示「手上的事情正在進行中」，是十分常見的口語表達方式。

I'm on it. 可以用於多種場合。例如，在上司吩咐你做某事的時候，如果你已經開始著手做了，就可以用 I'm on it 表示這項任務已經在進行中（如第一個對話中）；當你幫朋友做某事，而對方著急地催促你時，你也可以用 I'm on it 來告訴對方事情正在處理中，以平復其焦躁的情緒（如第二個對話中）；有時，你也可以用 I'm on it 作為拖延的藉口，表示「雖然還沒完成，但是你沒有停止工作」。例如："Haven't you made any progress on this project?" "No, but I'm (working) on it."（「這個項目你還是沒有任何進展嗎？」「沒有，但我正在努力。」）

 生字補充！ **Vocabularies & Phrases**

• **virus** [ˈvaɪrəs] 名 病毒

It beats me.

我說不上來。／把我難倒了。

A What's he trying to say?

A：他想說什麼呀？

B It beats me.

B：我也說不上來。

A Did they get married because they loved each other, or did they love each other because they got married?

A：他們是因為相愛才結婚，還是因為結婚才相愛啊？

B Beats me. This is a chicken and egg problem.

B：你難倒我了。這是個先有雞還是先有蛋的問題啊。

原來老外都這樣用！ Know it!

It beats me 或 Beats me 用於回答別人的問題時，可表示不知情、說不上來，相當於 You've got me (there)（你把我問住了），或 Don't ask me（別問我，我不知道），也可表示問題太難、無法理解。

除單獨成句外，It beats me 或 Beats me 還可放在句首，後接從句，表示「……我不明白、……我不知道」。如：It beats me how he could leave without a word.（我真不懂他怎麼能一句話都不說就走了。）Beats me what she's doing in his room.（真不知道她在他房間裡幹什麼。）

生字補充！ Vocabularies & Phrases

· **a chicken and egg problem** 片
先有雞還是先有蛋的問題（難以區分先後或因果）

It's no use.

白搭。／不行。

A Hurry up! We're running out of time!

B Oh, it's no use! I can't fix it!

A：快一點！我們沒時間了！

B：哦，不行！我修不好！

A Have you tried to persuade Mr. Riggs out of firing Chandler?

B It's no use. Mr. Riggs is one of the most stubborn persons I've ever met.

A I will try.

A：你有勸過里格斯先生不要解雇錢德勒嗎？

B：沒用。里格斯先生是我見過的最固執的人之一。

A：我去試試。

原來老外都這樣用！ **Know it!**

It's no use 表示說話的人認為不會成功而要停止做某事，可譯為「白搭、不行」。這裡的 use 作名詞，表示「用處、益處」。it's no use 後面可以加動名詞，變成 it's no use doing sth 的形式，表示「做某事沒用」，例如：It's no use complaining.（抱怨沒用。）

與之類似的說法有 it's no good (doing sth)，也表示「（做某事）沒用」。這裡的 good 是名詞，表示「用處、好處」。例如：It's no good telling him—he won't listen.（告訴他也沒有用──他不會聽的。）

生字補充！ **Vocabularies & Phrases**

- **fire** [faɪr] **動** 開除，解雇
- **stubborn** [ˈstʌbən] **形** 固執的

Leave me alone.

讓我靜一靜。

A I heard that you didn't pass the exam?

A：聽說你考試沒通過？

B No. I thought I could make it.

B：是沒通過。我本以為能過關呢。

A You will next time, you know, failure is the mother of success, and Albert Einstein...

A：下次會通過的，你知道，失敗是成功之母，而且阿爾伯特‧愛因斯坦……

B OK, OK, just leave me alone.

B：好了，好了，讓我自己靜一靜吧。

A I can't believe they canceled my reservation!

A：我真不敢相信他們竟然取消了我的預訂！

B Well, if you were not late, and if you were not that rude...

B：這個嘛，要是你沒遲到，態度沒那麼粗魯……

A Stop! Leave me alone!

A：別說了！離我遠一點！

原來老外都這樣用！ Know it!

Leave me alone 表示讓對方停止令人心煩的行為或停止批評的話語。其中 me 也可以由 him, her, Peter 等其他人代替。

也可以用 let 替換 leave，說成 Let me / him / her / Peter alone. 例如：Let Peter alone. He wasn't the one who broke the vase.（別說彼得了。不是他把花瓶打碎的。）

 生字補充！ Vocabularies & Phrases

• **reservation** [ˌrɛzɚˋveʃən] 名 預訂，預約

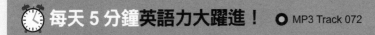

Let it go.
算了吧。／放下吧。

A I can't believe they've lost the game! They could have won it!

A：真不敢相信他們竟然輸掉了比賽！他們本來可以贏的！

B Honey, would you **let it go?** It's not that big a deal.

B：親愛的，算了吧？這不是什麼大事兒。

- -

A I just can't help thinking about her.

A：我總會不由自主地想起她。

B Hey, dude, **let it go.** It's time to move on and find someone new.

B：嘿，哥們，別想了。該放手去找下一個人了。

原來老外都這樣用！ Know it!

Let it go 是英語口語中用於勸說別人的常見表達，意為「算了吧，放下吧」。無論對方是因別人或自己的錯誤而耿耿於懷，還是因失戀而失魂落魄，你都可以用一句 Let it go 來勸他／她不要計較或放下包袱往前走。當有人因為對某件小事不滿意，一直在你耳邊抱怨時，你也可以說：Would you please let it go?（拜託你別沒完沒了行嗎？）這時說話的人的語氣帶有不耐煩的意味。在勸說別人放開某事時，和 Let it go 意思相近的表達還有 Get your mind off this.（別想了。）

風靡全球的動畫電影《冰雪奇緣》的主題曲便名為 Let It Go，歌曲表現了主角放下過去、打開心靈、勇敢前行的心理轉變，譯名為《放開手》。聽聽歌曲，可能會更容易理解這句話的含義呢。

生字補充！ Vocabularies & Phrases

- **dude** [djud] 名（稱呼）老兄，男孩，傢伙
- **move on** 片（在生活中）成長，長進

Let's get started.
我們開始吧。

A Sorry I'm late. The weather is terrible.

A：不好意思，我遲到了。天氣太糟了。

B Never mind. **Let's get started.**

B：沒關係，我們開始吧。

A **Let's get started**, Tom! We've got a really tight schedule.

A：我們動起來吧，湯姆！我們時間安排的很緊。

B OK, one minute.

B：好，馬上。

原來老外都這樣用！ **Know it!**

Let's get started 用於提議開始做某事，既可單獨成句，也可後接 on 引出具體要開始進行的事情，如：Let's get started on the wedding plans!（我們開始計畫婚禮吧！）

Let's get started 也可「變身」為 Gotta get started. 或 We should get started.，含義變化不是很大。另外，用於提議開始做某事的常見表達還有 Let's get down to business. 如：Stop fooling around! Let's get down to business.（別胡鬧了！我們做正事吧。）如果提議結束某事，則可以說 Let's call it a day. 或 That's all for today.，這兩種說法常用於老師宣布下課，當然也可以用在其他場合表示「收工」之意。

生字補充！ **Vocabularies & Phrases**
- **tight** [taɪt] 形 （時間）緊的
- **schedule** [ˈskɛdʒul] 名 計畫表，時間安排

Looks that way.

貌似是那樣。

A Lucy went to the library?

B Yes, she told me that she would go there for some references.

A So she really started to study hard?

B Looks that way.

A：露西去圖書館了？

B：是的，她跟我說要去圖書館查些資料。

A：所以說她真的是要開始好好學習了？

B：貌似是那樣。

A He didn't say anything at the meeting.

B I think he may side with us.

A Looks that way.

A：開會的時候他什麼也沒說。

B：我覺得他可能會支持我們。

A：貌似是那樣。

原來老外都這樣用！ **Know it!**

Looks that way 表示根據表面現象推測，「看起來是那樣」，有不確定的意味。look 主要有兩種意思。一種表示「看似」（如上述兩個對話中），再例如：The future of his career is looking good.（他的職業前景看似一片光明。）另外一種表示「從外表看上去」，例如：You look sad. What happened?（你看上去很傷心，發生什麼事了？）

 生字補充！ **Vocabularies & Phrases**
- **reference** [ˋrɛfərəns] **名** 參考書目
- **side** [saɪd] **動** 支持

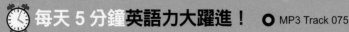
No hard feelings?

沒生氣吧？／別生我的氣。

(A) You promised me!

A：你答應過我的！

(B) I'm sorry it didn't work out, but **no hard feelings**, eh?

B：很抱歉那不行，但別生我的氣，好嗎？

(A) So that means I'm not qualified for that position?

A：所以這就意味著我沒有資格得到那個職位？

(B) That's what the company rules say. But I'll try to get you another chance. **No hard feelings?**

B：公司規定是這樣說的。不過我會為你爭取別的機會。沒生氣吧？

(A) Of course not. Thank you, John. You're always helpful.

A：當然沒有。謝謝你，約翰。你總是這麼樂於幫忙。

原來老外都這樣用！ **Know it!**

hard feelings 意為「生氣，憤怒」，如：We'd known each other too long for hard feelings.（我們認識太久了，彼此之間不會心生嫌隙。） no hard feelings 就是「沒有生氣」，問句 No hard feelings? 意為「沒生氣吧？別生我的氣。」

再看幾個與 feeling 相關的常用搭配。the feeling is mutual 意為「對方感覺也一樣」，例如：My dad hated my boyfriend, and the feeling was mutual.（我爸爸對我男朋友反感，我男朋友也討厭我爸爸。） with feeling 表示「情緒激動地，充滿感情地」，例如：Chang spoke with great feeling about the injustices of the regime.（張情緒激動地講述了該政權的種種不公。） bad / ill feeling 意為「（尤因爭論或不公正的決定產生的）反感、惡感、不滿」，例如：The changes have caused a lot of ill feeling among the workforce.（這些變革引起了職工的強烈不滿。）

Not at all.

不用謝。╱一點兒也不。

A Thank you for lending me your bike.

B Not at all.

A：謝謝你借我單車。

B：不用謝。

A The rain is letting up.

B Yes. Hope it'll be clear soon. Do you mind if I stay a little longer?

A Not at all.

A：雨變小了。

B：是的。希望很快會放晴。你介不介意我再待一會兒？

A：當然不介意。

原來老外都這樣用！ Know it!

Not at all 主要用於禮貌地回應他人的感謝（如第一個對話中）或者強調說話的人的否定態度，例如對他人所要求之事表示毫無異議（如第二個對話中）。與之類似的回答還有 You're welcome.（不客氣。）和 That's / It's all right.（不用謝。╱沒關係。）這兩句。You're welcome. 僅用於回應對方的感謝，比如："Thank you so much for your help." "You're welcome."（「萬分感謝您的幫助。」「不用客氣。」）That's / It's all right. 除了用於回應他人的致謝外，還可以回應對方的致歉，例如："Sorry, I forgot to call you." "That's all right."（「對不起，我忘了打電話給你。」「沒關係。」）

 生字補充！ Vocabularies & Phrases

• **let up** **H** 減弱，緩和

Now you're talking.

這就對了。╱正合我意。

A What do you say about the reelection?

B I've made up my mind to run for the town council reelection.

A Now you're talking.

A：你對改選這件事有什麼想法嗎？

B：我已決定參加市民代表改選了。

A：這就對了。

A We have been working so hard recently. Let's go out for a drink.

B Now you're talking.

A：我們最近工作太辛苦了，出去喝一杯吧。

B：正合我意。

原來老外都這樣用！ **Know it!**

Now you're talking 表示他人的提議正合你的心意，讓你感到高興。

That's more like it. 和 Now you're talking. 類似，也是表示滿意和認可，但不僅可用於對他人的提議，而且 That's more like it. 強調某種對比，表示說話的人因為事情有了改進而感到滿意。例如：That's more like it! You're really starting to study hard.（這樣才對嘛！你真的是開始用功讀書了。）That's more like it! Real food—not the instant noodles.（這還差不多！終於好好吃真的飯菜，而不是泡麵了。）

 生字補充！ **Vocabularies & Phrases**

- **reelection** [ˌriəˋlɛkʃən] 名 再次選舉
- **make up one's mind** 片 下決心

Pick yourself up.

站起來。／振作起來。

A Hey, buddy, **pick yourself up!** There are plenty of beautiful girls out there.

B I'll pick myself up tomorrow. But today, just let me drown my sorrows.

A：嘿，哥們，振作點兒。天涯何處無芳草。

B：我明天再振作吧。今天且讓我借酒澆愁。

A **Pick yourself up!** Nobody is flawless. It was just a small mistake.

B Thank you. Actually, I feel a lot better now after a good sleep.

A：你要振作起來！人無完人。那不過是個小失誤。

B：謝謝。其實好好睡了一覺之後，我已經覺得好多了。

原來老外都這樣用！ **Know it!**

pick oneself up 的意思是「（跌倒後）站起來」，它既可以指真的跌倒後站起來，也可以是指遇到挫折後重新振作起來。例如：Carol picked herself up and brushed the dirt off her coat.（卡蘿爾站起身，拍去外套上的灰塵。）直接對別人說 Pick yourself up! 就是在鼓勵對方不要氣餒，振作精神。

pick sb up 可以表示「（藥物或飲料）使某人感覺好些，使振作精神」，相應的名詞 pick-me-up 就是指「提神的飲料、藥品、興奮劑」。pick up the pieces / threads (of sth) 指「（使某事物）重整旗鼓，恢復正常」，例如：Thousands of victims of the earthquake are now faced with the task of picking up the pieces of their lives.（數以千計的地震災民現在面臨著重建生活的重擔。）

生字補充！ **Vocabularies & Phrases**

• **flawless** [ˋflɔlɪs] 形 無缺點的，完美的

Pigs might fly!

太陽還能從西邊出來呢！／不可能！

A Did Jack pay you back?

A：傑克還錢給你了嗎？

B Not yet, but he promised he would pay me back on Saturday.

B：還沒，不過他保證週六的時候就會還。

A Yeah, and **pigs might fly!**

A：是呀，太陽還能從西邊出來呢！

A Remember to submit your paper next Monday. It's the deadline.

A：下週一記得提交論文。那是最後期限了。

B I'll have finished it by tomorrow.

B：我明天之前就能寫完了。

A And **pigs might fly!**

A：能寫完才怪！

原來老外都這樣用！ **Know it!**

Pigs might fly! 用來表示說話人認為某事完全沒有可能發生，和中文裡「太陽還能從西邊出來呢！」是一個意思。除了 pigs might fly，還可以說 when pigs fly，there's a pig flying by 等，有時可起到幽默嘲諷的作用。例如，一個考試總是不及格的人忽然考了第一名，身邊的同學就會說：Hey look! There's a pig flying by!（快看啊！太陽從西邊出來了！）下屬滿懷信心地保證一個不可靠的計畫會成功，老闆也會說：Yeah, when pigs fly.（是啊，等太陽從西邊出來吧。）

生字補充！ **Vocabularies & Phrases**

- **pay back** 片 償還（欠款）
- **submit** [səb`mɪt] 動 提交
- **deadline** [`dɛd͵laɪn] 名 最後期限，截止時間

See you around.
再見。／改天見。

Ⓐ It was a lot of fun hanging out with you.

Ⓑ Same here. **See you around.**

A：跟你出來玩真開心。

B：我也一樣。改天見。

- -

Ⓐ So, I guess I'll **see you around.**

Ⓑ All right. Call me and ask me out again.

Ⓐ OK, I'll call you.

Ⓑ Oh, wait. You haven't got my phone number.

A：那就再見吧。

B：好。你還要打電話約我出來喲。

A：好，我會打給你的。

B：哦，等等。你還沒有我的電話號碼呢。

原來老外都這樣用！ **Know it!**

See you around 意為「再見，改天見」，用於沒有約定再次見面時間的道別。類似的表達還有 See you / ya 或 I'll see / See you later. 如果分別時約定了再見面的時間，則可說：I'll see / See you at six / tomorrow / next week / at work.（六點見／明天見／下週見／上班見。）

需要注意的是，See you around 有時會帶些敷衍的意味。比如在美劇中，英俊瀟灑的男主角常常會對某個跑龍套的花癡女說 I guess I'll see you around, 但結果往往是再也沒有下文了。同樣常見的謊話還有 I'll call you.（見第二個對話中）。當然，真正看對眼的就另當別論了喲。

生字補充！ **Vocabularies & Phrases**

- **hang out (with sb)** 片（與某人）打發時間，廝混
- **ask sb out** 片 邀請某人出去

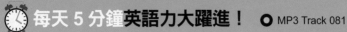 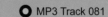

Take a hike!
一邊兒待著去！

Ⓐ Pass me that bottle.

A：把那個瓶子遞給我。

Ⓑ Here you are.

B：給你。

Ⓐ Pass me that newspaper.

A：把那份報紙遞給我。

Ⓑ **Take a hike!** I'm watching football!

B：一邊兒待著去！我正在看足球賽呢！

Ⓐ Will *Transformers: Age of Extinction* be shown next month?

A：《變形金剛 4：絕跡重生》下個月會上映嗎？

Ⓑ I guess it will, and I am so excited that I will buy a ticket as early as possible.

B：我覺得會，好興奮啊，我會儘早買票的。

Ⓐ Can you buy me one?

A：你能買一張給我嗎？

Ⓑ **Take a hike!**

B：哪兒涼快哪兒待著去！

原來老外都這樣用！ Know it!

在英語口語中，**Take a hike!** 這句話主要表示「走開，不要過來打擾」之意（如第一個對話中）。當然，這句話雖然氣勢十足，但多少有些不禮貌，所以對你在乎的人還是要三思而後說哦！

朋友之間也可以用開玩笑的口吻說出 Take a hike! 這句話，此時說話的人不是真的不耐煩，而是為了凸顯親密的關係（如第二個對話中）。再舉個例子，你換了個新髮型，好友總是拿你開玩笑，那麼你就可以直接回敬說：Take a hike!（一邊兒待著去！）

That's a relief!

真叫人鬆了一口氣！

A I heard that you had a backache. What's the matter?

B Oh, nothing serious. I bumped my back on a low beam, but now it doesn't hurt anymore.

A That's a relief!

A：我聽說你背痛。怎麼了？

B：哦，不要緊。之前後背撞到了一根低矮的橫樑，不過現在已經不痛了。

A：那我就放心了！

A I'm so sorry, but I forgot to bring your sunglasses.

B I knew it, so I got another pair.

A That's a relief!

A：真是對不起啊，我忘記把你的太陽眼鏡帶來了。

B：我就知道會這樣，所以我又帶了一副呢。

A：那我就放心了！

原來老外都這樣用！ **Know it!**

That's a relief! 中的 relief 表示「寬慰、安心、解脫」，這句話意為「真叫人鬆了口氣！終於放心了！」，可用於表示懸著的心終於落地了。

What a relief! 可用於同樣的語境。例如："The meeting on Saturday has been cancelled." "What a relief!"（「週六的會議已經取消了。」「總算能鬆口氣了！」）what a relief 還可以後接不定詞，例如：What a relief to finally get away from the party.（謝天謝地，終於從聚會裡逃出來了。）可以後接不定詞的還有 it's a relief，例如：It's a relief to finally get away from the party.（終於從聚會裡逃出來了，總算能鬆一口氣。）

That's the spirit.

這就對了。

A Hey, are you OK? I'm sorry for last night's match.

B It's OK. Failure is the mother of success.

A That's the spirit!

A：嗨，你還好吧？昨晚的比賽很可惜。

B：沒事，失敗乃成功之母嘛。

A：這就對了！

A My goal is to go to Cambridge!

B Then you will have no time for TV, films, novels...

A Nothing is more important than realizing my goal!

B That's the spirit!

A：我的目標是考上劍橋！

B：那你就沒時間看電視、看電影、看小說……

A：沒什麼比實現我的目標更重要！

B：要的就是這股勁！

原來老外都這樣用！ Know it!

That's the spirit 這句話用於認可某人的行為或態度，意為「這就對了，這種態度才對」。和 spirit 有關的口語還有一句也很常用，那就是 The spirit is willing.（心有餘啊。）這句話的完整版是：The spirit is willing, but the flesh is weak.（心有餘而力不足。）不過 The spirit is willing 這半句也可以表示整句的意思。比如，同事建議你再接管一個專案，可是你已經忙得分身乏術了，那麼就可以用 The spirit is willing. 表示你已經沒有多餘的精力來做更多的工作了。

生字補充！ Vocabularies & Phrases

• realize [ˋriəˌlaɪz] 動 實現

There you are.

給你。／我說對了吧。

A This is the freshly baked bread.

A：這是新烤好的麵包。

B Can I have two slices?

B：我可以要兩片嗎？

A There you are.

A：給你。

A I gave my girlfriend the present that you'd suggested, and she forgave me. Thank you!

A：你之前建議我買的禮物，我買了送給我女朋友，然後她原諒我了。謝謝你！

B There you are, I told you she'd love it!

B：我說對了吧，就說她肯定會喜歡！

原來老外都這樣用！ Know it!

There you are 這句話常可以用 There you go. 替換，主要用於以下幾種場合：1. 給某人其索取之物（如第一個對話中）。2. 為某人做了某事，例如："I want to give this to my classmate as a present." "There you go. I'll just put it into the box for you."（「我想把這個送給同學當禮物。」「我這就幫你裝進盒子裡給你。」）3. 認為自己所說的話是正確的（如第二個對話中）。

此外，There you go (again) 還用於強調對方再次說了惱人的話或做了氣人的事情，例如：There you go again, leaving me with all the housework!（你又這樣，家事全留給我做！）

生字補充！ Vocabularies & Phrases

- **bake** [bek] **動** 烘，烤
- **slice** [slaɪs] **名** 片，薄片

This is weird.

這可怪了。

A I saw Susan leave her office for the parking lot just now.

B **This is weird.** I told her to wait for me five minutes ago!

A：我剛才看見蘇珊離開辦公室去停車場了。

B：這可怪了。五分鐘前我還讓她等我的呢！

A I have packed all my things and I'm ready to go at any time.

B Wow, **this is weird!** It's so not like you.

A：我把行李都收拾好了，隨時可以出發。

B：哇，這可怪了！太不像你了。

原來老外都這樣用！ **Know it!**

This is weird 用於感嘆某件事奇怪或出乎意料。其中的 weird 是口語中常用的一個字，表示「古怪的，奇怪的」，如：He's a weird bloke.（他是個奇怪的傢伙。）Something weird happened last night.（昨晚發生了件怪事。）

funny 這個字也可以用來感嘆某事奇怪，如：That's funny. I was sure I had put the keys in my pocket, but they're not here now.（真奇怪，我明明把鑰匙放口袋裡了，可是現在不見了。）當然，funny 還可以表示「有趣的」，如果你用 funny 來形容某人或某事，別人則有可能問你：Funny weird or funny ha-ha?（是奇怪還是有趣？）

 生字補充！ **Vocabularies & Phrases**

· **parking lot** Ｈ 停車場

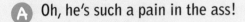

Watch your tongue.

注意你的言辭。／說話小心。

A Oh, he's such a pain in the ass!

A：哦，他真討厭！

B **Watch your tongue.** That's your boss you're talking about!

B：注意你的言辭。你可是在說你的上司啊！

A I don't like the new secretary. She's such a bitch!

A：我不喜歡新來的祕書。她就是個潑婦！

B **Watch your tongue.** Walls have ears.

B：說話小心一點。隔牆有耳喲。

原來老外都這樣用！ Know it!

Watch your tongue 或 Watch your mouth / your language / what you say 用於警告別人注意言辭，說話小心。它們既可以單獨成句（如上述兩個對話），也可以用在句子中，如：You should watch what you say in personal emails.（在私人電子郵件中，你要注意自己的措辭。）當然，當對方對你出言不遜時，你也可以用 Watch your tongue. 酷酷地警告他／她嘴巴放乾淨點。

Watch your tongue 中的 watch 表示「留心，注意」的意思，類似的用法還有 watch yourself / your weight / what you eat / the steps（小心／注意體重／吃東西小心／注意臺階）等等。如：A mother cat can be very protective of her kittens, so you'd better watch yourself.（貓媽媽有時很護著小貓，你最好小心點。）

 生字補充！ **Vocabularies & Phrases**

- **bitch** [bɪtʃ] 名 潑婦
- **Walls have ears.** 片 隔牆有耳。

每天 5 分鐘英語力大躍進！ 🔘 MP3 Track 087

Way to go!

幹得好！

A I got straight A's in the final exam.

B Way to go!

A：我的期末考試成績全都是 A。

B：幹得好啊！

A We hammered Manchester United 5-0.

B Way to go! Let's have a drink!

A：我們隊以 5 比 0 大敗了曼聯隊。

B：幹得漂亮！我們去喝一杯吧！

原來老外都這樣用！ **Know it!**

Way to go! 意為「幹得好！」，表示對對方所做事情的讚許。表達相似的含義還可以說 Well done! 或 Good job!

看幾個與 way 相關的常用表達。you can't have it both ways 意為「（兩種決定或行動的好處）不可兼得」，例如：It's a choice between the time and the money—you can't have it both ways.（這是時間和金錢之間的選擇—你不能兩者兼得。）if I had my way 意為「要我說（用於告訴某人什麼辦法最好）」，例如：If I had my way, we'd leave this place tomorrow.（要我說，我們明天就應該離開這個地方。）that's the way 意為「就是這樣，就這麼做（用於告訴某人其做法正確）」，例如：Now bring your foot gently off the clutch—that's the way.（現在讓你的腳慢慢地鬆開離合器——對了，就是這樣。）

 生字補充！ **Vocabularies & Phrases**

• hammer [`hæmə`] 動（在體育比賽中）徹底擊敗

每天 5 分鐘英語力大躍進！　○ MP3 Track 088

What a coincidence!

太巧了！

Chapter
03

三字句

A I'm going to the Macy's this afternoon.

B **What a coincidence!** I'm going there too. I can give you a lift.

A：我今天下午要去梅西百貨。

B：好巧啊！我也要去那裡。我可以順便開車載你去。

A You know, Jenny's dad gave her the exact same thing that she gave us for our wedding.

B **What a coincidence!**

A：你知道嗎，珍妮的爸爸給她的東西和她給我們的結婚禮物一模一樣。

B：太巧了吧！

原來老外都這樣用！ **Know it!**

What a coincidence! 是英語口語中常見的一句話，用於感嘆某一巧合的發生，例如你和同事乘坐同一班飛機出去度假，或你和某個同學被同一所大學錄取。

另外一個類似的常用說法是 It's a small world!（世界真小啊！）它用於在外地遇見認識的人，或發現某人跟自己有意想不到的關係時表示驚訝。如：My roommate's sister went to school with my sister. It's a small world, isn't it?（我室友的姐姐和我姐姐是同學。世界真小啊，是不是？）"I never thought of seeing you here!" "Well, it's a small world."（「真沒想到會在這裡見到你！」「嗯，世界很小嘛。」）

 生字補充！ **Vocabularies & Phrases**

• **give sb a lift** 片 讓某人搭便車

109

What's your sign?

你是什麼星座的？

A What's your sign? I guess you might be a Leo.

B Well, in fact I'm a Scorpio. My birthday is October 25th.

A：你是什麼星座的？我猜你有可能是獅子。

B：哦，其實我是天蠍。我的生日是 10 月 25 日。

A What's your sign?

B Oh, can't you see? I'm a typical Gemini. I'm not superstitious, but sometimes astrology does make sense.

A：你是什麼星座的？

B：哦，你看不出來嗎？我是典型的雙子呀。不是我迷信哦，有時候星座還是挺有道理的。

原來老外都這樣用！ Know it!

談論星座時最常用到的就是 What's your sign?（你是什麼星座的？）回答這個問題的時候，通常說 I'm a / an...（我是……座的人）。如果要說某人是個典型的……座，則可說 sb is a typical...（見第二個對話）。

十二星座中英文名稱對照：Aries（白羊）、Taurus（金牛）、Gemini（雙子）、Cancer（巨蟹）、Leo（獅子）、Virgo（處女）、Libra（天秤）、Scorpio（天蠍）、Sagittarius（射手）、Capricorn（摩羯）、Aquarius（水瓶）、Pisces（雙魚）。需注意的是，十二星座的英文名稱既可代表星座，也可代表屬這個星座的人，但有些星座的人有兩種叫法：金牛座的人 Taurus (Taurean)；巨蟹座的人 Cancer (Cancerian)；天秤座的人 Libra (Libran)；射手座的人 Sagittarius (Sagittarian)；水瓶座的人 Aquarius (Aquarian)；雙魚座的人 Pisces (Piscean)。

 生字補充！ **Vocabularies & Phrases**

• **superstitious** [ˌsupɚˈstɪʃəs] 形 迷信的
• **astrology** [əˈstrɑlədʒɪ] 名 占星術

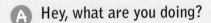

Where were we?

我們剛才談到哪裡了？

A Hey, what are you doing?

B I'm trying to persuade Lily to go shopping with me.

A She's already agreed to go to the cinema with me!

B Don't interrupt me when I'm talking. Now **where were we**, Lily?

A Now, **where were we?** Oh, yes. I asked if you are available tomorrow evening.

B I need to buy my girlfriend a birthday present.

A OK, let's go for a drink next time.

A：喂，你在幹什麼？

B：正説服莉莉和我去逛街呢。

A：她已經答應和我去看電影了！

B：我説話的時候別打岔。莉莉，我們剛才説到哪裡了？

A：剛才我們説到哪裡了？哦，對。我問你明晚是不是有空。

B：我必需去幫女朋友買生日禮物。

A：好吧，我們下次再去喝一杯吧。

原來老外都這樣用！ Know it!

Where were we? 在口語中用來詢問「剛才說到哪裡了？」，它的使用情境一般有兩種：一是說話的人並沒有真的忘記剛才說到哪裡了，只不過講話被人打斷後需要有個引子才能接著剛才的話題說下去，算是給自己找個「臺階」下；二是說話的人真的忘了剛才的話題，就是所謂的「一打岔就忘了」，需要回想一下或者對方提醒一下才能想起來。

要是真的想問「我們這是在哪裡？」，英文該怎麼說呢？很簡單，將 Where were we? 換成一般現在式，即 Where are we? 就可以了。

You don't say!

真的嗎？／我早就知道了！

A Let's go to a movie next Monday.

A：我們下週一去看電影吧。

B Monday?

B：週一嗎？

A Yeah, I'm sure we won't have to wait in line for tickets.

A：對啊，我們肯定不用排隊買票了。

B But I'm starting a new job next Monday.

B：但是下週一我要開始新的工作了。

A You don't say!

A：真的嗎？

A Two apples cost me five yuan. Prices are getting high.

A：兩個蘋果就花了我五塊錢。物價真是越來越貴了。

B You don't say!

B：你才知道啊！

原來老外都這樣用！ **Know it!**

可不要誤把 You don't say! 當成「你別說！」，那就要鬧笑話了。這句話其實可以表達兩種截然不同的意思：一是對聽到的話表示驚訝（如第一個對話），二是對聽到的話並不感到驚訝（如第二個對話）。在表示驚訝時，You don't say! 並不是不相信的意思，而是說話的人有禮貌地表示驚奇或感興趣。例如，很久沒聯繫的朋友突然告訴你她進階當媽媽了，你就可以說 You don't say!（真的嗎？），回應中包含欣喜的成分。有時候，You don't say! 還有諷刺的作用，是對對方缺乏常識等的嘲笑。例如："Guess what? There's a country called South Africa." "You don't say!"（「你猜怎麼了？有個國家叫南非。」「真的呢！」）

You made it!

你成功了！／你趕上了！

A Mom! I won the tennis game this morning!

B You made it! You made it! That's my good boy!

A：媽媽！今天早上的網球比賽我贏了！

B：你成功了！你成功了！真是我的好兒子！

A Hey, darling!

B Hey, Mom! You made it. Great!

A Of course, this is your wedding! I'm so glad I made it!

A：嘿，寶貝！

B：嘿，媽媽！你趕到了，太好了！

A：當然，這可是你的婚禮呀！真高興我趕上了！

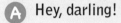 **原來老外都這樣用！** **Know it!**

You made it!（或 You did it!）是一句常用的鼓勵、讚揚之語，用來誇獎對方渡過難關、獲得成功，或是在困難情況下準時趕到等，含有「真了不起」的驚喜之意。

要想說一口道地的英文，就要學會利用 make 和 do 這種簡單的字來表達豐富的含義。例如：He will never make it as a professional singer.（他永遠也成不了職業歌手。）Can we have two cups of coffee? Oh, no, make that three.（請給我們兩杯咖啡好嗎？不對，是三杯。）I usually make do with a cup of coffee for breakfast.（我早餐通常喝杯咖啡就算了。）Oh yes, I certainly did my time in the army.（哦，沒錯，我當然在部隊待過。）靈活運用這些表達，會使你的口語增色不少。

 生字補充！ **Vocabularies & Phrases**

• **tennis game** 片 網球比賽

You never know.

這很難說。

A It was so cloudy today.

A：今天真是烏雲密佈啊。

B Yeah, so I plan to cancel the picnic tomorrow.

B：是啊，所以我打算取消明天的野餐。

A Oh, no. It might turn into a beautiful day—**you never know.**

A：哦，不，也許會轉晴呢，這可說不定。

A I decided to try asking Susan out again.

A：我決定再試著約蘇珊一次。

B The girl who turned you down last time?

B：上次拒絕你的那個女孩？

A Yep, any suggestions?

A：對，有什麼建議嗎？

B I'm on your side. **You never know,** she might change her mind.

B：支持你。誰知道呢，也許她改主意了！

原來老外都這樣用！ **Know it!**

You never know 單獨成句時強調有發生好事的可能，即便這個可能性微乎其微。當對方因某事而憂心忡忡或意志消沉時，這句話傳遞的是一種積極樂觀的正能量，可以給人以安慰或讓人重新燃起拼搏的鬥志。試想一下，當你因擔心自己的面試而情緒低落時，朋友及時地說一句：You never know—they might give you the offer.（誰知道呢—他們也許就會錄取你呢。）這時你的心情是不是會好一些呢？

但是切記，如果 you never know 不是單獨使用而是後接從句的話，那就僅僅表示「說不準會有怎樣的情況發生」，這個情況可能是好的，也可能是不好的。例如：You'd better be nice—you never know when you might need her help.（你最好友善一些——說不定什麼時候你就需要她的幫助了。）

You're kidding me!
你開玩笑的吧？

A I've got Kobe Bryant's autograph!

A：我拿到了柯比・布萊恩的簽名！

B That basketball player?
You're kidding me!

B：打籃球的那個柯比？你開玩笑的吧？

A Let's have a walk in the park.

A：我們去公園散散步吧。

B In such bad weather?
You're kidding me!

B：這鬼天氣去散步？你開玩笑的吧？

原來老外都這樣用！ **Know it!**

You're kidding me! 表示說話的人對某人的話持懷疑態度（如第一個對話）或不贊成的態度（如第二個對話）。You're kidding me! 有多種可替換的表達方式，例如：Are you kidding? You've got to be kidding! You must be kidding! No kidding? 其中，no kidding 也可以用肯定的語氣說出，但含義就變了，表示的是強調某事是真的。試比較：I won the Employee of the Month! No kidding!（我獲得了「每月最佳員工」的稱號！是真的！）I won the Employee of the Month? No kidding?（我獲得了「每月最佳員工」的稱號？真的嗎？）

生字補充！ **Vocabularies & Phrases**

• autograph [ˈɔtəˌɡræf] 名（名人的）親筆簽名

You're telling me!

那還用說！／沒錯！

A It's such a pain to live with him!

A：跟他一起生活太痛苦了！

B You're telling me!

B：那還用説！

A It's cold in here!

A：這裡真冷啊！

B You're telling me! It's freezing cold!

B：沒錯！凍死人了！

原來老外都這樣用！ **Know it!**

You're telling me! 用於表示你早就知道對方所說的情況，而且強烈贊同，相當於中文裡的「那還用說！」

表達強烈贊同的說法還有不少，例如：Ditto.（沒錯。我也一樣。）Absolutely!（絕對的！）Exactly!（正是如此！）You can say that again!（說得沒錯！）看幾個例句："I hate this course." "Ditto."（「我討厭這門課。」「我也是。」）"There was a big argument!" "You can say that again."（「吵得真厲害！」「沒錯！」）如果對方問了個問題，你表示強烈肯定，則可用 I'll say! 如：「Was there a big argument?" "I'll say!"（「吵得很厲害嗎？」「是啊！」）

 生字補充！ **Vocabularies & Phrases**

· **freezing** [ˈfrizɪŋ] 形 極冷的

You've got me (there).

我不知道。╱你把我問倒了。

🅐 Hey! What's on this video tape?

🅑 **You've got me.** Put it in and see.

> A：嘿！這錄影帶裡是什麼呀？
>
> B：我也不知道。放進去看看。

🅐 How did things get so complicated?

🅑 Well, **you've got me there.**

> A：事情怎麼變得這麼複雜了？
>
> B：唉，你可把我問倒了。

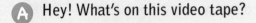

原來老外都這樣用！ **Know it!**

You've got me (there) 用於表示你不知道對方所問問題的答案。在日常會話中，這個說法往往簡化成 You got me 甚至 Got me. 如："Who are these people?" "Got me."（「這些人都是誰啊？」「不知道啊。」）

類似的說法還有：Don't ask me.（別問我，我不知道。）It beats / Beats me.（可把我問倒了。）其中，It beats / Beats me 還可以表示「不懂，不理解」的意思，如："What's he saying?" "Beats me."（「他在說什麼？」「我也搞不清楚。」）Beats me why she has to go.（我不明白她為什麼非要走。）下次再說「不知道」時，別只用 I don't know 或 I've no idea 了，也試試這些新表達吧！

生字補充！ **Vocabularies & Phrases**

- **video tape** 片 錄影帶
- **complicated** ['kɑmpləˌketɪd] 形 複雜的

Don't be (such) an ass.
別蠢了。／別惹人厭了。

A Maybe someday she'll come back to me.

A：說不定哪天她還會回到我身邊呢。

B Don't be an ass. She'll end up with someone much better.

B：別蠢了。她肯定會找個比你好得多的人。

A I think I should introduce myself to the actress.

A：我覺得我應該向那個女演員介紹一下我自己。

B Don't be such an ass. She wouldn't care.

B：別惹人厭了。人家才不稀罕呢。

原來老外都這樣用！ Know it!

Don't be (such) an ass 用於告訴別人別做蠢事、別討人嫌，是一種不太禮貌的說法。其中的 ass(或 arse)意為「又蠢又煩人的傢伙」，如：He's a pompous ass.（他是個自負的蠢驢。）它的同義字是 asshole（或 arsehole），不過這個字會給人一種很粗魯的感覺，淑女們最好不要輕易嘗試。

類似的表達還有：Don't make an ass / a fool of yourself.（別出洋相了。）Stop clowning around!（別到處胡鬧了！）這些說法大多都有些不禮貌，為避免傷人自尊，大家要慎用哦。

 生字補充！ **Vocabularies & Phrases**
• **end up** 片（尤指經歷一系列意外後）最終處於，到頭來

Don't get me wrong.

別誤會我的意思。

A You sent me these flowers?

B Yes. **Don't get me wrong—** they are the flowers of friendship.

A：這些花是你送我的？

B：是的。別誤會——這是友誼之花。

A Look at Norman's electric car! I'm sure it can save energy.

B It sucks!

A You don't like electric cars?

B **Don't get me wrong**—I'm not against environmental protection per se... I just hate Norman!

A：快看諾曼的電動車！這車一定節能。

B：真差勁！

A：你討厭電動車？

B：別誤會我的意思——我並不反對環保……我只是討厭諾曼！

原來老外都這樣用！ Know it!

Don't get me wrong，意思是「別誤會我的意思」，後面往往會接解釋說明性的話。

get sb / sth wrong 表示「誤解某人／某事」，例如：This isn't it. We must have got the address wrong.（不是這裡，我們肯定把地址搞錯了。）還可以加一個 all 表示強調，變成 get it all wrong 的形式，例如：No, no—you've got it all wrong. We are just friends.（不，不一你完全搞錯了。我們只是朋友。）還有一個類似的表達 take sth the wrong way，表示「誤解某句話」。

生字補充！ Vocabularies & Phrases

• **energy** [ˈɛnədʒɪ] 名 能源
• **per se** [pɝˈse] 副 本身，就本身而言

Don't give me that!

少來！／別跟我來這套！

A We worked until 9:30 in the office...

B Don't give me that! I know exactly where you have been!

A：我們一直在辦公室工作到 9 點半……

B：少來！你去了哪裡我一清二楚！

A It's the lowest price I can offer. Look at the cut! Look at the design! Look at the material!

B Don't give me that! I know only too well about women's clothing.

A：這是我能開的最低價了。看看這剪裁！看看這設計！看看這面料！

B：別跟我來這套！我太瞭解女裝這回事了。

原來老外都這樣用！ Know it!

Don't give me that! 用於表示不相信某人的解釋或藉口，可譯為「別給我來那一套！」，言外之意是「我們明人不說暗話，你不要廢話了」。

don't give me that 後面還可以接 look, face, smile, smirk 這類字彙，意思稍有變化。例如：Don't give me that look! It's not my fault!（別那麼看著我！又不是我的錯！）Don't give me that smile. It seems like you know something I don't know!（別給我露出那種微笑，好像你知道什麼我不知道的事情似的！）

 生字補充！ Vocabularies & Phrases
- **design** [dɪˋzaɪn] 名 設計，圖案
- **material** [məˋtɪrɪəl] 名 料子，素材

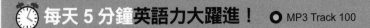
Don't waste your breath.
別白費口舌了。

A Ten people can make a team. We need one more member if we want to enter the contest.

A：10 個人才能組隊。想參賽的話，我們還需要一名隊員。

B How about asking Lily for help?

B：找莉莉幫忙怎麼樣？

A Don't waste your breath. I've already asked her and she said no.

A：別白費口舌了。我已經問過她了，她沒答應。

A I have to talk to Mike in private.

A：我得和麥克私下談談。

B I heard that he was going to resign.

B：我聽說他要辭職。

A That's the reason for the talk. I'll try to make him change his mind.

A：我就是為了這個才要和他談談。我要勸他改變主意。

B He won't listen to you. Don't waste your breath.

B：他不會聽你的。別白費口舌了。

原來老外都這樣用！ Know it!

Don't waste your breath 是非常好記的一句話，主要用於讓對方放棄要勸說別人的想法。如果說話的人肯定對方無法說服某人，認為對方沒有嘗試的必要，就可用這句話，有時也說成 Save your breath。

如果說話的人是想評價對方正在進行的勸說行為，表示「你是在白費口舌」，那麼可以用 You're wasting your breath. 這句話的主詞不是非 you 不可，可以根據情境自由替換，例如：She / He is wasting her / his breath.（她／他是在白費口舌。）只不過 You're wasting your breath 更為常用。

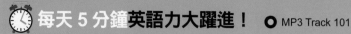
First come, first served.

先到者先得。／先來者先被服務。

A How can I buy a ticket?

A：怎麼買票呢？

B Tickets are available on a "**first come, first served**" basis.

B：先到先買，售完為止。

A What's it on the board? I can't see that clearly. I forgot to wear my glasses.

A：公告板上面寫了什麼？我看不清。我忘了戴眼鏡了。

B It's about the lecture. It says— Conducted in Cantonese. Free admission. **First come, first served.**

B：是關於講座的通知。上面寫著——講座以粵語進行。免費入場，座位先到先入座。

A Then we have to get there before 6:00. Let's have dinner now.

A：那我們必須 6 點前趕到。我們現在就去吃晚餐吧。

原來老外都這樣用！ **Know it!**

First come, first served 的意思是「先到先得，先來者先被服務」，一般在表示「按先來後到的順序排隊，不能插隊」時使用，也可以表示某活動或服務「不接受預訂，當天請早」。這個表達中逗號兩邊的分句都以 first 開頭，位置對稱，使得整句話讀起來朗朗上口，對比的含義也很明顯。

英文中有不少習慣用語或固定表達都運用了這種表現形式，來看幾個例子：Easy come, easy go 意為「來得容易，去得容易」，指太容易得來的東西不被珍惜，也就容易失去，常被用來指金錢和感情。Like father like son 意為「有其父必有其子」，指兒子的行為和其父親一樣，尤其被用來形容缺點。More haste, more waste 意為「欲速則不達」。No pain, no gain 意為「沒有付出就沒有回報」。Out of sight, out of mind 意為「眼不見為淨」。

How are you doing?

最近如何？／你好嗎？

A Hey, Julie, **how are you doing?**

A：嗨，朱莉，近來可好？

B Um, I don't know. I mean, my boyfriend has been away on business for one month, and I miss him.

B：呃，我也不知道。我的意思是，我男朋友已經出差一個月了，我很想他。

A How are you doing?

A：你最近好嗎？

B I'm just a little sad.

B：我就是有點難過。

A What's the matter?

A：怎麼了？

B I saw my ex-boyfriend going out with another girl.

B：我看到前男友和別的女孩約會了。

原來老外都這樣用！ Know it!

How are you doing? 是日常口語中常用的寒暄語之一，用來詢問對方近況，表示「近來可好？最近過得怎麼樣？」通常肯定的答覆有：Fine, thanks!（還不錯，謝謝！）Very well, thank you.（相當不錯，謝謝！）

How are you? / How are things going? / How's it going? 和 How are you doing? 都是用來詢問對方近況或進展，通常可以互換使用。How are you? 偏重關注對方身體狀況，但通常也只是表示禮貌性的問候。

生字補充！ Vocabularies & Phrases

- **on business** 片 出差
- **go out (with sb)** 片 （和某人）約會，交往

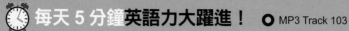

I can't follow you.
我不懂你說的。

A I can't follow you. Can you slow down a little?

B All right. I may have been pushing you too hard.

A：我不懂你說的。你能放慢一點嗎？

B：好。我可能逼你逼得太緊了。

A How did you like my presentation yesterday?

B It was too complicated. I couldn't follow you.

A：你覺得我昨天的報告做得如何？

B：太複雜了，我都沒聽懂。

原來老外都這樣用！ **Know it!**

I can't follow you 用於表示跟不上對方的談話，或無法理解對方所講的事情。這裡的 follow 是「理解，明白」的意思，如：The plot of the story is a little difficult to follow.（故事情節有點難以理解。）

反過來，當你為對方講述事情時，也可用 follow 的這種用法來詢問他／她能否跟上、聽懂：Can you follow me? Are you following me? You follow me? 如："Go along the street, turn right at the second crossing, and then left at the first crossing. You follow me?" "I think so. First right, then left."（「沿著這條街走，第二個路口右轉，然後第一個路口左轉。聽懂了嗎？」「我覺得懂了。先右轉，再左轉。」）

 生字補充！ **Vocabularies & Phrases**

- push [puʃ] **動** 督促，逼迫
- presentation [ˌprizɛnˋteʃən] **名** 報告，介紹

I can't help it.

我忍不住。

A You seem rather nervous.

A：你看起來相當緊張。

B Yeah, I still don't know whether I will be recruited.

B：是啊，我還不知道能不能被錄取。

A I'm sure you'll make it. Stop biting your nails!

A：我肯定你會被錄取的。別咬指甲了！

B I can't help it.

B：我忍不住。

A You smoked again! I can smell it.

A：你又抽菸了！我能聞到菸味。

B Sorry, but I couldn't help it.

B：對不起，我忍不住。

原來老外都這樣用！ Know it!

I can't help it 意為「我忍不住」，表達的是說話的人無可奈何的心情，但有時候也是由於自制力不夠，給人一種「江山易改，本性難移」的感覺。此外，sb can't help it if... 也比較常用，表示「如果……怪不了某人」。比如：He couldn't help it if anger took charge of him.（如果他生氣了的話，那也怪不了他。）

日常生活中，在表示「忍不住做某事」之意時，sb can't help (doing) sth 是常用的表達。比如，工作的時候，老闆總是挑你的毛病，你是做什麼錯什麼，那麼你就有理由說：I can't help thinking that my boss was finding fault with me.（我總覺得老闆是在找我麻煩。）

生字補充！ Vocabularies & Phrases

- **recruit** [rɪ'krut] 動 招收
- **nail** [nel] 名 指甲

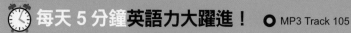

I couldn't agree more.

我再同意不過了。／我萬分同意。

A The two kids would make a perfect couple!

B I couldn't agree more.

A：這兩個孩子真是天生一對！

B：我完全同意。

A Never try to change your boyfriend. When it comes to relationship, making choices is much more important than making changes.

B I couldn't agree more. I learned it the hard way.

A：永遠不要嘗試改變你的男朋友。在戀愛的關係中，選擇比改變重要太多了。

B：我再同意不過了。這是我的血淚經驗。

原來老外都這樣用！ Know it!

I couldn't agree more 中的 I 可以省略，寫成 Couldn't agree more. 這句話的字面意思是「我不能同意更多了，我不能更同意了」，也就是同意的情緒達到了頂點，表示「無比同意，萬分同意」。這句話是一種虛擬語氣，所以要用 couldn't，不用 can't。如果想表示同意某人某事，還可以加上 with sb，如：I couldn't agree with you more.

還有一些用法能表示「完全同意，你說得太對了」的含義，例如：You can say that again!（你說得真對！）You said it!（沒錯！說得對！）Right on!（完全正確！）That makes two of us.（我跟你的情況一樣。我有同感。）來看幾個例子："It's cold in here." "You can say that again!"（「這裡好冷。」「說得沒錯！」）"Let's go home." "You said it! I'm tired!"（「我們回家吧。」「同意！我也累了！」）"But I don't know anything about children!" "Well, that makes two of us."（「可是我一點也不瞭解小孩！」「好吧，我也一樣。」）

I didn't mean it.

我不是故意的。

(A) What you said yesterday really hurt my feelings.

(B) I'm sorry. **I didn't mean it.**

A：你昨天說的話真的讓我很受傷。

B：對不起。我不是故意的。

(A) He kept me waiting for three hours that day. It really upset me.

(B) Oh, I'm sure **he didn't mean it.**

A：那天他讓我等了三個小時。我很生氣。

B：哦，我肯定他不是故意的。

原來老外都這樣用！ **Know it!**

I didn't mean it 用於做錯事後的解釋，告訴對方你不是故意要讓他／她生氣或難過。如果你不是為自己而是為別人解釋，則可以說：I'm sure he / she didn't mean it（如第二個對話）。類似的表達還有：I didn't mean this to happen at all.（我並不想發生這樣的事。）若要表示某人本是好意，並不想傷害、冒犯對方，則可以用 mean no harm / offence / disrespect，或 mean well / it for the best。如：He may sound a little rude, but I'm sure he means well.（他的話可能聽起來有點粗魯，但我肯定他是出於好意。）

需要注意的是，I didn't mean it 的肯定形式 I mean it 表示「我是認真的，我說到做到」之意。如：I like her. And I mean it.（我喜歡她。我是認真的。）I'm going to teach you a lesson. I mean it.（我要好好給你個教訓。我說到做到。）

生字補充！ **Vocabularies & Phrases**

• upset [ʌpˋsɛt] 動 使（某人）心煩意亂，使生氣

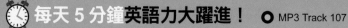

I don't blame you.

我不怪你。

A I'm sorry.

A：對不起。

B **I don't blame you.** I can't give you what you want.

B：我不怪你。我無法給你你想要的。

A I've never thought we would come to all this. I still remember the day when we started this company.

A：我從沒想過我們會走到今天這一步。我還記得我們剛剛成立公司的那天。

B It's all my fault. I screwed up everything.

B：都是我的錯。我把一切都搞砸了。

A **I don't blame you.** I only have myself to blame.

A：我不怪你。要怪只能怪我自己。

原來老外都這樣用！ **Know it!**

I don't blame you 表示說話的人認為對方做某事可以理解、情有可原，不應該受到指責，可以譯為「我不怪你」。don't blame 後不僅可以加第二人稱 you，也可以加第三人稱和第一人稱。例如："She left her husband." "I don't blame her, after the way he treated her."（「她離開她丈夫了。」「他那樣對她，也難怪她這麼做。」）後加第三人稱時，還可以表達為 You can hardly blame him / her / them。

don't blame me 意為「不要怪我」。它不僅能用於認為自己沒有錯，讓對方不要責怪自己，還可以用於勸阻別人而又認為別人不會聽的時候，例如：Buy it then, but don't blame me when it breaks down.（那你就買吧，不過壞了別怪我。）

 生字補充！ **Vocabularies & Phrases**

• **screw up** 片 搞砸，弄糟

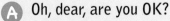

I got your back.

我挺你。

A Oh, dear, are you OK?

B I just can't get this paper done! Tomorrow is the deadline!

A You can do it! **I got your back.**

A Just do it, son. **I got your back!**

B Thank you, Dad.

A：哦，親愛的，你還好嗎？

B：我這篇論文寫不完了！明天就是截止日了！

A：你能寫完的！我挺你。

A：去做吧，兒子！我挺你。

B：謝謝爸。

原來老外都這樣用！ **Know it!**

I got your back 是口語中常見的一句加油鼓勵的話，用於告訴對方「我挺你，我會支持你渡過難關」。這句話的本意是指在別人專注於面前的事物時幫他／她盯著身後的情況，常用於體育活動中，後來逐漸演變為一句鼓勵用語。

類似的表達還有：I'll back you up.（我會支持你的。）I'm on your side.（我站在你這邊。）如：I'll back you up at the concert.（我會去演唱會幫你加油鼓勵的。）Don't worry. I'm on your side.（別擔心，我是站在你這邊的。）

 生字補充！ **Vocabularies & Phrases**

• **paper** [ˋpepɚ] **名** 論文

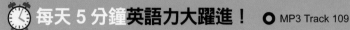

I told you so.

我早就告訴過你。

A My daughter fell off her new bike and broke her leg!

B **I told you so.** She's too young to ride a bike alone.

A：我女兒從新的自行車上摔下來，把腿摔壞了！

B：我早就告訴過你的，她太小了，不能獨自騎自行車。

A You broke up with Peter? What a pity!

B Don't play possum! I suppose you've come to say "I told you so."

A：你跟彼得分手了？好可惜啊！

B：別裝蒜了！我猜你來就是為了跟我說句「誰叫你不聽勸」的吧。

原來老外都這樣用！ **Know it!**

當你早就提醒過別人某件不好的事情可能發生，而如今這件事真的發生了時，你就可以對對方說：I told you so.（我早告訴過你的。）這一表達往往帶有責備或洋洋自得之意（「誰叫你不聽我的！」）。

I told you so 可簡化為 I told you 或 Told you / ya. 如："There was a terrible traffic jam this morning!" "I told you! Why didn't you leave home earlier?"（「今早塞車塞得真嚴重！」「早跟你說了的！你為什麼不早點出門？」）"She's a real bitch!" "Told ya!"（「她真是個潑婦！」「早跟你說過的！」）

 生字補充！ **Vocabularies & Phrases**

- **fall off** 片 從……上掉下來
- **play possum** 片 裝蒜，裝糊塗

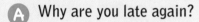

I wasn't born yesterday.

我又不是三歲小孩。

A Why are you late again?

A：你為什麼又遲到了？

B My car broke down.

B：我的車拋錨了。

A The same excuse! Come on, **I wasn't born yesterday.**

A：又是這個理由！拜託，我又不是三歲小孩兒。

A This is your birthday present.

A：這是你的生日禮物。

B A bottle of perfume?

B：一瓶香水？

A A bottle of perfume from France.

A：一瓶來自法國的香水。

B **I wasn't born yesterday,** you know! I know what "Made in China" means.

B：你要知道我又不是三歲小孩！我知道「Made in China」是什麼意思。

原來老外都這樣用！ Know it!

I wasn't born yesterday 通常可以用於表示說話的人並非無知到會相信對方，即沒有那麼容易被騙。如果想要描述他人，表示「他／她可不傻」的話，把主詞 I 換成相應的 he / she 即可。一般情況下，這種用法並沒有什麼貶低之意，但是，Were you born yesterday? 這個問句有時還是會讓對方不高興，因為它含有嘲諷對方無知的意思。

生字補充！ Vocabularies & Phrases

- **break down** 片 （車或機器）停止運轉，出現故障
- **perfume** [ˋpɝfjum] 名 香水

I won't be long.

我很快就好。／我去去就來。

A Where are you going? Dinner's ready.

B I'm just going to make a call—I won't be long.

A：你去哪裡？晚餐都做好了。

B：我只是去打個電話，不會太久的。

A Just wait downstairs—I won't be long!

B Last time I was kept waiting for almost two hours!

A Sorry for that, but I promise I'll be ready within 10 minutes!

A：在樓下等我一下——很快就好！

B：上次我可是等了快兩個小時！

A：上次很抱歉，不過這次我保證 10 分鐘就好！

原來老外都這樣用！ Know it!

I won't be long 用於告知對方自己做某事不需要很長時間，即對方不需要等待很久，類似於中文裡的「我很快就好，我去去就來」。如果想表示某事物準備好或發生不需要很長時間，可以用 It won't be long.（馬上就好。）例如："Mom, is lunch ready?" "It won't be long now."（「媽，午餐好了嗎？」「馬上就好了。」）當然，也可以直接說：Lunch won't be long now.（午餐馬上就準備好了。）在日常口語中，be long 表達這種含義時僅用於否定句或疑問句中，用來表明某人或某事準備好、到達或發生不需要很長時間，或詢問是否需要很長的時間。例如，室友讓你先去教室，那麼你就可以問：Will you be long, or shall I wait?（你需要很久的時間嗎？要不要我等你？）

 生字補充！ **Vocabularies & Phrases**

- **downstairs** [ˈdaʊnˈstɛrz] 副 在樓下
- **promise** [ˈprɑmɪs] 動 承諾，保證

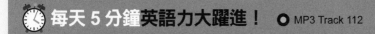

每天 **5** 分鐘英語力大躍進！　◯ MP3 Track 112

I'll check it out.

我確認一下。／我去看看。

A I think I smell gas coming from the kitchen.

B What? **I'll check it out.**

A：我覺得我聞到廚房那邊有煤氣味。

B：啊？我去看看。

A Hey, here's an interesting website about cooking!

B Really? Send me the link and **I'll check it out.**

A：嘿，這裡有個關於做菜的網站很有意思！

B：是嗎？把連結發給我，我去看看。

原來老外都這樣用！　**Know it!**

I'll check it out 是口語中非常常見的一句話，表示說話的人要去查看、確認或瞭解某一情況。check it out 也可以放在句子中，在表示「核實」的意思時後接 with sb 表示核實的人事物，如：Check it out with your boss before you make any important decision.（做任何重大決定前都要請示一下老闆。）

check it out 在表示「查看」時還有一個常見用法，就是單獨成句，用來引起對方注意，相當於「看，瞧」，如：Check it out! Check it out! Here's my new bag!（看呀，看呀！我的新包包！）在一些英文 rap（饒舌）歌曲中，我們也常聽到 rapper（說唱歌手）反覆吟唱：Hey! You! Check it out! Hey! You! Check it out!... 只不過這時的 check it out 並不是「看」的意思，而是已經蛻變成一句無意義的口頭禪啦。

 生字補充！　**Vocabularies & Phrases**

- gas [gæs] 名 瓦斯，天然氣
- link [lɪŋk] 名（網際網路檔中的）連結

I'm lost for words.
我說不出話來。／我不知道說什麼好。

A The performance is fabulous!

A：演出太精彩了！

B Yeah, **I'm lost for words.**

B：是啊，我說不出話來了。

A What did Norman say to you?

A：諾曼跟你說什麼了？

B He said that he had lied to me.

B：他說他騙了我。

A Oh my gosh.

A：天啊。

B For once in my life, **I was lost for words.**

B：我平生頭一次不知道說什麼才好。

原來老外都這樣用！ Know it!

be lost for word 表示「說不出話來，不知道說什麼才好」。在特別驚訝或難過而說不出話的時候，你都可以說 I'm lost for words.

跟 **I'm lost for words** 含義相近的表達還有 I'm speechless. speechless 意為「（因憤怒、難過等）說不出話的，啞口無言的」，例如：His comments left me speechless with rage.（他的那番話氣得我說不出話來。） I was speechless when confronted with the lawyer's new evidence.（面對律師出示的新證據，我無言以對。）

 生字補充！ Vocabularies & Phrases
• **fabulous** [ˈfæbjələs] 形 極好的，絕妙的

I'm on a diet.

我在節食。

A Would you like some toffees?

A：你要一些太妃糖嗎？

B No, thanks. **I'm on a diet.**

B：不用了，謝謝。我正在節食。

A I'm so sorry. We didn't know you would come home tonight, and we've eaten up all the food here.

A：太不好意思了。我們不知道你今晚回來，就把家裡的食物都吃光了。

B Never mind. **I'm on a diet**, anyway. Out of sight, out of mind.

B：沒關係，反正我在節食呢。正好眼不見為淨。

原來老外都這樣用！　**Know it!**

be on a diet 意為「在節食」，我們在談論減肥的話題時常會用到這個表達。其他與減肥有關的常用表達還有不少呢。put on weight（或 gain weight）意為「體重增加，變胖」，例如：He had put on weight since she last saw him.（與她上次見到他時相比，他體重增加了。）lose / shed weight 意為「體重減輕，變瘦」。watch one's weight 意為「（通過健康飲食）控制體重」。get / keep one's weight down 意為「減輕體重，減肥」，例如：How can I keep my weight down?（我要如何才能減輕體重呢？）

再看幾個與 diet 相關的常用表達吧。go on a diet 意為「開始節食」，例如：I really ought to go on a diet.（我真的應該節食了。）follow a diet 意為「按照規定飲食」，例如：You will feel better if you follow a low-fat diet.（你如果採用低脂食譜會感覺好一些。）a crash diet 意為「快速減肥」，例如：It's better to lose weight gradually than to go on a crash diet.（慢慢減肥比快速減肥好。）

生字補充！　**Vocabularies & Phrases**

• **toffee** [ˋtɔfɪ] 名 太妃糖

I've got to go.

我該走了。

A I've got to go. The yoga class is at four.

B And I've got a belly dance class. I'll catch you in the gym later.

- -

A Got to go. Mom will freak out if I stay on the computer too long.

B OK. We can have another video chat tomorrow.

A:我該走了。四點鐘有瑜伽課。

B:我也該去上肚皮舞課了。待會兒健身房見。

A:我該撤了。要是在電腦前待太久,我媽會發飆的。

B:好的。我們可以明天再視訊聊天。

原來老外都這樣用! Know it!

I've got to go 用於告訴對方你要離開(如第一個對話)或結束通話(如第二個對話),也可簡化為 I got to go 或 Got to go. 這裡的 have got to do sth 相當於 have to do sth(不得不做某事)。

除單獨成句外,I've got to go 後面還可以接各種成分,用來陳述離開的理由,如:I've got to go home / upstairs / to work / to the bathroom / to pick up my son...(我該回家了/我該上樓去了/我該上班去了/我該去洗手間了/我該去接我兒子了……)

 生字補充! Vocabularies & Phrases

- **gym** [dʒɪm] 名 健身房
- **freak out** 片 產生強烈反應,心煩意亂
- **video chat** 片 視訊聊天

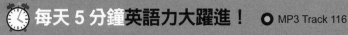

每天5分鐘英語力大躍進！ ○ MP3 Track 116

It serves you right.

你活該。／你罪有應得。

Chapter 04

四字句

A She kicked me!

B It serves you right, teasing her like that.

A：她踢我！

B：活該，誰叫你那樣取笑她。

A I only got a C. All my friends got A's or B's.

B It serves you right. You never take studying seriously.

A I want to catch up. Will you help me?

B Of course.

A：我考試只得了 C。我所有的朋友都是得 A 或 B。

B：活該。你學習從來都真不認真。

A：我想追上他們。請你幫我好嗎？

B：當然好。

原來老外都這樣用！ Know it!

It serves you right 意為「你活該，你罪有應得」。表達相似的含義還可以使用：You asked for it. You had it coming. You deserve it. You just got what you deserve.

看幾個與動詞 serve 相關的常用表達吧。serve sth out 意為「服滿刑期，做到期滿」，例如：Dillon's almost served out his sentence.（狄龍快服完刑了。）serve sth up 意為「（為某人）端上，提供（食物）」，例如：What are you serving up tonight?（今晚你給大家吃什麼？）serve the purpose 意為「適用，有用」，例如：A large cardboard box will serve the purpose.（一個大紙板箱就解決問題了。）serve customers 意為「為顧客服務」，例如：There was only one girl serving customers.（只有一個女孩在接待顧客。）serve in the army / air force / navy 意為「在軍隊／空軍／海軍服役」，例如：He returned to Greece to serve in the army.（他回到希臘服兵役。）

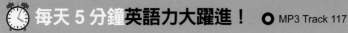

It slipped my mind.
我忘了。

A Have you bought me a birthday present?

A：幫我買生日禮物了嗎？

B Sorry, it slipped my mind.

B：對不起，我忘了。

A I thought as much.

A：我已經料到了。

A Did you call your sister to pick you up at the airport?

A：你打電話給你姐姐請她來機場接你了嗎？

B Oh, no! It totally slipped my mind.

B：哦，不！我徹底給忘了！

原來老外都這樣用！ Know it!

slip 有「滑落，脫落」之意，所以 It slipped my mind 的字面意思就是某事「從我的頭腦滑落」，即表示「我忘了」。It slipped my memory. 可以和 It slipped my mind. 互換使用，有時也可以加上 totally, completely 等副詞表示「我徹底忘了」（如第二個對話）。所以，以後再回答別人說「我忘了」時，不要總用 I forgot it 了，It slipped my memory 或者 It slipped my mind 也是不錯的選擇哦！

此外，關於 slip 還有兩個實用的片語應該牢記：let sth slip (through one's fingers)（錯過機會），例如：Don't let a golden opportunity slip through your fingers.（千萬不要錯失良機。）a slip of the tongue / pen（口誤／筆誤），比如：She said it was a slip of the tongue.（她說那是口誤。）

 生字補充！ **Vocabularies & Phrases**
• **pick up** 片 搭載，接載

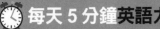

It's a long story.

說來話長。

A I'm leaving for Canada tomorrow.

A：我明天動身去加拿大。

B Why all this hurry?

B：為什麼這樣匆忙？

A Well, **it's a long story.** Let's go for lunch first.

A：嗯，說來話長。我們還是先去吃午餐吧。

A I lost my credit card last night.

A：我昨晚弄丟了我的信用卡。

B Really? How'd it happen?

B：真的嗎？怎麼回事？

A Well, **it's a long story.**

A：哦，說來話長啊。

原來老外都這樣用！ **Know it!**

It's a long story 可是聊天時用來逃避話題的利器，但只要說話的人不想詳細說明的時候，這句話就可以用來禮貌地表明其不想再說下去的態度。例如，遇到八卦人士打聽你的私人情況，問你為什麼和女朋友分手了呢；昨天老闆找你說了什麼呀……這時用這句神回足以巧妙地回避不想細談的話題。

作為一個有「故事」的人，下面這些有關「故事」的說法都是值得一記的。當以前經常發生的糟糕情況再次發生時，可以說：It's the same old story.（情況還是跟過去一樣。）表示有更多資訊可以提供時，可以說：That's not the whole story.（情況還不止這樣。）向別人感慨總是時運不濟時，可以說：That's the story of my life.（這就是我的命。）

 生字補充！ **Vocabularies & Phrases**

• **credit card** 片 信用卡

It's up to you.
聽你的。／你決定。

A When shall we leave?

B **It's up to you.** I'm ready when you are.

A：我們什麼時候走呀？

B：聽你的。我隨時可以走。

A What shall we eat tonight?

B **It's up to you.** I don't feel like eating anyway.

A：今晚我們吃什麼？

B：你決定吧。反正我也不想吃。

原來老外都這樣用！ **Know it!**

當別人就某事徵詢你的意見，而你覺得怎樣都行時，就可以用 It's up to you 表示把決定權交給對方。

it's up to you 既可單獨成句，又可放在句子中，如：It's up to you to decide who will stay.（誰留下由你說了算。）... as you like 可表達類似的含義，意為「隨你……」，如：You can choose as you like.（你可以隨意選擇。）另外，如果要表示「某事由某人說了算」，就可用 it's up to sb，如：You may have to pay the rent monthly or quarterly. It's up to the landlord.（你的房租可能是每月一付或每季一付。由房東說了算。）

 生字補充！ **Vocabularies & Phrases**

- **ready when you are** 片 我準備好了，就等你了
- **feel like (doing) sth** 片 想要（做）某事

Let's not rush things.
別太心急。／讓我們慢慢來。

A We'd better make the decision today.

B Let's not rush things. I'll bring it up at the weekly meeting, and listen to the opinions of other committee members.

A：我們最好今天就作出決定。

B：我們不要太心急。我會在週會上把這個事情提出來，然後聽聽其他委員會成員的意見。

A What was it like when you and mom first met?

B When we first met, neither of us wanted to rush things.

A：你剛跟媽媽認識的時候，是什麼樣的情況？

B：我們剛認識時，誰也不想太心急。

原來老外都這樣用！ Know it!

rush 在這裡是動詞，意為「倉促行事，匆匆決定」，例如：He does not intend to rush his decision.（他不想倉促作出決定。）I'm not rushing into marriage again.（我不急於再婚。）She rushed through her script.（她匆匆讀完稿子。）

Let's not rush things 是一種委婉的勸說，意為「我們不要太心急，讓我們慢慢來」。想表示類似含義，還可以瞭解一下其他的表達方式。take one's time 意為「不著急，慢慢來」，例如：Marie took her time cutting my hair and did it really well.（瑪麗仔細地幫我剪頭髮，剪得非常好。）(there is) no hurry 意為「不用著急」，例如：Pay me back whenever you can. There is no great hurry.（隨便什麼時候還我錢都行，不用太著急。）More haste less speed. 意為「欲速則不達」，也可以說成 Haste makes waste.。

生字補充！ Vocabularies & Phrases

• **committee** [kə`mɪtɪ] 名 委員會

My phone just died.

我手機沒電了。

A You were half an hour late!

B I'm really sorry. There was heavy traffic on the roads.

A So you were too busy directing traffic to give me a call?

B Er... my phone just died.

A：你遲到了半個小時！

B：萬分抱歉，路上太堵了。

A：所以你忙著指揮交通，沒工夫給我來個電話是吧？

B：呃……我手機沒電了。

A I've been trying to call you the whole morning. Why did you turn off your phone?

B My phone just died.

A I think "I lost my phone" is a better excuse.

A：我打了一早上的電話。你為什麼關機？

B：我手機剛好沒電了。

A：你還不如編「我手機丟了」這個理由呢。

原來老外都這樣用！ **Know it!**

My phone just died 可以被用來當作不接電話的藉口。

在平常使用時，手機還可能經常出現當機的問題。例如，你可以向維修人員抱怨說：Why does my phone always freeze?（為什麼我的手機總是當機？）

生字補充！ **Vocabularies & Phrases**

· **turn off** 片 關上，關掉

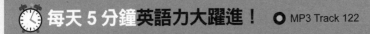

Need to go somewhere.
我要上廁所。

A Would you please keep an eye on the luggage for me? Need to go somewhere.

A：你能幫我看一下行李嗎？我想去廁所。

B No problem!

B：沒問題！

A Are you OK? You look so nervous.

A：你沒事吧？你看起來很緊張。

B I'm fine. I just need to go somewhere.

B：我沒事，就是想上廁所。

原來老外都這樣用！ Know it!

I need to go somewhere（I 可以省略）在口語中通常表示「我要上廁所」的意思。如果約會時聽到對方說這句話，可別一臉疑惑地問：Where? 在公共場合中，人們通常不會直白地說 I need to go to the toilet.（我要去廁所。）除了 I need to go somewhere，I need to powder my nose 也可以表示這層含義。從字面上看，powder one's nose 是「往鼻子上塗粉」，即「補妝」之意，實際上就是「上廁所」的委婉說法。正因為和補妝有關，I need to powder my nose 通常是女性使用的說法，不過有些幽默的男士也會這麼說。如果想去廁所又實在想不起這兩句「委婉」的說法，怎麼辦呢？那就記住下面這句簡單的吧：I need to go to the bathroom.（我要去洗手間。）

生字補充！ Vocabularies & Phrases

- **keep an eye on (sth / sb)** 片 照看，照料（某物／某人）

Right back at you.

你才是呢。／原話奉還。

A You're such a cruel, selfish and mean woman!

A：你這個殘酷、自私、刻薄的女人！

B **Right back at you!** You're such a cruel, selfish, mean and old woman!

B：原話奉還！你這個殘酷、自私、刻薄的老女人！

A You are so adorable!

A：你真可愛。

B **Right back at you.** Everybody loves you.

B：你才是呢。人人都愛你。

原來老外都這樣用！ Know it!

back 在這裡是副詞，表示「回到原處，回應，歸還」，例如：call back 是「回電話」，pay back 是「還錢」，shout back 是「大聲回答」，hit back 是「還手（打人）」，give (sth) back 是「歸還（某物）」，have / get (sth) back 是「拿回（某物）」，answer / talk back 表示「頂嘴，回嘴」。

right 在這裡也是副詞，表示「恰恰，正好，不偏不倚」，例如：right in front of 是「在……正前方」，right here / there 表示「就在這裡／那裡」。合起來 Right back at you 在口語中表示「你才是呢，原話奉還」，是指將對方的話原封不動地還給他／她。別人攻擊你時你可以用這句話回擊對方，別人誇獎你時你也可以用這句話予以回應。

生字補充！ Vocabularies & Phrases

- **mean** [min] 形 刻薄的
- **adorable** [ə`dorəbl] 形 可愛的，討人喜歡的

Same old, same old.
還是老樣子。

A How are you doing, dude?

A：最近怎麼樣，老兄？

B Same old, same old.

B：老樣子啦。

A Hey, Alice! Haven't seen you for ages. How are you?

A：嘿，愛麗絲，好久不見。你好嗎？

B Same old. All my time has been spent on the kids.

B：還是老樣子。時間都花在孩子身上了。

原來老外都這樣用！ Know it!

在日常寒暄中，當別人問你最近怎麼樣時，如果你想表示「沒什麼變化，還是老樣子」，就可以用 Same old 或 Same old, same old.

很多人初學英語時，面對別人 How are you? 的提問，就只能想到 Fine, thank you. And you? 這一種回應。其實回應的方式很多，大家平時可以留心記憶幾種，到時候就可以信手拈來了。例如：It's just wonderful!（感覺好極了！）I feel like a million bucks.（我感覺棒極了。）Never felt better. / Better than ever.（再好不過了。）Great.（非常好。）Fine, thank you for asking.（很好，謝謝關心。）Pretty good.（挺好的。）Not bad.（還不錯。）Fair to middling.（還過得去。）So-so.（一般般。）Can't complain.（沒什麼好抱怨的。）I'm hanging on. / Surviving.（還活著呢。）有時候甚至可以直接用 How are you? 去回應。

 生字補充！ Vocabularies & Phrases

• **for ages** 片 很長時間，很久

That's fine by / with me.

我沒問題。／我不介意。

A Please don't tell my offer to anyone.

B If you want to keep it a secret, that's fine with me.

A：請不要把我的報價告訴任何人。

B：如果你想保密，那我沒意見。

A Some of the members are carsick. So shall we take subway?

B That's fine with me.

A Thank you for your understanding.

A：有些成員暈車，所以我們坐地鐵好嗎？

B：我沒問題。

A：謝謝您的理解。

原來老外都這樣用！ Know it!

That's fine by me 或 That's fine with me 表示說話的人不介意某事，意為「我沒問題，我不介意」。表達類似的意思還可以使用：I don't mind. That's OK with / by me. That's good for me.

形容詞 fine 在這裡表示「令人滿意的，可以接受的」，它還有不少常用的表達。looks / seems / sounds fine 意為「看起來／似乎／聽起來不錯」，例如：In theory, the scheme sounds fine.（理論上，這個計畫聽起來不錯。）it's fine as it is 意為「這樣就可以了，不用再麻煩了」，例如："Do you want chili sauce on it?" "No, it's fine as it is, thanks."（「你要淋上辣椒汁嗎？」「不用了，這樣子就很好，謝謝。」）I'm fine (thanks / thank you) 意為「我夠了（謝謝／謝謝你）」，例如："More coffee?" "No, I'm fine, thanks."（「再來點兒咖啡嗎？」「不了，我夠了，謝謝。」）大家請注意，I'm fine 不僅可以在回答別人的 How are you? 時使用，還可以表示「我夠了」哦。

That's more like it.

這還差不多。／那還比較像樣。

Ⓐ Here's the money you lent me last month, and this is the thank-you gift.

Ⓑ **That's more like it!**

Ⓐ：這是你上個月借我的錢，還有一份謝禮。

Ⓑ：這還差不多！

Ⓐ I've considered your suggestion.

Ⓑ And?

Ⓐ I can raise my offer to 20,000 yuan.

Ⓑ Now, **that's more like it!**

Ⓐ：我考慮過你的建議了。

Ⓑ：結果呢？

Ⓐ：我可以把報價提高到兩萬元。

Ⓑ：嗯，這還比較像樣嘛！

原來老外都這樣用！ **Know it!**

當先前讓你不滿的情況發生改變而符合你的心意時，就可以用 That's more like it! 這句話表示你對這種改善感到滿意（如上述兩個對話）。不滿的情況發生改變也包括錯誤得到改正。例如，餐廳服務生上錯了菜，但他／她意識到錯誤之後馬上表示歉意並換上正確的菜，這時你就可以說：That's more like it!（這才對嘛！）

此外，That's more like it! 這句話也可以用於表揚他人。例如，好友的英語成績提高了，你就可以鼓勵他／她說：That's more like it! You're really starting to improve.（很不錯嘛！你現在真的開始進步了。）

生字補充！ **Vocabularies & Phrases**

• **raise** [rez] 動 增加，提高
• **offer** [ˈɔfɚ] 名 報價，開價

That's not the point.

這不是重點。

A Mom, I'm sorry I failed the exam.

B **That's not the point.** The point is that you lied to us about it.

A：媽媽，對不起，我考試不及格。

B：這不是重點。重點是你對我們撒謊。

A Isn't she good enough for you?

B Er... I don't find her attractive. But **that's not the point.** The point is, I'm already in love with a girl.

A：對你來說她還不夠好嗎？

B：呃……我不覺得她多有魅力。不過這不是重點，關鍵是我已經有喜歡的女孩了。

原來老外都這樣用！ **Know it!**

That's not the point 用於告訴對方之前所說的話並不是問題的關鍵，後面往往會跟一句解釋：The point is...（關鍵在於……）這裡的 point 是「關鍵，重點」之意，例如在跟別人理論的過程中你可以說：I think you've missed the point.（我想你沒搞清楚；我想你沒搞懂問題的關鍵。）

另外，point 也可指對話中的「觀點，論點」，例如你贊同別人的看法，就可以說 You have a point (there) 或 I take your point (about...). 如：I take your point about travel.（我贊同你關於旅行的看法。）還可以說 Good point!（好觀點！好想法！）

 生字補充！ **Vocabularies & Phrases**
• attractive [əˋtræktɪv] 形 有魅力的，漂亮的

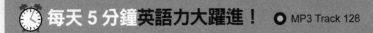
We need to talk.

我們需要談一談。

A I think **we need to talk.**

B I don't want to talk right now.

A Perhaps you want to talk to your father?

B All right. What do you want to talk about?

A：我想我們需要談一談。

B：我現在不想說話。

A：或許你想跟你父親談談？

B：好吧。您想談什麼？

A Everything's going smoothly. If we...

B Dick, **we need to talk.**

A Anything wrong?

B I'm afraid so.

A：一切都很順利。如果我們……

B：迪克，我們得談談。

A：出了什麼問題嗎？

B：恐怕是的。

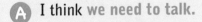 **Know it!**

動詞 talk 在這裡可不是「聊天」的意思，它是指「討論，商談（嚴肅、重要的話題）」。看幾個例子：Is there somewhere we can talk in private?（有什麼地方我們可以去私下談談嗎？）You should talk to a lawyer.（你應該諮詢律師。）We've been talking about getting married.（我們在談結婚的事了。）

We need to talk 常常在以下兩種情況中使用：一種是有重要的或嚴肅的事情要跟對方說；另一種是對對方有所不滿，要與之說道，有興師問罪的意思。例如，母親強壓著怒火對孩子說 We need to talk.，孩子就應該做好心理準備，十有八九要挨一頓罵了。

We'd better be off.

我們還是走吧。／我們該出發了。

A It's getting dark. Is it going to rain?

B Maybe, and we'd better be off.

A：天越來越黑了，是不是要下雨啊？

B：有可能，我們還是走吧。

A Hurry up! We'd better be off, otherwise we'll miss the train.

B Wait a minute! I'm almost ready.

A：快點！我們該出發了，不然就趕不上火車了。

B：等一下！我馬上就好了。

原來老外都這樣用！ Know it!

We'd better be off 這句話中，我們應重點關注 had better 的用法。此處的 better 為副詞，had better 的主詞是人，後面可以什麼都不接，或接動詞原形，表示「某人最好（做某事）」。例如："I'll do the homework right now." "Yeah, you'd better."（「我馬上就去寫作業。」「對，就該這麼做。」）You'd better hurry up—the movie will start in ten minutes.（你最好快一點——電影 10 分鐘後開演。）

有時，had better 還含有威脅的意味。比如：They'd better not go out smoking when I told them not to.（我不讓他們出去抽菸的時候他們最好別去。）

在日常口語中，had 常常可以省略不讀。以第一個對話為例，B 也可以這樣回答：Maybe, and we better be off.（有可能，我們還是走吧。）

 生字補充！ **Vocabularies & Phrases**

• otherwise [ˈʌðəˌwaɪz] 副 否則，要不然

What do you say?

你覺得怎麼樣？

A The supplier said the discount rate couldn't be higher than 20 percent.

B John and I can accept anything above 10 percent. **What do you say?**

A It's OK with me.

A：供應商説折扣不能低於八折。

B：約翰和我覺得九折以下都可以接受，你覺得怎麼樣？

A：我也沒問題。

A I think it is appropriate to split this report into three parts. **What do you say?**

B I agree with you, but I think we'd better discuss it with the other teammates.

A OK, let's do it after lunch.

A：我覺得這份報告分成三部分比較合適，你的看法呢？

B：同意，但是我覺得最好和其他組員討論一下。

A：好，我們午餐後討論吧。

原來老外都這樣用！ **Know it!**

What do you say? 在口語中常用來詢問他人是否同意所提的建議（如上述兩個對話）。what do you say 除了獨立成句外，還可以就某個具體行為徵求對方的意見，此時表示具體行為的動詞要用原形。例如：What do you say I learn a second foreign language?（我學一門第二外語，你覺得怎麼樣？）What do you say we have dinner together?（我們一起吃晚飯怎麼樣？）另外，在口語中詢問某人對某事的看法還可以用 What would you say to sth? 的句型。例如：What would you say to a pajama party?（你覺得睡衣派對怎麼樣？）

What're you talking about?

你在說什麼？

A You were late again this morning!

A：你們今天早上又遲到了！

B What're you talking about? We got there in plenty of time.

B：你在說什麼？我們很早就到那裡了。

A I'd need at least a week to complete the project.

A：我至少需要一週的時間完成這個項目。

B What are you talking about? How could it take a week?

B：你在說什麼？怎麼可能需要一週？

原來老外都這樣用！ **Know it!**

What're you talking about? 用來指對方說的話愚蠢或錯誤，可譯為「你在說什麼？」想表達類似的意思，有時還可以用 Are you listening to yourself? 它的字面意思是「你在聽自己說的話嗎？」暗藏著的含意就是「如果你在聽，怎麼能說出這麼愚蠢或錯誤的話呢？」，其實也就是「你在說什麼啊？」的意思。例如："I think 2,000 dollars may be enough for me to live there for a week." "Are you listening to yourself? Maybe 2,000 by 10 will do."（「我想2,000元夠我在那裡生活一星期。」「你在說什麼呀？2,000乘以10還差不多。」）

 生字補充！ **Vocabularies & Phrases**

・**plenty of** 片 充足的，大量的

You asked for it!

你自找的！

A The waiter served me such a huge bowl of ice cream! I've just finished my dinner!

A：服務生竟然上了這麼大一碗冰淇淋！我剛吃完晚餐耶！

B You asked for it!

B：這可是你自己點的。

A But it is only a pocket-sized bowl on the menu!

A：但是看菜單上它才那麼一小碗呀！

A The manager scolded me again! I guess he may fire me soon!

A：經理又罵了我一頓！我猜他可能很快就會把我炒了！

B It's all about the careless way you do your job. You asked for it!

B：還不是因為你工作不認真，你自找的！

原來老外都這樣用！ Know it!

我們常說某人是自討苦吃，這個「自討苦吃」在英語裡就可以用 You asked for it! 來表達，只不過具體也分兩種情況。一種情況為這個「苦」是你自己要求的，常用於點餐中（如第一個對話）。再例如，當朋友抱怨點的菜不好吃時，你可以回一句：You asked for it.（這可是你自己要吃的。）還有一種情況是表示做錯事情理應受到批評或懲罰（如第二個對話）。再如，孩子不僅沒有完成作業還撒謊，媽媽教訓他時可能會說本來不想打你，但是 You asked for it!（這是你自己找打的！）

 生字補充！ Vocabularies & Phrases

- **bowl** [bol] 名 一碗之量
- **scold** [skold] 動 責罵，訓斥
- **careless** ['kɛrlɪs] 形 粗心的

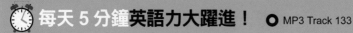

You owe me one.

你欠我個人情。

A How's it going between you and Judy?

A：你和茱蒂相處得如何？

B Great! And I have to say, I would never have chased her if you hadn't encouraged me.

B：很好！不得不説，要是沒有你的鼓勵，我根本就不會去追她。

A Well, **you owe me one.**

A：嗯，那你欠我個人情啦。

A You have to help me this time. **You owe me one** when I talked your wife out of selling the house.

A：你這次必須幫我。上回我説服你妻子不賣房子，所以你欠我個人情。

B Fair enough. I'll see what I can do.

B：説得有道理。我來看看我能幫什麼忙。

原來老外都這樣用！ **Know it!**

動詞 owe 在這裡指「應該做，應給予，對……負有……的義務」。**You owe me one** 意為「你欠我一個人情」。當然，當你欠別人人情的時候，就可以把話反過來説：I owe you one.（我欠你個人情。）

owe 的常見含義還有「欠（錢），負債」，如：I owe her $50.（我欠她 50 美元。）owe 還有「把……歸功於，有……是由於」的意思，常表示為 owe sth to sb，如：She owes her life to him.（他對她有救命之恩。）Sophie owes her success to her parents.（蘇菲把自己的成功歸功於父母。）

 生字補充！ **Vocabularies & Phrases**

- **talk sb out of doing sth** 片 説服某人不做某事
- **fair enough** 片 有道理，説得對

You've got a point.

你說的對。

A I was told to work overtime this weekend.

A：我被告知這週末要加班。

B Again?

B：又加班？

A Yeah, but I've decided that no extra pay no overtime!

A：是啊，不過我已經決定了，不給加班費就不加班！

B You've got a point!

B：你說的對！

A I don't think that he will give us a lower offer.

A：我覺得他不會給我們更低的報價。

B You've got a point. That's why I insist on negotiating with other suppliers.

B：你說的沒錯，所以我才堅持要和其他供應商進行洽談。

原來老外都這樣用！ **Know it!**

You've got a point 這句話可以和 That's a point 互換使用，表示說話的人認為某人說得有道理。I see your point（我明白你的意思）和 You've got a point 字面意思相近，在日常口語中也比較常用，但是前者暗含否定之意，尤其用於並不贊同對方的時候。例如，在第二個對話中，如果改用 I see your point. 來回答，則後面通常會跟一個「但是」：I see your point, but I insist on not changing the partner.（我明白你的意思，但是我堅持不換合作夥伴。）

關於 point 還有一點大家要牢記，當它用於表示「（試圖表達的）觀點，看法」時，只有單數形式，千萬不要用複數形式哦！例如，可以說 What's your point?（你想說什麼？），但 What are your points? 則是錯誤的。

You've got some nerve!
你真厚臉皮！

A I've called our team leader!

A：我打電話給我們隊長。

B For what?

B：為了什麼事？

A I've called to ask him to invite me to the party.

A：我打電話告訴他，請他邀請我參加宴會。

B You've got some nerve!

B：你真厚臉皮！

A I forgot my wallet, so this is your treat!

A：我忘記帶錢包了，所以這頓就你請吧！

B You've got some nerve!

B：你臉皮可真厚！

原來老外都這樣用！ Know it!

You've got some nerve! 中的 nerve 是「放肆，厚顏無恥」之意，所以這句話是強調某人臉皮厚，也可以說成 You have some nerve! 此外，What a nerve! 也可表示此意。例如："Then he demanded to see the president!" "What a nerve!"（「他還要求見董事長！」「真不要臉！」）

有一點需要特別記住，由於 nerve 還可表示「信心，勇氣」，have the nerve 就有了兩種截然不同的意思。例如：He didn't have the nerve to ask her for a date.（他沒有勇氣約她出去。）He had the nerve to take the credit for my work.（他竟然搶我的功勞，真不要臉。）通常來說，當 nerve 和表示「需要，缺少」之意的字彙搭配使用時，大都表示「信心，勇氣」，反之就是「厚顏無恥」之意啦！

Part 2

傳情達意好用句

He won't bite.

他又不會咬你。／他又不會吃人。

A Could you tell Mr. Kutche that I won't make it to the meeting next week?

A：你能告訴庫奇先生我出席不了下週的會議嗎？

B You can tell him yourself. He's just over there discussing something with the secretary. Come on. **He won't bite.**

B：你可以自己跟他說啊。他就在那邊跟祕書討論事情呢。去吧，他又不會咬你。

A Boss hasn't replied to me. Has he received my email?

A：老闆還沒回覆我。他有沒有收到我的郵件啊？

B Well, go and ask him—**he won't bite!**

B：去問問他吧——他又不會吃人！

原來老外都這樣用！ **Know it!**

動詞 bite 通常意為「咬」，既可以是及物的，也可以是不及物的，如：bite one's nails（咬指甲），bite one's lip（咬嘴唇），bite through sth（咬穿某物），bite sth off（咬掉某物），A barking dog doesn't bite.（會叫的狗不咬人。）sb won't bite 意為「某人又不會咬你」，用於表示不用害怕某人，尤指有權有勢的人。

再來看幾個跟「咬」有關的動詞，感受一下它們跟 bite 的異同。chew 表示「（不停地）嚼」，如：Helen was chewing a piece of gum.（海倫嚼著口香糖。）gnaw 表示「（動物）啃，咬」，如：The dog was in the yard gnawing on a bone.（那狗在院子裡啃骨頭。）nip 表示「輕咬」，如：When I took the hamster out of the cage, it nipped me.（我把倉鼠抓出籠子時，它咬了我一口。）nibble 表示「啃，一點點地咬」，如：A fish nibbled at the bait.（一條魚咬餌了。）chomp 表示「大聲地咀嚼」，如：The donkey was chomping on a carrot.（那頭驢當時正大口大口地嚼著胡蘿蔔。）

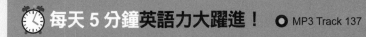

I've been there.

我也經歷過這種情況。

A Did you see how mad Diane was? Do you think she'll ever forgive me?

B I'm sure she will. Look, **I've been there.** Fight, then make up—it's quite common among couples.

A：你看到戴安娜有多生氣了嗎？你覺得她還會原諒我嗎？

B：她肯定會原諒你的。聽我說，我也經歷過這種情況。小倆口吵吵架，再和好，很正常的事嘛。

A I hate being forced to dance! I've never felt so awkward!

B Oh, I know. **I've been there.**

A：我討厭被人逼著跳舞！我從來沒這麼尷尬過！

B：哦，我懂的。我也經歷過。

原來老外都這樣用！ **Know it!**

在安慰別人時，我們常常會用到「感同身受」這一招，而 I've been there. 就是一個很好的表達。有時它甚至可以簡化為 Been there，短短的一句話讓對方知道你也經歷過同樣的難題。

我們經常用來安慰別人的另一招則是弱化事態的嚴重性，讓人覺得沒那麼可怕。比如你可以說：It's just one of those things.（這是常有的事。）That happens. / Happens.（天有不測風雲嘛。）不過，為了避免讓對方覺得你是「光嘴巴會說」，最好還是配合第一招「感同身受」一起使用喲。

生字補充！ **Vocabularies & Phrases**

- **mad** [mæd] 形 生氣的
- **make up** 片 和好，和解
- **awkward** [ˋɔkwəd] 形 緊張的，不舒服的

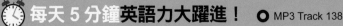

It was meant to be.

這是註定的。

A He dreamed about being a chemist when he was a child, but he studied political economy at university.

A：他小時候的夢想是成為化學家，但是大學時卻學了政治經濟學。

B Is he an economist now?

B：那他現在是經濟學家嗎？

A No, but he just won a Nobel Prize in chemistry. He's a world renowned expert in the field.

A：不是，但是他剛贏得了諾貝爾化學獎。他是該領域中享譽世界的專家。

B It was meant to be.

B：這是註定的。

A They met after ten years' separation and finally got married.

A：他們分開 10 年後又遇見彼此，並且終於結了婚。

B Well, it was meant to be.

B：嗯，他們註定是要在一起的。

原來老外都這樣用！ Know it!

It was meant to be 表示因為人力無法控制的因素，某事註定會發生。其中的 it 也可以用某具體事物來替換。比如，在第二個對話中，最後一句可以替換為 Their love was meant to be.（他們註定是要相愛的。）這個口語也可以根據其意思用 meant to be... 的句型來替換。例如，在第一個對話中，最後一句可替換為 He was meant to be a world renowned expert in the field.（他註定要成為該領域享譽世界的專家。）

 生字補充！ **Vocabularies & Phrases**

• **separation** [ˌsɛpəˈreʃən] **名** 分開，分離

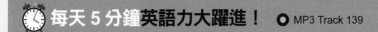

It's their loss.

那是他們的損失。

A I was rejected by that company.

A：我被那家公司拒絕了。

B Sorry to hear that. But I think **it's their loss**, and you still have many good opportunities.

B：真替你感到惋惜。但我覺得這是那家公司的損失，你還是有很多好機會的。

A How was your audition?

A：你的試鏡如何？

B I failed.

B：沒戲唱了。

A You must be very depressed now.

A：你現在肯定很沮喪吧。

B I'm OK. **It's their loss.**

B：還好，不用我是他們的損失。

原來老外都這樣用！ Know it!

It's their loss 可以用來安慰遭到拒絕的人（如第一個對話），也可用來表示說話人對於失敗的不在乎（如第二個對話）。除了獨立成句，it's / that's sb's loss 還可以和 if 從句搭配，表示「如果……某人就會利益受損」。例如，你想勸朋友一起做生意，在說了一大堆這生意會如何賺錢之後，你可以再強調一句：If you don't participate, it's your loss.（如果不加入的話，那可就是你的損失。）

此外，有個特別容易被表面字義誤導的表達大家要注意：loss leader 可不是指人，而是指「為了吸引顧客進店消費而虧本銷售的產品」。

 生字補充！ Vocabularies & Phrases
- **opportunity** [ˌɑpəˈtjunətɪ] **名** 機會
- **audition** [ɔˈdɪʃən] **名** 試鏡

Things will work out.

情況會好起來的。

A I lost my job, my house was broken into, and here's the terrible cold—everything seems wrong with me lately.

B Cheer up! **Things will work out.**

A：我丟了工作，家也遭竊，又加上重感冒——最近好像什麼都不對勁。

B：開心點！情況會好起來的。

A It seems that **things won't work out** between Jenny and me.

B Oh, don't let it get you down. I'm sure there's someone else out there who's just right for you.

A：看樣子我和珍妮是有緣無分了。

B：哦，別為這事情難過。肯定還會有適合你的人的。

原來老外都這樣用！ Know it!

安慰某人說「一切都會好起來的」時，最常用的表達之一就是 Things will work out. work out 後還可以加上各種修飾詞，如 work out OK / for the best 等。也可以用 work itself out 這一結構，如：I'm sure everything will work itself out.（我確信一切都會好起來的。）如果是表示「（某些人之間的問題）得到解決」，則可以用 work out for sb，如：I hope it all works out for the two of us.（我希望我倆之間的一切問題都能得到解決。）

相反，如果要表示問題解決不了，則可以說 things won't / don't / didn't work out（如第二個對話）。這時，傾訴對象就要和 B 一樣，說些溫柔體貼的話來安慰對方啦。

 生字補充！ **Vocabularies & Phrases**

• **break into** 片 闖入（行竊）
• **get sb down** 片 使某人傷心，使某人沮喪

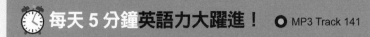

Better luck next time!

祝你下次好運！

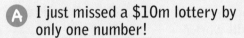

A I just missed a $10m lottery by only one number!

A：我差一點就中 1000 萬的大獎了！就差一個數字！

B Better luck next time!

B：祝你下次好運！

A How is your final exam?

A：你期末考試考得怎麼樣？

B I've done my best, but still failed to outdo John.

B：我盡全力了，但還是沒超過約翰。

A Better luck next time!

A：祝你下次好運！

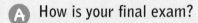 **原來老外都這樣用！** **Know it!**

Better luck next time! 主要是用來安慰並祝願對方下次能夠如願以償，此時說話人的語氣應該是鼓勵、肯定的。但有的時候這句話也可以用來嘲笑他人的失敗，語氣粗魯或諷刺。例如，某人跑步比你快，你不服輸要求再比一次，結果還是對方贏，此時對方就可能不屑地說：You thought you could get ahead of me? Better luck next time!（你還以為能跑過我？下次吧！）

如果遭遇失敗，你也可以用 Just my luck!（我就這運氣！）來表示「一點也不奇怪為什麼會這樣，因為運氣一直不好」之意。例如，你買了彩票沒中，就可以說：Just my luck! I've never won a lottery!（我就這運氣！從來就沒中過彩票！）

 生字補充！ **Vocabularies & Phrases**

• **lottery** [ˈlɑtərɪ] **名** 獎券，彩票

每天 **5** 分鐘**英語力大躍進！** ○ MP3 Track 142

There is no harm in trying.
不妨去試試。／試一試又不會有損失。

A I'm thinking about selling our fruit online. Do you think it will work?

A：我在考慮把我們的水果放到網路上去賣。你覺得可行嗎？

B Let's just do it. **There is no harm in trying.**

B：我們就做吧。反正試一試又沒有損失。

A Do you think I should let her know that I like her?

A：你覺得我該不該讓她知道我喜歡她呢？

B Why are you hesitating?

B：你在猶豫什麼呢？

A She once said she wouldn't accept boys who are younger than her.

A：她曾說過不會接受年紀比她小的男生。

B Go ask her out, you dumb boy. **There is no harm in trying.**

B：去約她吧，傻小子。試試又不會有損失。

原來老外都這樣用！ **Know it!**

當看到朋友為一件事情糾結猶豫、瞻前顧後、裹足不前的時候，如果採取積極的行動也不會有太大風險的話，你就可以鼓勵他／她去嘗試一下，因為一旦成功了豈不是更好，萬一失敗了也沒有什麼損失。There is no harm in trying 就是適合這時候用的表達。

名詞 harm 指「損害、傷害、危害」，句型 there is no harm in doing sth 表示「不妨做某事」，用於建議和鼓勵他人，還可以表達為 it does no harm to do sth，意思完全一樣，例如：It does no harm to ask.（不妨去問問。）

it wouldn't do sb any harm to do sth 的意思也差不多，表示「做某事對某人並無害處」，例如：It wouldn't do you any harm to get some experience first.（你不妨先積累點經驗。）

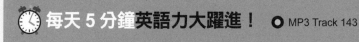

Time heals all wounds.

時間能治癒一切創傷。／時間是療傷的良藥。

A I hate him! I'll never forgive him!

A：我恨他！我永遠不會原諒他！

B Don't hate him. It's not worth it. **Time heals all wounds.** You'll forget him very soon.

B：不要恨他。不值得。時間會治癒一切，你很快就會忘記他的。

A I'm worried about Lucas. He seems so broken-hearted.

A：我很擔心盧卡斯。他看起來那麼傷心。

B Don't worry. **Time heals all wounds.**

B：別擔心。時間是療傷的良藥。

A That's right. Nobody can really help him right now.

A：對。現在沒人能真正幫得了他。

B Lucas is a strong boy. He'll be all right.

B：盧卡斯是個堅強的孩子。他會沒事的。

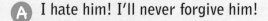

原來老外都這樣用！ **Know it!**

在受到創傷的當下，無論是別人的勸慰還是自己的努力，可能都無法減輕創傷帶來的痛苦。好在時間是療傷的良藥，只要時間夠久，大部分創傷都可以得到治癒，再刻骨銘心的痛苦也會得以緩解。所以當你不知道說什麼來安慰別人，或者覺得任何安慰都是沒有用的，你就可以說一句：Time heals all wounds. 把一切都交給時間。同樣的意思還可以用 Time is a great healer. 來表達。名詞 healer 在這裡指「撫平創傷的事物」。

另外一個相關的表達是 get over, 它可以指「從不愉快的經歷中恢復過來」，如：It took her three years to get over the death of her boyfriend.（她男朋友死後三年，她才漸漸看開。）

You're not the only one.

並非只有你是這樣。／我也是這樣。

A I have to take five exams in two days! Can you imagine that?

B **You're not the only one!** I think we should have a party after all these exams.

A：我兩天之內要參加五場考試！你能想像得到嗎？

B：我也是呀！我覺得考完之後我們應該辦個派對慶祝一下。

A Guess what? I failed to buy the train ticket again! The third time!

B **You're not the only one!** I've decided to get one from a scalper.

A The Spring Festival travel rush!

A：你猜怎麼了？我又沒買到火車票！買了三次都沒買到！

B：我也是啊！我決定找黃牛買一張。

A：這「農曆春節的交通」啊！

原來老外都這樣用！ **Know it!**

You're not the only one 通常用於表示安慰的場合，意思就是說「你不是一個人，我們都面臨著同樣的困境或令人不愉快的局面」。有時，這句話也可後接從句以具體說明面臨的困境或局面。例如，組員向作為項目負責人的你抱怨週末加班，那麼你就可以回應說：You're not the only one who works overtime at the weekend.（不是只有你週末加班。）We're in the same boat 與 You're not the only one 類似，表示「大家處境相同」。略微不同的是，它還含有「同舟共濟，共同面對」的意思。例如：We're in the same boat, so we need to trust each other.（我們處境相同，所以我們要彼此信任。）

 生字補充！ **Vocabularies & Phrases**
• scalper [ˋskælpɚ] 名 黃牛

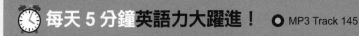

He is such a miser!

他是個小氣鬼！

A My husband always complains that I'm spending too much money, but I'm not! He never gives me any money.

A：我老公總抱怨我太會花錢，可是我並沒有啊！他從來不給我錢。

B He is such a miser!

B：他可真是個守財奴啊！

A Ashton said it was his treat yesterday.

A：昨天艾希頓說他請客。

B I can't believe it! He is such a miser!

B：我真不敢相信！他那麼小氣！

A When we finished eating, he went to the bathroom.

A：當我們吃完飯後，他就去洗手間了。

B Hah, there he goes again.

B：哈，他又來這套。

原來老外都這樣用！ Know it!

名詞 miser 意為「吝嗇鬼，小氣鬼，守財奴」。能表達相似含義的名詞還有 skinflint, tightwad, cheapskate 等，例如：We waited for the old skinflint to find his wallet and pay us our money.（我們等著那個老吝嗇鬼找到他的錢包，把錢還給我們。）Joe is such a tightwad—he won't even buy his own newspaper!（喬真是小氣啊—他連他自己的報紙都不買！）Howard called the taxi, he rode with us, and then the cheapskate didn't even offer to pay any of the fare!（霍華德叫了計程車，他跟我們一起搭車，然後這個吝嗇鬼居然一分錢都不打算出！）

要想表達「吝嗇的，小氣的」之意時，可以用下列形容詞：stingy, mean, tight, tight-fisted, miserly。看幾個例句：They are rich, but they are terribly stingy.（他們雖然有錢，但小氣極了。）He is the meanest man I have ever worked for!（他是我服務過最小氣的雇主！）She is really tight with money and only puts the heating on when it's freezing cold.（她特別吝嗇，只有天氣非常冷的時候才肯開暖氣。）

That's low.

這招真夠低級的。

A Snitching on David? **That's low.**

A：打大衛的小報告？這招真夠低級的。

B Oh, come on. He might have done the same to us.

B：哦，拜託，換成是他說不定也會這樣對我們呢。

- -

A You know what? I sneaked into his room and put a rat in his closet!

A：你知道嗎？我偷偷溜進他的房間，在他的壁櫥裡放了一隻老鼠！

B Wow! **That's low.**

B：哇！這招真夠低級的。

原來老外都這樣用！ **Know it!**

當別人做了或打算做一件你認為有點缺德的事時，你可以用 That's low 來表達對他／她的鄙視。當然，根據具體情境和語氣的不同，這句話既有可能是真正的批評，也可能只是開玩笑的。

提醒大家注意這裡 that 的用法（代指一種無須明說的情況），在英文中恰當使用 that 能使語言簡潔而道地。例如有人說了一句傷害你的話，你可以簡單地回一句：Ouch! That hurts!（哎喲！這話可真傷人哪！）當某人做出莫名其妙的舉動時，你則可以皺著眉頭問道：What's that (all) about?（你這是演哪一齣啊？）

 生字補充！ **Vocabularies & Phrases**

- **snitch on sb** 片 打某人的小報告
- **sneak into** 片 偷偷溜進
- **closet** ['klɑzɪt] 名 壁櫥

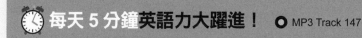

Who do you think you are?

你以為你是誰啊？

Chapter **02**

鄙視、鄙夷

A Stop pointing the finger at me, OK? **Who do you think you are?**

A：別對我橫加指責可以嗎？你以為你是誰啊？

B Well, I'm just trying to help.

B：嗯，我只是想幫幫忙嘛。

A I can't put up with the noise anymore! I'm going to the city council to make a complaint!

A：我受不了這噪音了！我要去市議會投訴！

B Just let it go. **Who do you think you are?** The President of the United States?

B：別多管閒事了。你以為你是誰，美國總統啊？

原來老外都這樣用！ Know it!

當一個人試圖做超越自己職責或能力範圍的事，而讓你感到不爽時，你就可以翻白眼對他／她說：Who do you think you are?（你以為你是誰呀？你算老幾呀？）後面還可以像第二個對話中那樣配上一句追問：The President of the United States? / Superman?（你以為你是美國總統／超人啊？）進一步提醒對方不要自不量力、多管閒事，增加諷刺的意味。

不過，這句話殺傷力較強，有可能傷到對方的自尊心，使用時應該格外謹慎小心。

生字補充！ Vocabularies & Phrases

• **point the / a finger at sb** 片 指責某人，責怪某人
• **put up with** 片 忍受
• **make a complaint** 片 投訴

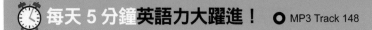
He's just an expert at betraying his colleagues to the manager.

他老是向經理打同事的小報告。

A How did the manager know who wrote that letter?

B I saw John go into the manager's office yesterday afternoon.

A He's just an expert at betraying his colleagues to the manager.

A：經理怎麼會知道那封信是誰寫的？

B：昨天下午我看到約翰去了經理的辦公室。

A：他老是向經理打同事的小報告。

- -

A It seems that the other colleagues don't like Williams.

B Ah, Williams, he's just an expert at betraying his colleagues to the manager.

A：其他同事好像都不喜歡威廉斯。

B：喔，威廉斯啊，他就是個愛跟經理打同事小報告的人。

原來老外都這樣用！　Know it!

He's just an expert at betraying his colleagues to the manager 這句話用於鄙視某個總是在主管面前打小報告的人。其實不僅是在工作中，我們從上學開始，身邊肯定就不乏向老師打小報告的人，這些學生雖然深得老師喜愛，卻容易遭其他同學所排擠。談到這類人時，你也可以套用上面的句型，用鄙視的語氣說：He / She's just an expert at betraying his / her classmates to the teacher.（他／她就會向老師打同學的小報告。）

另外，be an expert at doing sth（是一個做……很在行的人）是個非常有用的句型，在不同的語境中可以表達嬉笑怒罵等不同的語氣。例如，對於身邊常常製造髒亂的孩子，你就可以說：He's just an expert at making a mess.（製造髒亂這種事他最擅長。）

Don't play innocent with me.

少跟我裝無辜。

A Why did you take money from my wallet?

A：你為什麼從我錢包裡拿錢？

B What money?

B：什麼錢？

A Don't play innocent with me!

A：少跟我裝無辜！

A You betrayer! She's already known my secret!

A：你這個叛徒！她已經知道我的祕密了！

B I didn't say anything to her.

B：我什麼也沒和她說過。

A Don't play innocent with me!

A：你別跟我裝無辜！

原來老外都這樣用！　Know it!

Don't play innocent with me 用於鄙視對方裝無辜。儘管對方裝作不知情，但說話的人基本上已經能確定對方和某件事有關。Don't play...（別裝作……）這一句型在口語中可以用於多種場合。例如，和別人吵架的時候不滿第三者充當和事佬，此時你可以說：Don't play the peacekeeper.（用不著你裝和事佬。）再如，某人背著你很囂張，但是當著你的面又表現出很緊張的樣子，那麼你可以說：Don't play nervous！（別在這兒裝緊張！）

Don't play... 句型可以後接名詞或形容詞，接名詞時別忘了在前面加個定冠詞哦！

 生字補充！ **Vocabularies & Phrases**
• **betrayer** [bɪˋtreɚ] 名 叛徒

You are all talk and no action.

你總是光說不練。

A I'm going to shed some pounds and squeeze myself into the pants.

A：我要減肥，讓自己能擠得進那條褲子裡。

B How many times have you failed? You are all talk and no action.

B：你都失敗多少次了？總是光說不練。

A I love you baby. We'll get married sooner or later.

A：我愛你，寶貝。我們遲早會結婚的。

B You are all talk and no action. I'm not waiting for you any longer.

B：你總是嘴上說說而已。我不會再等你了。

原來老外都這樣用！ Know it!

You are all talk 可以表達說話的人對對方的鄙視。類似的說法還有：That's easier for you to say 意為「你說得倒容易」，例如："Why not try to persuade the directors?" "That's easier for you to say!"（「為什麼不去說服董事們呢？」「你說得倒容易！」）Talk is cheap 意為「說起來容易」，表示說話的人認為對方做不到他們說的話，例如："I'll buy you a big house and we can live there with your mom when we're married." "Talk is cheap."（「我會買一棟大房子給妳，等我們結婚了，我們可以和妳媽媽一起住在那裡。」「說起來容易。」）

與 talk 相比，action 就實際多了，俗話說得好，Actions speak louder than words.（行動勝於言辭。）take action 表示「採取行動」，put ideas into action 表示「將想法付諸行動」，spring / swing / leap into action 表示「突然採取行動」，immediate / prompt / swift action 表示「迅速的行動」。

 生字補充！ **Vocabularies & Phrases**

• shed [ʃɛd] 動 去除，擺脫
• squeeze [skwiz] 動 擠進，塞入

He never knew his place.

他從沒有自知之明。

A I never thought that Jack would make that suggestion at the meeting.

A：我從沒想過傑克會在會議上提出那樣的建議。

B He never knew his place.

B：他從沒有自知之明。

A John said his English was much better than mine.

A：約翰説他的英語比我厲害多了。

B Did he?

B：他這麼説了嗎？

A Yeah, and besides, he said he would be the interpreter for the conference instead of me.

A：是的，而且他還説要取代我成為這次會議的口譯員。

B He never knew his place.

B：他從沒有自知之明。

原來老外都這樣用！ **Know it!**

He never knew his place 這句話意為「他從沒有自知之明，他從不知道自己所處位置」，其中 know one's place 是指某人「清楚自己的地位，有自知之明」，一般為幽默用法。

此外，當 place 用作動詞時，有兩句日常口語中的常用句型。一句是 How are you placed for sth?（你是否有足夠的某物？）例如：How are you placed for clothes?（你的衣服夠不夠？）另外一句是 How are you placed for doing sth?（你能否做某事？）例如：How are you placed for helping me paint the walls?（你能不能幫我粉刷牆壁？）

生字補充！ **Vocabularies & Phrases**

• interpreter [ɪnˋtɝprɪtɚ] 名 口譯者

He's always sucking up to the boss.

他老是拍老闆的馬屁。

A Look at George! Don't you think it's a bit over the top?

A：你看看喬治！你不覺得這樣做有點過頭了嗎？

B You've got to get used to it. **He's always sucking up to the boss.**

B：你得習慣。他總是這樣拍老闆的馬屁。

A **He's always sucking up to the boss!**

A：他老是拍老闆的馬屁！

B Don't be so mean. I think he's just an ambitious hard-working young man.

B：別這麼刻薄嘛。我覺得他只是個有野心又勤奮的年輕人而已。

原來老外都這樣用！ Know it!

suck up to sb 意為「奉承某人，巴結某人，拍某人的馬屁」，含有貶義，例如：I hate people who suck up to the manager.（我討厭巴結經理的人。）Sucking up to the teacher doesn't mean you'll pass the exams.（拍老師的馬屁並不意味著能通過考試。）

與「奉承，巴結，拍馬屁」相關的表達還有不少。kiss up to sb 與 suck up to sb 的含義基本相同，例如：If you say that, it'll look like you're kissing up to me.（你如果這麼說，就好像是在拍我馬屁似的。）動詞 grovel 指「（因有求於人而）卑躬屈膝」，例如：I groveled to the customer and begged him to forgive me.（我向客戶卑躬屈膝，求他原諒我。）動詞 brown-nose 也指「拍馬屁，巴結」，它的名詞形式 brown-noser 更常見，指「拍馬屁的人」，例如：He's always telling the boss what a wonderful company this is to work for—what a brown-noser!（他總跟老闆說在這家公司工作有多麼好——真會拍馬屁啊！）

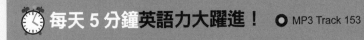

每天 5 分鐘英語力大躍進！ ○ MP3 Track 153

Don't be such a coward.

別這麼懦弱。／別像個懦夫。／別做膽小鬼。

02

鄙視、鄙夷

A **Don't be such a coward**, Adam. Is it that difficult to admit defeat?

A：別像個懦夫，亞當。承認失敗就這麼困難嗎？

B You're right. At the end of the day, I'll have to face it.

B：你說得對。最終我必須要面對現實。

A I know Tracy is not a good choice for me, but...

A：我知道崔西對我來說不是一個好的選擇，但是……

B **Don't be such a coward**, Simon. Tell her you want to break up.

B：別這麼沒種，西蒙。告訴她你想分手吧。

原來老外都這樣用！ **Know it!**

Don't be such a coward 指「別這麼懦弱，別像個懦夫，別做膽小鬼」。

名詞 coward 意為「膽小鬼，懦夫」，如：He called me a coward, because I wouldn't fight.（他說我是個懦夫，因為我不肯戰鬥。）be a coward about 指「在……方面是個懦夫，在……事情上膽小」，如：I knew I was an awful coward about going to the dentist.（我知道我不敢去看牙醫，這太膽小了。）

形容詞 cowardly 意為「膽小的，（像）懦夫（一樣）的」，如：His friends thought it was cowardly of Sam not to admit he had once been to prison.（山姆的朋友們認為他不承認自己曾坐過牢是懦夫的行為。）spineless 與 cowardly 有些相似，它意為「沒有骨氣的，懦弱的」，例如：The president has been accused of being spineless in the face of naked aggression.（總統被指責面對赤裸裸的侵略時軟弱無力。）

生字補充！ **Vocabularies & Phrases**

• **at the end of the day** 片 最終，到頭來，不管怎麼說
• **face** [fes] 動 正視，面對，接受（困難局面）

He's a stupid good-for-nothing.

他是個一無是處的窩囊廢。

A Do your parents often fight?

B Oh, yes, they often call each other names. My mom says **my dad's a stupid good-for-nothing.**

A：你父母會經常吵架嗎？

B：哦，是的，他們常常謾罵對方。我媽媽説我爸爸是個一無是處的窩囊廢。

A What's wrong with Jim? He just sat around while others were busy working.

B There's no need to be angry with him. **He's a stupid good-for-nothing** and he'll soon be kicked off the team.

A：吉姆是怎麼回事？別人都在忙著工作，他就那麼閒坐著。

B：沒必要生他的氣。他是個一無是處的飯桶，很快會被踢出團隊的。

原來老外都這樣用！ Know it!

good-for-nothing 在這裡作名詞，意為「懶散無用的人，一無是處的人」，它不只強調「無用」，而且表示這種無用是由於「懶惰」造成的。它也可以作形容詞，表示「懶散無用的，一無是處的」，例如：His father is an idle good-for-nothing drunk. (他父親是個懶惰無用的酒鬼。)

要表示「無用的」這層含義，還可以用 useless，它可用來形容某人「差勁的，無能的」，例如：Don't ask Maggie to do the calculation. She's completely useless. (別叫瑪姬來算，她根本不行。)

要表示「懶惰的」這層含義，還可以用形容詞 lazy (懶惰的)。也可以用 shiftless，它表示「懶惰的，不求上進的，得過且過的」，例如：His parents were shiftless farm people. (他父母是那種不求上進的農民。) idle 表示「懶散的，不認真的」，例如：Average students who work hard usually do better than clever students who are idle. (資質平平但勤奮的學生，往往比聰明但懶散的學生成績好。)

He's a bad loser.

他是個輸不起的人。

A That player threw his bat away.

A：那個球員把球棒給扔了。

B Perhaps **he is a bad loser**, or he was unfairly treated.

B：也許他是個輸不起的人，也許他受到了不公正的對待。

A Hey, come play cards this afternoon.

A：嘿，下午來打牌吧。

B Will Steve be there, too?

B：史蒂夫也會去嗎？

A Perhaps. Why?

A：可能吧。怎麼啦？

B Then I won't go. **He's a bad loser.** I don't want to hear his grumbling.

B：那我不去了。他可輸不起了，我不願意聽他抱怨。

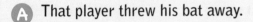

原來老外都這樣用！ **Know it!**

如今在中文情境裡，我們能經常聽到有人直接用 loser 這個字，它可以指「（在工作、生活、感情、人際關係等方面）屢屢失敗的人，失敗者」。例如：I lost my job, my wife left me, my parents are disappointed by me—I am a complete loser.（我丟了工作，妻子離開了我，父母對我失望——我是個徹底的失敗者。）也可以指「（競爭、比賽、選舉等中的）失敗者，輸家」。

此外，名詞 loser 還可以表示「不幸的人，受害者」，例如：If the strike continues, the students of the town will be the real losers.（如果罷工持續下去，鎮上的學生將會成為真正的受害者。）與 loser 處境或遭遇相反的人則可用 winner 表示。

生活中，有的人在競爭、比賽等中失敗後表現得特別沒有風度，例如擺臉色、摔東西、向對手冷嘲熱諷、詆毀勝利者等，我們將這些人稱為 bad loser，即「輸不起的人」。相反，good loser 指即使失敗也能保持風度的「輸得起的人」，例如：Janet clapped and shook the winner's hand to show that she was a good loser.（珍妮特鼓了掌，並與勝利者握手，表現出了良好的風度。）

177

The movie almost sent me to sleep.

電影太無聊，讓我昏昏欲睡。

A Have you seen the latest movie directed by Kevin Spacey?

B Yeah. **The movie almost sent me to sleep,** but the crying kid beside me kept me awake.

A：你看凱文執導的新電影了嗎？

B：看了。那電影很乏味，讓我昏昏欲睡。但是旁邊的小孩一直哭，我又沒睡著。

A How did it go with Sammy last night?

B **The movie almost sent me to sleep.**

A Who cares about the movie? I mean you two guys.

B We just went to see the movie together.

A：昨晚你跟山米怎麼樣？

B：電影太無聊，我都快睡著了。

A：誰關心電影啊？我是問你們兩個怎麼樣啦？

B：我們就是一起去看了場電影而已。

原來老外都這樣用！ Know it!

send sb to sleep 的本義是「使某人入睡」，它可以表示「（某事物極其無聊）讓人昏昏欲睡」。

還有哪些表達可以用來形容無聊乏味呢？形容詞 boring 指「無趣的，無聊的，乏味的，令人生厭的」，例如：He always ends up telling us one of his boring stories about the war.（他最後總是會講一個有關於他的無聊的戰爭故事。）其動詞形式 bore 表示「使厭煩」，如 bore sb to death / tears 指「使人厭煩得要命，讓人無聊得想死／想哭」。形容詞 long-winded 表示「冗長乏味的，絮絮叨叨的」，例如：His speeches tend to be rather long-winded.（他的演說往往都很冗長乏味。）形容詞 tedious 表示「枯燥乏味的，冗長的」，例如：Introducing too many characters at the beginning of a story makes it tedious and confusing.（在故事開頭就介紹太多人物會顯得冗長無聊，也容易讓人搞混。）

I don't like the look / sound of it.

看起來／聽起來有些不妙。

A We should turn back now.

A：我們應該馬上回去。

B Why?

B：為什麼？

A Look at the sky. **I don't like the look of it.**

A：你看看天空，看起來不大妙的樣子。

B Yes, it's getting dark and there are so many rain clouds.

B：對，天越來越黑，還烏雲密佈的。

A There's been a slight change in our plans.

A：我們的計畫有點小小的變動。

B **I don't like the sound of it.**

B：這消息聽起來不大好啊。

原來老外都這樣用！ Know it!

not like the look of... 表示「不喜歡……的樣子」，後面可以接 sb，也可以接 sth，不喜歡的原因是從某人／某物的樣子判斷，認為可能已經發生或即將發生不好的事情。例如：

- I don't like the look of that rash on your chest.
  （你胸口的疹子看起來不大好。）

- Don't let anyone into your home that you don't like the look of.
  （不要讓任何看起來可疑的人進入你家。）

not like the sound of... 的含義差不多，不過不是「看起來不妙」，而是「聽起來不妙」，後面多接 sth。例如："They say that tanks are massing close to the border." "I don't like the sound of it—that could mean war."（「他們說坦克已在邊境集結。」「聽起來讓人憂心—這可能意味著要開戰了。」）

What's eating him?

他在煩什麼呢？

A Allan didn't make any comments at the morning meeting.

A：艾倫在早晨的會議上一言未發。

B I saw him frown from time to time.

B：我看見他不時皺著眉頭。

A What's eating him?

A：他有什麼煩心事嗎？

B Maybe it's the pressures of work.

B：可能是工作壓力的原因吧。

A You look unhappy. What's eating you?

A：你看上去不太高興，有什麼煩惱嗎？

B Nothing. I just feel tired.

B：沒有，就是覺得累。

原來老外都這樣用！ Know it!

What's eating him? 表示詢問某人有什麼苦惱，其中的 him 可以根據不同的詢問物件而進行相應的改變（比如第二個對話）。例如，有個女同事最近總是短歎長吁，你和別人聊天時就可以問：What's eating her?（她心裡煩什麼呢？）回答這類問句的時候，可以用 be eaten up 這個片語來表示某人深陷某種情緒（尤其是不良情緒）。例如，別人問你 What's eating you? 時，你就可以說：I was given some unfair treatment, so I was eaten up by anger.（我受到了不公平的對待，真是氣死我了。）當然，在你問別人之前，也可以先加一句 I was eaten up with curiosity（我特別好奇），以表達你想知道答案的迫切心情。

 生字補充！ Vocabularies & Phrases

- frown [fraun] 動 皺眉
- pressure [`prɛʃɚ] 名 （工作或生活中的）壓力

What are the kids up to?

孩子們在搞什麼名堂呢？

A Have you seen Mike? He's not in his room.

B No, and Lucy is not in her room either.

A What are the kids up to?

A：你看見麥克了嗎？他不在房間裡。

B：沒看見，露西也不在她自己的房間裡。

A：這兩個孩子搞什麼名堂呢？

A It's already half past eight, but where are the kids?

B What are the kids up to? I'll give them a call.

A：已經八點半了，孩子們去哪兒了？

B：這些孩子在搞什麼鬼呢？我打電話給他們。

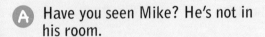 **Know it!**

What are the kids up to? 意為「孩子們在搞什麼名堂呢？」，表達的是說話的人疑慮或擔憂的心情。這句話中的 the kids 可以換成其他任何主詞。例如，下屬最近經常請假，老闆心裡就會嘀咕：What is he / she up to?（他／她搞什麼鬼呢？）好友 Lily 最近常常神祕消失，你感到擔心，就會問另一位好友：What is Lily up to?（莉莉在偷偷幹什麼呢？）在日常英語中，be up to sth 暗指在做不好的或祕密的事。例如：He's so quiet recently, and I know he's up to something.（他最近太安靜了，我知道他一定是在搞什麼鬼。）

與之相關的用法還有 be up to no good，這個表達強調的是「進行不好的勾當」，比如：I'm sure he's up to no good.（我敢肯定，他一定沒幹好事。）

I have a lot on my mind.
我有很多煩心的事。

A Have you brought my book?

B Sorry, I forgot. **I have a lot on my mind** at the moment.

A：我的書你帶來了嗎？

B：不好意思，我忘了。我最近心事太多了。

A Do as I said. Right now!

B Can you just stop yelling? I never thought you are so quick-tempered.

A Sorry. Nothing personal. **I have a lot on my mind.**

A：照我說的做。馬上！

B：你可以別大呼小叫的嗎？我從來不知道你脾氣這麼急躁。

A：對不起。不是針對你的。我最近有好多煩心的事。

原來老外都這樣用！ Know it!

have something on one's mind 的意思是某人一直在思考或擔憂某事，也就是有煩心事，有事情要操心。例如：My teacher looked as though she had something on her mind.（我的老師看起來好像有心事。）那 have a lot on one's mind 當然就是「有很多煩心事」的意思。

上述兩個片語都是以人作主詞，如果以事物作主詞，可以用 prey on sb's mind 這個表達，表示某事「使某人苦惱不堪，折磨某人」，例如：Try to forget about the accident. You can't let it prey on your mind.（忘記那場事故吧，你不能讓它一直折磨你。）The old woman's warning preyed on Mia's mind as she continued her journey.（在後續的旅途中，老太太的警告一直讓米婭苦惱不已。）

 生字補充！ Vocabularies & Phrases
· **quick-tempered** [ˋkwɪkˋtɛmpəd] 形 火爆脾氣的，急性子的

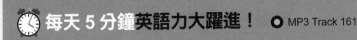
It's for your own good!

這可是為了你自己好！

A Have you taken your medicine?

A：你吃藥了嗎？

B Not yet.

B：還沒。

A Here you are. Take it—**it's for your own good!**

A：給你。把藥吃了——這可是為了你自己好！

A Here is your coat, and also a pullover.

A：這是你的外套，還有件套頭毛衣。

B Mom, there's no need to take both of them.

B：媽，用不著兩件都帶。

A Just in case! **It's for your own good!**

A：以防萬一嘛！這可是為了你自己好！

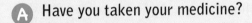 **原來老外都這樣用！** **Know it!**

It's for your own good! 是日常口語中的常用句，用於表示關切，勸說對方做某事，通常譯為「這可是為了你自己好！」但是有一點要切記，如果有人對你說 You're too clever for your own good. 這句話，這可不是在誇你聰明，而是說「你聰明過了頭」。這是因為 too + 形容詞 + for your own good 句型的意思是「過分……對你沒好處」。比如，朋友總是心軟借錢給那些長期不還的人，你就可以對朋友說：You're too nice for your own good.（你這樣過分善良對你沒好處。）

 生字補充！ **Vocabularies & Phrases**

• **pullover** [`pulovə] **名** 套頭毛衣

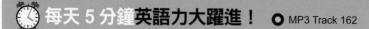

I have a hang-up about my nose—I think it's too big.

我的鼻子讓我很苦惱——我覺得它太大了。

A You're so beautiful, Emma. You'll make a great model. But you don't seem confident.

B I have a hang-up about my nose—I think it's too big.

A：艾瑪，你真美，你會成為很棒的模特兒。但是你似乎不太有自信。

B：我的鼻子讓我很苦惱——我覺得它太大了。

A I thought you were near-sighted. Why do you wear glasses every day?

B Glasses are my shield. I have a hang-up about my nose—I think it's too big.

A：我還以為你近視呢。那你為什麼每天都戴著眼鏡？

B：眼鏡是我的防護罩。我很在意我的鼻子——我覺得它太大了。

原來老外都這樣用！ **Know it!**

名詞 hang-up 指「（不必要的、無根據的）擔憂，苦惱，困擾」，這種困擾基本都是由於當事人本身鑽牛角尖造成的，在他人看來完全沒有必要擔憂。例如：The consultant had cured him of all his hang-ups.（顧問消除了他所有不必要的困擾。）I want the children to understand sex and grow up without hang-ups.（我希望孩子們能夠理解性，在成長過程中不要有不必要的苦惱。）表示「因……而擔憂」可用 have a hang-up about…，例如：She's got a real hang-up about her body.（她為自己的身體非常苦惱。）

形容詞 hung-up 表示「對某事想得過多的，過度擔心的」，可使用 be hung-up about / on sth 的表達。但片語動詞 hang up 並沒有這種類似含義，hang up 可表示：1. 掛斷電話；2. 掛起（衣服）；3. hang up one's hat / football boots / briefcase etc.（離開某一工作／掛起靴子／退休等）。

I have butterflies in my stomach.

我緊張死了。／我心裡好慌啊。

A Waiting for the result? You look quite calm. I think you did a good job and have every reason to be confident.

A：在等結果？你看起來很鎮定。我覺得你表現得很好，有理由有自信。

B Oh, I have butterflies in my stomach. I'm just good at putting on a poker face.

B：哦，我緊張死了，我不過是擅長裝得面無表情罷了。

A I have butterflies in my stomach. I've never performed before such a big audience.

A：我好慌啊，我還從來沒在這麼多觀眾面前表演過呢。

B Don't worry. When the light goes on, the audience are in the dark, and you will not see them clearly.

B：不用擔心，等燈光亮起，觀眾在暗處，你根本看不清他們。

原來老外都這樣用！ Know it!

have / get butterflies in one's stomach 的字面意思是「胃裡有蝴蝶（在抖動翅膀）」，顯然這是一個讓人很難受的狀態。其實這個表達是指「（在做某事前）焦慮不安，精神緊張，心裡發慌」，in one's stomach 可以省略。例如：It was the morning of the World Cup Final and most of the players had butterflies in their stomachs.（世界盃決賽的早上，多數球員都緊張不安。）Some actors never have butterflies before going on stage.（有些演員上臺前從不緊張。）I always get butterflies before exams.（我考試前總是很心慌。）

英語中還有一個表達 have a bee in one's bonnet (about sth)，也是說某物裡面有個昆蟲，不過這次不是「胃裡有蝴蝶」，而是「帽子裡有蜜蜂」，意為「一心想著（某事），念念不忘（某事）」。例如：Felix has got a bee in his bonnet about buying a motorcycle.（菲力克斯總是想著要買臺摩托車。）

Can you just leave it?

別問了可以嗎？／你別管了可以嗎？

A Why did you come home so late last night?

B I went to the bar with John.

A But John was at home when I called him!

B Mom, **can you just leave it?**

A：你昨晚怎麼那麼晚才回來啊？

B：我和約翰去酒吧了。

A：可是我打電話給約翰的時候他在家啊！

B：媽，你可以別再問了嗎？

A To whom on earth did you lend the money?

B **Can you just leave it?**

A：你到底把錢借給誰了？

B：你別管了可以嗎？

原來老外都這樣用！ Know it!

Can you just leave it? 用於表示讓對方到此為止，不要再追問或再插手某事。要表達同樣的意思還可以用 Leave it alone! 這句話，二者都有因心裡不爽而阻止對方繼續做某事之意。

Leave it alone! 有兩層意思：1. 表示不要碰某物，例如：It's my new shirt! Leave it alone!（那是我新買的襯衫！別碰它！）2. 表示勸對方不要再抓住某事不放，例如：He has tried his best, so why don't you just leave it alone?（他已經盡力了，你就不能高抬貴手嗎？）在表示第二個意思時，它可以和 Can you just leave it? 互換。例如：He has tried his best, so can you just leave it?（他已經盡力了，這件事就到此為止不行嗎？）

 生字補充！ Vocabularies & Phrases

• bar [bɑr] 名 酒吧

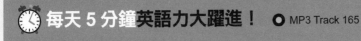

Don't get on my nerves!

別煩我！

A Would you please stop screaming? **Don't get on my nerves!**

B Uh-oh, I'm sorry.

A：你可以不要尖叫嗎？別煩我！

B：哎喲，對不起。

- -

A Honey, do I look better in this green dress, or the blue one?

B Oh, **don't get on my nerves** with the same questions every morning!

A：親愛的，我穿這條綠裙子好看，還是那條藍裙子好看？

B：唉，別每天早上都用同樣的問題煩我可以嗎！

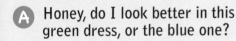

原來老外都這樣用！ **Know it!**

Don't get on my nerves! 是一種不太客氣的說法，用於警告別人別煩你，離你遠一點等等。其中的 nerve 本義為人體中的「神經」，用作複數時則可指人擔心的情緒，get on sb's nerves 就是「煩擾某人」的意思。你有沒有聯想到《傲慢與偏見》中神經兮兮、整天抱怨 Oh, my poor nerves! 的 Mrs. Bennett 呢？

意為「別煩我」的表達還有 Quit bothering me! Leave me alone! 等。如：I'd like to take a good rest. Just leave me alone!（我想好好休息一下，別煩我了！）使用這幾個表達時要注意對象，不然很容易傷感情哦。

生字補充！ **Vocabularies & Phrases**

• **uh-oh** [ʌˋo] 感 哎喲，哎呀（表示做錯了事或感到有麻煩）

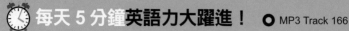
Will you hold your tongue?

你能少說幾句嗎？

A Keep the following things in mind: don't touch my computer, don't use my Kindle, don't watch TV, don't...

A：記住以下事情：不要碰我的電腦，不要用我的 Kindle 電子書閱讀器，不要看電視，不要……

B Will you hold your tongue?

B：你能少說幾句嗎？

- -

A Where did you go last night?

A：你昨晚去哪裡了？

B I need some privacy.

B：我需要有隱私。

A Did you go out with John?

A：你是和約翰去約會了嗎？

B Will you hold your tongue?

B：你能少問幾句嗎？

原來老外都這樣用！ **Know it!**

Will you hold your tongue? 可用來請求對方別再說下去了，表達了說話的人厭煩的情緒，可以用於朋友之間、父母和子女之間等多種場合。例如，當對方跟你提了一大堆要求時，可以用這句話表示希望對方別再嘮叨；當對方不斷盤問質疑時，可以用這句話表示你不想再回答任何問題；當兩人吵架時，其中一方咄咄逼人，另一方一直忍讓，作為旁觀者的你也可以使用這句話，意在告知咄咄逼人者這麼吵下去對解決問題無益。

Will you watch your tongue? 和 Will you hold your tongue? 相似，但是前者主要用於提醒對方其言語過於無禮，不要再說無禮的話了；後者則多半是不希望對方繼續嘮叨，或是不希望對方談論原話題。

生字補充！ **Vocabularies & Phrases**

· privacy [`praɪvəsɪ] **名** 隱私

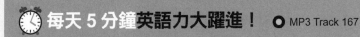

I've been under a lot of strain.
我壓力很大。／我很焦慮。

A Justin, you're drinking a little too much recently.

A：賈斯汀，你最近酒喝得有一點多啊。

B Sorry, I've been under a lot of strain. I'll control myself.

B：對不起，我最近壓力很大。我會控制自己的。

A I've been under a lot of strain lately and I need a vocation to unwind.

A：我最近壓力好大啊，我得休假放鬆一下。

B Summer will be our busiest season. You may take a vocation in September or October.

B：夏季會是我們最忙的季節。你可以在九月或十月休假。

原來老外都這樣用！　Know it!

strain 在這裡作名詞，意為「焦慮，緊張」，如果一件事情對你造成很大的壓力，引起緊張的情緒，你就可以將它形容為 a strain，例如：Did you find the job a strain?（你覺得這工作緊張嗎？）put / place a strain on sb 表示「使某人感到有壓力」，例如：The long studying hours put a severe strain on the students.（長時間的學習讓學生們嚴重焦慮。）如果更嚴重一點，某人因壓力大而崩潰，可以說 crack / collapse / buckle under the strain，例如：I could see that the fund manager was beginning to collapse under the strain.（我能看出那名基金經理開始承受不住壓力了。）

名詞 stress 與 strain 的含義相似，表示「壓力，憂慮，緊張」，這兩個字可放在一起用，stresses and strains 意為「緊張和壓力」，是一種固定表達。under stress 也表示「承受壓力」。

生字補充！　Vocabularies & Phrases
• unwind [ʌnˋwaɪnd] **動** 放鬆，鬆弛

I'm on pins and needles.
我坐立難安。／我如坐針氈。

A You look anxious.

B Yes, **I'm on pins and needles.** My husband is three hours late, and he didn't answer my calls.

A：你看起來很不安。

B：是的，我坐立不安。我老公遲到了三個小時了，打他電話也不接。

A **I'm on pins and needles** waiting to hear if I have passed the exam.

B You need to forget the exam for a moment. Let's go shopping.

A：我在等考試結果，真是如坐針氈啊。

B：你需要暫時忘記考試。我們去逛街吧。

原來老外都這樣用！ **Know it!**

be on pins and needles 表示「如坐針氈，坐立不安」，尤指是因為在等待重要的事發生，或等待得知某個結果。be on pins and needles 的字面含義是「在釘子和針上」，這和中文的「如坐針氈」在意境上很契合。

pins and needles 還可以指因長久保持同一個姿勢，血流不暢，而產生的「痠痛，發麻，針刺感」，這種感覺常出現在腿上或腳上。例如：I'll have to move because I'm starting to get pins and needles in my foot. （我得動一動了，我的腳已經開始發麻了。）

be on tenterhooks 的含義與 be on pins and needles 相似，例如：She had been on tenterhooks all night, expecting her daughter to return at any moment. （她整晚都心神不寧，盼著她女兒隨時可能回來。）

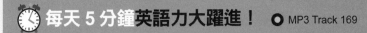
It made me squirm with embarrassment.

那令我窘得無地自容。

A I'm really sorry. I don't know what was wrong with me. **It made me squirm with embarrassment.**

A：真的很抱歉，我也不知道我當時是怎麼了，想起來真是覺得無地自容。

B Forget about it. It was just a coincidence. Nobody will blame you.

B：別在意，那只是個巧合而已。沒人會怪你的。

A The tall guy reminds me of the silly mistake I made at the opening ceremony.

A：那個高個子的人讓我想起了我在開幕式上犯的愚蠢錯誤。

B Oh, your face blindness. It was...

B：哦，你的臉盲症嘛。當時……

A Don't even go there! **It made me squirm with embarrassment.**

A：別再提了！想起來我就窘得無地自容。

原來老外都這樣用！ **Know it!**

動詞 squirm 可以指「極度窘困，羞愧難當」，尤其是因為說了蠢話或做了蠢事，有點像我們常說的「想找個地洞鑽進去」。例如：Whenever I think back to what I said at the party it really makes me squirm.（一想起我在派對上說的話，我就覺得羞愧難當。）squirm 常和 with embarrassment 連用，強調了尷尬，在上面兩個對話中都是這樣用的。再看一例：The little boy squirmed with embarrassment when his mother told him off in front of his friends.（小男孩的媽媽當著他朋友們的面訓斥他時，他窘得無地自容。）

大家需要注意，squirm 的基本含義是「扭動，蠕動，扭來扭去（因為不舒服、緊張或想掙脫某物）」，例如：The girl squirmed uncomfortably in her chair.（女孩在椅子上不自在地扭來扭去。）

I nearly died. /
I could have died.

我尷尬死了。／我尷尬得要命。

A You said you saw your daughter go out with a middle-aged man?

B Oh, it was so embarrassing. **I nearly died** when I found out it was my ex-husband! I think I need a pair of new glasses.

A Her father? I thought he was in Mexico.

B They didn't tell me he had come back!

A：你說你看到你女兒和一個中年男人在一起？

B：啊，太丟臉了。我發現那居然是我前夫，簡直尷尬得要死！我想我得配副新眼鏡了。

A：她爸爸？我還以為他在墨西哥呢。

B：他們沒告訴我他已經回來了！

A Why is Rose mad at you?

B I was talking to her mom, saying she had some problems catching up with the rest of the class. Suddenly I saw her standing right behind me and she had heard every word I'd said—honestly, **I could have died!**

A You know, teens are sensitive.

A：蘿絲為什麼生你的氣？

B：我正在跟她母親談話，談到她跟不上班級其他同學的進度。突然發現她就站在我身後，我說的話她都聽見了——說真的，我真是尷尬死了。

A：青少年都是很敏感的。

原來老外都這樣用！ **Know it!**

I nearly died 和 I could have died 在這裡是誇張的用法，表示某事造成的痛苦程度之強，而這種痛苦主要是由於尷尬而造成的。

die of embarrassment 同樣表示「尷尬得要命」，但是因為直接出現了 embarrassment，所以比較容易理解。例如：The room was such a mess, I just died of embarrassment.（房間裡這麼亂，我真是尷尬得要命。）

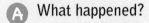
My face turned bright red.
我滿臉通紅。

A What happened?

A：怎麼了？

B Someone yelled, "Mary is like a little pig!" They all started laughing at me and my face suddenly went bright red.

B：有人喊「瑪麗像隻小豬！」他們都開始笑我，我一下子就漲紅了臉。

A Ha-ha, Pig Mary is adorable!

A：哈哈，小豬瑪麗很可愛！

A Congratulations!

A：恭喜你！

B Thank you. I'm sure my face turned bright red on the stage.

B：謝謝。我在臺上時臉肯定都紅透了。

A You always feel uncomfortable when you are praised in public.

A：你每次當眾被表揚時都覺得不自在。

B Yes, ever since I was a pupil!

B：是，從小學開始就這樣！

原來老外都這樣用！ **Know it!**

sb's face turns red 指「某人臉紅」，尤其是指因為尷尬或氣惱造成的。bright 用來形容顏色時指「鮮豔的，鮮亮的」，bright red 即指「鮮紅的」。合起來 sb's face turns bright red 是指「某人的臉紅透了」。其中 's face 可以省略，sb 後面可以直接加 turn / go red，例如：Every time you mentioned his name, she goes bright red.（每次你提到他的名字，她的臉都會漲得通紅。）

動詞 blush 也可以表示「臉紅」，例如：Joan blushed at the unexpected compliment.（突如其來的誇獎讓喬安臉紅了。）

193

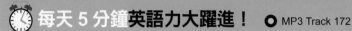
I'm really self-conscious about my weight.

我很在意自己的體重。

A You need to have one more piece of bread. You're too thin!

B No, thanks. **I'm really self-conscious about my weight.** One more pound will get me upset.

A：你要再吃一片麵包。你太瘦了！

B：不用了，謝謝。我很在意自己的體重，多長一公斤的肉就能讓我心煩意亂。

A You'll look gorgeous in that red dress. And there is a discount!

B I don't wear dresses. Or skirts. Never.

A Why?

B Because **I'm really self-conscious about my weight.** I don't want people to see my bare legs.

A：你穿那件紅連衣裙一定非常美。而且還有折扣呢。

B：我不穿連衣裙。半身裙也不穿。從來不穿。

A：為什麼？

B：我對自己的體重感到不自在。我不想讓別人看到我的腿露在外面。

原來老外都這樣用！ Know it!

形容詞 conscious 可表示「關注的，有意識的，注重的」，例如：politically / socially / environmentally conscious（有政治／社會／環保意識的），再如：health-conscious / fashion-conscious / safety-conscious（有健康／時尚／安全意識的）。

self-conscious about sth 指「（因顧慮某事物而表現得）彆扭的，扭捏的，不自然的」，這個「某事物」常常是指自己的外表或別人對自己的看法。例如：Young adolescents tend to feel very self-conscious about their appearance.（青少年往往對自己的外貌特別在意。）

Now I really have egg on my face!

我現在真的覺得丟臉死了！

A I was so drunk yesterday that I did something stupid.

B What?

A I told John that I loved him, and now I really have egg on my face!

A：我昨天醉得很厲害，做了件蠢事。

B：怎麼了？

A：我告訴約翰我愛他，我現在真的覺得丟臉死了！

A I mistook Carlos for Reese.

B Actually they were once asked whether they were twins.

A But the way I said hello was not that polite, and now I really have egg on my face!

A：我把卡洛斯錯當成里斯了。

B：其實還有人問過他們是不是雙胞胎呢。

A：但是我打招呼的方式不怎麼禮貌，我現在真的覺得丟臉死了！

原來老外都這樣用！ Know it!

Now I really have egg on my face 主要用於表示尷尬、難為情的場合。have egg on one's face 意為「丟臉，出醜」，在口語中很常用，此外，片語 with egg on one's face 也可以表達同樣的意思，例如：I took the game lightly and ended up with egg on my face.（我對這場比賽掉以輕心，結果出了醜。）egg on one's face 常用於指有權威的一方，可以是人，也可以是機構等，例如：The organization has been left with egg on its face.（該機構顏面盡失。）

 生字補充！ Vocabularies & Phrases

• **mistake** [mə`stek] 動 把⋯⋯錯當成

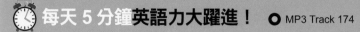

I often feel awkward about telling people my true feelings.

向別人袒露心聲常讓我感到尷尬。

A Since I graduated from college, I've seldom had chances to have a real talk with my father.

B Me too. It's just that I often feel awkward about telling people my true feelings.

A：自從大學畢業後，我很少有機會能跟父親好好談談心。

B：我也是。我只是覺得向別人袒露心聲常讓我感到尷尬。

A I often feel awkward about telling people my true feelings. I envy those guys who can speak their minds.

B That's the problem with you grown-ups. We kids don't have that problem.

A：向別人袒露心聲常讓我感到尷尬。我很羨慕那些心裡想什麼就能說什麼的人。

B：那是你們成年人的問題。我們小孩就沒有那問題。

原來老外都這樣用！ **Know it!**

形容詞 awkward 可以指「令人尷尬的，使人難堪的」，例如：There was an awkward moment when she didn't know if she should call him James or Mr. Nolan.（她不知道該叫他詹姆斯還是諾蘭先生，一時之間非常尷尬。）Adam's remarks put me in an awkward position.（亞當的話將我置於很尷尬的境地。）表示某人「感到尷尬的，彆扭的」可以用 feel awkward，例如：I always feel awkward when I'm with Greg—he's so difficult to talk to.（我跟葛列格在一起時總覺得尷尬—他太難接近了。）

形容詞 uncomfortable 也可以表達類似的含義，它指「不自在的，不安的」，例如：She always feels uncomfortable in her father's presence.（她父親在場時她總覺得不自在。）

Some people have all the luck.
有的人就是比別人幸運。／有的人就是命好啊。

A Have you heard that Daniel's parents spent 800,000 dollars on his luxury wedding ceremony?

B A rich family, a top university, a good job, and a beautiful wife— some people have all the luck.

A：你聽説了嗎？丹尼爾的父母為他的豪華婚禮花了 80 萬美金。

B：富裕的家庭、名校、好工作、漂亮的妻子——有的人就是比別人幸運。

A It's said that the whole department will have to work overtime next week.

B Oh, our group is going to London for a business meeting next week.

A What? Some people have all the luck!

A：聽説下週整個部門都要加班。

B：哦，我們小組下週要去倫敦開個商務會議。

A：什麼？有的人就是命好啊！

原來老外都這樣用！　Know it!

名詞 luck 意為「好運，幸運」，例如：You're not having much luck today, are you?（你今天運氣不太好，是不是？）He's had good luck with his roses this year.（今年他種玫瑰的運氣不錯。）have all the luck 就是「擁有了所有的好運」。Some people have all the luck 這句話表達了說話的人對別人好運的羨慕，隱含之意就是 Others have no luck, or only bad luck.

再來看幾個與 luck 相關的常用表達。wish sb（the best of）luck（祝某人好運），例如：She wished me luck in the exam, then left.（她祝我考試好運，然後就走了。）just my luck（我總是不走運），例如：I didn't get to the phone in time. Just my luck!（我沒來得及接那通電話。我總是不走運！）luck is on sb's side（某人走運或交好運），例如：Luck was on my side; all the traffic lights were green.（我很走運，一路全是綠燈。）

That's the way it goes.
這是沒辦法的事。／這就是命啊。

A My boyfriend built a snowman for me on my birthday.

B Wow, so romantic!

A But it melted in warm weather.

B That's the way it goes.

A：我男朋友在我生日那天為我堆了個雪人。

B：哇，真浪漫哪！

A：但是天氣一暖它就化了。

B：那也沒辦法啊。

- -

A Romeo and Juliet loved each other so much but ended tragically.

B That's the way it goes.

A：羅密歐和茱麗葉如此相愛卻以悲劇收場。

B：這就是命啊。

原來老外都這樣用！ Know it!

That's the way it goes 主要用於兩種場合：表示事情的發展趨勢就是這樣（如第一個對話），此時 That's the way it goes 多含有安慰他人之意。還可以表示天意如此（如第二個對話），此時 That's the way it goes 多含有對命運不由人的無奈感嘆。That's (just) the way it is 可以與 That's the way it goes 互換使用。

That's (just) the way sb is 則表示「某人就是這樣」，強調其特點不會改變。例如：Sometimes he wants to be alone. That's just the way he is.（有時候他想一個人獨處。他就是那個樣子。）

 生字補充！ Vocabularies & Phrases
- **romantic** [ro`mæntɪk] 形 浪漫的
- **melt** [mɛlt] 動 （使）融化
- **tragically** [`trædʒɪkl̩ɪ] 副 悲慘地，不幸地

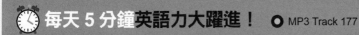

每天 5 分鐘英語力大躍進！　**○** MP3 Track 177

Something happens when you get older.

歲月不饒人啊。

Chapter
06

感
慨
、
感
嘆

A She is still beautiful and elegant, but you can see the wrinkles once you get close to her.

A：她還是那麼美麗優雅，但是一旦近距離就能看到皺紋。

B After all, she is over 50 now. **Something happens when you get older.**

B：畢竟她都 50 多歲了。歲月不饒人啊。

A I didn't get up until noon today.

A：我今天到中午才起床。

B You stayed up for the football match?

B：你熬夜看足球賽了？

A Yeah, I still feel sleepy right now. **Something happens when you get older!**

A：是啊，我現在還是很睏。真是歲月不饒人啊！

原來老外都這樣用！ **Know it!**

Something happens when you get older 主要是說話的人感慨時光的無情流逝，可以用於感嘆他人變老（如第一個對話），也可以用於感嘆自己青春不再（如第二個對話）。There's something that happens as you get older 也可以用來表達此意。說到歲月催人老，最明顯的就是表現在皮膚方面，那麼下面介紹幾個和皮膚有關的常用字彙：rough 用來形容皮膚粗糙；slack 或 sagging 表示皮膚鬆弛，fragile 是皮膚敏感脆弱，皮膚有彈性可用 elastic，wrinkle 是皺紋，粉刺是 pimple，雀斑是 freckle。

生字補充！ **Vocabularies & Phrases**
• wrinkle [ˈrɪŋkl] **名** 皺紋

199

A win is a win.

贏了就是贏了。

A My shoes hurt my feet, or I would have run faster than you.

B **A win is a win!** Last time you said you lost because you were hungry.

A：我的鞋子讓我腳痛，不然我會跑得比你快。

B：我贏了就是贏了！上次你還説你是因為肚子餓才輸了呢！

A I heard you've won the race. Congratulations!

B Thanks! That was a narrow victory, you know. I was ahead of the second-place finisher by only one second.

A **A win is a win!** It is worth celebrating!

A：聽説你在賽跑中得了第一名。恭喜呀！

B：謝謝！但是你知道其實贏得很驚險，我僅僅領先第二名 1 秒。

A：贏了就是贏了！這值得慶祝！

原來老外都這樣用！ Know it!

A win is a win 主要用於兩種場合：一種是說話的人強調不管怎樣都是自己贏了，讓對方不要不服氣（如第一個對話）；另一種是說話的人肯定對方的勝利，強調只要是勝利，都是值得慶祝的（如第二個對話）。能贏當然是好事，但是總有一些時候，不論你怎麼努力，結果都是 You can't win.（你註定失敗。／你怎麼做都不好。）例如，遇到挑剔的客戶，不管你設計出什麼樣的方案，對方總是不滿意，此時你就可以對同事抱怨說：Whatever I do, she isn't satisfied—you just can't win.（不管我怎麼做，她都不滿意——真是怎麼做都不對。）

 生字補充！ **Vocabularies & Phrases**

• **celebrate** [ˈsɛləˌbret] **動** 慶祝

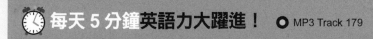

It's too good to be true.

美好得不像是真的。

A It says buy one get two free.

A：買一送二耶。

B It's too good to be true.

B：這太好了，不像是真的。

A You look absolutely great now!

A：妳看起來過得很幸福。

B Yes, Mrs. Stone. It is too good to be true. You know, when I left home, I never thought I could have all these—a loving husband, two adorable kids, and a decent job. It never happened in my wildest dream.

B：是的，史東女士。這美好得不像是真的。妳知道嗎，當我離開家時，我從來沒想到我能擁有這一切——愛我的丈夫、兩個可愛的孩子、體面的工作。我做夢也沒想過。

A You deserve it, Cathy. You are the most intelligent and hard-working girl I've ever known.

A：這是妳應得的，凱西。妳是我認識的所有人中，最聰明、最用功的女孩了。

原來老外都這樣用！ Know it!

副詞 too 在這裡表示「太，過分」，it is too... to do sth 表示「太過於……以至於不能做某事」，或者說「對於做某事而言，太過於……」，所以 too good to be true 所表達的意思就是「太過於美好，以至於（看起來）不像是真的」。如果你遇到了完全超過預期和想像的好事，你就可以說：It's too good to be true.（這太好了，簡直不像是真的。）但也有人說過，如果一件事好得不像是真的，那它大概就不是真的。所以，當你對「天上掉下來的餡餅」或「免費的午餐」之類的好事表示懷疑時，也可以說 It's too good to be true.

該句型中 too 之後的形容詞可以根據實際情況進行替換。例如感嘆「此景只應天上有」，可以說：It's too beautiful to be true.（這景色太美了，都不像是真的了。）再如，學生離開校園後體會到工作的不易，可以感嘆：It's too cruel to be true.（職場太殘酷了，讓人無法置信。）

每天 **5** 分鐘**英語力大躍進！** ⊙ MP3 Track 180

Time and tide wait for no man.

歲月不饒人。／時不我與。

A Twenty years has passed. We're both old men now.

A：二十年過去了，我們都老了。

B It is a true saying that time and tide wait for no man.

B：歲月不饒人啊。這句話一點也不假。

A You're so young. How can you accomplish so many things?

A：你這麼年輕，是怎麼完成這麼多事情的？

B I always remind myself that time and tide wait for no man.

B：我一直提醒自己時不我與。

原來老外都這樣用！ **Know it!**

Time and tide wait for no man 的含義是「歲月不等人」。它可用於勸誡人們珍惜時間、把握機遇，同時表達了說話者對歲月無情、青春易逝的慨歎。英文中關於珍惜時間的表達很多，例如：

- You cannot have two forenoons in the same day.（人無法在一日之內擁有兩個早晨。）
- The day is short but the work is much.（工作多，時間迫。）
- Time flies.（光陰似箭。時光易逝。）
- Time is money.（時間就是金錢。一寸光陰一寸金。）
- Time marches on.（時間永不回頭。）
- The morning sun never lasts a day.（好景不常在。）
- You may delay, but time will not.（人拖時不拖。歲月不饒人。）

 生字補充！ **Vocabularies & Phrases**
- accomplish [əˈkɑmplɪʃ] **動**（尤指通過努力）完成，實現

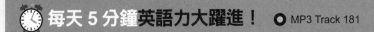

Every dog has its / his day.

人人都能出頭天。／每個人都有機會成功。／
風水輪流轉。

A The hard-working and frugal couple who have never stepped out of the small town they live in sent their son to one of the top universities in China.

B Wow, every dog has its day.

A：那對辛勤節儉的夫妻從來沒有邁出過他們生活的小鎮，但他們把兒子送進了中國的一所頂尖大學。

B：哇，人人都能出頭天。

A Did you watch the One-day's Star Show yesterday evening?

B Yes, I saw old Jim on the television!

A I'm so happpy for him. He finally got the chance to sing with his idol on stage. Every dog has his day!

A：你昨晚有看「一日明星秀」嗎？

B：看了，我看到老吉姆上電視了！

A：我真為他高興。他終於有機會和他的偶像在臺上　起唱歌了。人人都有閃亮的瞬間啊！

原來老外都這樣用！ **Know it!**

Every dog has its / his day 這句話是指，即使是最平凡普通的人，也會有屬於他們的美好時光，有他們得意的時候。在一定的情境下，大家常說的「野百合也有春天」「輸家也有逆襲的瞬間」等說法，也可以用 Every dog has its / his day 來表達。

狗是西方人熟悉和重視的寵物，英文中有不少關於狗的表達。be going to the dogs 意為「（國家或機構）每況愈下，趨於衰敗」，例如：After a series of donation scandals, the foundation is going to the dogs.（在一系列的捐款醜聞之後，該基金會每況愈下。）a dog in the manger 意為「占著茅坑不拉屎的人」，例如：He held the remote all the time, but he wasn't really watching TV! Such a dog in the manger.（他一直拿著遙控器，但其實沒在看電視！真是占著茅坑不拉屎。）

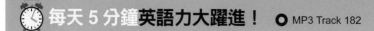
Beauty is only skin-deep.

外表的美麗是膚淺的。／內在美比外在美更重要。

A Betty is a good girl.

A：貝蒂是個好女孩。

B But she is not good-looking.

B：可是她長得不好看。

A Beauty is only skin-deep. I like her because she is nice and brave.

A：內在美比外在美更重要。我喜歡她是因為她善良又勇敢。

A All your girlfriends are pretty and silly.

A：你所有女朋友都是又美又傻的。

B Yeah, I like pretty girls.

B：對，我喜歡漂亮的女孩。

A But beauty is only skin-deep.

A：但美貌只是外在的一張皮。

B I am a superficial man.

B：我就是個膚淺的男人。

原來老外都這樣用！　Know it!

Beauty is only skin-deep 意指美貌是膚淺的東西，外在美沒有內在性格重要。當你見到有人因過分追求外在美貌，忽視內在美的重要，最終嚐到惡果，這時你就可以感嘆一句：Beauty is only skin-deep. 還有一句話勸人們別以貌取人：Don't judge a book by its cover. 字面意思是說「別透過封面來判斷一本書的優劣」，意指「勿只憑外表作判斷」。下面來看看英文中各式各樣形容美貌的表達吧。

【女性常用】beautiful（美麗的），pretty（漂亮的），lovely（美麗的、可愛的），stunning（極具吸引力的、極漂亮的），ravishing（非常美麗的、十分標緻的），elegant（優雅的）

【男性常用】cute（性感迷人的），hunky（魁梧性感的），rugged（粗獷而英俊的），dashing（風度翩翩的、時髦的）；男女通用：good-looking（好看的），handsome（英俊的、健美的），attractive（有魅力的），striking（吸引人的、惹人注目的）

There's no doubt about it!

毫無疑問！

A It's a quarter to ten. Can she arrive on time?

B There's no doubt about it! She's never late.

A：差 15 分鐘就 10 點了，她能準時到嗎？

B：一定可以！她從不遲到。

A He is the cleverest student in our class.

B There's no doubt about it! There is nothing he doesn't know.

A：他是我們班上最聰明的學生。

B：毫無疑問！他無所不知。

原來老外都這樣用！ Know it!

There's no doubt about it! 也可以直接說 No doubt about it! 它主要表示某事是毋庸置疑的，既可以是強調自己的觀點（如第一個對話），也可以是強調對他人觀點的贊同（如第二個對話）。without question 也表示「毫無疑問」的意思，但是它主要是用來強調自己的觀點。比如：She was the best storyteller in our class, without question.（毫無疑問，她是我們班上最會講故事的人。）

如果想表達「我不這麼認為」該怎麼說呢？用 I doubt it. 即可。例如：「Do you think they will win the basketball match?" "I doubt it."（「你認為他們會打贏籃球比賽嗎？」「我看是不行。」）

 生字補充！ **Vocabularies & Phrases**

• **quarter** [ˋkwɔrtɚ] 名 一刻鐘，十五分鐘

Not while I breathe air.

絕對不行。

A I want to have another piece of chocolate.

B Your doctor said the less sugar the better.

A Only one more!

B Not while I breathe air!

A：我想再吃一塊巧克力。

B：你的醫生說過糖吃得越少越好。

A：就再吃一塊！

B：絕對不行！

A Our car is too old. How about having a new one?

B No, we still have so many bills to pay.

A But a new car...

B Not while I breathe air!

A：我們的車太舊了，買輛新的如何？

B：不行，我們還有很多帳單沒付呢。

A：但是買輛新車的話……

B：說不行就是不行！

原來老外都這樣用！ Know it!

Not while I breathe air 用於表示說話者堅決否定的態度。與之類似的一句常用口語是 Over my dead body!（除非我死了！）只不過這句話表達的情緒更加強烈，用於氣憤地告訴對方永遠不會允許某事發生，和電視劇、電影或小說中經常出現的臺詞「那你就踩著我的屍體過去吧」是同樣地意思。

下面就再多學幾句跟 breathe 相關的常用口語，動詞 breathe 意為「呼吸」，breath（氣息）是名詞形式。Don't hold your breath.（你有得等了。／不會很快。）也是一句常用口語，用於告訴對方不要期待某事會很快發生。例如：The system's due for an update, but don't hold your breath.（系統應該要更新了，不過你有得等了。）

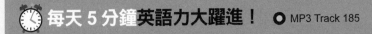

You can say that again.

你說的沒錯。

A That was an absolutely delicious dinner!

A：真是一頓美味的晚餐啊！

B You can say that again!

B：你說的沒錯！

A The rain finally stopped.

A：雨終於停了。

B Yeah, it's good to have a sunny day.

B：是啊，晴天真好。

A You can say that again!

A：沒錯！

原來老外都這樣用！ **Know it!**

You can say that again 表示說話的人非常贊同對方說的話，完全沒有異議。You said it. 也表示同樣的意思，例如，同學說這次考試真難，如果你也這麼認為的話就可以回應：You said it.（我同意。）但是，You said it 還有另外一層意思，表示雖然同意對方的話，但是自己不便說出，因為這麼說不合適或者不禮貌。例如，同事向你吐苦水說 I've made such a mess of my life.（我把生活搞得一團糟。）你就可以用 You said it.（這可是你自己說的。）來表示同意，而不用 You can say that again.

注意不要將上述表達和 You could say that. 搞混了，後者是對某人提出的問題表示肯定，但又不想說更多的細節。例如："Is she your friend?" "You could say that."（「她是你的朋友嗎？」「也可以這麼說。」）

生字補充！ **Vocabularies & Phrases**

• **absolutely** [ˈæbsəˌlutlɪ] 副 完全地，絕對地

每天5分鐘英語力大躍進！ O MP3 Track 186

Take my word for it.
相信我（的話）。

A How's Linda getting on at school? I'm kind of worried about her.

A：琳達在學校裡怎麼樣？我有點兒擔心她。

B Oh, she's doing very well. You can take my word for it.

B：哦，她表現非常好。你可以相信我。

A It won't happen again. Take my word for it.

A：這種事不會再發生了。相信我。

B Well, I never know whether to believe what you say or not.

B：唉，我從來不知道該不該相信你的話。

原來老外都這樣用！ **Know it!**

Take my word for it 用於向別人承諾、保證，讓對方相信你的話。同樣意思的表達還有 You have my word. 和 I give you my word. 如：I'll give you a big surprise. You have my word.（我會給你一個大驚喜。我保證。）I give you my word that I'll never be late again.（我向你保證，我再也不遲到了。）

再看幾個關於 word 的表達。如果誇一個人言而有信，則可以說 He's a man of his word. / She's a woman of her word. 或 His word is his bond. / Her word is her bond. 若表示「食言、違背諾言」，則可用 go back on one's word。另外要注意，eat one's words 可不是中文裡的「食言而肥」，而是「承認自己說錯話」之意，如：I'm going to make you eat your words.（我要讓你承認自己說錯話了。）千萬不要被字面意思誤導哦。

 生字補充！ **Vocabularies & Phrases**
· **kind of** 片 有一點，有幾分

I'd do the same thing again.

即使時光倒流，我還是會這麼做。

A Are you sorry you left home so young?

A：你年紀那麼小就離開家了，你現在會後悔嗎？

B Oh no, **I'd do the same thing again.**

B：哦，不。就算時光倒流，我還是會這麼做。

A They say you were very beautiful when you were young, and you could have chosen a better man than dad...

A：他們説你年輕時特別漂亮，本來可以選擇比爸爸更好的男人⋯⋯

B If I could turn the clock back **I'd do the same thing again.**

B：即使時光能夠倒流，我還是會和你爸爸在一起。

原來老外都這樣用！ **Know it!**

I'd do the same thing again 表明了說話的人對做過的事情和選擇——尤其是指生命中重大的事件和選擇－沒有半分的後悔和遺憾，即使時光倒流，再給一次選擇的機會，他／她還是會做同樣的事情。這句話也可以說成 I'd do the same。

not regret, not be sorry, have no / few regrets 等表達也可以表示與 would do the same thing again 相似的含義。例如：I still miss him sometimes, but I don't regret ending the relationship.（我有時還是會想他，但我並不後悔結束那段戀情。）She wasn't sorry to leave her job—she hated it.（辭掉工作她一點也不遺憾－她討厭那份工作。）Even though it's hard work they have few regrets about setting up their own business.（雖然很辛苦，但他們一點也不後悔自己去創業。）

I would give my right arm to be with him.

為了跟他在一起，我不惜一切代價。

A Your parents won't let you marry Nicolas.

A：你父母不會讓你嫁給尼古拉斯的。

B He is the love of my life. I would give my right arm to be with him.

B：他是我今生的最愛，為了跟他在一起我不惜一切代價。

A Peter will be transferred to Paris, and I'll go with him.

A：彼得將被調去巴黎，我要跟他一起走。

B You mean you'll give up your job? At this point when you're to be promoted? You said you would give your right arm to get that promotion!

B：你是說要放棄你的工作？在你馬上要升職的這個時候？你不是說只要能升職，拿什麼換都行嗎！

A No. I would give my right arm to be with him.

A：不。是只要能跟他在一起，拿什麼換都行。

原來老外都這樣用！ Know it!

sb would give their right arm to do sth 意為「某人為了做某事而不惜任何代價」。right arm 指「右手臂」，人的右手臂是人身上非常重要的部位，通常寫字、提東西、拿武器等都要依靠它，為了做某事寧願犧牲自己的 right arm，可見真的是意志堅決，不惜一切。

同樣能表達「不惜一切代價，堅決要做某事」的還有 at any price，它表示「不惜任何代價，無論如何」，例如：She was determined to have a child at any price.（她決心不惜任何代價都要生一個孩子。）go to the ends of the earth to do sth，表示「竭盡所能」之意，例如：I'd go to the ends of the earth to be with him.（哪怕走到天涯海角，我也要和他在一起。）

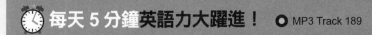

 每天 5 分鐘英語力大躍進！　◯ MP3 Track 189

I have a phobia about snakes.

我怕蛇。

A Hey, why are you so angry? It's just a joke.

B I have a phobia about snakes. Take your silly fake snake away!

A：嘿，幹嘛這麼生氣？只是開個玩笑嘛。

B：我怕蛇。把你那可笑的玩具蛇拿走！

A Look at my new bag! It's a limited edition of the snakeskin tote bag.

B Oh my God, I got goosebumps. I have a phobia about snakes.

A：看我的新包包！是限量版的蛇皮托特包。

B：天啊，我起雞皮疙瘩了。我怕蛇。

原來老外都這樣用！　Know it!

名詞 phobia 指「恐懼，恐懼症」，表示對某種事物具有極端或反常的恐懼感無法克服，例如怕蛇、怕搭電梯、怕在公開場合講話等。例如：Some children suffer from school phobia.（有些兒童對上學有恐懼症。）have a phobia about 表示「對……有恐懼（症）」，如：She has a phobia about answering machines and never leaves a message.（她很怕電話答錄機，所以從來不留言。）

be afraid / scared / frightened / terrified of 也可以表示「害怕／恐懼……」，例如：It's amazing that so many people are afraid of spiders.（居然有這麼多人害怕蜘蛛，真叫人吃驚。）He's terrified of heights.（他恐高。）They always travel by boat because Jimmy's frightened of flying.（他們總是搭船旅行，因為吉米害怕坐飛機。）

生字補充！　Vocabularies & Phrases

- **fake** [fek] 形 偽造的，冒充的
- **edition** [ɪˋdɪʃən] 名 版本
- **tote bag** 片 托特包，大袋子

I got / had cold feet.

我臨陣退縮了。

A You didn't sign up for the competition?

A：你沒報名參加競賽？

B No, I had cold feet.

B：沒有，我臨陣退縮了。

A Look, who's this? Our bridegroom! How was the wedding ceremony?

A：看看這是誰啊？我們的新郎官！婚禮怎麼樣啊？

B There was no wedding ceremony, actually.

B：其實沒有舉行婚禮。

A Oh... I'm sorry... why?

A：哦……對不起……為什麼啊？

B I got cold feet at the last moment. I don't think I'm prepared for it.

B：事到臨頭我膽怯了，我覺得我還沒準備好。

原來老外都這樣用！ Know it!

get / have cold feet 的字面含義是「腳冷」，但其實是表示「臨陣退縮，膽怯」。與之含義相似的表達還有 chicken out，它表示某人在最後一刻因害怕而臨陣退縮，放棄已經計畫好的事情，例如：I hope nobody will chicken out tomorrow.（我希望明天誰也不要打退堂鼓。）I walked onto the ten-meter platform, but then I chickened out—it looked like a long way down to the water!（我走上十米跳臺，但我臨陣退縮了——從跳臺到水面的距離看起來好遠啊！）

 生字補充！ Vocabularies & Phrases
- **sign up for** 片 報名參加……
- **bridegroom** [ˈbraɪd,grʊm] 名 新郎

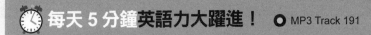

每天5分鐘**英語力大躍進！** 🔘 MP3 Track 191

I was scared out of my wits.

我被嚇傻了。／我太害怕了。

A What happened then?

B **I was scared out of my wits** when I saw the car coming straight towards me.

A：然後發生什麼事了？

B：我看到那輛車直直地朝我開過來，我都嚇傻了。

A I knew someone was following me.

B Why didn't you call your parents?

A **I was scared out of my wits.** Then my phone rang. It was my father. When I was talking to my father, I found the man disappeared.

B Oh, thank goodness.

A：我當時知道有個人在後面跟著我。

B：你為什麼不打電話給你父母？

A：我都嚇傻了。接著我的電話就響了，是我爸爸打來的。當我跟我爸爸說話時，我發現那個人不見了。

B：哦，謝天謝地。

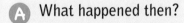 **Know it!**

形容詞 scared 表示「害怕的，驚慌的」。複數名詞 wits 意為「機智，領悟力」，例如：Alone and penniless, I was forced to live on my wits.（孤身一人又身無分文，我只好靠我的機智生活。）

be scared 本身就可以表示「害怕的」，加上 out of one's wits 的修飾後這種情緒得以加強。be scared 還常被「加強」為 be scared stiff（被嚇呆了）和 be scared to death（被嚇得要死），例如：You must have been scared stiff when you saw the car coming straight towards you.（看到那輛車直直朝你開過來，你一定被嚇得都不會動了。）

形容詞 panic-stricken 可以表達類似的含義，它是指「驚慌失措的、恐慌萬分的」，表示某人害怕到無法清晰思考、理智行事，例如：She suddenly looked panic-stricken.（她突然表現得驚慌失措。）

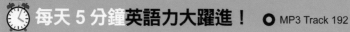
I don't know if I am being paranoid.

我不知道是不是自己疑神疑鬼。／不知道是不是我自己嚇自己。

A **I don't know** whether they are trying to murder me or whether **I am being paranoid**.

A：我不知道是他們真的想謀殺我，還是我在疑神疑鬼。

B Anyway, you have to leave this country, as soon as possible.

B：無論如何，你必須離開這個國家，越快越好。

A Look, nobody's following you, you're just getting paranoid.

A：看，沒有人跟蹤你，你只是在自己嚇自己。

B **I don't know if I am being paranoid**, but I saw some man in black around my house five times in a week.

B：不知道是不是我自己在疑神疑鬼，但我一週內已經五次看見有個穿黑衣服的男人出現在我家附近了。

原來老外都這樣用！ **Know it!**

形容詞 paranoid 指莫名地不信任他人，毫無根據地覺得別人要害你，總是懷疑別人會對你不利。例如：One of my clients got really paranoid, deciding that there was a conspiracy out to get her.（我的一個客戶變得疑神疑鬼，認定有什麼要害她的陰謀。）要表示「對……疑神疑鬼，在……方面多疑」，可以在 paranoid 後面加 about，例如：My boss has always been paranoid about his personal security.（我的老闆總是對他的人身安全疑神疑鬼的。）在醫學上，paranoid 表示「患偏執狂的，患妄想症的」。

形容詞 neurotic 與 paranoid 的含義有些相似，它表示「神經質的，神經過敏的」，用於形容某人總是無端地感到害怕或焦慮緊張，例如：Very talented people are often neurotic as well.（特別天才的人往往也很神經質。）neurotic 也可作名詞，指「神經質的人」。

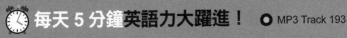

It gives me the creeps.

它讓我心裡發毛。／它使我毛骨悚然。

A A strange old man lives alone in that house. It gives me the creeps.

A：一個奇怪的老頭獨自住在那棟房子裡。那房子讓我心裡發毛。

B Oh, it must be Mr. Salisbury's house. He has scares on his face, but he is a nice man.

B：哦，那肯定是索爾茲伯里先生的房子。他臉上雖然有傷疤，但是一個好人。

A Look at this stuffed owl. It's so cool!

A：看這個貓頭鷹標本。太酷了！

B I don't think so. Let's get out of this place. It gives me the creeps.

B：我不覺得。我們快出去。這個地方使我毛骨悚然。

原來老外都這樣用！　Know it!

give sb the creeps 表示「（因奇怪）使某人緊張或害怕」，可用來形容人或地方，例如：Sue hates being left alone in the office with Daniel—he gives her the creeps.（蘇討厭單獨和丹尼爾待在辦公室裡——他讓她心裡發毛。）The house gives me the creeps—it's so dark and quiet.（這房子使我毛骨悚然——房子又黑又靜。）

同樣能表達這種含義的有形容詞 creepy 和 spooky，它們都可表示「使人毛骨悚然的」，另外後者還有「陰森恐怖的」之意，例如：The house looks OK from the outside, but inside it is all dark and creepy.（這房子從外面看還好，可是裡面一片漆黑，使人毛骨悚然。）The wood is really spooky at night.（這片樹林在晚上的時候真是陰森恐怖啊。）

生字補充！ **Vocabularies & Phrases**
• **stuffed owl** 片 貓頭鷹標本

每天5分鐘**英語力大躍進！** ○ MP3 Track 194

I don't want to live in fear of that.

我不想生活在恐懼之中。

A I'm going to tell my boss everything.

B You don't have to. He may never know.

A But he may know it one day. I don't want to live in fear of that.

A：我要對老闆坦白一切。

B：你用不著這麼做。他也許永遠不會知道。

A：但他也許有一天會知道。我不想生活在恐懼之中。

A Listen, I don't want to be the whistle-blower, but they're always threatening me with violence. I don't want to live in fear of that.

B I totally understand.

A：聽著，我不想做個告密者，但我總是受到他們的暴力威脅。我不想生活在這種恐懼中。

B：我完全理解。

原來老外都這樣用！ **Know it!**

名詞 fear 意為「害怕，恐懼，擔憂」，live in fear of 指「生活在對⋯⋯的恐懼中，處在對⋯⋯的恐懼中」，其中 live 也可以替換為 be。如：After leaking the secret document, Mary lived in fear of being found out.（瑪麗洩露了祕密檔案後一直害怕被查出來。）The surgeon lives in constant fear of slipping up in an operation when he's tired.（那位外科醫生一直害怕他疲勞時手術會出差錯。）

關於 fear 還有很多常見表達。shake / tremble with fear 意為「嚇得發抖」，如：The shopkeeper was shaking with fear after being held at gunpoint.（那名店主被槍口指著，嚇得渾身發抖。）be gripped by fear 表示「非常害怕」，如：The passengers were gripped by fear as the boat was tossed around by the waves.（船被波濤晃來晃去，乘客們害怕極了。）be paralyzed with fear 指「嚇呆了」，如：I was paralyzed with fear when I stood behind the microphone.（我站在麥克風後面時都嚇呆了。）

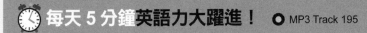

每天 **5** 分鐘**英語力大躍進！**　○ MP3 Track 195

It made my hair stand on end.

嚇得我汗毛都豎起來了。／嚇得我毛骨悚然。

A Did Henry tell you about the murder?

B Yes. **It made my hair stand on end!**

A：亨利跟你講過那起謀殺案嗎？

B：講過了。聽得我毛骨悚然！

A What's the TV series about?

B It's about what a psycho husband does to his wife.

A Oh, are there any horrific scenes?

B Yes. **It made my hair stand on end.**

A：那部電視劇是關於什麼的？

B：是關於一個精神病丈夫如何對待他妻子的。

A：哦，有什麼恐怖的場景嗎？

B：有，看得我毛骨悚然。

原來老外都這樣用！ **Know it!**

下面介紹幾個非常生動的表達，用於表示「令人恐懼的」。對話中的表達就是其中之一，make sb's hair stand on end 意為「讓某人汗毛豎起，使某人毛骨悚然」，指特別害怕。再看一個例句：If you hear some of the things that happened in the prison camp, they'll make your hair stand on end.（如果聽聽發生在戰俘營裡的一些事，它們會讓你嚇得汗毛都豎起來的。）

spine-chilling 的字面意思是「使人背脊發涼的」，也就意為「令人毛骨悚然的」，它多用來形容故事或電影，例如：The collection includes a spine-chilling ghost story by Edgar Allan Poe.（該選集收錄了艾德格·愛倫坡寫的一篇令人背脊發涼的鬼故事。）blood-curdling 的字面意思是「使血液凝固住的」，其實就是「令人心驚膽戰的，讓人毛骨悚然的」，常用來形容尖叫聲，例如：Chris went upstairs to look for Hope and seconds later I heard a blood-curdling scream.（克里斯上樓去找霍普，幾秒鐘後我聽到了令人毛骨悚然的尖叫聲。）

I just couldn't care less.
我一點也不在乎。／我完全無所謂。

A If you don't lend me that novel, I will tell mom that you drank beer last night.

B Just do it! **I just couldn't care less.**

A：你要是不借我那本小說，我就告訴媽媽你昨晚喝啤酒了。

B：去說吧！我一點也不在乎呢。

A I will fly to London next Tuesday.

B But it is my birthday.

A Sorry, honey, this is business, and my manager said...

B OK, OK, you can go wherever you want! **I just couldn't care less!**

A：下週二我要坐飛機去倫敦。

B：可是那天是我的生日。

A：親愛的，對不起啊，這是公事，經理説……

B：好吧，好吧，你愛去哪就去哪！我完全無所謂！

原來老外都這樣用！ **Know it!**

I just couldn't care less 這句話強調說話的人認為某事不重要，所以完全不在乎。有時，說話的人雖然表現出冷漠或無所謂的態度，但其實是因為處於憤怒或不開心的情緒中，並不是真的不在乎。所以如果有人對你說這句話，說不定對方其實非常在乎呢！

As if I cared! / See if I care! 和 I couldn't care less 的用法是一樣的。例如，第一個對話中的 B 也可說：Just do it! As if I cared!（去說吧！我又不在乎！）第二個對話中的 B 也可說：OK, OK, you can go wherever you want—see if I care!（好吧，好吧，你愛去哪就去哪，我根本不在乎！）

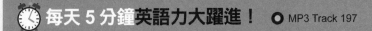
It's none of your business.

不關你的事。

A I like chocolate cake so much!

B How much do you weigh?

A It's none of your business!

A：我真是太喜歡巧克力蛋糕了！

B：你體重多少？

A：跟你無關！

A You're wearing makeup?

B Yeah, I'm going to start a new life.

A Are you seeing someone?

B It's none of your business.

A：你化了妝？

B：是啊，我要開始新生活。

A：你是不是在戀愛？

B：不關你的事。

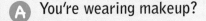 原來老外都這樣用！ **Know it!**

It's none of your business 指說話的人態度冷漠，意思是不該你問的不要問，不該你管的不要管。同樣的表達還有 Mind your own business. 和 That's my business. 這兩句。例如，好友八卦地問你是不是喜歡隔壁班那個清秀的男生，你就可以回答：Mind your own business!（少管閒事！）你在班上的對手問你會不會競選班長，不想回答的話就可以直接說：That's my own business!（那是我的事！）

 生字補充！ **Vocabularies & Phrases**

• **weigh** [we] 動 稱，量
• **makeup** [ˋmek,ʌp] 名 化妝品

I don't give a shit.

我才不在乎。

A You're the only one who failed the mid-term exam.

B Just a mid-term exam—I don't give a shit!

A：期中考只有你一個人不及格。

B：不就是一次期中考試嘛──我才不在乎！

A We'd better stop making fun of Nick, or his brother will teach us a lesson.

B His brother? I don't give a shit.

A He is a boxer!

B Oh no!

A：我們最好不要取笑尼克了，不然他哥哥會教訓我們的。

B：他哥哥？我才不在乎。

A：他哥哥可是個拳擊手！

B：哦，不會吧！

原來老外都這樣用！ **Know it!**

I don't give a shit 用於表示對某人或某事物毫不在意，同樣的意思也可用 I don't give a damn 來表達。因為 shit 本身就是粗魯用語，所以和 shit 有關的用法基本上也都是不禮貌的，大家可以瞭解一下，但是不要輕易使用。例如，朋友遇到倒楣的事情，Shit happens（這種倒楣事誰都可能發生的）可以用來安慰朋友；No shit（不會吧／真的）可以用來表示吃驚或質疑，也可以用來強調所說屬實或同意某人的說法，例如：He had like, no shit, over sixty packets of cigarettes.（真的，他有 60 多包香菸。）如果你聽不慣某人總是滿嘴胡說，也可以對他／她說：You're full of shit.（你總是胡扯。）

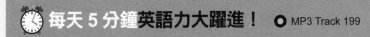
How should I know?

我怎麼會知道？

A Where's my English book?

A：我的英文書呢？

B How should I know?

B：我怎麼會知道？

A You were not with Mike yesterday after school?

A：昨天放學後你沒和麥克在一起？

B Nope, I went home and he went to the bookstore.

B：沒有，我回家了，他去書店了。

A Why did he go there alone?

A：他為什麼自己去書店了？

B How should I know?

B：我怎麼會知道？

原來老外都這樣用！ **Know it!**

How should I know? 用於表示說話的人不知道或不在乎某事。當然，有時說話的人可能知道答案，但是因為種種原因不想告訴對方，那麼此時也可以用這句話作為回答，只不過有點「嗆人」，可能會被對方指責態度不好。

再介紹一個含有 should 的表達吧。I should think / hope / imagine so 這句也經常用於日常口語中，常用於以下兩種場合：一種是表示認為或希望某事屬實卻又不太肯定，例如："I guess he will be the winner." "I should imagine so."（「我猜他會贏。」「我想是的。」）；另一種是強調對別人告知的事情不感到意外，例如："He did apologize." "I should hope so, after the way he behaved."（「他道歉了。」「他那樣的行為，理應道歉。」）

It amounts to the same thing.

結果都一樣。

A Is she mad at me?

B It doesn't matter whether she is mad or not. It amounts to the same thing—she's gone, and she'll never come back again.

A：她生我的氣了嗎？

B：她生不生氣都不重要了。結果都一樣——她已經走了，而且再也不會回來了。

A Did you talk to your mother?

B It amounts to the same thing. She won't listen. She will do what she thinks is good for me.

A You should tell her what you're thinking about.

B I've tried. But it's like banging my head against a brick wall.

A：你有沒有跟你媽媽談一談？

B：結果都是一樣的。她不會聽的。她會做她認為對我好的事。

A：你應該告訴她你的想法。

B：我試過了。根本就是白費口舌。

原來老外都這樣用！ **Know it!**

amount to the same thing 表示「結果或效果都一樣」。這裡 amount to 可以替換為 come to，意思不變。

Same difference 的含義相似，表示雖然行為或表現不同，但最終結果相同。例如："We could take a train or drive to the city tomorrow morning." "Same difference. We still won't get there on time." （「我們明早可以乘火車或開車去那個城市。」「都一樣。反正都來不及了。」）

生字補充！ **Vocabularies & Phrases**

• bang [bæŋ] **動** 撞擊

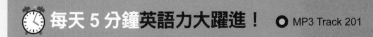
That's not my problem.
那不是我的問題。／我不管。

A Please help me! If I can't pay the debt this time, they'll seize my house!

B That's not my problem.

A：請幫幫我！如果我這次還不了欠款，他們會查封我的房子！

B：那又不是我的問題。

A Jeremy is in trouble now.

B That's not my problem.

A Friends should help each other!

B Me and Jeremy were never friends.

A：傑瑞米有麻煩了。

B：那不是我的問題。

A：朋友之間應該互相幫助！

B：我和傑瑞米從來不是朋友。

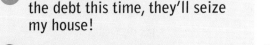 **原來老外都這樣用！** **Know it!**

That's not my problem 或 It's not my problem 意為「那不是我的問題」，表示某事與自己無關，自己對某事沒有責任或義務，所以不願意提供幫助。

That's your / his etc problem 的含義與 That's not my problem 相近。它的隱含之意是「不要麻煩我，我不會幫忙的」。例如：If you can't afford a house, that's your problem.（如果你買不起房子，那是你自己的問題。）

 生字補充！ **Vocabularies & Phrases**

- **debt** [dɛt] 名 債務，欠款
- **seize** [siz] 動 沒收，查封

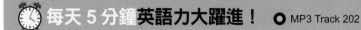

I don't have a clue.
我不知道。／我毫無頭緒。

A Do you know how to turn this thing off? It's too noisy.

B I don't have a clue.

A：你知道怎麼把這東西關掉嗎？太吵了。

B：我不知道。

A How do you plan to tell her the bad news?

B I have absolutely no clue. It's too cruel for her.

A：你打算怎麼把這個壞消息告訴她？

B：我完全不知道啊。這對她來說太殘酷了。

原來老外都這樣用！ **Know it!**

I don't have a clue 用於回答別人的問話，表示你毫不知情或毫無辦法。也可以說 I have（absolutely）no clue（如第二個對話）。除單獨成句外，這個表達還可以放在句首，後接從句，如：I have no clue what she is talking about.（我完全不知道她在說什麼。）

另外，not have a clue / have no clue 還可以表示對某事一竅不通，或做起某事來很愚蠢、很笨拙。如：I haven't a clue about physics.（我對物理一竅不通。）He has no clue how to please girls.（他完全不懂得怎麼取悅女孩子。）

生字補充！ **Vocabularies & Phrases**
- **turn sth off** 片 關閉（電視機、引擎、電燈等）
- **cruel** [ˈkruəl] 形 殘忍的，殘酷的

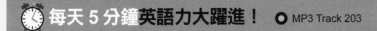

I get all mixed up.

我搞糊塗了。／我腦袋一片混亂。／ 我感到非常迷茫。

A It's such a mistake that I chose law as my major. I get all mixed up whenever I try to memorize those provisions of law.

A：我選擇法律專業真是個錯誤啊。我每次想記住那些法條，腦子就一片混亂。

B I'm not good at memorizing things either. But I think I'll be a good lawyer.

B：我也不擅長記東西。但我覺得我能成為一個好律師。

A Did you go to John's home yesterday?

A：你昨天去約翰家了嗎？

B Yes. What I found out made me upset. His parents are divorced and his father does't care about him at all.

B：去了。我覺得很難過。他的父母離婚了，而且他父親一點也不關心他。

A No wonder he is so mixed up.

A：難怪他在情感上這麼迷茫。

原來老外都這樣用！ Know it!

形容詞片語 mixed up 可以指「困惑的，糊塗的，頭腦混亂的」，例如因為某事繁瑣複雜、細節太多，讓人無法應付處理（如在第一個對話），也可以指「情感錯亂的，感情迷茫的」（如在第二個對話），這時也可寫成 mixed-up。再看兩個例子：I got all mixed up over the money I spent when I was traveling in Paris.（關於上次在巴黎旅行的花費，我完全是一團混亂。）She is just a crazy mixed-up kid.（她不過是一個情感迷茫的傻孩子。）

mixed up 還有其他的含義。be / get mixed up in sth 表示「被捲入某事，被牽連進某事中」，例如：He is the last person I'd expect to be mixed up in something like this.（他是我最想不到會牽涉進這種事情的人。）be / get mixed up with sb 表示「與某人廝混」，例如：After he entered college, he got mixed up with some wrong people.（上了大學後，他結交了一些不三不四的人。）

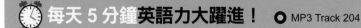

It's beyond me.
我真搞不懂。／我無法理解。

A Have you seen Jennifer's new look in that magazine?

B Yeah. She had that beautiful hair. It's beyond me why she had it all cut.

A：看見雜誌裡珍妮佛的新造型了嗎？

B：看見了。她以前頭髮那麼美，真搞不懂她幹嘛要全部剪掉。

A Why do they keep living together when they're always arguing?

B Oh, it's beyond me.

A Perhaps that's true love.

A：他們總是爭吵，為什麼還要住在一起？

B：哦，我無法理解。

A：也許那是真愛。

原來老外都這樣用！ Know it!

be beyond sb 表示「超出某人的理解能力」，要表達「超出某人的理解能力」的含義，還可用：

1. be over sb's head，如：It was obvious from their blank expressions that what I was saying was over their heads. （一看他們迷茫的表情就知道我說的東西他們根本聽不懂。）為表強調，可以在 over 前加上 way，如：We started watching a science documentary, but it was way over our heads, so we watched a comedy film instead. （我們開始看一部科學紀錄片，但根本看不懂，所以就換了一部喜劇電影。）

2. be out of sb's depth，如：Then they started discussing Greek philosophy and it was completely out of my depth, so I left. （接著他們開始討論希臘哲學，我完全無法理解，所以就走了。）

 生字補充！ Vocabularies & Phrases
• look [luk] 名（服裝、頭髮、傢俱等的）時尚，風格，樣式

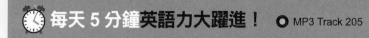

I'm still none the wiser.

我仍然不明白。╱我還是不明白。

A Sorry, I'm still none the wiser.

A：對不起，我還是不明白。

B Never mind. Let me put it this way.

B：沒關係，我換種方式說吧。

A I just can't start this stupid machine.

A：我沒辦法發動這個討厭的機器。

B Have you read the manual?

B：你看過使用手冊了嗎？

A I've read it but I'm still none the wiser.

A：看過了，但還是不明白。

原來老外都這樣用！　Know it!

"none the + 比較級」表示「一點也沒有變得更……」，例如：She seems none the worse for her experience.（這次經歷好像對她沒有什麼不良影響。）none the wiser（也可以寫為 not any the wiser）表示「並沒有比以前瞭解得更多、更深」，即「仍然不明白，還是沒理解」。例如：Unfortunately her detailed explanations of how to use the eye shadow brushes left me none the wiser.（非常不幸，她詳細解釋了如何使用眼影刷之後，我仍然不明白。）

none the wiser 還有另外一種含義，表示「（某人做的壞事）誰也不會知道」，如：He could easily have taken the money and no one would have been any the wiser.（他本可以輕輕鬆鬆把錢拿走，不會有人知道的。）

生字補充！　Vocabularies & Phrases

• **manual** [ˈmænjʊəl] 名 說明書，使用手冊

I'm (all) at sea.

我茫然不知所措。

A Dad, which one should we buy for Mom? This essence, or that lotion, or that cream?

B Don't ask me. **I'm all at sea.**

A：爸爸，我們該幫媽媽買哪一個呢？這個精華液，還是那個乳液，還是那個面霜？

B：別問我。我完全糊塗了。

A Can you help me with these forms?

B Sure. What's the problem?

A Should I fill out all these three pages, or just choose one of them? **I'm all at sea.**

B These forms are confusing. Let me help you.

A：你能幫我看看這些表格嗎？

B：當然。有什麼問題？

A：我是要把這三頁全部填了，還是選擇一頁就可以了？我很茫然。

B：這些表格確實令人感到困惑。我幫你吧。

原來老外都這樣用！ **Know it!**

be (all) at sea 意為「困惑，茫然不知所措」，注意這個表達跟 be lost at sea 的區別，後者指「葬身大海」。

再來看幾個常見的形容 sea（海）的方式：blue sea 指「蔚藍的大海」，如：The sun shone brightly upon the clear blue sea.（明媚的陽光灑在清澈蔚藍的海面上。）be rough 指「浪大的」，如：The sea was too rough to swim in.（海上浪太大了，不能游泳。）be calm 指「無浪的，平靜的」。be choppy 指「波浪起伏的」，如：The wind was starting to pick up and the sea was becoming choppy.（風大了起來，海面開始蕩漾波浪。）heavy seas 指「洶湧的大海」，如：The tanker split apart and sank in heavy seas.（油輪斷裂，沉入了洶湧的大海。）stormy sea 指「波濤翻滾的大海」。

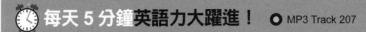

I don't know the first thing about that.

對此我一竅不通。／那方面我一無所知。

A Oh, shit! The car broke down again. Do you know how to fix it?

A：哦，該死！這車又拋錨了。你知道怎麼修嗎？

B Sorry. I don't know the first thing about that.

B：不好意思。這方面我一竅不通啊。

A How was your date with that biologist?

A：你跟那個生物學家的約會怎麼樣啊？

B Oh, it bored me to tears. He talked on and on about the physiology of the brain, and I don't know the first thing about that.

B：哦，無聊得我都要哭了。他一直在講腦部的生理機能。我一點都不懂啊。

A Sounds interesting.

A：聽起來挺有趣的。

原來老外都這樣用！ Know it!

don't know the first thing about 意為「對……一竅不通，對……一無所知」，first thing to know 的意思是「關於某事物首先應該瞭解的東西」，也就是最基本的知識或常識。如果連這個都不知道，那就是說某人一竅不通、一無所知了。

don't know what sb is doing 的含義與 don't know the first thing 相似，表示「沒有處理某事的技術或經驗」，例如：I don't really know what I'm doing when it comes to cars.（說到汽車，我可是一點都不懂。）

生字補充！ Vocabularies & Phrases

- **biologist** [baɪˋɑlədʒɪst] 名 生物學家
- **bore** [bor] 動 使厭煩
- **physiology** [ˌfɪzɪˋɑlədʒɪ] 名（人或動物的）生理機能，生理

每天 5 分鐘**英語力大躍進！** **O** MP3 Track 208

I can't make sense of it.

我搞不懂這個。／我無法理解。

A Do you know why he said that before he left?

B No. I can't make sense of it.

A：你知道他離開之前為什麼說了那些話嗎？

B：不，我無法理解。

A Can you make sense of this slogan?

B I can't make sense of it. It's Japanese, not Chinese.

A：你能看懂這句口號嗎？

B：看不懂。這是日語，不是中文。

原來老外都這樣用！ **Know it!**

make (some) sense of 意為「理解，搞懂（尤指困難或複雜的事物）」，如：Police are trying to make sense of a bizarre note left by the murderer.（警方正在試圖弄清楚一張行兇者留下的古怪紙條。）How can anyone make sense of the huge volume of news information that bombards us daily?（誰搞得懂每天轟炸我們的大量新聞資訊啊？）

以上表達是以人作主詞，當以事物作主詞時，make sense 可表示以下三種含義：1.「有意義，表述清楚，易於理解」，如：Read this and tell me if it makes sense.（讀讀這個，告訴我通不通。）2.「是明智的，是合乎情理的」，如：Would it make sense for the city authorities to further restrict parking?（市政當局進一步限制停車的做法是否合乎情理？）3.「解釋得通，有道理」，如：Why did she do a thing like that? It doesn't seem to make sense.（她為什麼要那麼做？這似乎解釋不通啊。）

 生字補充！ **Vocabularies & Phrases**
• slogan [ˈslogən] 名 口號，標語

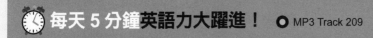
My throat is killing me.

我的喉嚨痛死了。

A Ouch, my throat is killing me.

A：哎呀，我的喉嚨痛死了。

B I think this is a sign of flu.
You'd better go and see a doctor.

B：我覺得這是流感的跡象。你最好去看醫生。

A You look pale and weary.

A：你看起來臉色蒼白，疲憊不堪。

B I barely ate anything today.

B：我今天一天幾乎沒吃東西。

A What's the matter?

A：你怎麼了？

B My throat is killing me. It hurts so much when I swallow.

B：我的喉嚨痛死了。吞東西時特別痛。

原來老外都這樣用！ Know it!

由 My throat is killing me 舉一反三，想表達「……痛死了」就可以用 ... is killing me 這一句型。例如：My back is killing me.（我的背痛死了。）這裡的 kill 強調的是痛的程度，而不是真的要殺死之意。

也常很見 I'll kill him / her / them（我要殺了他／她／他們）之類的表達，這裡所說的殺也不是真的要取人性命，而是表達對某人感到非常憤怒。例如，有人刮花了你的愛車，你可能就會咬牙切齒地說：Wait until I get my hands on him! I'll kill him.（等我抓到他，非殺了他不可！）

生字補充！ **Vocabularies & Phrases**

• **flu** [flu] 名 流感
• **weary** [`wɪrɪ] 形 非常疲勞的
• **swallow** [`swɑlo] 動 吞下，嚥下

I can't feel my legs / feet.

我的腿／腳麻了。

A She's been sleeping with her head in my lap for two hours and **I can't feel my legs** now!

B Why don't you wake her up?

A：她把頭靠在我的腿上睡了兩小時了，我的腿都麻了！

B：你為什麼不叫醒她呢？

A The shoes are so tight that **I can't feel my feet.**

B Well, try another pair.

A：這雙鞋太緊了，綁得我腳都麻了。

B：好，那再試試別雙吧。

原來老外都這樣用！ **Know it!**

I can't feel my legs / feet 從字面上看是「我感覺不到我的腿／腳了」的意思，其實就是生動地表達「我的腿／腳麻了」之意。人體的不少部位都可以用於這個句型中，如：I can't feel my hands / fingers / tongue / ears.（我的手／手指／舌頭／耳朵麻了。）

若表示身體某部位非常不舒服，還可以說：My throat is killing me!（我的喉嚨痛死了！）My legs are killing me!（我的腿難受死了！）如果只是泛泛地表示身體不舒服，則可以說：I don't feel quite myself today.（我今天身體不太舒服。）另外，not feel oneself 也可以表示「心情不好」的意思哦。

 生字補充！ **Vocabularies & Phrases**
• **wake sb up** ﬁ 叫醒某人

I'm starving.

我快要餓死了。／我餓極了。

A I skipped breakfast, and only ate an apple for lunch. Now **I'm starving.**

A：我早餐沒吃，午餐只吃了一個蘋果。我現在快要餓死了。

B Poor kid. Dinner will soon be ready.

B：可憐的孩子。晚餐馬上就好了。

A **I'm starving.** Let's grab something to eat.

A：我餓死了。我們去弄點東西吃吧。

B I have some cookies on the desk. You can eat them.

B：我有一些小甜餅放在書桌上。你可以吃。

A That's far from enough! I could eat a horse!

A：那根本不夠。我餓得能吃下一頭牛！

B I'll make noodles when you eat the cookies.

B：你先吃甜餅，我去煮麵。

原來老外都這樣用！　**Know it!**

動詞 starve 意為「（使）挨餓，（使）餓死」，例如：I saw pictures of starving children.（我看到了飢餓兒童的照片。）Thousands of people will starve if food doesn't reach the city.（如果食物不能運到那座城市，成千上萬的人就要挨餓。）It looked like the poor cat had been starved.（那隻可憐的貓看起來一直在挨餓。）

be starving 的字面意思是「正在挨餓」，它常在口語中表示「感覺很餓，餓極了」，如：You must be starving!（你們肯定餓壞了！）be ravenous 的含義與 be starving 相近，也表示「餓極了」。口語中還有一種很形象的表達方式，用 could eat a horse 來表示「餓極了」，例如：I'm so hungry, I could eat a horse!（我餓得能吃下一頭牛！）當然，be hungry 也是很常見的表示飢餓的方式。

I'm dying of thirst.

我快渴死了。／我好渴。

A Don't drink that coke. Remember that you're on a diet.

B I'm dying of thirst.

A The coke will only make you even thirstier.

A：別喝可樂。記住，你在節食呢。

B：我要渴死了。

A：喝可樂只會讓你更渴。

A Do you have anything to drink? I'm dying of thirst.

B Tea or coffee?

A I want both! Thank you so much!

A：你有什麼東西可以喝嗎？我要渴死了。

B：你要茶還是咖啡？

A：都要！太謝謝你了！

原來老外都這樣用！ **Know it!**

名詞 thirst 意為「渴，口渴」，如：The patient woke up with a raging thirst.（病人醒來時感到口乾舌燥。）be dying of 意為「都快要……死了」，表示程度強烈，如：be dying of hunger（都快要餓死了），be dying of boredom（都快要厭煩死了）。所以 I'm dying of thirst 就是表示「我都快要渴死了，我渴極了」。

形容詞 thirsty 表示「渴的，口渴的」，例如：She'd been working on the playground and was very hot and thirsty.（她一直在操場上工作，又熱又渴。）be parched 可表示「（嗓子）渴得冒煙」，例如："Hurry up with that coffee,"she said,"I'm absolutely parched."（「咖啡快一點上，」她說，「我渴得嗓子都冒煙了。」）還可以用 dry 來形容嗓子或嘴巴等，表示「乾燥的」，例如：My throat is so dry I could hardly speak.（我的喉嚨很乾，都說不出話來了。）

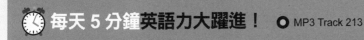

My teeth are chattering.

我凍得牙齒直打顫。／我冷得牙齒咯咯作響。

A I'm frozen. How about you?

A：我凍僵了。你呢？

B Can't you hear? **My teeth are chattering.**

B：你聽不見嗎？我凍得牙齒咯咯作響。

A Can I have one more blanket? **My teeth are chattering.**

A：能再給我一條毯子嗎？我凍得牙齒直打顫。

B Take this quilt. I've turned up the heat, and you'll get warm very soon.

B：把這床被子拿去。我已經把暖氣調大了，你很快就會暖和起來的。

原來老外都這樣用！ **Know it!**

teeth are chattering 指上下牙齒因冷得發抖而碰在一起發出咯咯的聲音。表示「冷得發抖」還可以用 shiver 這個字，它意為「顫抖，哆嗦」，例如：I'm so cold that I can't stop shivering.（我冷得發抖，根本停不下來。）When they pulled him out of the sea, he was shivering with cold.（當他們把他從海裡拉上來時，他凍得直發抖。）

下面再介紹幾個與「冷」相關的表達。be / feel cold 表示「很冷／感覺冷」，例如：Tell me if you feel cold, and I'll turn the heat up.（覺得冷的話告訴我，我把暖氣開大點。）be frozen 表示「凍僵，特別冷」，例如：He's only got shorts on—he must be frozen.（他只穿著短褲——一定凍僵了。）be blue with cold 指「凍得發紫」，例如：He huddled into his coat, his face blue with cold.（他蜷縮在外套裡，凍得臉色發紫。）

生字補充！ **Vocabularies & Phrases**
- **blanket** [ˋblæŋkɪt] **名** 毯子
- **quilt** [kwɪlt] **名** 被子

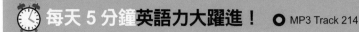
It's stifling (hot) here.

這裡悶熱得讓人喘不過氣來。

A It's too hot, isn't it?

A：太熱了，是吧？

B Yes, it's stifling here.

B：是啊，這裡悶熱得讓人喘不過氣來。

A Are you OK? You look pale.

A：你還好嗎？你看起來臉色蒼白。

B I find it a bit hard to breathe.

B：我覺得有點喘不過氣來。

A It's stifling hot here. Come and sit by the window. I'll get you some water.

A：這裡很悶熱。過來靠窗坐。我去幫你拿點水。

原來老外都這樣用！ Know it!

hot 指「熱的」，stifling hot 指「又悶又熱，讓人喘不過氣來」，而 stifling 本身就可以表示「悶熱的，令人窒息的」，例如：We sat inside the hut, but it grew so stifling in there that we had to come out again.（我們在小屋裡坐下，但那裡變得越來越悶熱，我們只好又出來了。）

形容詞 oppressive 也可以表示「悶熱的，令人煩悶的」，例如：As the sun climbed higher the heat grew more oppressive.（隨著太陽漸漸升高，熱氣讓人變得越來越悶了。）

如果形容人很熱，喘不過氣來，可以用：I'm really hot, and find it difficult to breathe.（我覺得特別熱，有點喘不過氣來了。）

 生字補充！ **Vocabularies & Phrases**
• pale [pel] 形 蒼白的

It's still a little tender.

還是一碰就有點痛。

A Don't touch my arm. It's still a little tender where I bruised it.

A：別碰我的手臂。被我擦傷的地方現在還是一碰就有點痛。

B I'm sorry. Let me carry this for you.

B：對不起。我幫你拿這個吧。

A How's your leg? Can you walk now?

A：你的腿怎麼樣了？你現在可以走路了嗎？

B Yes. But it's still a little tender.

B：可以。但還是一碰就有點痛。

原來老外都這樣用！ **Know it!**

表示「疼痛」的概念時，我們最常用的字應該有 hurt, pain（painful），ache，例如：My back hurts like hell.（我的背痛死了。）I'm in a lot of pain.（我疼痛萬分。）Is your arm very painful?（你的手臂很痛嗎？）I'm aching all over.（我渾身都痛。）I have a terrible headache.（我頭非常得痛。）

還有一些表達可以生動地表示很具體的疼痛，It's still a little tender 就是其中之一。形容詞 tender 在這裡表示「一觸即痛的」，一般是指原來受過傷的地方現在還沒有完全復原，被碰到還是會痛。動詞 sting 可以表示「（使）刺痛，（使）短時間劇痛」，例如形容被洋蔥辣到眼睛的刺痛等，例如：Antiseptic stings a little.（消毒劑稍有刺痛感。）現代人常趴坐在桌前，經常覺得肩頸僵硬，這時可以用 stiff 來形容，例如：After working the whole morning, my left shoulder is painful and stiff.（工作了一上午，我的左肩又僵硬又痛。）形容喉嚨疼痛時常用形容詞 sore，例如：I had a sore throat.（我喉嚨痛。）

I don't feel (very) well.

我覺得身體不太舒服。／我感覺有點難受。

A I don't feel very well. Can I leave now?

B Of course. I'll call a taxi for you.

A：我覺得身體不大舒服。我可以現在就走嗎？

B：當然可以。我幫你叫輛計程車。

A Are you OK? It looks like you're ready to drop. You'd better go home now.

B I don't feel well. I'll take a break, but I'll stay here, waiting for the result.

A：你還好嗎？你看起來好像就要累倒了。你最好現在就回家。

B：我感覺不大舒服。我會休息一會兒，但還是要留在這裡等結果。

原來老外都這樣用！ Know it!

如果你覺得身體不舒服，但不知道是不是真的生病了，或者你不想明確說出哪裡不舒服，這時 not feel (very) well 就是一個特別好用的表達，表示「感覺身體不太舒服」。well 在這裡作形容詞，意為「健康的」。例如：If you don't feel well, the best thing to do is to stay in bed.（如果你感覺不舒服最好躺在床上休息。）

feel funny 也可以表達相似的含義，例如：I feel a bit funny—I wonder if it is that fruit I ate.（我覺得不大舒服——不知道是不是因為吃的水果有問題。）under the weather 也可以表示「身體不大舒服」，例如：You look a bit under the weather. You'd better take a break.（你看起來不大舒服。你最好休息一下。）not feel oneself 不但可以表示「身體不舒服」，也可以表示「心情不好」，例如：I don't know what's wrong. I just don't feel quite myself.（我不知道怎麼回事，就是感覺很不好。）

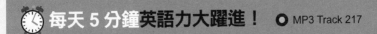

My head is swimming.

我覺得天旋地轉。／我頭暈。

A **My head is swimming** after looking at the screen all day.

A：一整天盯著螢幕，我的頭都暈了。

B Get out of your chair. Let's take a walk.

B：別坐在椅子上了。我們出去散散步吧。

A How did you fall?

A：你怎麼會摔倒的？

B **My head was swimming**, and the floor seemed to be moving up and down, and the next thing I knew I was lying on the floor.

B：我感到天旋地轉，地板好像忽高忽低的，接著不知怎麼地我就躺在地上了。

原來老外都這樣用！ Know it!

head swims 表示「頭暈」，如果按字面理解，意為「頭在游泳」，頭都在游泳了，那肯定暈得不輕啊。例如：He stood up, his head swimming, and found himself unable to move for fear of falling over.（他站起來，感到天旋地轉，不敢動彈，怕一動就要摔倒。）動詞 swim 在表示「思維或視覺不清」這層含義時，如果以「頭」作主詞，它意為「發暈，眩暈」；如果以物作主詞，它意為「（生病、疲勞或喝醉時眼前物體）晃動，旋轉」，這時也能表現出「頭暈」的意思，例如：The figures swam before my eyes.（那些數字在我眼前晃動。）

形容詞 dizzy 和 giddy 也能表示「頭暈目眩的」之意，例如：If you feel dizzy or short of breath, stop exercising immediately.（如果你覺得頭暈或呼吸短促，要馬上停止鍛鍊。）She suddenly felt giddy and had to find somewhere to sit down.（她突然覺得頭暈，不得不找地方坐下來。）

I feel sick to my stomach.
我覺得噁心反胃。／我想吐。

A Do you want some coffee?
It smells great.

B No, thanks. I feel sick to my stomach.

A Do you want to go out with us this evening?

B I feel sick to my stomach. I want to go to bed early today.

A Perhaps it's because of the steak we had. I'll ask my mom to give you some medicine.

A：你要來點咖啡嗎？聞起來很香。

B：謝謝，不用了。我有點反胃。

A：你今晚想和我們一起出去嗎？

B：我覺得反胃噁心。我今天想早點上床睡覺。

A：可能是我們吃的牛排有問題。我請我媽媽拿藥給你。

原來老外都這樣用！ **Know it!**

be / feel sick to one's stomach（或 feel sick）表示「反胃，噁心，作嘔」。注意它跟 be sick 的區別，後者指「嘔吐」，例如：He dashed into the bathroom and was sick again.（他衝進廁所，又吐了。）

形容詞 queasy 和 nauseated 也可以表示「感到噁心的，想吐的」，例如：Just the thought of all that food has made me feel quite queasy.（一想到那些食物我就覺得很噁心。）His head was aching and he felt feverish and nauseated.（他的頭很痛，他覺得發熱，並且想吐。）

我們常說的女性懷孕初期的「晨吐反應」，英文中用 morning sickness 表示，例如：Morning sickness usually disappears after the third month of pregnancy.（通常晨吐反應會在懷孕三個月後消失。）

I'm ready to drop.

我累得都站不住了。／我要累倒了。

A George, it's a good day today. Let's go to the zoo.

B Oh, I want to have a rest. I didn't get a wink of sleep last night, and **I'm ready to drop.**

A：喬治，今天天氣不錯，我們去動物園吧。

B：哦，我想休息一下。昨晚我一夜都沒闔眼，現在快要累倒了。

A Thank you so much, David. I would never have made it without your help.

B Glad I could help. **I'm ready to drop.** Let's have a good meal.

A：太感謝你了，大衛。如果沒有你的幫忙我是不會趕上的。

B：很高興我能幫上忙。我快累趴了。我們好好吃頓飯吧。

原來老外都這樣用！ Know it!

動詞 drop 在這裡指「倒下」，通常是由於筋疲力盡所致，例如：We are going to shop till we drop.（我們要逛街購物直到走不動為止。） be ready to do sth 含有「可能快要做某事」的意思，例如：She looked ready to burst into tears.（她看樣子就要哭出來了。）合起來 be ready to drop 則意為「就快要累倒了，累得站都站不住了」。

與之含義相近的一個表達是 be dead on one's feet，例如：After 14 hours of non-stop work I was dead on my feet.（連續工作了 14 個小時後，我累極了。）

另外，be (dead) beat, be bushed 和 be pooped 在口語中都可以表示「很累，筋疲力盡」的意思，例如：I'm sorry I can't go any further, I'm dead beat.（對不起，我實在走不動了，我累壞了。）The whole team was bushed after three weeks of grueling training.（經過了三週緊張的訓練後，整個隊伍都已筋疲力盡。）The taxi driver was really pooped at the end of the day.（一天下來那計程車司機真是筋疲力盡。）

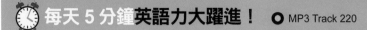
I tossed and turned last night.

我昨晚翻來覆去睡不著。／我昨夜輾轉反側。

A I tossed and turned last night, regretting what I had done in math class.

B Don't worry. Go and say sorry to Miss Jackson. She'll forgive you.

A：我昨晚翻來覆去睡不著，後悔我在數學課上的所作所為。

B：別擔心。去跟傑克森小姐道歉吧，她會原諒你的。

A Did you stay up again? Look at the dark circles under your eyes.

B I tossed and turned last night, and didn't fall asleep until 2 am this morning, although I went to bed early.

A Bad habits die hard.

A：你又熬夜了嗎？看看你的黑眼圈。

B：雖然昨晚很早就上床了，但我翻來覆去，直到凌晨 2 點才睡著。

A：壞習慣很難改。

原來老外都這樣用！ Know it!

動詞 toss 有「翻轉不停」的意思，動詞 turn 有「轉動，轉身」的意思，toss and turn 指「（睡不著而在床上）翻來覆去」，也許是因為不睏，也許是因為腦子裡一直想著事情。

再看看其他表示「睡不著，沒睡好」之意的表達。lie awake 指「躺在床上睡不著」，尤其指為了某事擔憂或興奮得睡不著，例如：Martin was a nervous teenager, often lying awake and worrying about the future.（馬丁是一個容易焦慮的少年，常常躺在床上為未來而擔憂，無法入眠。）can't get to sleep 指「睡不著」，尤其指因為噪音、焦慮、疼痛等原因，例如：David couldn't get to sleep because of all the noise.（大衛被噪音吵得睡不著覺。）not get much sleep 表示「沒怎麼睡著，睡得不多」，例如：The people next door are having a big party tonight, so I don't suppose we'll get much sleep.（隔壁的人今晚要辦一個大聚會，我想我們別想睡好覺了。）

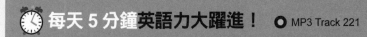

每天５分鐘**英語力大躍進！** ○ MP3 Track 221

Don't push me around!

別對我呼來喝去！

Chapter
12
譴責、不贊同

🅐 Give me a cup of tea!

🅑 Here you are.

🅐 Give me a glass of water, and I also need...

🅑 I'm not your servant! **Don't push me around!**

A：給我一杯茶。

B：給你。

A：給我一杯水，我還要……

B：我不是你的僕人！別對我呼來喝去的！

🅐 This is your to-do list, and do remember the deadline!

🅑 **Don't push me around!** I have my own business to deal with!

A：這個單子上都是你要做的事情，一定要按時完成！

B：不要把我呼來喝去的！我有自己的事情要處理呢！

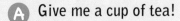 **Know it!**

> **Don't push me around!** 用於表示譴責，抗議對方呼來喝去地支使自己，同樣的意思也可以用 Don't push me about! 來表達。除了 push sb around / about，日常口語中還有 boss sb around / about 和 order sb around / about 可以表示「支使某人」。其中，boss sb around / about 可以直接用 boss sb 表達。例如：How dare you boss me like that?（你怎麼敢那樣使喚我？）

 生字補充！ **Vocabularies & Phrases**

- **servant** [ˈsɝvənt] 名 僕人
- **deadline** [ˈdɛdˌlaɪn] 名 截止時間，最後期限

243

You scared the hell out of me!

你嚇得我魂都飛了！

A Ha, I'm here!

B You scared the hell out of me!

A：哈，我在這呢！

B：你嚇得我魂都飛了！

A Where have you been? I've been calling you for about one hour!

B Sorry, my phone is in silent mode.

A Don't do that again! You scared the hell out of me!

A：你去哪裡了？我打你電話打了有 1 個小時！

B：對不起，我的手機關靜音了。

A：別再這樣了！你嚇得我魂都飛了！

原來老外都這樣用！ **Know it!**

You scared the hell out of me! 用於表示譴責，譴責對方嚇了自己一大跳，意為「你嚇得我魂都飛了」。這句話還可以和 You scared the life out of me! 互換使用。如果譴責的程度沒這麼深，可以只說 You're scaring me.（你嚇到我了。）

在日常用語中，動詞 + the hell out of sb 的句型比較常見，可以用於多種場合。例如，如果被某人惹急了，你就可以說：You irritated the hell out of me!（我被你煩死了！）某人想給你個驚喜，結果只有驚沒有喜，那麼你就可以說：You surprised the hell out of me!（真是被你嚇死了！）在比賽之前，你可以豪氣萬丈地說：We are here to beat the hell out of the opposition!（我們這次就是要把對手打得屁滾尿流！）不過要注意這些說法通常都不太禮貌哦。

 生字補充！ **Vocabularies & Phrases**

• **silent** [ˋsaɪlənt] 形 無聲的
• **mode** [mod] 名（機器、設備的）狀態，模式

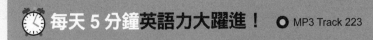
You're ripping me off!

你這是在敲我竹槓！／你搶錢啊?!

A How much is it?

B 90 dollars.

A You're ripping me off!

A：這個多少錢？

B：90 美金。

A：你搶錢啊！

A You're ripping me off!

B Calm down. The price includes three meals and free use of the swimming pool.

A That's more like it.

A：你這是在敲我竹槓！

B：別激動啊。這價格包括三餐費用和游泳池的使用費。

A：這還差不多。

原來老外都這樣用！　Know it!

rip sb off 在這裡表示「敲……竹槓」，相當於 overcharge sb，例如：The agency really ripped us off.（代理商狠狠敲了我們一筆。）在買東西討價還價時，You're ripping me off! 是非常好用的一句話，意思是「你這是在敲我竹槓！你這是搶錢啊！」，表示說話的人認為賣家要價太高，很不合理，言外之意就是「要再便宜一點」。名詞 rip-off 意為「索價過高的物品」。

再來看幾個關於討價還價的常用表達：The price is much too high.（價格太高了。）Give me a good price.（給我便宜一點。）Can you give me a discount?（能幫我打個折嗎？）Can you give me this for cheaper?（你能算我便宜一點嗎？）This is the best price.（這是最低價了。）That's a special offer.（這是特價。）I have to cover the cost.（我必須夠成本啊。）

rip off 除了表示「敲……竹槓」外，還有其他兩種含義。一種是「盜取，盜竊」，例如：Someone had come in and ripped off the TV and stereo.（有人進來偷走了電視機和音響。）另一種含義是「剽竊」，相當於 plagiarize。

You are going too far.
你太過分了。

A I don't want to work today.

A：我今天不想工作。

B You're going too far. I won't cover for you this time.

B：你太過分了。這一次我不會再替你説謊了。

A Look, I've used the money this month, and I'll pay it back next month, without Harry even knowing it.

A：你看，我這個月用了這筆錢，下個月再還清，哈利甚至不會知道。

B You're going too far. It's stealing!

B：你太過分了。你這是偷竊！

原來老外都這樣用！ **Know it!**

You are going too far 字面的意思是「你走得太遠了」，太遠了就是表示超過了合適的範圍，也就是「你太過分了」的意思。如果說一個人 go so far / as far as to do sth，指的是「竟然做某事，甚至做某事」，其實也有「過分」的意思，例如：The government went so far as to try to arrest opposition leaders.（政府竟然企圖逮捕反對黨領導人。）

再看一些意為「過分」的表達：1. take / carry sth too far / to extremes / to excess，例如：I don't mind a joke, but this is carrying it too far.（我不介意開玩笑，但這個也太過分了。）Problems only occur when this attitude is taken to extremes.（只有當這種態度走向極端時，問題才會發生。）2. over the top，例如：Her dress was completely over the top—really not appropriate for a business dinner.（她的裙子太過火了──真不適合在商務晚宴上穿。）3. too much，例如：I can't stand him any longer. It's too much!（我再也忍受不了他了。真是太過分了！）4. go overboard，例如：I hope the politicians will not go overboard in trying to control the press.（我希望政客們不會在控制媒體方面做得太過分。）

Where are your manners?

你的禮貌到哪裡去了？

A Damn it! He just doesn't know how to play football!

A：他媽的！他根本就不會踢足球！

B Good heavens, child, where are your manners?

B：天呀，孩子，你的禮貌呢？

A Stop yelling, Emily. Where are your manners?

A：別大呼小叫的，艾蜜莉。你的禮貌到哪去了？

B Sorry, Mom. I'm just too excited.

B：不好意思，媽媽。我只是太興奮了。

原來老外都這樣用！ Know it!

manners 在這裡指「禮貌，禮儀」，good manners 指「有禮貌」，bad manners 指「沒禮貌」，have no manners 也是指「沒禮貌」，table manners 指「餐桌禮儀」，impeccable manners 指「無可挑剔的禮儀」。看幾個例句：Her children all had such good manners.（她的孩子都很有禮貌。）It's bad manners to talk with your mouth full.（吃東西時講話是不禮貌的。）Dad gave us a lecture about our table manners.（爸爸對我們的餐桌禮儀教育了一番。）

Where are your manners? 的意思是「你的禮貌呢？你的禮貌哪裡去了？」，其實是指責對方沒有注意禮貌，提醒對方要注意禮儀。還有一種提醒別人注意禮儀的表達是 Mind your manners. 例如：You mind your manners, young man!（你要注意點禮貌，年輕人！）

manners 還可以表示「習俗，風俗」，是比較正式的用法，例如：She gave me a book about the life and manners of Victorian London.（她給了我一本關於維多利亞時期倫敦的生活和風俗的書。）

Our teacher always plays favorites.

我們老師總是偏心。

A Mr. Bush praised Samantha again.

A：布希先生又表揚薩曼莎了。

B Not surprised. **Our teacher always plays favorites.**

B：不覺得意外。我們老師總是偏心。

A **Our teacher always plays favorites.** Some kids have performed at the ceremony twice or three times, some have never had that chance.

A：我們老師總是偏心。有的孩子都在典禮上表演過兩三次了，有的卻從來得不到機會。

B That's why I don't like him.

B：所以我才不喜歡他。

原來老外都這樣用！ **Know it!**

favorite 在這裡是名詞，意思是「受寵的人，寵兒」，例如：You always were Dad's favorite.（你一直是爸爸的寵兒。）play favorites 意為「偏心，偏寵」，常用在老師、父母、長輩、領導身上，指他們對某些人比對另一些人更好。用動詞 favor 也可以表達「偏袒」的含義，例如：This tax cut obviously favors rich people.（這項減稅明顯偏向富人。）The judicial system of this country favors men over women.（該國的司法制度祖護男性。）形容詞 partial 和 biased 也能表達出類似的含義，它們都能表示「偏向一方的，偏袒的」，例如：Of course I'm biased, but I thought my daughter's paintings were the best.（當然我有偏心，但我還是覺得我女兒的畫最好。）

favorite 除了「受寵的人，寵兒」的含義，還可表示「特別喜愛的東西」和「最有希望獲勝者，最被看好的參賽者」，例如：Can we have strawberries? They are my favorite.（能給我們一點草莓嗎？我最喜歡草莓了。）He was the hot favorite for the Booker Prize.（他是布克獎最熱門的人選。）

Be nice.

友善一點吧。／不要這麼刻薄。

A Jim didn't finish his homework again! I should really teach him a lesson!

A：吉姆又沒完成家庭作業！我真該好好教訓他一頓！

B Hey, be nice! He's only nine years old.

B：嘿，別這麼凶嘛！他才九歲而已。

A I'll make a complaint against that waiter.

A：我要投訴那個服務生。

B What's the matter?

B：怎麼了？

A He mixed up the orders twice!

A：他竟然兩次都上錯菜！

B Be nice! He didn't mean it.

B：別這麼刻薄嘛！他也不是故意的。

原來老外都這樣用！ Know it!

形容詞 nice 在這裡意為「友好的，友善的，禮貌的」。Be nice! 在英語口語中非常常見，主要用來勸說他人態度要好一些、不要發脾氣等，可用於多種場合。如果想表達「對……好一點」，可以在 be nice 後面加上 to sb，例如：Be nice to the cat!（對那隻貓好一點！）

mean 與這裡的 nice 恰恰相反，它可表示「殘酷的，不善良的，刻薄的」，例如：I felt a bit mean asking him for help.（我覺得讓他來幫忙有點殘忍。）It was mean of him not to invite her.（他不厚道，沒邀請她。）所以 Don't be so mean 與 Be nice 的含義相近。

生字補充！ Vocabularies & Phrases

- **complaint** [kəmˋplent] 名 投訴
- **order** [ˋɔrdɚ] 名（餐廳裡）所點的菜餚飲料

Women tend to get a raw deal from employers.

女性常常受到雇主不公平的對待。

A Things are not easy for a woman who wants to have her own career.

A：女人想要擁有自己的事業可不容易啊。

B Yes. Women tend to get a raw deal from employers.

B：是啊。女性常常受到雇主不公平的對待。

A Generally speaking, men and women are now equally treated in the workplace.

A：總之，現在男性和女性在職場中能得到平等的對待。

B I don't think so. I think women tend to get a raw deal from employers.

B：我不這麼認為。我認為女性常常受到雇主不公平的對待。

原來老外都這樣用！ Know it!

raw deal（或 rough deal）指「不公平待遇」，用法類似於 unfair treatment，例如：Customers are getting a raw deal and are rightly angry.（顧客受到不公平的對待，生氣是理所當然的。）名詞 deal 在這裡指「待遇」，例如：Our nurses deserve a better deal.（我們的護士應該得到更好的待遇。）The prime minister promised farmers a new deal.（首相向農民保證推行一項新政策。）

說到因性別受到不公平對待這個話題，我們再來看看其他一些相關表達：widespread sex discrimination against women in the job market（就業市場上普遍存在著對婦女的性別歧視），sexism in the workplace（工作場所的性別歧視），sexual harassment（性騷擾），prenatal gender selection（產前性別選擇），prenatal gender inequality（產前性別不平等），marriage and childbirth（婚姻與生育），promotion and pay raise（升職與加薪）。

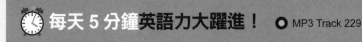

No more excuses.

別再找藉口了。／別狡辯了。

A You haven't finished your 5,000 meters running yet. You didn't finish yesterday either.

A：你還沒完成 5,000 米跑步呢。你昨天也沒有完成。

B I have a headache today.

B：我今天頭痛。

A No more excuses. Go on running. Right now.

A：別再找藉口了。繼續跑。趕快。

A I love you, baby. She's only a friend.

A：我愛你，寶貝。她只是一個朋友。

B No more excuses. I'm past caring about that.

B：別再找藉口了。我已經不在乎了。

原來老外都這樣用！　Know it!

句型 no more sth 表示「不要再有某事，不會再有某事」，例如：No more dreary winters—we're moving to Florida.（不會再有沉悶的冬天了一我們就要搬到佛羅里達去了。）名詞 excuse 可指「辯解的理由，托詞，藉口」，表示「對於某事的藉口」可以用 excuse for sth 或 excuse to do sth，例如：I need an excuse to call her.（我需要一個給她打電話的藉口。）The conference is just an excuse for a holiday in New York.（這個會議只是去紐約度假的藉口。）如果你對某人說 No more excuses，那就說明對方之前給過理由或藉口，現在你不想再聽任何藉口或解釋了。

再看幾個 excuse 表示「藉口」的表達。make up / think up / invent an excuse（編造藉口），例如：I made up some excuse about my car breaking down.（我編了個藉口，說我的車拋錨了。）make excuses for sb / sth（為某人 / 某事找藉口），例如：His mother was always making excuses for her son's behavior.（他媽媽總是為兒子的行為找藉口。）use sth as an excuse（拿某事物當藉口），例如：She never complained or used her illness as an excuse.（她從不抱怨，也從不拿自己的病當藉口。）

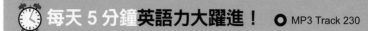

Don't take it out on me.

別拿我出氣。／別把我當成出氣筒。

A It's time to have lunch.

A：該吃午飯了。

B I've told you not to talk to me when I'm working.

B：告訴過你我工作時不要跟我說話。

A Don't take it out on me just because you've had a bad day.

A：不要因為你一天過得不順心就拿我來出氣。

A Why are you still watching TV at this time? Go do your homework.

A：都這個時候了你怎麼還在看電視？去做作業。

B I know you're in a bad mood Mom, but don't take it out on me.

B：媽媽，我知道你心情不好，但你別拿我出氣啊。

原來老外都這樣用！ Know it!

take it out on sb 表示「向某人發洩不滿，拿某人出氣，把某人當出氣筒」，其中 it 可替換為 anger, frustration 等字彙，例如：Irritated with herself, she took her annoyance out on Nick.（她生自己的氣，就把怒氣發洩在尼克身上。）

說到「出氣筒」，我們可以來看看 punching bag 和 doormat 這兩個表達。punching bag 的基本意思是「沙包，（拳擊）吊袋」，是拳擊的訓練工具，拳擊手會戴上手套猛擊吊袋，也有人把它當成發洩脾氣的道具，心情不好了就去打兩下。所以 punching bag 常被用來指「出氣筒」，例如：He is willing to be my punching bag.（他願意做我的出氣筒。）doormat 的本義是「門口的地墊」，可引申為「出氣筒，受氣包」的意思，很好理解，出氣筒和受氣包就像門口地墊，誰都可以上去踩兩腳，例如：He has been treating his secretary like a doormat.（他一直把他的祕書當成出氣筒。）

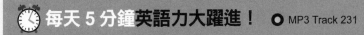

Are you going to bleed me dry?

你是要把我榨乾嗎？

A Honey, this is the bill to pay.

A：親愛的，這是要付的帳單。

B Are you going to bleed me dry? I just paid one yesterday.

B：你要把我榨乾嗎？我昨天剛付了一張。

- -

A Julie, would you please lend me 500 yuan?

A：茱莉，你能借我 500 塊錢嗎？

B Again? Are you going to bleed me dry? I'm just a student!

B：又借？你是不是想把我榨乾？我只是個學生啊！

原來老外都這樣用！ Know it!

Are you going to bleed me dry? 這句話通常用於表示氣憤或不滿，是對對方花錢過於誇張的指責（如第一個對話中）。不過，有時這句話也是一種誇張幽默的說法，說話者並不是氣憤或不滿，而是想表達「你明明知道我沒有錢，怎麼還找我借錢」這樣的意思（如第二個對話）。這句話裡的 bleed sb dry 強調的是「拿走某人所有的錢或財產等」，而 bleed 也可以只和 sb 連用，強調的則是「一段時期內勒索或榨取錢財」。例如：He'll do nothing but bleed them for every penny they can get.（他唯一會做的就是盡可能榨乾他們的每一分錢。）

生字補充！ Vocabularies & Phrases

- **yesterday** [ˈjɛstɚde] 副 昨天
- **please** [pliz] 感 請求

253

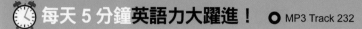
You're putting words into my mouth.

我沒說過這種話。

A You must help me do the homework! You promised!

B You're putting words into my mouth!

A：你必須幫我做作業！你保證過的！

B：我沒說過！

A Don't forget to bring your skates!

B Why?

A You said you would go skating with me today.

B You're putting words into my mouth!

A：別忘了把你的溜冰鞋帶來！

B：為什麼？

A：你說過今天會陪我去溜冰。

B：我沒說過這種話！

原來老外都這樣用！ **Know it!**

put words into sb's mouth 意為「硬說某人說過某些話」用於譴責對方捏造自己並沒有說過的話或是歪解自己所說之話的含義。

另外有兩句和 word 有關的日常口語也很常用，大家可以在此一併記下。一句是 Take my word for it（相信我的話），通常用於向對方強調自己說的話是完全真實的。例如：Take my word for it, you're my best friend!（相信我的話，你是我最好的朋友！）另外一句是 Words fail me.（我不知道說什麼好。）通常用於強調驚訝或憤怒的情緒。例如：I'd never thought I would see you here. Words fail me!（我從未想過會在這裡看見你。我不知該說什麼了！）

 生字補充！ **Vocabularies & Phrases**

• **skate** [sket] **名** 溜冰鞋

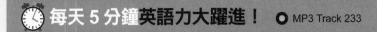

It is really hurtful.

太傷人了。

A This is your birthday present. I chose it for you.

B A teddy bear? It looks as stupid as you.

A Why are you always so sharp-tongued? It is really hurtful!

A：這是你的生日禮物。我為你選的。

B：玩具熊？看起來和你一樣傻。

A：你怎麼總是這麼毒舌？太傷人了！

A How could he be so heartless? We've been together for five years.

B Forget him! You deserve someone better!

A It is really hurtful.

A：他怎麼能這麼無情？我們都在一起 5 年了。

B：忘了他！你值得擁有更好的人！

A：他這麼做太傷人了。

原來老外都這樣用！ Know it!

It is really hurtful 意為「太傷人了」，通常僅用於表示感情上的傷害與冒犯。在日常口語中，表示「傷害」的常用動詞有 hurt, injure 和 wound，它們適用的場合各不相同。

- hurt 是日常英語中比較常用的，可表示傷了某人或傷害感情。例如：He hurt his knee playing basketball.（他打籃球時傷了膝蓋。）

- injure 強調的是在事故或打鬥中受傷。比如：Several people have been slightly injured on the highway.（一些人在公路上受了輕傷。）

- wound 既可以表示用刀、槍等武器傷害身體，又可以表示傷害感情。例如：That girl was deeply wounded by the treachery of her friend.（朋友的背叛深深地傷害了那個女孩。）

I thought we were closer than that.

我還以為我們關係很好呢。

A Vicky has changed a lot since she got married.

B Wait a minute! Vicky's married but she never told me? I thought we were closer than that!

A：薇琪自從結婚之後變了好多。

B：等等！薇琪結婚了都沒告訴我？我還以為我們關係很好呢！

A Why didn't you tell me you were in trouble? I thought we were closer than that.

B I just didn't want you to be involved in it.

A：你怎麼不跟我說你有麻煩了？我還以為我們關係很好呢。

B：我就是不想讓你被捲進來。

原來老外都這樣用！ Know it!

當別人不顧你和他／她之間的關係，做了讓你失望的事（尤其是有事瞞著你）時，你就可以酸酸地說一句 I thought we were closer than that.（我還以為我們關係很好呢。）如果想把話說得再重些，則可以說 I thought we were friends.（我還以為我們是朋友呢。）暗示對方現在這樣做就是不把你當朋友。不過，有可能傷感情的話還是要謹慎使用。

值得注意的是這裡 that 的用法，它指的是一種無須明說的情況，英語口語裡經常這樣使用。如：I'm not the girl I used to be anymore. With him, I am so much more than that.（我再也不是以前那個女孩了。和他在一起，我的人生豐富了好多。）

 生字補充！ Vocabularies & Phrases

・in trouble 片 在危險／困難的處境中

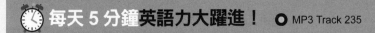

You're just saying that.

你不過是哄我開心罷了。

A This song I wrote is terrible. Nobody will like it.

A：我寫的這首歌真是爛透了。沒人會喜歡。

B Are you sure? It sounds fine to me.

B：你確定嗎？我聽了覺得還不錯啊。

A Oh, come on, I know **you're just saying that.**

A：哦，算了啦，我知道你不過是哄我開心罷了。

A I think you've made huge progress this semester.

A：我覺得你這學期進步了很多。

B Really? **You're not just saying that** to make me feel better?

B：真的嗎？你不會是為了安慰我才這麼說吧？

原來老外都這樣用！　Know it!

當別人安慰或讚揚你時，如果你覺得對方只是出於好意而口頭說說，其實心裡並不這麼想，就可以用 You're just saying that 這個表達。你既可以簡單地說：You're just saying that!（你只是嘴上這麼說罷了！）也可以說：You're just saying that to cheer me up / make me feel better / save my face etc.（你這麼說只是為了讓我振作起來／安慰我／幫我挽回面子等等。）

相反地，如果你在陳述一個事實時加上一句 I'm not just saying that，則可以表達「我不只是嘴上說說，我是真心的」之意。如：You're the best mom ever. And I'm not just saying that.（你是世上最棒的媽媽。我這話可不是隨便說的。）

 生字補充！　Vocabularies & Phrases

• **progress** [ˈprɑgrɛs] 名 進步

每天 **5** 分鐘**英語力大躍進！** ○ MP3 Track 236

I feel like an idiot.
我覺得自己像個白癡。

A How did you feel when you proposed to your girlfriend in the street?

B Oh, **I felt like an idiot.** I lost the ring, and there was a dog barking all the time. And worst of all, she turned me down.

A：在大街上跟女朋友求婚感覺如何呀？

B：哦，我覺得自己就像個白癡。我把戒指弄丟了，還有一隻狗一直在那裡叫。最糟的是她還拒絕了我。

A I'm sorry I messed up your plan. **I feel like an idiot.**

B Oh, no, it's not your fault. You didn't know.

A：真抱歉我把你的計畫搞砸了。我覺得自己像個白癡。

B：哦，不，不是你的錯。你又不知道。

原來老外都這樣用！ **Know it!**

I feel like an idiot 是口語中很常見的一句話，用於做了傻事之後的自嘲（如第一個對話），或做了錯事之後的自我批評（如第二個對話）。I feel terrible / awful 也可以用來表達類似這種糟糕的心情。

feel like 是一個非常好用的表達自我感覺的片語。如：I feel like home now.（我現在覺得自在了。）I feel like I'm a hundred years old.（我覺得自己老得像一百歲了似的。）另外，feel like (doing) sth 還可以表示「想要（做）某事」，如：I feel like a cup of tea.（我想喝杯茶。）

 生字補充！ **Vocabularies & Phrases**
- **propose** [prə`poz] 動 求婚
- **turn down** 片 拒絕
- **mess up** 片 搞砸，弄糟

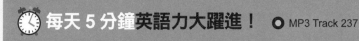 每天 5 分鐘**英語力大躍進！**　○ MP3 Track 237

I'm not in the mood.

我沒那個心情。

A How about a movie tonight?

A：今晚一起去看場電影怎麼樣？

B I'm sorry, but **I'm not in the mood.**

B：對不起，我沒有心情。

A You look so sad. Is it about your boyfriend?

A：你看起來很難過。和你男朋友有關嗎？

B Yeah, we had a quarrel yesterday.

B：是啊，我們昨天吵了一架。

A Let me sing Justin Bieber's "Boyfriend" for you, and I hope you'll feel better.

A：我唱首小賈斯汀的《男朋友》給妳聽吧，希望妳心情會好一點。

B Oh, thank you, but **I'm really not in the mood** now.

B：哦，謝謝你，但是我現在真的沒心情聽。

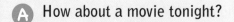 **Know it!**

名詞 mood 表示「心情，心境」的意思，be in the mood 意為「有心情……，有意……」。be not in the mood 表示沒心情或不想做某事，通常用來婉轉地拒絕某人。如果想要明確表示不想做某件事，可以用介系詞 for 引出具體的事情。例如，朋友邀請你一起去游泳，你不想去的話就可以說：I'm really not in the mood for swimming.（我真的沒有心情去游泳。）

I'm in a mood 可不是說有心情做某事，它的意思是「我心情不好，我感到生氣」。例如：I'm sorry for the yelling, but I was in a mood.（很抱歉和你大吼，我當時心情不好。）其主詞可以換成 she, he 等任何人。例如：Just leave her alone when she's in a mood.（她心情不好的時候不要去煩她。）

259

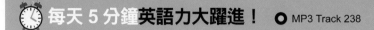

I cried myself to sleep.

我哭到睡著了。

A It was the first time I left home.

A：那是我第一次離開家。

B It must be hard for a little girl.

B：那對一個小女孩來說一定很難。

A Yes. I remember the very first night, **I cried myself to sleep.**

A：是的。我記得第一天晚上，我是哭著睡著的。

A **I** had a fight with my parents and **cried myself to sleep.**

A：我和我爸媽大吵一架，結果哭到睡著。

B So did they agree?

B：所以他們同意了沒有？

A This morning, they said I could go as long as I came back home before nine.

A：今天早上他們同意我去，只要在晚上九點前回家即可。

B Great!

B：太棒了！

原來老外都這樣用！ Know it!

cry oneself to sleep 指的是「哭到睡著」。例如某人一直哭，停不下來，直到哭累了就睡著了。這是人特別傷心的表現。

cry one's eyes out 和 cry one's heart out 也表示哭得特別傷心，含義基本相同，前者可譯為「哭得眼睛都紅了」，後者可譯為「哭得傷心欲絕」。例如：It was such a sad movie. I cried my eyes out.（這部電影太悲情了，我哭得眼睛都紅了。）Peter came round later, crying his heart out, asking me to forgive him.（後來彼得來了，哭得傷心欲絕，求我原諒他。）

It broke my heart.
我的心都碎了。／我非常傷心。

A My dog died last month, and **it broke my heart.**

A：我的狗上個月死了，我很傷心。

B Oh, baby, I know what it feels like.

B：哦，寶貝，我知道這種感受。

A Do you know Zach is going to get married?

A：你知道查克快要結婚了嗎？

B Yeah, I've heard about it.

B：嗯，我聽說了。

A He's such a bastard!

A：他真是個渾蛋！

B **It broke my heart** when I found out he had been cheating on me.

B：我發現他劈腿的時候簡直心都要碎了。

原來老外都這樣用！ Know it!

break sb's heart 意為「使某人非常傷心」，例如：She is a beautiful girl but she is cruel, and one day she'll break your heart. （她是個漂亮女孩，但她很狠心，總有一天她會讓你心碎的。）It breaks my heart to see the children starving. （看到孩子們挨餓真是讓我心如刀割。）

再來看一些相關表達。名詞 heartbreak 意為「悲傷，極度失望」；形容詞 heartbreaking 和 heartrending 意為「使人悲傷的，使人極度失望的」；形容詞 heartbroken 和 broken-hearted 意為「極度傷心的」；a broken heart 意為「破碎的心」。例如：The old man told a heartrending story of pain and suffering. （老人講述了一個充滿痛苦和磨難的故事，令人心碎。）When his parents separated he was heartbroken. （他父母分開時他傷心欲絕。）Broken-hearted fans camped outside the singer's house when she announced the end of her career. （該歌手宣佈退出歌壇時，心碎的歌迷在她家外面搭起了帳篷。）They said the woman died of a broken heart. （他們說那女人是傷心過度而死的。）

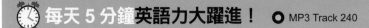
There was a lump in my throat.

我哽咽了。／我的喉嚨哽住了。

Ⓐ At least say something, please.

Ⓑ **There was a lump in my throat** and I didn't speak because I knew I would cry.

A：至少說點什麼，拜託。

B：我的喉嚨哽住了，我沒說話是因為我知道我一開口就會哭的。

Ⓐ Have you visited the professor?

Ⓑ Yes. He was very weak.

Ⓐ Did you cry?

Ⓑ **There was a lump in my throat** but I managed to fight back my tears.

A：你去看教授了嗎？

B：去了。他很虛弱。

A：你哭了沒？

B：我哽咽了，但忍住了眼淚。

原來老外都這樣用！ **Know it!**

名詞 lump 指「不定形的塊狀物」，如：Melt a lump of butter in the frying pan.（把一塊奶油放入煎鍋裡化開。）a lump in one's throat （或 a lump to one's throat）就是指喉嚨裡好像有塊東西，即「某人喉嚨哽住，某人哽咽得要哭了」。例如：The sight of the fresh green fields of my homeland brought a lump to my throat.（看到了故鄉綠油油的田野，我哽咽欲泣。）

想表達「快要哭了，但還沒有真的哭出來」這種含義，還可以使用 be close to tears 或 be on the verge of tears，例如：The lesson was going very badly and our new teacher was close to tears.（講課的效果非常不好，我們的新老師快要哭了。）My aunt's hands were shaking. She was on the verge of tears but my uncle didn't realize that.（我嬸嬸雙手顫抖，馬上就要哭出來了，但我叔叔沒有看出來。）

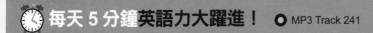

We're made for each other.

我們真是天生一對。

Chapter 14 深情、熱愛

A I love you so much, babe.

A：我好愛你，親愛的。

B I love you, too. We're made for each other.

B：我也愛你。我們真是天生一對。

A How's it going with Stephen?

A：和史蒂芬相處得怎麼樣？

B Oh, couldn't be better. I think we're probably made for each other.

B：哦，非常好。我覺得我們大概是天生一對。

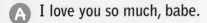 **Know it!**

be made for each other 用於形容夫妻或情侶非常般配、天生一對，是秀恩愛或誇讚別人幸福的常用表達。這個表達可以配合各種修飾語使用，如第二個對話中的 probably，又如 Jack and Jill are perfectly made for each other（傑克和吉爾真是天造地設的一對）中的 perfectly。

類似的表達還有 be / make a perfect / good match，名詞 match 在這裡意為「一對（配偶）」，如：They're a perfect match.（他們是非常般配的一對。）片語 a match made in heaven 也能夠表達「天造地設的一對」之意。另外，be / make a(n)... couple 也很常用，修飾的形容詞可以是 great, perfect, ideal, hot, amazing, incredible, attractive, happy 等。

 生字補充！ **Vocabularies & Phrases**

- **babe** [beb] 名 親愛的，寶貝
- **couldn't be better** 片 非常好，再好不過

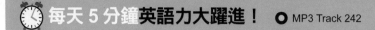

I can't take my mind off you.

我無法停止想你。

A Oh, Tom! Why're you here? I thought you were leaving for Boston this morning!

B Well, **I couldn't take my mind off you** all night, so I thought I'd drop in on you for a good-bye kiss before I ran to the airport.

A：哦，湯姆！你怎麼來啦？我以為你今天早上就動身去波士頓了呢？

B：嗯，我一晚上都止不住想你，所以想在趕去機場之前先來跟你吻別。

A Just hear me out, OK? **I can't take my mind off you** and it's driving me crazy.

B Trust me, dear. It's not a good time to be sentimental.

A：就聽我把話說完，好嗎？我一直在想你，都快瘋了，

B：相信我，親愛的，現在可不是感情用事的時候。

原來老外都這樣用！ Know it!

向愛慕之人表達思念之情時，除了直接說「我好想你」（I miss you so much / You're always on my mind...）之外，還可以試著換個角度，說「即使努力不去想你也做不到」，即上面兩個對話中的 I can't take my mind off you.（我止不住想你。／我無法關上思念之門。）

電影 Closer《偷心》的插曲中，歌手反覆吟唱著：I can't take my eyes off you... I can't take my mind off you... 將愛情中的依戀和絕望表現到了極致。配上電影的情節，是不是讓人覺得既心酸又浪漫呢？

 生字補充！ **Vocabularies & Phrases**

- **drop in on sb** 片 順道拜訪某人，臨時拜訪某人
- **sentimental** [sentʌˈmentl] 形 多愁善感的，感情用事的

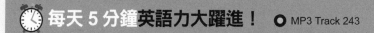
You mean the world to me.

你就是我的一切。／你對我非常重要。

A I can't believe you anymore.

B I'll never do anything to hurt you—**you mean the world to me.**

A：我再也不能相信你了。

B：我永遠不會傷害你的 ——你就是我的一切。

A Darling, I love you.

B I love you, too. **You mean the world to me**—you and our kids.

A：親愛的，我愛你。

B：我也愛你。你們就是我的一切——你和孩子們。

原來老外都這樣用！ **Know it!**

mean the world to sb 的字面含義是「對某人來說意味著全世界」，也就是指「對某人來說非常重要，為某人所深愛」，例如：My children mean the world to me.（我的孩子們就是我的全部。）要表達類似「你對我非常重要」這種含義還可以用：You mean everything to me. / You mean a lot to me. / You are very important to me. / You are my VIP.

think the world of sb 與 mean the world to sb 含義相同，但是主詞和賓語是相反的，即 You mean the world to me 與 I think the world of you 含義相同。再看兩個例子：We all thought the world of Isaac and were devastated when he died.（我們都特別愛艾薩克，他的死讓我們悲痛欲絕。）Don't be nasty to Sharon—she thinks the world of you, you know.（不要對莎朗這麼凶——她那麼愛你，你知道的。）

生字補充！ **Vocabularies & Phrases**

• **anymore** [ˈɛnɪmɔr] 副 再也不

I've been swept off my feet.
我已神魂顛倒。／我被迷住了。

A Do you love me?

A：你愛我嗎？

B Of course! **I've been swept off my feet!**

B：當然！我已經神魂顛倒了！

- -

A So you think Peter is your Mr. Right?

A：所以你覺得彼得就是你的真命天子？

B Yes! **I've been swept off my feet** by him. I can feel the chemistry between us.

B：是的！我已經被他迷住了。我能感到我們之間很來電。

原來老外都這樣用！ **Know it!**

be / get swept off one's feet 意為「被一下子迷住，神魂顛倒」，這是一種非常強烈的情緒，不是理性和慢熱的感情，而是既迅速又熱烈的。如果要強調被誰迷住、為誰神魂顛倒，可以在後面加上 by sb。例如：My niece has been swept off her feet by an older man.（我侄女被一個年長的男人迷住了。）She's just waiting to get swept off her feet by a handsome stranger.（她等待著邂逅一個英俊的陌生人，談一場轟轟烈烈的戀愛。）

英文中有很多關於愛戀的表達，而在熾熱程度上能跟 be swept off one's feet 媲美的並不多，be madly in love 也許是其中之一。be madly in love 表示「陷入瘋狂熱戀之中」，例如：Sarah and Greg are still madly in love.（莎拉和葛列格還處在熱戀之中。）be / fall head over heels in love with sb 也能表示「深深地愛著某人／突然愛上某人」，例如：Keith fell head over heels in love with the drummer in his band.（凱斯深深愛上了他樂隊的鼓手。）

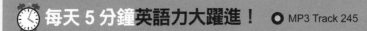
I fell in love with you at first sight / glance.

我對你一見鍾情。

A When did you fall in love with me?

A：你什麼時候愛上我的？

B I fell in love with you at first sight.

B：我對你是一見鍾情。

A I fell in love with you at first sight then.

A：我當時對你一見鍾情。

B You're kidding! You refused to shake hands with me, and you were rather rude. I thought you didn't like me.

B：你開玩笑吧！你拒絕跟我握手，還對我很無禮。我還以為你討厭我。

A I was just nervous.

A：我只是太緊張了。

原來老外都這樣用！ **Know it!**

fall in love with sb 意為「愛上某人，與某人陷入愛河」，fall in love with sb at first sight / glance 指「一見鍾情」。love at first sight 是其名詞片語形式，例如：When I met Tracy, it was love at first sight.（我一見到崔西就愛上她了。）He thought love at first sight would never last long.（他認為一見鍾情不會長久。）

與「一見鍾情」相對的是「日久生情」。「對……日久生情」可以表達為 grow to love...，例如：It wasn't exactly love at first sight but I did grow to love John.（我對約翰並沒有一見鍾情，但確實漸漸喜歡上了他。）這裡的動詞 grow 指「逐漸改變看法，逐漸產生某種感覺」，後面常可接 to love / like / hate / respect 等，例如：After a while the kids grew to like Miss Riggs.（過了一會兒，孩子們開始喜歡里格斯小姐了。）如果想表示「（某事物）逐漸為某人所喜歡」，可以用 grow on sb，例如：I hated his music at first, but it grows on me.（我一開始討厭他的音樂，可慢慢地卻越來越喜歡。）

I had a crush on him.

我迷戀過他。

A I saw Mr. Smith last week. He's still so charming.

A：我上週見到了史密斯先生。他還是那麼迷人。

B Oh, Mr. Smith! **I had a crush on him** back in high school.

B：哦，史密斯先生！我高中時迷戀過他。

A Are you going to Justin's concert?

A：你要去賈斯汀的演唱會嗎？

B Of course! **I had a crush on him.** I would like to hear all the old songs.

B：當然！我迷戀過他。我想聽那些所有的老歌。

原來老外都這樣用！ Know it!

have a crush on sb 意為「迷戀某人，癡情於某人」，常常指的是年輕人迷戀某個比自己年長、自己並不熟識，而且幾乎沒有機會能與之發展真正戀情的人。隨著年齡增長，人變得成熟，這種衝動而難以控制的迷戀和癡情往往也就煙消雲散了。看兩個例句：It is quite normal for adolescents to have crushes on pop stars. （青少年迷戀流行歌星是很常見的事。）The only reason I went to church every Sunday was that I had a crush on the minister. （我每週日去做禮拜的唯一原因就是我迷戀那位牧師。）

名詞 crush 也可以指「（不太熟識的）熱戀的物件，癡迷的物件」，例如：My brother is going to have the first date with his crush. How lucky he is! （我弟弟要去跟他心儀的對象初次約會了。他可真走運啊！）

 生字補充！ Vocabularies & Phrases

• **charming** [ˈtʃɑrmɪŋ] 形 迷人的，有魅力的

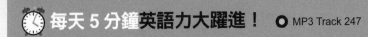

Get out of my face!

滾開！

A Hey, Mike. Sorry to hear that you've failed math.

B Don't talk to me as if you cared. Just **get out of my face.**

A：嘿，麥克。聽說你數學不及格，真遺憾啊。

B：別說得好像你在乎一樣。給我滾開。

A What if he just walks in here and asks for money?

B Well, I'll tell him to **get out of my face.**

A：要是他直接大搖大擺過來要錢怎麼辦？

B：嗯，那我就叫他滾開。

原來老外都這樣用！ **Know it!**

當一個人非常憤怒、想叫面前的某人滾開時，最常用的表達自然是 Get out! / Get out of here!（或 Piss off!）不過，上面兩段對話中的 get out of my face 則能夠更為生動地表達此意——「從我眼前消失」。但不論哪種說法，叫人滾開都是較粗魯的行為，要謹慎使用。

有趣的是，英語中還有一個與 get out of sb's face 對應的片語—— get in sb's face，意思是「惹怒某人」。例如：He totally got in my face by saying that.（他那麼說徹底把我惹火了。）

生字補充！ **Vocabularies & Phrases**

- **fail** [fel] **動** 不及格，未能通過
- **as if** **片** 彷彿，好像（用於強調某事不是真的或不會發生）

What's wrong with you?
你怎麼回事呀？

A **What's wrong with you?** Why aren't you outside playing like other boys?

B I'm sorry, Dad, but I just prefer my books.

A：你怎麼回事啊？怎麼不跟其他男孩子一樣在外面玩？

B：不好意思，老爸，相較之下我更喜歡跟書待在一起。

A Hey, Sophie! Fancy a drink after work?

B **What's wrong with you**, Bob? I think I've made it quite clear that I'm not into you.

A：嘿，蘇菲！下班後去喝一杯嗎？

B：你怎麼回事啊，鮑伯？我覺得我已經說得很清楚了，我對你沒興趣。

原來老外都這樣用！ **Know it!**

當某人的行為不合常理或某人做了你認為不對的事而讓你感到氣憤時，你就可以用 What's wrong with you? 來質問他／她。配上憤怒的語氣，對方一定明白你不是真的在詢問他／她出了什麼事，而是被惹怒了。

在這種情況下還可以說：What's your problem? 其語氣比 What's wrong with you? 更為直接。如：What's your problem? You should have left hours ago!（怎麼回事呀你？你好幾個小時之前就應該離開了！）

 生字補充！ **Vocabularies & Phrases**

- **fancy** [ˈfænsɪ] **動** 想要，喜歡
- **be into sb / sth** **片** 喜歡某人／某事物

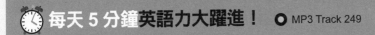
Read my lips.

你給我聽好了。

A Mom, can I have more ice cream?

A：媽，我能再吃一點冰淇淋嗎？

B Read my lips: you're not having any more.

B：你給我聽好了：不准再吃了。

A Did you really break up with John?

A：你真的和約翰分手了嗎？

B Yes, and it was his fault.

B：是的，而且都是他的錯。

A But John said he loved you...

A：可是約翰說過他愛你……

B Read my lips! Do not mention his name any more!

B：你給我聽好了！不要再提他的名字！

原來老外都這樣用！ Know it!

名詞 lip 是「嘴唇」的意思，Read my lips 意為「你聽好了，我說話算數」，表達的是說話的人強勢的態度，旨在告訴對方某事已經決定好了，不能再更改了。這句話通常用於「約法三章」的場合，向另一方表明什麼事是絕對不能做的。Listen here（給我聽著）和 Read my lips 有異曲同工之妙，二者都可以用來引起某人的注意，讓其仔細聽你接下來要說的話，只不過 Listen here 尤其是用在生氣的時候，而且後面通常還要加上 you，young lady 等對對方的稱呼。例如，你在商場裡看中一雙鞋，殺完價正要給錢的時候，老闆忽然又反悔了，還想提高價錢，那麼你就可以氣憤地說：Listen here, you, I'm not paying any more than we agreed.（你給我聽著，比原先議定價格多一分錢我都不會付的。）

You pissed me off!

我會被你氣死！

A Mom, I'm sorry I came home late last night.

A：媽媽，對不起，我昨晚太晚回來了。

B This is your third time this week! **You** really **pissed me off!**

B：這已經是本週第三次了！你真把我氣死了！

A Why are you so upset?

A：你怎麼這麼不開心呀？

B It's Carol. **The way she treats me pisses me off.**

B：是因為卡蘿。她對待我的方式讓我很生氣。

原來老外都這樣用！ **Know it!**

piss sb off 在英語口語中很常用，意為「使某人生氣，激怒某人」。這一結構還可以變形為 be / get pissed off doing sth 或 be / get pissed（off）with / at sb / sth，此時的主詞也相應從激怒別人的「罪魁禍首」變為被激怒的對象。如：You get really pissed off applying for jobs all the time.（不停地找工作真的讓人很煩。）It seems that everybody's pissed at me.（好像人人都生我的氣了。）

另外，piss off 還有「滾開」或「不行」之意。如：Just piss off and leave me alone!（滾開，讓我一個人靜一靜！）"Can I have five pounds?" "Piss off!"（「能給我五英鎊嗎？」「不行！」）要注意 piss off 是較粗魯的語言，大家應慎用。

 生字補充！ **Vocabularies & Phrases**
· **upset** [ʌpˋsɛt] 形 不快的，煩惱的

每天 **5** 分鐘英語力大躍進！ ● MP3 Track 251

The way he treats her really burns me up.

他那樣對待她，實在讓我很火大。

A Have you seen how John treats Maria?

B Yeah, he's a little bossy.

A The way he treats her really burns me up.

- -

A You beat your sister's boyfriend?

B The way he treats her really burns me up.

A：你看到約翰怎麼對瑪麗亞了嗎？

B：看到了，他有點專橫。

A：他那樣對待她，實在讓我很火大。

A：你打了你妹妹的男朋友？

B：他那樣對待她，實在讓我很火大。

原來老外都這樣用！ **Know it!**

The way he treats her really burns me up 中的 burn sb up 指「使某人非常氣憤」。burn up 在日常英語中可以用於多種場合，用於人時，除了上述對話中的用法，還可以用 be burning up 表示「發燒」，比如：He is burning up.（他發燒了。）用於某事物時，可以表示「燒光，消耗」，比如：The fire has burned up tens of thousands of acres of timber.（那場大火燒光了數萬英畝的木材。）Exercises can help you burn up a lot of calories.（運動能幫助消耗很多熱量。）在表示「消耗」之意時，burn off 可以和 burn up 互換使用。例如：Exercises can help burn off a lot of calories.（運動能幫助消耗很多熱量。）

 生字補充！ **Vocabularies & Phrases**

• **bossy** [ˋbɑsɪ] 形 愛發號施令的，專橫的

To hell with her!

讓她見鬼去吧！

A Eve just called me to cancel the interview on Sunday.

B Again? **To hell with her**, I will never ever interview her again!

A：伊芙剛打電話給我取消週日的採訪。

B：又取消？讓她見鬼去吧，我再也不採訪她了！

A I have a message for you.

B From whom?

A Janey.

B **To hell with her**, I don't want to hear any message from her!

A：我有個訊息要告訴你。

B：誰的？

A：珍妮。

B：讓她見鬼去吧，我不想聽她的任何訊息！

原來老外都這樣用！ **Know it!**

To hell with her! 通常可譯為「讓她見鬼去吧！」這句話的重點在於 to hell with 結構，它在口語中經常使用，可以後接人或事物，均表示說話者無所謂、不在乎的態度，但也是一種不禮貌的用法。例如，麥克要求做主持人，否則就不來參加晚會，那麼晚會負責人可能就會說：To hell with Mike, who cares if he comes or not!（讓麥克見鬼去吧，誰在乎他來不來！）你計畫去看電影，但是朋友找你商量事情，結果電影都快開演了還沒商量出結果，那麼你也可以說：To hell with this, I'm going to see the movie!（讓這事見鬼去吧，我要去看電影了！）當然，如果關係沒那麼親近，還是不要用這句話了，容易傷感情，你說呢？

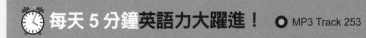

I blew my top / stack / cool.

我大發雷霆。／我勃然大怒。

A When I saw him beating that kid, **I blew my top.**

A：我看到他在打孩子，頓時勃然大怒。

B Scum like that should be locked away.

B：像這種人渣就應該關起來。

A Did they give your money back?

A：他們還你錢了嗎？

B At first they said it was not their fault. **I blew my top.** Then they gave me the money back.

B：一開始他們說不是他們的錯。我大發脾氣。然後他們就把錢還給我了。

原來老外都這樣用！ **Know it!**

blow one's top / stack / cool 的意思是「大發雷霆，勃然大怒，突然發火」，例如：Yesterday I blew my stack and hit him.（昨天我發火，就打了他。）

have / throw a fit 也能表示「大發脾氣」，其中名詞 fit 指「（感情的）衝動，一陣發作」，例如：When Tommy saw the mess his friend left, he had a fit.（湯米看到他朋友留下的一片狼藉後，大發了一陣脾氣。）go through / hit the roof 意為「暴跳如雷，火冒三丈」，例如：You can't tell Dad we crashed his car—he'll hit the roof.（你不能告訴爸爸我們把他的車撞壞了——他會大發雷霆的。）還有，go crazy / nuts 意為「氣得發瘋」，例如：Betty would go crazy if she found out you'd been seeing him.（貝蒂如果發現你一直在跟他交往的話，她會氣瘋的。）

生字補充！ **Vocabularies & Phrases**

• **scum** [skʌm] **名** 社會渣滓，人渣
• **lock away** **片** 把⋯⋯關進監獄

They really get under my skin.

他們真叫我惱火。

A Some people just will talk while you're trying to concentrate on your work.

A：有些人就是會在你努力專心工作時說話。

B Yes, **they really get under my skin.**

B：是啊，他們真叫人惱火。

A Why do the Smiths always make so much noise on weekend mornings? **They really get under my skin.**

A：史密斯他們家為什麼總在週末的早晨那麼吵？真讓人惱火。

B They get up early in the morning and play soccer in the yard.

B：他們一早起來在院子裡踢足球。

原來老外都這樣用！ Know it!

說某些人 get under sb's skin，是指這些人的某種做法讓你特別討厭、氣憤。這種做法可能並不會遭到所有人的討厭，但卻會讓你特別生氣，也就是說，這是你特別不能容忍的行為。例如在第一個對話中，在別人專心工作時說話的行為，可能不是所有人遇到都會氣憤，但至少會惹對話中的 B 生氣。

再來看兩個與 skin 相關的表達。have (a) thin / thick skin 指「臉皮薄／厚」，例如：This is not a job for someone with thin skin.（臉皮薄的人做不了這個工作。）by the skin of one's teeth 指「好不容易才……，差點就沒……」，例如：The other player in his team also made it by the skin of his teeth.（他隊上的另一名隊員也勉強通過了。）

 生字補充！ Vocabularies & Phrases
• concentrate ['kɑnsn̩‚tret] 動 專注，集中注意力

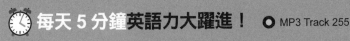

I was mad, but I didn't want to make a scene.

我確實氣得要命，但我不想大吵大鬧。

A That waitress was so rude! She really pissed me off! Why didn't you let me teach her a lesson?

A：那個服務生也太無禮了！真是把我氣死了！你幹嘛不讓我教訓教訓她？

B I was mad too, but I didn't want to make a scene.

B：我也很生氣，但我不想在公共場合大吵大鬧。

- -

A Let's talk about that Emily.

A：我們來談談那個艾蜜莉吧。

B Baby, I didn't know you were unhappy at the party.

B：寶貝，我不知道你在聚會上不高興了。

A I was mad actually, but I didn't want to make a scene.

A：我其實很生氣，但我不想在外面大吵大鬧。

原來老外都這樣用！ Know it!

形容詞 mad 在這裡表示「生氣的」，而它也可表示「瘋狂的，行為失控的」。形容詞 crazy 和 nuts 在這一點上與之相像，也是既可以表示「生氣的」，也可以表示「瘋狂的」。看幾個例子：Why are you mad at me?（你為什麼生我的氣？）The music is driving me crazy.（那音樂快把我逼瘋了。）Dad will go nuts when he knows about this.（爸爸知道這件事的話會發火的。）

make a scene 意為「（尤指在公共場合）大吵大鬧」，而且這種大庭廣眾下的爭吵會讓人覺得尷尬、丟臉。例如：Jamie could see that Andrea was getting annoyed with the shop assistant and prayed that she wouldn't make a scene.（傑米能看出來安德莉雅被店員惹火了，他祈禱她不要跟人家大吵大鬧。）I'm not telling my husband about Jackie skipping school; he'll only make a scene.（我不打算告訴我老公傑基翹課的事，他知道了只會大吵大罵。）

Do what I tell you, or else!

照我說的做，不然有你好看的！

A Never tell Mom that I drank last night!

B Mom said a good boy would never lie!

A Do what I tell you, or else!

A：千萬別把我昨晚喝酒的事告訴媽媽！

B：媽媽説過好孩子從來不會説謊的！

A：叫你別説就別説，不然有你好看的！

A Here is my telephone number, but remember not to tell others.

B What if they ask me?

A Do what I tell you, or else!

A：這是我的電話號碼，但是記住，不要告訴別人。

B：要是他們問我呢？

A：照我説的做，不然有你好看的！

原來老外都這樣用！ Know it!

Do what I tell you, or else! 在口語中用於威脅他人，強調「不按照我説的辦就後果自負」，這裡威脅的語氣主要通過 or else 表現出來。通常情況下，or else 的威脅之意可以通過兩種方式表達：一種是 or else 獨立成句，不明確表達出具體威脅的內容（如上述兩個對話）；另一種則是在 or else 後面説出到底是哪種後果，例如：Give me back those documents, or else I'll scream!（把那些文件還給我，否則我就叫人了！）

or else 在警告、威脅他人時，還常常與 you'd better... 連用以起到強調的作用。例如：You'd better do as we tell you, or else!（你最好照我們的話去做，否則有你好看的！）

Just you wait!

你等著！／你就等著瞧吧！

Ⓐ You broke my favorite pen!

Ⓑ So what?

Ⓐ I'll tell your mom on you, **just you wait!**

Ⓐ What about your project?

Ⓑ Almost done!

Ⓐ So happy for you!

Ⓑ Thank you! It will be a great success, **just you wait!**

A：你把我最喜歡的鋼筆弄壞了！

B：那又怎樣？

A：我要到你媽媽那裡去告你一狀，你等著！

A：你的項目怎麼樣了？

B：快完成了。

A：真為你高興！

B：謝謝！它會大獲成功的，你就等著瞧吧！

原來老外都這樣用！ Know it!

Just you wait! 主要用於兩種場合：用於威脅或警告某人（如第一個對話）；用於告訴某人某事肯定會發生（如第二個對話）。在表示威脅或警告時，如果自己起不到威懾作用，還可以靠第三方。例如，小孩子不聽奶奶的話，一直在看電視而不寫作業，奶奶就可以說：Just you wait until / till your mother gets home!（等你媽回來！）言外之意就是說，再不寫作業，你媽媽回來一定會收拾你的！估計這個殺手鐧一出，小朋友們都會乖乖聽話了。所以也請記住just you wait until / till...這個句型，專門用來警告某人再不停止不好的行為就會有麻煩的。

生字補充！ Vocabularies & Phrases
• **tell on sb** 片 告發，打某人的小報告

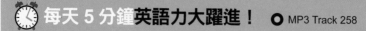
I'll get even with you one day.

總有一天我會找你算帳的。

A I'll get even with you one day!

B Hey man, it's not my fault. Don't be mad at me!

A：總有一天我會找你算帳！

B：嘿，老弟，這不是我的錯，別跟我生氣啊！

A I'll get even with you one day!

B Did I do something wrong?

A I know it's you who bad-mouthed me behind my back.

B This must be a misunderstanding!

A：總有一天我會找你算帳的！

B：我做錯什麼了嗎？

A：我知道是你在背後說我壞話。

B：這一定是個誤會！

原來老外都這樣用！ Know it!

get even with sb 表示「向某人報復，跟某人算帳」，I'll get even with you one day 用於表示威脅的場合，意為「總有一天我會找你算帳的」，和 I'll be even with you one day. 可以互換使用。當然，算帳的對象也可以是他、她，或其他任何人。例如：I'll be / get even with him / her / them one day.（總有一天我會找他／她／他們算帳的。）同樣可以表示威脅的還有 I'll get revenge on you one day.（總有一天我會找你報仇的。）不過，這句話更加正式，而且感情也更強烈一些。另外，revenge 也可以用於表示在比賽中一雪前恥。例如：He took revenge for his defeat here last time.（他報了上次在這裡被擊敗的一箭之仇。）

生字補充！ Vocabularies & Phrases

- **bad-mouth** [`bæd͵mauθ] **動** 說……的壞話
- **misunderstanding** [͵mɪsʌndɚˋstændɪŋ] **名** 誤會

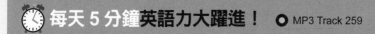

每天5分鐘英語力大躍進！ 🔴 MP3 Track 259

Don't you dare!

你敢！

Chapter
16

威脅、挑釁

A Julie is such a selfish person!

B I'll tell her what you said about her!

A Don't you dare!

A：茱莉真是個自私的人！

B：我要把你的話告訴她！

A：你敢！

A Can I borrow your new laptop?

B Of course not!

A OK, I'll use it while you're not at home.

B Don't you dare!

A：能借我你新買的筆記型電腦嗎？

B：當然不能！

A：好吧，等你不在家的時候我再用。

B：你敢！

原來老外都這樣用！ **Know it!**

Don't you dare! 這句話用於表示威脅的場合，警告某人不要做某事以免惹你生氣。在日常口語中，也常常用 Don't you dare do sth! 來表示「你敢……！」的意思。例如：Don't you dare laugh at me!（你敢嘲笑我！）言外之意就是說「你嘲笑我試試，我肯定讓你吃不完兜著走」。與之類似的一句是 How dare you!（你怎麼敢！），但這句強調的是對他人行為或言辭的震驚和憤怒。例如，同學問你這次的好成績是不是抄來的，你就可以憤怒地說：How dare you! I've been studying hard for the whole month!（你竟敢這麼說！我可是整整用功了一個月！）How dare you do sth!（你竟敢……！）也可表達同樣的意思。例如：How dare you use my laptop without telling me!（你竟敢不告訴我一聲就用我的筆記型電腦！）

281

I will smash you next time.

下次我會殺你個片甲不留。／
下次我會輕鬆打敗你。

Ⓐ I will smash you next time!

Ⓑ Hah, I'll wait for you.

A：下次我會殺你個片甲不留！

B：哈，我等著。

Ⓐ Oh, it's so easy. I won again.

Ⓑ I will smash you next time!

A：哦，這太容易了。我又贏了。

B：我下次一定會打敗你！

原來老外都這樣用！ **Know it!**

動詞 smash 在這裡指「在比賽或選舉中打敗、擊敗對手」，例如：
The company strategy was to form an alliance to smash the competing companies.（公司策略是建立聯盟，擊潰競爭對手。）能表達類似含義的動詞不少，這裡僅舉幾例：We didn't expect to win the game, but we thrashed them 9-0.（我們沒想到會贏得比賽，結果以 9-0 打敗對手。）James was bowling extremely well and we routed the Susan side.（詹姆斯在保齡球比賽中打得非常好，我們輕鬆擊潰了蘇珊那一方。）Your dad skunked me at fishing again.（你爸爸釣魚又輕鬆贏過了我。）Chicago hammered Boston in a game on Saturday.（芝加哥隊在週六的一場比賽中打得波士頓隊落花流水。）

 生字補充！ **Vocabularies & Phrases**
• **wait for sb** 片 等待某人

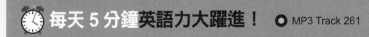
Try me.

你可以考我。／我隨便你考。

A You can match all the countries with their respective capital cities? I don't believe that.

A：你能把所有國家和其首都對應起來？我不信。

B Come on. **Try me.**

B：來啊，來考我啊。

A I can tell from your face whether you're lying or not.

A：我看你的臉就能知道你是不是在說謊。

B Really? You are a fan of *Lie to Me*?

B：真的？你喜歡看《別對我說謊》？

A You can **try me.**

A：你可以考我啊。

原來老外都這樣用！　Know it!

當別人不相信你能做到某事，而你自信滿滿時，就可以跟對方說 Try me，意思是「不相信的話你可以隨便考我，隨你怎麼考都行」。

動詞 try 在這裡是「試驗，試探」的意思。try sb's patience 指「考驗某人的耐心」；try one's hand at sth 指「嘗試某事」；try one's luck 指「試一試運氣」；try it on with sb 可指「故意表現惡劣以試探某人」。看 兩 個 例 句：After she lost her job, she thought she'd try her hand at writing a novel. （她丟掉工作後想嘗試寫小說。）After the war my grandfather went north to try his luck. （戰爭結束後我祖父北上去試試運氣。）

生字補充！　Vocabularies & Phrases

• **respective** [rɪˋspɛktɪv] 形 各自的

I'm walking on air.
我高興得像飛上了天。

A You just did a good job!

B I'd never thought I could beat him.

A Excited now?

B Actually, **I'm walking on air!**

A：你剛才表現很棒！

B：我從來沒想過能贏他。

A：現在很興奮吧？

B：說實在的，我高興得像飛上了天！

A Since his successful application for the job, **he's** been **walking on air.**

B Yeah, I can see that.

A：自從他成功地申請到那份工作，他就一直高興得像飛上了天。

B：是啊，我看出來了。

原來老外都這樣用！ Know it!

I'm walking on air 這句話主要用於表達說話的人喜悅或興奮的心情，通常譯為「我高興得像飛上了天」。但是在日常的使用中，要特別記得，這句話說的是一種狀態，所以只能用進行式時態：想表達此刻的心情就用現在進行式（如第一個對話）；想表達一直以來的狀態就用現在完成進行式（如第二個對話）；想表達之前某一時刻的狀態，就用過去完成進行式，但此時一般用 felt like 代替 was，例如：When he got the job offer, he felt like walking on air.（拿到工作邀約時，他高興得像飛上了天。）

還有一點相信大家已注意到了，句子的主詞不是「非我莫屬」，可以根據實際情況相應變化哦！

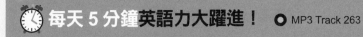
I can't wait to get off work!
我等不及要下班了！

A I can't wait to get off work! I'm leaving for New Zealand tonight!

B Oh, lucky you!

A：我等不及要下班了！我今晚就要前往去紐西蘭了！

B：哦，你真幸運啊！

A The dinner is gonna be so great with Mom's homemade pizza!

B Yeah, **can't wait!**

A：這一頓飯肯定很棒，有媽媽自己做的比薩！

B：是呀，我等不及要吃了！

原來老外都這樣用！ **Know it!**

can't wait to do sth 用於表達等不及要做某事的興奮心情。在說話雙方都明確所期待的內容時，也可簡化為 Can't wait!（如第二個對話）。如果期待的事物是名詞或動名詞，則要用 can't wait for sth，如：I can't wait for their wedding.（真想快點參加他們的婚禮。）

不過，can't wait 也可以用在反話上，表示你覺得某事可能非常乏味、不想去做。如："There's a concert tonight, Mozart and Beethoven. Will you come?" "Oh, classical music? Can't wait!"（「今晚有一場音樂會，演出莫札特和貝多芬的曲子。你要來嗎？」「哦，古典音樂嗎？我可等不及了！」）具體是何種情緒就要通過說話人的語氣和表情去判斷了。

生字補充！ **Vocabularies & Phrases**

- **leave for** 片 前往去某地
- **homemade** ['hom`med] 形 自製的，家裡做的

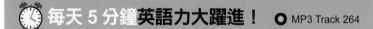
It's too exciting for any words.
讓人興奮到無法言喻。

A A ticket for Madonna's concert? **It's really too exciting for any words!**

A：瑪當娜演唱會的門票？這真是讓人激動得說不出話來！

B I knew you would like it!

B：我就知道你會喜歡！

A You're chosen to be the representative of our school to attend the ceremony.

A：你被選為我們學校的代表參加此次典禮。

B ...

B：……

A What's the look on your face? Anything to say?

A：你那是什麼表情啊？想說些什麼嗎？

B It's too exciting for any words.

B：太讓人興奮了，不知說什麼好。

原來老外都這樣用！ **Know it!**

too... for words 表示「太……而無法用言語表達」，It's too exciting for any words 這句話用於表達激動或興奮，即「太令人興奮了而無法用語言形容，讓人興奮得說不出話來」。一般說來，在「夢想成真」「天上掉下餡餅」之類的場合會用到這句話（如上述兩個對話），但是有的時候這句話也可以作為「沒有反應」的藉口。例如，女朋友告訴你國慶日已經訂好了雙人旅遊，但其實你只想宅在家裡做個「安靜的美男子」，所以當女朋友質問你為何沒有什麼激動的反應時，你就可以說：It's too exciting for any words.

另外，It's too exciting that I couldn't say a word 也能表達相同的意思，可替換使用。當然，也可以用人作主詞，修飾的形容詞相應變換。例如：I'm too excited for any words.（我興奮得不知說什麼好。）

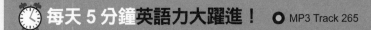
I jumped for joy.
我高興得跳了起來。

A I heard you were very excited at the news that your school took the championship.

A：我聽說當你得知你們學校奪冠時特別興奮。

B Yeah, I jumped for joy.

B：是啊，我高興得跳了起來。

A I have been recruited as a member of the football team.

A：我入選足球隊了。

B Congratulations!

B：恭喜！

A I really jumped for joy at the news.

A：聽到這個消息的時候我真的高興得跳了起來。

B Yeah, after all, you've been practicing so hard.

B：是啊，畢竟你苦練了這麼久。

原來老外都這樣用！ Know it!

I jumped for joy 用於形容說話的人特別高興。這句話可以用於兩種場合：一種是真的高興得跳了起來；另外一種強調的是非常高興的狀態，並沒有真的跳起來。

另外，如果大家聽到 jump up and down 這個用法，可不要想當然地以為就是高興得跳起來的意思。雖然也是「跳了起來」，但 jump up and down 可以根據不同的情境表達「欣喜若狂，非常激動，暴跳如雷」等多種意思。例如：They jumped up and down and said, "We won!"（他們欣喜若狂地說：「我們贏了！」）

 生字補充！ Vocabularies & Phrases

• **recruit** [rɪˋkrut] **動** 招收（新成員）

I'm excited like I won the jackpot.

我興奮得像中了大獎似的。

A You really love your wife.

B Everybody says that. When she said "yes," I was excited like I won the jackpot.

A When the host called my name, I even screamed. I was excited like I won the jackpot.

B Well, it's very much like the jackpot. It's a chance of 1: 15,000.

A：你真的很愛你太太。

B：人人都這麼說。當她說「願意」的時候，我像中了大獎一樣興奮。

A：當主持人叫到我名字時，我甚至尖叫了起來。我興奮得像中了大獎似的。

B：嗯，這跟中大獎差不多。是 1:15,000 的機率。

原來老外都這樣用！ Know it!

英文和中文裡都會用「像中了大獎似的」來形容喜悅和興奮的心情。英文裡的一個字 jackpot，意為「（碰運氣遊戲中的）頭獎，最大獎」，就非常適合用來指「中了大獎」中的這個「大獎」。a $50,000 jackpot 指「五萬美元的頭獎」，jackpot winner 指「頭獎得主」，而「中獎」除了可以說成 win the jackpot，還可以說成 hit the jackpot。hit the jackpot 除了字面意思「贏得大筆獎金，中頭彩」之外，還可以泛指「大獲全勝」，例如：Owens hit the jackpot in his first professional game with the Cowboys.（歐文斯在加盟牛仔隊後的第一場職業賽中便大獲全勝。）

提到中獎，我們很容易會想到 lottery 這個字。名詞 lottery 指「摸彩、樂透」，a lottery ticket 即指「彩券」，所以「中獎」也可以說成 win the lottery。

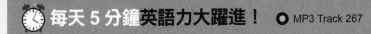
I'm happy as a clam.

我高興得不得了。

A The job is demanding. The pay is not very good. But you seem happy with it.

A：這份工作很辛苦，收入也不高，但你看起來還挺滿意的。

B I'm happy as a clam, as long as I can work with my idol.

B：只要能和我的男神一起工作，我就開心得不得了。

A Now you have your own pet store, and you have two employees helping you. Everything seems perfect.

A：現在你有自己的寵物店了，還有兩個店員幫忙。一切看來都很完美。

B Yes, I'm happy as a clam.

B：是啊，我高興得不得了。

原來老外都這樣用！ Know it!

clam 的意思是「蛤蜊，蜆」，clamshell phone 指的就是翻蓋手機。as happy as a clam 字面上的意思就是「跟蛤蜊一樣開心」，可是為什麼要用「像個蛤蜊」來形容「開心」呢？蛤蜊和開心有什麼關係？其實這個表達的完整說法是 as happy as a clam at high tide（像漲潮時的蛤蜊一樣快樂），at high tide 就是「漲潮時」。（也有 happy as a clam in / at high water 的說法。）人們通常在退潮時才會去海灘撿拾蛤蜊，所以漲潮時的蛤蜊既不用擔心生命安全，又可以飽食海中的浮游生物，當然很開心。沿用到後來，at high tide 被省略，就用 as happy as a clam 來形容一個人開心得不得了。這個表達雖然比較古老，但現在仍然很常用，在輕鬆幽默的情境中使用可以顯得語言很生動。

 生字補充！ Vocabularies & Phrases

- **demanding** [dɪˋmændɪŋ] 形 要求高的，費力的
- **idol** [ˋaɪdl̩] 名 偶像

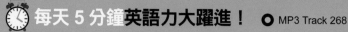

It cracks me up.

我被逗得捧腹大笑。

A Why do you like watching cartoons?

A：你為什麼喜歡看動畫片？

B Because they crack me up.

B：因為動畫片能逗我笑。

A Have you read my novel? How do you like it?

A：你看過我的小說了嗎？你覺得怎麼樣？

B I love it. It cracked me up.

B：我很喜歡。看得我捧腹大笑。

A But it isn't supposed to be funny!

A：可是這並不是搞笑的小說呀！

原來老外都這樣用！ Know it!

crack up 可表示「（因為覺得有趣而）捧腹大笑」，例如：Everyone in the class just cracked up.（全班哄堂大笑。）crack up 還可以表示「吃不消，精神崩潰」，例如：I was beginning to think I was cracking up.（我開始覺得我快要精神崩潰了。）「使某人捧腹大笑」可以表示為 crack sb up，上面兩個對話裡就是這種用法。

break sb up 也可以表示「使某人大笑」，例如：Mr. Bean really breaks us up. He's so funny.（豆豆先生真是讓我們笑破了肚皮，他太好笑了。）

 生字補充！ Vocabularies & Phrases

• **cartoon** [kɑr`tun] 名 卡通（片），動畫片

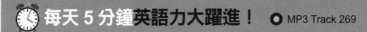

每天5分鐘**英語力大躍進！** ● MP3 Track 269

We had a great laugh together.

我們一起玩得很開心。

A How was the camping?

B The other campers were nice, and we had a great laugh together.

A：露營活動怎麼樣？

B：其他露營的人都很友善，我們一起玩得很開心。

- -

A Do you remember our trip to Disneyland?

B Yeah. Anne, Chloe, Mia, you and I, we had a great laugh together. I miss the girls so much!

A：你還記得我們那次去迪士尼樂園玩嗎？

B：記得，安妮、克蘿伊、米雅、你和我，我們一起玩得特別開心。我好想這些女孩們啊！

原來老外都這樣用！ **Know it!**

名詞 laugh 在這裡意為「開心愉快的事」，例如：We all went to the beach last night—it was a really good laugh.（昨晚我們都去海灘了——真好玩啊。）It was a great holiday with lots of laughs.（假期很愉快，有許多好玩的事。）have a great laugh 表示「玩得很開心」，就如對話中的用法。

英文中有許多表達可以表示「玩得很開心」，僅舉幾例供大家學習。have a good / great / wonderful / marvelous / terrific time，如：David and Johnnie said they had a great time playing football with their old neighbors.（大衛和強尼說他們和老鄰居踢球踢得很開心。）have fun，如：We had great fun trying to guess who Mel's new girlfriend was.（我們猜梅爾的新女友是誰，猜得很開心。）have a blast，如：A few guys came to my apartment after the game—we had a blast!（比賽後幾個哥們來到我的公寓——我們玩得很開心。）

It gives me a thrill.
這讓我覺得很興奮／激動／刺激。

A **It gives me a thrill** to watch all the street lamps light up at the same time.

B Yeah. Looking down from here, they are really beautiful.

A：看著所有的路燈同時亮起會讓我覺得很激動。

B：是啊。從這裡往下看，它們的確很漂亮。

- -

A Wouldn't you feel bored and tired looking at the numbers day after day?

B No. **It gives me a thrill** whenever I see them going up.

A：你一天天地盯著這些數字不煩嗎？

B：不會啊。每當我看到它們上升就會覺得很興奮。

原來老外都這樣用！ Know it!

thrill 在這裡作名詞，意為「（突然而又強烈的）激動，狂喜」或「讓人激動的事」，如：Winning first place must have been quite a thrill. （贏得第一名一定會讓人覺得非常興奮。）give sb a thrill 指「（某事物）讓某人覺得興奮／激動／刺激」，上面兩個對話中就是這種用法。

名詞 kick 也可以表示「極大的樂趣或刺激」，因此「（某事物）讓某人覺得興奮／激動／刺激」也可以表達為 give sb a kick，如：It gives her a kick to get you into trouble. （給你惹麻煩讓她覺得開心。）但 kick 所表示的樂趣或刺激有時會帶有負面的含義。

thrill 和 kick 還有兩個極相似的常用表達：get a kick / thrill out of / from (doing) sth，意為「由於（做）某事而感到激動」，如：Even though I've been acting for years, I still get a thrill out of acting on stage. （儘管我演了多年的戲，上臺演出仍然讓我感到很激動。）do sth (just) for kicks / for the thrill of it，意為「（僅）為了尋求刺激而做某事」，如：Rich kids who turn to crime do it just for kicks, and not because they need the money. （有錢的孩子們犯罪只是為了尋求刺激，並不是因為缺錢。）

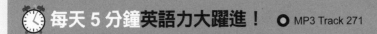
He's as tough as nails.

他特別堅強。／他吃苦耐勞。

A He is a warm and friendly person, but **he is** also **as tough as nails.**

B I like him.

A：他是個溫暖親切的人，但也特別強韌。

B：我喜歡他。

A Do you know Adam Johnson?

B **He is** a good man to have on your side—**tough as nails**, from what I hear.

A：你認識亞當強森嗎？

B：我聽說他吃苦耐勞，你隊伍中有這麼一個人應該不錯。

原來老外都這樣用！ **Know it!**

形容詞 tough 在這裡表示「堅強的，吃苦耐勞的」，指身體或精神強韌，可以應付艱苦嚴峻的環境，例如：When Aunt Agnes caught cholera out in India, we all expected her to die—but she's a tough old lady and she pulled through.（當愛格妮斯嬸嬸在印度染上霍亂時，我們都覺得她性命不保了——但這位老太太非常堅韌，挺了過來。）as tough as nails 的字面意思是「像釘子一樣堅韌」，它指的是 very tough，即「非常堅強的，能吃苦的」。這裡的 nails 可以替換為 old boots，含義不變，看來人們覺得舊靴子在堅韌程度上與釘子比起來也不遑多讓。

形容詞 resilient 與 tough 的含義有相似之處，表示「堅韌的，有復原能力的，適應力強的」，指能適應艱苦嚴峻的環境，吃苦之後還能恢復如初，例如：Amy will soon be out of hospital—children of her age are very resilient.（艾美很快就能出院——她那個年紀的孩子恢復力都很強。）

He knows the ropes.

他很內行。

A Do you think he can handle the work?

B He works repairing streets, and knows the ropes when it comes to safety.

A：你覺得他能搞定這個工作嗎？

B：他是維修道路的，在安全方面很在行。

A Can I trust Mr. Ford?

B Yes. He is a decent manager who knows the ropes.

A：我能信任福特先生嗎？

B：能，他是一位經驗豐富的優秀經理。

原來老外都這樣用！ **Know it!**

名詞 rope 的基本含義是「繩子」，而在這裡 the ropes 指「（進行某項工作的）訣竅，竅門」，例如：Miss McGinley will show you the ropes and answer any questions.（麥金莉小姐會教你怎麼做，並解答你所有問題。）know the ropes 意為「內行，對自己的工作非常在行」，說一個人 know the ropes，那是對他專業知識的一種肯定和稱讚。

來看看其他與 know 相關且表示「內行，在行」含義的表達：1. know what sb is talking about，例如：The staff are dedicated people who clearly know what they are talking about.（這些員工有敬業精神，而且非常內行。）2. know what sb is doing，例如：The young lawyer seemed to know what he was doing.（那位年輕律師似乎很有兩把刷子。）3. know one's job / subject / stuff 指「對自己的工作／學科／懂得的事物很在行」，例如：The young professor who just gave us a lecture really knows the subject.（剛剛幫我們做講座的年輕教授對這個學科非常在行。）4. know a thing or two 指「非常瞭解」，例如：My cousin knows a thing or two about golf.（我的表弟對高爾夫球很在行。）

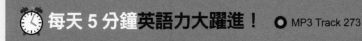

He can hold his own.
他毫不遜色。

A He could be the dark horse of this year.

B Yeah, he can hold his own against the top seed.

A：他可能成為今年的「黑馬」。

B：是的，他可以和頂尖種子選手抗衡。

A Is it too early to put little Tommy in the advanced class?

B He's very intelligent. I believe he can hold his own, even in the advanced class.

A：現在就讓小湯米上高級班會不會太早了？

B：他非常聰明。我相信他即使在高級班也會毫不遜色的。

原來老外都這樣用！ Know it!

當某人在比賽、競爭等局面中處於劣勢（例如對手更成熟、更有經驗等），但依然能固守陣地，與別人針鋒相對，表現得毫不遜色，這時就可以說 He can hold his own. 如果要表現出較量的人或事，則可在後面加 with / against sb。例如：He was a good enough singer to hold his own against the pros.（他是個很好的歌者，可以與職業歌手媲美。）He can hold his own with the best players in the league.（他可與聯賽中最好的選手一較高下。）

動詞 rival 可表示類似的含義，指「與……匹敵，可與……媲美」，例如：There was no one else who could rival her in terms of sheer talent.（單就天賦而言，沒有人能與她匹敵。）

生字補充！ Vocabularies & Phrases

- **dark horse** 片 「黑馬」，出人意料的獲勝者
- **top seed** 片 頂尖種子選手
- **advanced** [əˋvænst] 形（課程）高深的，高級的

He is the salt of the earth.

他是個高尚的人。

A He is an honest, hard-working man.

B Yes, he is the salt of the earth.

A：他是個誠實、勤勞的人。

B：是啊，他是高尚的人。

A Old Jim was the salt of the earth. He was kind to everyone.

B Yes. I will remember him forever.

A：老吉姆是個高尚的人。他對所有人都很好。

B：是啊。我會永遠懷念他的。

原來老外都這樣用！ Know it!

the salt of the earth 意為「世上的鹽」，指高尚、品行誠實良好的人，社會的中堅份子。古時候鹽很稀少，就顯得特別珍貴，所以就用 salt 來比喻這些勤勞、善良、正直的「好人」。例如：Those aid workers are marvelous—the salt of the earth.（那些救援人員太偉大了，他們是高尚的人。）

還可以如何形容這樣的「好人」呢？最簡單的方式就是用 good，如：They were good people, and helped the girl and her baby.（他們是好人，幫助了那個女孩和她的孩子。）形容詞 decent 描述人時可指「正派，規矩的」，也是形容平凡普通的「好人」，如：Mel's a decent ordinary hard-working civil servant.（梅爾是一名勤奮正派的普通公務員。）I decided his uncle was a decent guy after all.（我認為他叔叔畢竟是個好人。）

 生字補充！ **Vocabularies & Phrases**

• **hard-working** [ˌhɑrdˈwɝkɪŋ] 形 勤勞的，努力的

He is a natural.

他很有天份。／他是天才。

A Look at the way he swings that golf club. **He's a natural.**

B Like father like son.

A：你看他揮桿的動作。他有天份。

B：有其父必有其子。

A John should settle into teaching quite quickly. **He's a natural** with small children.

B Yeah. Children love him.

A：約翰應該很快就適應當老師的。他天生對小朋友有一套。

B：對，孩子們喜歡他。

原來老外都這樣用！ Know it!

natural 在這裡是名詞，意為「有天份的人，天才」，例如：People think I'm a natural, but I've had to work at it.（人們覺得我是天才，但我也是得努力的。）

natural 作形容詞時可表示「天賦的，天生具有某種素質或技能的」，例如：The teachers were amazed at his natural ability with figures.（老師們對他的數位天份嘖嘖稱奇。）形容詞 natural-born 的含義與之相似，a natural-born singer 指「天生的歌手」，a natural-born story-teller 指「天生會講故事的人」。單獨用形容詞 born 也可以，例如：She has all the right qualities—she's a born leader.（她具備所有應有的素質——她是個天生的領導者。）

 生字補充！ Vocabularies & Phrases

- **golf club** 片 高爾夫球桿
- **settle into** 片 適應，習慣

She's her own woman.

她很有主見。／她有自己的想法。

A I love Jenifer so much. I hope one day I'll be like her.

B Me too. **She's her own woman**, and she'll do whatever she wants.

A：我非常愛珍妮佛。希望有一天我能像她一樣。

B：我也是。她很有主見，想做什麼就去做什麼。

- -

A Though my sister is no more than 15, **she is her own woman**, and has already decided on a career.

B She always seems to know what she wants.

A：雖然我妹妹才 15 歲，但她有自己的想法，她已經決定好未來的職業了。

B：她似乎一直知道自己想要什麼。

原來老外都這樣用！ **Know it!**

be one's own man / woman 意為「有自己的想法，有主見」，主詞是男性就用 man，是女性就用 woman，例如：He is very much his own man. He'll listen to everyone and then make up his mind for himself. （他特別有主見。他會傾聽大家的建議，然後自己做決定。）

have a mind of one's own 和 know one's own mind 也能表達「有主見，有自信，能自主決定」的含義，例如：That's what he thinks. He's got a mind of his own, that boy. （這就是他的想法。那個小子有自己的主見。）Margaret has a mind of her own. I always enjoy talking to her. （瑪格麗特很有自己的想法，我一直喜歡跟她聊天。）He's successful and competent, and knows his own mind. （他成功、能幹，而且有主見。）

 生字補充！ **Vocabularies & Phrases**

· **career** [kəˋrɪr] **名** （終身的）職業、生涯

It's really a good buy.

這東西買得真划算。

A You've given your old car to your son?

B Yes. It's really a good buy. I've never had any trouble with it.

A：你把你的舊車給你兒子了？

B：是的。那輛車買得真划算，一直沒有出過任何問題。

A Guess how much it is.

B Give me a hint.

A A hint? Hmm, it's really a good buy.

A：猜猜這個多少錢？

B：給點暗示吧。

A：暗示？嗯，這東西買得很划算。

原來老外都這樣用！　Know it!

buy 在這裡作名詞，意為「划算的東西」。一般我們說某樣東西買得划算，指的是它物美價廉，或有升值空間等。我們可以說 It is a good buy / an excellent buy，還可以說 It is a best buy，後者指「最划算的東西」。

能表示「划算」的表達還有不少，僅舉幾例：The meal was really good value—we got at least six courses all for under $30.（這頓飯吃得真划算──六道菜才花了不到 30 美元。）We got a coffee table and three chairs for quite a good price in the market.（我們在市場以非常划算的價格買到了一張咖啡桌和三把椅子。）The price of the holiday includes free use of the tennis courts. It's really a good deal.（度假的價格包括了使用網球場的費用，真是很划算。）The Rolling Stones played for over three hours and the fans certainly got their money's worth.（滾石樂隊表演了三個多小時，對粉絲們來說絕對是值回票價了。）

 生字補充！　**Vocabularies & Phrases**

• hint [hɪnt] **名** 暗示

Generosity is my father's middle name.

慷慨是我爸很大的優點。

A I find that your dad always vies to pay for a meal outside.

B Of course! **It's my father's middle name.**

A：我發現你爸爸在外面吃飯總是搶著買單。

B：當然！慷慨是我爸很大的優點。

A Have you heard that an earthquake happened in the region last week?

B Yes. My father has donated a sum of money.

A Wow, awesome!

B **Generosity is my father's middle name.**

A：你聽説那個地區上週地震了嗎？

B：聽説了，我爸已經捐款了。

A：哇，真棒！

B：慷慨是我爸很大的優點。

原來老外都這樣用！ Know it!

Generosity is my father's middle name 表示誇讚、讚賞「爸爸」慷慨這一特質。middle name 本義是指「中間名」，即名和姓之間的名字，例如，前美國總統歐巴馬的全名是貝拉克侯賽因歐巴馬（Barack Hussein Obama），中間的這個「侯賽因（Hussein）」就是 middle name。sth is sb's middle name 表示某事物是某人的突出個性，因此你想誇別人的時候，也可以將 generosity 替換成 frankness，discretion 等其他表示人物美好、積極特質的名詞。例如：Don't worry. She won't tell anyone. Discretion is her middle name.（別擔心，她不會跟任何人說的。小心謹慎是她很大的優點。）

 生字補充！ **Vocabularies & Phrases**
• vie [vaɪ] 勔 （與某人）競爭

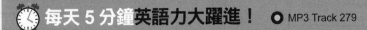

The smell is making my mouth water.

那香味讓我口水直流。／那味道讓我垂涎欲滴。

A Do you want to have a cupcake? They're hot from the oven.

A：要一個杯子蛋糕嗎？熱乎乎剛出爐的。

B Yes! **The smell is making my mouth water.**

B：要！這香味讓我直流口水。

A Is Mom cooking in the kitchen?

A：媽媽在廚房煮飯嗎？

B I guess so. **The smell is making my mouth water.**

B：我猜是的。那香味讓我直流口水。

原來老外都這樣用！ **Know it!**

make one's mouth water 指某食物「讓人流口水，讓人垂涎欲滴」。上面兩個對話中說的都是香味引起食慾的例子，其實看到或想到食物的樣子，也會讓人流口水，例如：The roast fish that restaurant serves is my favorite dish. Just the thought of it can make my mouth water.（那家飯店的烤魚是我最喜歡的菜，一想到它就讓我口水直流。）The photographs in that new recipe book really make little Tommy's mouth water.（新食譜裡的圖片讓小湯米饞得直流口水。）

mouth-watering 是形容詞，表示「令人垂涎欲滴的，誘人的」，例如：The waitress came round with a tray of mouth-watering cheese cakes.（女服務生端著托盤走來，托盤裡裝著誘人的芝士蛋糕。）形容詞 appetizing 和 tempting 也可表示「誘人的，讓人有食慾的」，例如：The soup didn't look very appetizing but it tasted delicious.（那湯看起來讓人沒什麼食慾，但其實很好喝。）The chocolate cake was tempting but I couldn't have any because of my diet.（巧克力蛋糕很誘人，但我在減肥不能吃。）

She has stood by him through thick and thin.

她和他甘苦與共。／她對他不離不棄。

A Did you see our boss's wife? She is rather ... plain.

B But she is a good woman. She has stood by him through thick and thin.

A：你看到老闆的老婆了嗎？長得真是……很一般。

B：但她是個好女人，一直和老闆同甘共苦。

A My mom said she wanted a divorce. I don't understand. I thought she loved my dad— she has stood by him through thick and thin!

B I never know my parents. The world of adults is beyond me.

A：我媽媽說她想離婚。我不明白。我以為她愛我爸爸——她一直跟他同甘共苦，不離不棄。

B：我一直不理解我的父母。成人的世界讓人搞不懂。

原來老外都這樣用！ Know it!

stand by sb 表示「繼續支持某人，對某人忠誠」，尤其是在受支持的這個人遇到了困難或犯錯時，可能有的支持者會背叛或離開，但有的支持者依然會 stand by sb。例如：My mom stood by me when I was dismissed from my job.（當我丟了工作時，我媽媽依然在身邊支持著我。）She did not really stand by Bert when his business fell apart.（伯特生意失敗時，她並沒有在他身邊支持他。）這裡的 stand 可以替換為 stick，含義不變，例如：Paul's girlfriend stuck by him when he was doing time for burglary.（保羅因入室竊盜在監獄服刑時，他的女友對他不離不棄。）

順道一提，主句裡出現的 through thick and thin 表示「不畏艱難，赴湯蹈火」，例如：At that time, families stuck together through thick and thin.（那個時候，家家戶戶團結一致，無懼艱難。）

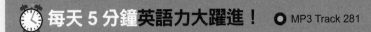

每天5分鐘英語力大躍進！ ○ MP3 Track 281

It's a real pain in the neck.
這真是討厭。

Chapter
19
厭煩、憎惡

A The application form is so complicated. **It's a real pain in the neck.**

A：這申請表這麼複雜，真讓人討厭。

B You'll soon get used to it.

B：你很快就會習慣的。

A **Bobby's** being a **real pain in the neck** today. I hope he can just go home.

A：巴比今天真煩人。我希望他趕快回家。

B I've called his father. He'll take him after lunch.

B：我已經打電話給他爸爸了。他午飯後就來接他。

原來老外都這樣用！ **Know it!**

be a pain in the neck 指「極其令人討厭」，有時候 in the neck 可省略，直接用 be a pain 也可以表達相同的含義，例如：It's a pain, having to go upstairs to make coffee every time.（每次都要上樓去煮咖啡，真討厭。）neck 也可以替換為「屁股」，表達為 be a pain in the ass / arse / backside / butt，意思是一樣的，但由於出現了「屁股」這種不雅的字彙，所以這種表達顯得比較無禮，大家要慎用。

be a nuisance 與 be a pain 相似，也表示「令人討厭」，名詞 nuisance 意為「討厭的、麻煩的人（或事物）」。例如：The dogs next door are a real nuisance.（隔壁那幾隻狗實在很討厭。）It's a nuisance having to get up that early on a Sunday morning.（週日早上還得那麼早起床，真討厭。）

生字補充！ **Vocabularies & Phrases**

· **complicated** [ˈkɑmpləˌketɪd] 形 複雜的

I've had enough of it.

我受夠了。

A When I got out of the office I just started to cry. **I've had enough of it!**

A：我一出辦公室就哭了。我受夠了！

B Relax, dear. Just let it be.

B：放輕鬆，親愛的。別再想了。

A All right, that's it. **I've had enough of it.** Waiter! These guys are trying to take our seats!

A：好，就這樣。我受夠了。服務生！這些人要搶我們的位子！

B Well... Sorry, sir, I'm afraid they came here first.

B：呃……對不起，先生，恐怕是他們先來的。

原來老外都這樣用！ Know it!

I've had enough of it 意為「我受夠了」，用於表示無法再忍受某人或某事物。如果要具體指出無法忍受的人事物，則可用 have enough of sb / sth, 如：I've had enough of him. I need a divorce.（我受夠他了。我要離婚。）I've just about had enough of their complaints.（我快聽不下去他們的抱怨了。）

表達「夠了」的說法還有：That's (quite) enough. / Enough is enough. 或簡單的一句 Enough. 如：There comes a point when you say enough is enough.（是時候了，你不該再忍下去了。）That's enough, boys. Just be quiet.（夠了，孩子們。靜一靜吧。）Enough! Enough! You can do whatever you like.（夠了！夠了！你愛怎麼樣就怎麼樣吧。）

 生字補充！ **Vocabularies & Phrases**

• **let it be** 片 順其自然，隨它去

每天 **5** 分鐘**英語力大躍進！** 〇 MP3 Track 283

I'm sick (and tired) of your excuses.

你的藉口我都聽膩了。

A I can explain.

B Save it. **I'm sick of your excuses.**

A：我可以解釋。

B：省省吧。你的藉口我都
聽膩了。

A I heard that you resigned.

B Yeah. **I'm sick and tired of** working for other people.

A：我聽說你辭職了。

B：是的。我厭倦了為別人
打工。

原來老外都這樣用！ **Know it!**

be sick of 表示「對某事感到厭煩、厭倦」，後面既可以接 sth，也可以接 doing sth，為表示強調，還可以和 tired 連用，以 be sick and tired of 的形式出現。be sick 可以表示「嘔吐」，feel sick 可以表示「反胃，噁心，作嘔」，例如：I think I'm going to be sick.（我覺得我就要吐了。）He dashed into the bathroom and was sick again.（他衝進浴室，又吐了。）As soon as the ship started moving I began to feel sick.（船一開動我就開始覺得噁心。）Virginia had a sick feeling in her stomach.（維吉妮亞感到有些反胃。）都又噁心又嘔吐了，難怪 be sick of 可以表示「厭煩，厭倦」。

添加的部分 be tired of 本身也可以表示「對（做）某事感到厭煩、厭倦」，例如：I'm tired of watching TV; let's go for a walk.（我看電視都看膩了，我們出去走走吧。）I was getting tired of the negative remarks.（我越來越厭倦充滿負能量的言論了。）

 生字補充！ **Vocabularies & Phrases**

• **resign** [rɪˋzaɪn] **動** 辭職

Everybody hates the sight of you.

人人都討厭你。

A Everybody hates the sight of you!

B I don't give a shit!

A：人人都討厭你！

B：我才不在乎呢！

A I'll never come back! You'll regret it!

B We won't miss you! Everybody hates the sight of you!

A：我再也不回來了！你們會後悔的！

B：我們不會想你的！人人都討厭你！

原來老外都這樣用！ **Know it!**

hate the sight of sb / sth 表示「非常不喜歡某人／某物，厭惡某人／某物」。名詞 sight 在這裡指「看見，見到」，例如：Just the sight of him made her go all weak.（一看到他，她就兩腿發軟。）Marcie will faint at the sight of blood.（馬西看到血會昏倒。）而 hate the sight of 就是「一見到……就討厭」，可見「不喜歡」的情緒多麼強烈了。

該句型中的 hate 還可以由別的動詞替換，例如 can't stand the sight of sb / sth 或 be sick of the sight of sb / sth。be sick of 表示「對某事感到厭煩、厭倦」，例如：I'm sick and tired of your excuses.（你的藉口我都聽厭了。）can't stand 意為「不能忍受」，例如：I can't stand people smoking around me when I am eating.（我受不了當我吃飯時有人在我旁邊抽菸。）

Don't push your luck!
別得寸進尺！／差不多就可以了！

A Should I ask for more money?

A：我是不是應該再多要一點錢？

B Don't push your luck—they've agreed to pay for your tickets!

B：差不多就可以了！他們不是已經同意幫你付車票錢了嘛！

A The report should be submitted by the end of next week.

A：這份報告下週末之前要交上來。

B Can I have one more week?

B：能再多給一週時間嗎？

A Don't push your luck—I've already given you a lot of time!

A：別得寸進尺——我已經給你很多時間了！

原來老外都這樣用！ **Know it!**

Don't push your luck! 就是告誡對方要見好就收，已經冒險做了某事，不要再試圖進一步碰運氣。例如，你逃了兩次課都沒有被教授點到名，於是決定繼續蹺課，這時好友可能就會提醒你說：Don't push your luck!（別再繼續冒險蹺課了！）此外，當有人不斷麻煩你幫忙時，你也可以用這句話表示拒絕，並提醒對方不要太過分。例如，某人找你借完電腦又借車，然後還想讓你先把油加滿，那麼你就可以說：Don't push your luck!（別得寸進尺啊！）

You're pushing your luck! 也可以表達出同樣警告的意味。例如，同學的自行車不太好用，但是因為沒出什麼事故所以一直拖著沒去修理，那麼你就可以提醒他說：You're pushing your luck!（等出事再去修就遲了！）

 生字補充！ **Vocabularies & Phrases**
• **submit** [səb`mɪt] **動** 提交

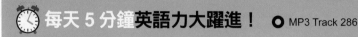

I've run out of my patience.

我已經沒耐心了。／我已經不耐煩了。

Ⓐ I'm afraid I need one more week.

Ⓑ **I've run out of my patience.** I need the result tomorrow.

A：恐怕我還需要一週的時間。

B：我已經沒耐心了。明天我就要知道結果。

Ⓐ **I've run out of my patience.** You don't want to piss me off, do you?

Ⓑ No! I've tried my best!

A：我已經不耐煩了。你不想惹惱我，對吧？

B：不想！我已經盡最大努力了！

原來老外都這樣用！　Know it!

名詞 patience 在這裡指「忍耐（力），忍受力，克制力」，例如：You'll need patience and understanding if you're going to be a teacher.（如果你想當老師，你就要有耐心並且能體諒他人。）It will take time and patience to get these changes accepted.（要讓這些變革為人接受，需要時間和耐心。）

run out of 表示「用完……，耗盡……」，例如：They ran out of money and had to abandon the project.（他們的錢用完了，不得不放棄這個項目。）He'd run out of ideas.（他已經想不出辦法來了。）run out of patience 表示的就是「失去耐心」，其中 run out of 也可以替換為 lose（動詞，意為「失去」）。如果想表示「對誰失去耐心」，還可以在後面加上 with sb，即 run out of / lose patience with sb，例如：I'm beginning to lose patience with you people.（我開始對你們這些人失去耐心了。）

run out 不僅可以用人作主詞，也可以用物作主詞，sth is running out 指的是「某物即將用完」，所以 My patience was running out 表示「我快沒耐心了」。

It really turns me off.
真倒胃口。／真讓我提不起興趣。

A You should try that restaurant. The decor is terrible, but the food is really good.

A：你應該試試那家餐廳。它的裝修風格慘不忍睹，但食物很好吃。

B I went there once. It really turned me off. Not the decor—I mean the flies in the air.

B：我去過一次。讓我大倒胃口。不是裝修風格——我指的是空中飛舞的蒼蠅。

A Did you buy the house?

A：你買那間房子了嗎？

B No. I like the house in some ways, but what really turned me off was those branches overhanging the front window.

B：沒有。從某些方面來說我還挺喜歡那房子的，但那些樹枝垂在前窗那裡，這點實在讓我失去了興趣。

原來老外都這樣用！　Know it!

turn sb off 指「使某人失去興趣」。該表達也常以被動形式 be turned off by 的形式出現，如：Any prospective buyer will be turned off by the sight of rotting wood.（任何潛在的買主看到腐朽的木頭都會失去興趣。）turn sb off 還可特指「讓某人失去性趣」，例如：Men who stink of beer really turn me off.（滿身啤酒味道的男人實在讓我沒那興趣。）

turn-off 是其名詞形式，可指「（尤指在性方面）使人失去興趣的東西」，例如：Pornographic pictures are a real turn-off to most women.（色情圖片對大多數女性來說是讓人大倒胃口的東西。）

turn sb on 與 turn sb off 意思正相反，指「使某人產生興趣」，例如：It was Cara who turned me on to Japanese cartoons.（是卡拉讓我喜歡上日本動畫的。）

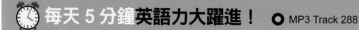
Stop going on at me!

別再煩我了！／別再嘮叨了！

A The dishes are still in the sink.

A：盤子還在水槽裡呢。

B Look, I'll do the dishes after I finish writing this letter. Just **stop going on at me!**

B：聽著，我寫完這封信就去洗碗。別再嘮叨了！

A When are you going to get married?

A：你打算什麼時候結婚啊？

B It's none of your business. **Stop going on at me.**

B：不關你的事。別再煩我了。

原來老外都這樣用！ **Know it!**

go on at sb 在這裡表示「數落某人，嘮叨某人，纏著某人」，而這種行為往往讓別人很厭煩，所以 Stop going on at me! 可以表現出說話的人希望對方不要繼續下去的不耐煩的心情。go on at sb 後面可接 about sth 或 to do sth，例如：Mom was always going on at me to do something with my music talent, but I was more interested in sports. （媽媽總是嘮叨著要我發展音樂天賦，但我對體育更感興趣。）He's always going on at me about fixing the door. （他總是纏著我要我修門。）

想表達相似的含義，還可以用動詞 nag 和 pester。這兩個詞都可以表示「跟……糾纏不休，嘮叨」，例如：Look, I don't want to keep nagging you, but could you move your car? （你看，我也不想嘮叨你，但是你能不能挪一挪你的車？）My children are always pestering me to get new story books. （我的孩子們總是纏著我買新的故事書。）

生字補充！ **Vocabularies & Phrases**

• sink [sɪŋk] 名 洗滌槽，洗碗糟

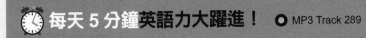
I almost made it.

我差一點就趕上了。／我差一點就成功了。

A Did you catch the bus yesterday?

A：你昨天趕上公車了嗎？

B I almost made it, but the bus arrived two minutes earier.

B：差一點就趕上了，但是公車早到了兩分鐘。

- -

A I almost made it.

A：我差一點就成功了。

B You mean what?

B：你指什麼？

A I planned to sneak out to go to the party, but my mother saw me.

A：我本打算溜出去參加聚會，結果被我媽看到了。

原來老外都這樣用！ Know it!

I almost made it 表示「我差一點就達成目標了」，可用於多種場合，且主詞可以相對地換成 you / she / he 等，表達遺憾、安慰等感情。例如，生活中，你自己烤蛋糕，出爐時的顏色和形狀很成功，結果一嘗才發現錯把鹽當糖了，此時你就可以遺憾地說：I almost made it.（差點就成功的做出美味的蛋糕了。）學習中，你發奮努力，總是想要超過對手，結果還是差了幾分，此時朋友就會說：Cheer up! You almost made it.（振作點！你差一點就超過他了。）看體育比賽時，你喜歡的選手因失誤未能拿到金牌，你也可以略帶遺憾地告訴別人說：He / She almost made it.（他／她差點就拿到金牌了。）

 生字補充！ **Vocabularies & Phrases**

- **sneak** [snik] 動 偷偷地走，溜

I regret saying that.
我很後悔那麼說。

A Did you really say that he was perfect for that job?

B Yeah, but I regret saying that now.

A：你真的說過他極其適合那個工作嗎？

B：是的，但是現在我很後悔那麼說。

A I heard Lily sobbing the whole night.

B It's my fault. I said she was so selfish that no wonder her boyfriend dumped her.

A Oh no...

B Now I regret saying that.

A：我聽莉莉整晚都在啜泣。

B：是我的錯。我說她太自私了，難怪男朋友會甩了她。

A：不是吧……

B：現在我很後悔那麼說。

原來老外都這樣用！ Know it!

I regret saying that 用於表示後悔曾經說過某句話。有道是「說出去的話，潑出去的水」，為了避免後悔，大家說話之前要三思哦！在這裡，注意不要混淆 I regret saying 和 I regret to say，前者是對說過的話表示後悔，後者是對將要說的話感到抱歉。例如：I regret to say his stubbornness is nothing new.（很遺憾，我不得不說他的頑固不化不是什麼新鮮事。）另外，表示「後悔做過某事」，要用 regret doing sth 的結構。例如：I don't regret helping her.（我不後悔幫了她。）當然，也可以說 I don't regret saying that.（我不後悔那麼說。）

 生字補充！ **Vocabularies & Phrases**
・**sob** [sɑb] 動 啜泣

每天 5 分鐘英語力大躍進！ ○ MP3 Track 291

I shouldn't have done it.
我真不該那麼做。

A How could you lie to me?

A：你怎麼能騙我？

B Sorry, I shouldn't have done it.

B：對不起啊，我真不該那麼做。

- -

A Why did your little brother cry last night?

A：你弟弟昨晚哭什麼？

B I scolded him for interrupting me while I was watching TV.

B：他打擾我看電視，我罵了他一頓。

A He's only six, and I think you were too harsh.

A：他才六歲，你太嚴厲了。

B Yeah, I shouldn't have done it.

B：是啊，我真不應該那麼做。

原來老外都這樣用！ Know it!

I shouldn't have done it 表示說話的人對做過的事情感到後悔。should not have 表示說話的人希望某事沒有發生過，但實際上已經發生了（比如上述兩個對話）；should have 表示說話的人希望某事發生了，但實際上沒有發生，例如：You should have done that yesterday!（你本該昨天就把它做完的！）

you should have heard 和 you should have seen 二者都強調所經歷之事有趣、令人震驚等，用於告訴對方「你該親耳聽聽……／你該親眼看看……」。例如：The baby started crying and she cried too. You should have seen them!（寶寶哭了起來，她也哭了。你真應該看看她們的樣子！）

 生字補充！ Vocabularies & Phrases

• **scold** [skold] 動 訓斥，責罵

I didn't see it coming.
我沒想到。

A John has resigned.

B What? How about our project?

A We have to find another partner.

B I didn't see it coming!

A I've just called the hotel and been told that there's no room available.

B Oh, no, I didn't see it coming!

A I told you to book in advance!

A：約翰辭職了。

B：什麼？那我們的項目怎麼辦？

A：我們得另尋搭檔了。

B：怎麼也沒想到他會辭職！

A：我剛給旅館打電話，被告知已經沒有空的房間了。

B：啊，不會吧，沒想到會沒房間！

A：告訴過你要提前預訂的！

原來老外都這樣用！ Know it!

I didn't see it coming 常用於表示悔恨的場合，懊惱於沒能預見到問題的發生。其中的 see sth coming 是日常口語中常用的表達，表示「意識到要出問題，看得出有麻煩了」。例如，朋友執意要和與自己性格迥異的人交往，那麼你就可以事先提醒說：You're going to have a lot of quarrels with him. I can see it coming. （你和他會經常鬥嘴的，這顯而易見。）容易與之混淆的 see sb coming 也很常用，它不是指預見到某人會來，而是指「看出某人容易上當受騙」。例如，同事說自己花 500 元在路邊買了一個香奈兒的太陽眼鏡，你可以感慨：The seller must have seen you coming! （賣東西的人肯定覺得你很好騙！）

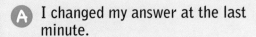

I could have kicked myself.

我後悔死了。

Chapter
20

遺憾、悔恨

A I changed my answer at the last minute.

B And your first answer was the correct one?

A Yes. **I could have kicked myself.**

A：我在最後一分鐘時把答案改了。

B：結果原來的答案是正確的？

A：是的。我真是後悔死了。

A Why didn't I do my homework earlier? Now I'll have to spend all my Sunday afternoon doing it. **I could have kicked myself.**

B Let me help you. Don't let your parents know.

A：我怎麼不早點寫作業？現在我要把整個週日下午都拿來寫作業。真是後悔死了。

B：我來幫你吧。不過別讓你爸媽知道。

原來老外都這樣用！ Know it!

could have kicked oneself 指對自己說過的蠢話、做過的蠢事超級後悔，自責萬分。例如：I was standing there joking about funerals when I suddenly remembered her father had died only last week. I could have kicked myself.（我站在那裡講關於葬禮的笑話，突然想起來她父親上個禮拜才去世。我真是被自己氣死了。）

could have kicked oneself 是由片語 kick oneself 變化而來的。kick oneself 意為「（因做了蠢事、犯了錯等）責備自己，生自己的氣」，例如：You'll kick yourself when I tell you the answer.（等我把答案告訴你，你會懊惱的。）

每天 5 分鐘英語力大躍進！ O MP3 Track 294

All my efforts were for nothing.

我所有的努力都白費了。

A All my efforts were for nothing. I'm a loser.

A：我所有的努力都白費了。我真是個失敗者。

B Your efforts have become your experience, which is important.

B：你的努力都已轉化成了經驗，而經驗是很重要的。

A ABC Company refused me. All my efforts were for nothing.

A：ABC 公司拒絕了我。我所有的努力都白費了。

B I'm interested in your plan. Can you show me the details?

B：我對你的計畫有興趣。能讓我看看細節嗎？

原來老外都這樣用！ Know it!

for nothing 表示「毫無結果，白白地」，指付出了努力卻未得到想要的結果，例如：We went all the way for nothing.（我們白白走了那麼遠的路。）come to nothing 的含義與之相似，表示「（計畫或行動）沒有結果，終未實現」，例如：The experiment cost the company $3 million and finally came to nothing.（此實驗耗費該公司 3 百萬美元，最終徒勞無功。）

in vain 也能表達「徒勞，無結果」之意，例如：Police searched in vain for the missing gunman.（警方搜尋失蹤的持槍歹徒，但毫無結果。）

另外，down the drain 表示「（時間、努力或金錢）白白浪費掉」，跟 for nothing 的含義也很相近，例如：Well, that's it. 18 months' work down the drain.（好吧，就這樣了，18 個月來白做工了。）

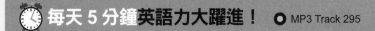

I missed out on all the fun.

我錯過了所有好玩的事情。

A When they were in town, you were on a business trip.

A：他們在城裡時，你出差去了。

B When I finally came back, they were about to leave. I missed out on all the fun.

B：等我終於回來，他們又要走了。我錯過了所有好玩的事情。

A I missed out on all the fun!

A：所有好玩的事情我都錯過了！

B We'll have a picnic next weekend. You can join us.

B：我們下週末要野餐，你可以加入我們。

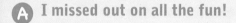 **Know it!**

miss out 表示「錯失了某個機會」，例如：Some children missed out because their parents couldn't afford to pay for school trips.（一些孩子因為父母負擔不起學校的旅行而錯失了機會。）如果想表達具體錯失了什麼樣的機會，可以在 miss out 後面加上 on sth，例如上面兩個對話中的用法。miss the boat 也是一個常用口語，同樣表示「錯過機會，坐失良機」，例如：You'll miss the boat if you don't marry him now.（如果你現在不嫁給他，那就是坐失良機。）

動詞 miss 本身就可表示「錯過（想去的地方或想做的事）」，例如：I'm absolutely starving—I missed the lunch.（我快要餓死了——我錯過了午餐。）sth is not to be missed 意為「某事不容錯過」，例如：A journey to Paris with your girlfriends is not to be missed!（和閨蜜們一起遊巴黎，這當然不能錯過！）

語研力 E017

超好學！每天 5 分鐘的英文會話課

利用零碎時間打造你的英語力，記得快、用得準、效率高！

作　　者	詹瑩玥、張帆、呂游
顧　　問	曾文旭
總 編 輯	黃若璇
編輯總監	耿文國
特約美編	Ariel
內文排版	張靜怡
文字校對	陳蕙芳、賴怡頻
法律顧問	北辰著作權事務所　蕭雄淋律師、嚴裕欽律師

初　　版	2017 年 10 月
出　　版	凱信企業集團 - 凱信企業管理顧問有限公司
電　　話	(02) 2752-5618
傳　　真	(02) 2752-5619
地　　址	106 台北市大安區忠孝東路四段 250 號 11 樓之 1
印　　製	世和印製企業有限公司

定　　價	新台幣 349 元 / 港幣 116 元
產品內容	1 書 + 1 外師親錄英語會話 MP3

總 經 銷	商流文化事業有限公司
地　　址	235 新北市中和區中正路 752 號 8 樓
電　　話	(02) 2228-8841
傳　　真	(02) 2228-6939

港澳地區總經銷	和平圖書有限公司
地　　址	香港柴灣嘉業街 12 號百樂門大廈 17 樓
電　　話	(852) 2804-6687
傳　　真	(852) 2804-6409

國家圖書館出版品預行編目資料

超好學！每天 5 分鐘的英文會話課／詹瑩玥，張帆，呂游合著 .-- 初版 .-- 臺北市：凱信企管顧問，2017.10
　面；　公分
ISBN 978-986-94331-9-8（平裝附光碟片）

1. 英語　2. 口語　3. 會話

805.188　　　　　　　　　　　　106016160

凱信企管

用對的方法充實自己，
讓人生變得更美好！

凱信企管

用對的方法充實自己，
讓人生變得更美好！